THE
CENTER
OF THE
UNIVERSE

THE CENTER OF THE UNIVERSE

BY RIA VOROS

KCP Loft

KCP Loft is an imprint of Kids Can Press

Kids Can Press gratefully acknowledges the financial support of the Government of Ontario, through the Ontario Media Development Corporation; the Ontario Arts Council; the Canada Council for the Arts; and the Government of Canada, for our publishing activity.

Published in Canada and the U.S. by Kids Can Press Ltd.
25 Dockside Drive, Toronto, ON M5A 0B5

Kids Can Press is a Corus Entertainment Inc. company

www.kidscanpress.com

The text is set in Minion Pro and Running Hipster.

Edited by Kate Egan
Designed by Emma Dolan

Printed and bound in Altona, Manitoba, Canada in 12/2018 by Friesens Corp.

CM 19 0 9 8 7 6 5 4 3 2 1

Library and Archives Canada Cataloguing in Publication

Voros, Ria, author
    The center of the universe / written by Ria Voros.

ISBN 978-1-5253-0038-7 (hardcover)

    I. Title.

PS8643.O76C46 2019   jC813'.6   C2018-901874-7

For my parents

All truths are easy to understand once they are discovered; the point is to discover them.

— Galileo Galilei

BIG DIPPER

PART ONE

1

The day my mother went missing turned out to be the hottest May tenth on record. Sidewalks could have fried eggs and kids were getting second-degree burns on playground equipment.

Something woke me up at 7:30 a.m. and I was already sweating. I lay there and tried to drag back the fading memory of the sound I'd heard. A dull noise, muffled.

There it was again — a thud against the wall.

Charlie. My little brother was kicking his soccer ball around the house.

I was about to get up and yell at him when my phone buzzed. I wondered why Iris would text me at this ungodly weekend hour. She slept in late any day she could, which was every day.

But it wasn't her.

Hey, it's Mylo. Do you think your mom would let me interview her for an English assignment? See you at the game? My cousin's playing.

Mylo McLean.

Until recently, just one of the good-looking guys at my school, one of those high-mass stars that so many people want to orbit like tidally locked planets. Mylo McLean, whom Iris had met at HackAttack, this coding class she'd started, and texted me to say she'd become friends with this guy who was into butterflies and wasn't that the best kind of awesome? Turns out he was more into the photography of butterflies, but the details ceased to matter after I realized this was the Mylo from my school, he of the perfect dark eyebrows, and Iris thought the three of us should hang out because she always wanted her people to meet. She's a connector.

She dragged us to her favorite ice cream parlor, and I sat across from him as he ate a banana split and talked about how photography made him whole and stuff, and his eyes softened when he talked about it. I got the feeling he was actually relaxed with us, which was unexpectedly flattering. And that's when he went full neutron star on me — or rather, I became aware of his neutron starriness. It was like I was looking at him through an intensely focused lens and found an undiscovered complexity. There was Iris beside me, chatting like we could all be BFFs because she fervently believed males and females could be just friends, and there I was, staring into my chocolate sundae, asking it to save me from his eyebrows.

Now I stared at his question on my phone. He wanted to interview my mother. Of course he did.

My thumbs became useless on the keypad and autocorrect had to save me. *Sure. She'd probably say yes.* Send. I stared out the window at the clear morning sky and considered my next move. Decided to melt a little more in the insistent sunlight. I imagined his family, neutron stars themselves, had a hard time with physical contact. All those magnetic fields.

My phone buzzed again. *Awesome. Could you possibly ask her for me? I can meet you guys at halftime.*

The thing was he was kind of uncategorizable now. Before the supernova at the ice cream parlor, he'd been a high-mass star I didn't really think about, but now he was someone from my French class + Iris's buddy from HackAttack + an insect photographer + an owner of beguiling facial features + really nice. The last guy I'd gone out with had been cute, too. We'd had way more in common, space- and snack-food-obsessed as we were. It'd been fun while it lasted, but there had been no butterflies, photographed or otherwise. Maybe caterpillars.

I read his text again. *Do you think your mom would let me interview her for an English assignment?*

I was not the girl who used her mother as an excuse to spend time with a neutron star. I tried not to bring my mother into anything at all.

"Grace?"

There she was standing in my doorway, clearing a raspy throat. Blue silk dressing gown, hair frazzled around her face, far smaller off-camera than on. *GG Carter, you look fabulous.* This tagline always played in my head. Months before, another broadcaster had said it to her with such a thick layer of kiss-ass fakery that it blew my mind, and I couldn't stop it from repeating like a bad meme.

There were dark smudges under her eyes. Fabulous.

"Charlie wants you to warm up with him," she said.

"Seriously?" I yawned. "It's not even eight."

"I know, honey, but he's excited. It'll be over by this afternoon."

"Why can't you do it?"

She looked more tired. "I can, but I had a late night, so I was hoping—"

"That you could go back to bed."

"Never mind. I'll ask your dad."

I got up, instantly five degrees cooler once I was out of the sunlight. "No, I got it. Go back to bed."

Pause. "Are you sure, honey?"

"Oh my God, really? You just asked me to and now you're asking if I'm sure?"

Now she was deflated. Not a molecule like the news anchor she had been on TV fourteen hours before. Suddenly I wanted to ask her about the stomach butterflies. If she'd ever had them with Dad, if that had been a determining factor. But I didn't. Couldn't. "I'm sure I can keep Charlie from exploding with soccer game anticipation," I said instead.

"Thank you."

I stretched my arms out in front of me and my shoulders popped. "But since we're kind of trading favors — a guy from school asked if he could interview you for a project."

She rubbed her exaggerated collarbones. "Yes, sure. When?"

"He wants to meet you during the game. It won't take long, I promise."

"He's a friend of yours?"

"Yeah."

Then she did something she hadn't done in a long time. She looked me in the eye and held me there. I felt both pinned and pulled. Her gravity was stronger than I expected. "That's fine, then," she said softly. "Anything else?"

"No," I said. "That's it."

∗

She'll do it. I sent the text from the kitchen, my bare feet cooling on the tile floor. Thought about breakfast to keep my mind occupied.

"There you are!" Charlie bounded in from the backyard. "Took you long enough. I only have two hours to get ready!"

"Two hours," I repeated. "That's a lot of warm-up time, Badger." He had a way of always living up to the nickname I'd given him when he was two, like it was a personal mission.

"But some of that will be taken up by eating and taking a dump. I have to practice my corner shot. *Come on.*"

I reached for a granola bar. "You may feel you're Messi in the making, but I'm starved. You can wait until I've ingested something."

He rolled his eyes. The same eyes as Mom's — a color that defied categorization but was best described as gray-green.

"By the way, she was up late last night. It's not very cool to wake the whole house up with your stupid enthusiasm."

"I was really quiet."

I snorted.

"I was. She said she came down for a glass of water and a Tylenol." His orange shirt was tucked perfectly into his shorts. I wondered if he'd been practicing that, too.

"You still woke her up."

He scowled and looked away. "Are you done yet?"

I took a big bite of the granola bar to show how committed I was to eating. "Go warm up for your warm-up. I'll be there in a minute."

He took off after only a second of pondering. His bright shirt flashed against the greenery of the backyard. He was a comet —

fast and oblivious, coming into others' orbits and then leaving
again. Always pulled back toward the sun.

2

Almost as soon as I was comfortable in the universe — the actual, measurable, astounding universe — I wanted to know it all. My space obsession had started on a vacation to California when I'd finished reading *A Wrinkle in Time* at the exact moment we pulled into the parking lot of the Lick Observatory and I'd spent an hour interrogating the poor PhD candidate who was our guide. Dad took Charlie back to the car because he was getting bored and making a mess in the gift shop, and Mom walked around the gallery in her hat and flowing linen vacation outfit. She didn't need to be in disguise because we were out of the country and she wasn't recognized yet anyway, just an up-and-coming reporter sharing ad space with other broadcasters. The guide answered my questions about planets and supergiant stars and black holes, and I felt like I was expanding in a way that could only be love. Cosmic butterflies for sure. The universe was around us everywhere — it *was* us. Like some celestial magic trick I'd only now figured out and would never be able to unsee.

All the way home from California, I bombarded my parents with information I'd learned and questions I still had. My dad humored me. My mother talked on the phone for half the time with her manager, who'd dumped a huge story on her lap. We'd just gone through the border crossing, and I was wondering aloud what matter would look like at the event horizon of a black hole when she squeezed my shoulder and said, "Why don't you google all this? I'm sure there are fantastic websites out there for kids. And ask your science teacher if you can do a project on space."

I knew what she meant. Get it out of my system. I'd had more than enough fleeting fantasies — paleontologist, veterinarian, spelunker — that she probably wouldn't put too much credence in this one.

Not until I asked for my first telescope.

3

The house phone rang as I came in from the backyard, where Charlie was laid out from his epic warm-up like an exhausted puppy.

Patricia Forsythe. Grandma. Mom's mom.

I was so not in the mood, but she always seemed to know when we screened her calls.

"Hi, Grandma," I said.

"Grace! How are you, darling?" Grandma was an actress. Her "darlings" were drawn out, even though she was Canadian like the rest of us. One of the first reviews I read of hers, when I was twelve, had said the smaller the town of origin, the more prima the donna.

"Okay," I said. "Did you want to talk to Mom?" Small talk was not something I could muster. "I think she's just upstairs."

"That's fine, honey, but I want to know how you are," she said. "How's school?" If her voice were a physical thing, it would have been a marshmallow.

She never understood why I was bored in half my classes and super excited about things I couldn't explain with an elevator pitch. "But what use is all that science going to be to you?" she'd said last time we talked, making "science" sound like "second-hand underwear."

Instead of answering her question, I asked, "Are you still at the same hotel with the infinity pool?"

"No, I'm in Palm Springs," she said. "Listen, Grace, I'm going to fly you and Charlie down here. You'll absolutely love it. You're seventeen now, aren't you? So it'll be fine for you to watch out for him."

"We're in school, Grandma. Until the end of June, like most kids." I climbed the stairs to my parents' bedroom.

"Oh, I know," she said. "I was thinking just for the long weekend."

"The one this month?"

"It gets awfully hot here if you wait too long. It won't interfere with your schedules at all."

"Yeah, it will. Charlie's got soccer and karate and there's a Star Club field trip that weekend —"

"Star Club? Sounds interesting. What stars do you talk about?"

"Not your kind of stars, Grandma."

"Oh, well, that sounds right up your alley, then. But listen, Grace, this is a special trip, just for you and Charlie. I've got a place booked and everything. You can do me this favor, can't you? The stars aren't going anywhere."

The sound of the phone smashing to pieces on the floor would be so satisfying. "I don't know if Mom would be okay with it," I said.

"I've already talked with your mother."

"You have? You guys never talk."

"Believe it or not, we have conversations outside of your house, Grace."

"And she wants us to go to *Palm Springs*?"

"She thought it was a fantastic idea."

The shower was running in the en suite. "Is she stressed about something?" It was a stupid question; Mom was always stressed — work or Charlie's eating habits or the gray roots she'd just noticed. But something was different here. Grandma and Mom rarely agreed on anything.

"It's just work stuff. Nothing that can't be sorted out. The truth is, I've booked her and your dad into a spa while you and Charlie are with me. It'll be a holiday for everyone."

"Or a holiday *from* everyone."

"What's that?"

"And Dad knows?"

"Of course. They both think you'll have a fantastic time down here. Really, you should see —"

"Just hold on a second." Hot steam hit my face.

Mom's still shape was obscured behind the frosted glass. She was probably standing right under the showerhead, the way she often did, her hair pouring down over her face. She said it relaxed her. I didn't know how she could breathe.

"Grandma's on the phone," I said. My voice bounced off the tiles.

Mom jumped, pressing against the tile wall of the shower for a moment. "God, you scared me, Grace."

"Sorry," I said. "It's Grandma."

"Sure. Just a minute, honey." She reached for the white towel hanging opposite the shower door and rubbed it over her wet hair, her face. Her shoulder blades stuck out.

"Bye, Grandma," I said into the phone. "Here she is."

"Bye, darling. See you soon!"

I held the phone away from my ear as Mom finished drying off, throwing her dressing gown back on. "Okay," she said, shoving her feet into flip-flops.

"Tell me you finally got the time off, Grace." Grandma's voice was tinny so far from my ear. "With the kids gone, you've got to use it. Has Andrew agreed to go?"

The phone was still in my hand, six inches from my face.

My mother was watching me, her eyes bloodshot. Her thin fingers reached out.

Grandma's voice was a thousand miles away. "Grace? Are you there?"

∗

The first day of preschool I introduced myself at circle time as sharing my name with my mother and grandmother (who uses her middle name) and everyone thought that was so neat. Three Graces in a row, and one of them a semi-famous actress.

Then I went to Mom's new work when she got the broadcaster job at ITV and saw how people were quizzical when our names matched but we didn't. She was thin and blond and I was solid and awkward and dark-haired. People always commented, always stared. Like the first day at my new school in Grade 4: kids wide-eyed when they recognized the Grace who picked me up — she of bus stop posters and evening TV — and then looked over at me.

By the beginning of high school, I was used to it, but I also had a shield: I was never going to be like her anyway. I took on our differences as if I'd chosen them all, and soon enough it felt like I had.

4

I first met Iris at Star Club, our astronomy group. She showed up the night we were looking at some images that the Hubble Space Telescope had taken. She walked in late, when the room was dark and we were all transfixed on an image of two galaxies colliding in swirls of green-blue gas. I was standing at the back, where the tall people were relegated, and Iris walked right into me.

"Jeez, sorry," she whispered. "Didn't know you were there."

"That's not what I usually hear," I whispered back, noticing in the faint light from the screen that her ponytail was almost on the top of her head. She exuded the smell of cinnamon gum.

"Is that Claudia?" she asked, pointing to the front, where Claudia was explaining the image.

"Yeah. She's a kick-ass astronomer."

"I know. She's my mom's friend. I'm doing a project on hot Jupiters, and she said I should come check this out."

"What school do you go to?"

"It's a self-directed project," she said. "I homeschool. I interviewed Elizabeth Tasker last week."

That got my attention enough that I forgot to whisper. "You talked to Elizabeth Tasker the astrophysicist? How?"

The guy beside me shushed us.

"I emailed her and then we Skyped," Iris whispered. "She was really nice, too."

As Claudia moved on to the next image, I turned back around, astounded that the girl who'd just walked in had interviewed my favorite exoplanet researcher *via Skype*.

"I'm Iris Falino, by the way," she breathed in my ear. She must have been balancing on tiptoes.

I bent down a little. "I'm Grace Carter. You sound like you have superpowers."

"Ha, no. Just time to geek out."

The guy beside me cleared his throat at us.

"Grace Carter," Iris murmured.

I ground my teeth, waiting for her to make the connection.

"I love the name Grace," she said. "It's so classic."

*

I texted Iris as we pulled into the parking lot overflowing with soccer parents and players and, inexplicably, a group of kids dressed as *Star Wars* characters.

Mylo's going to meet us.

In front of me, Mom murmured something to Dad. He shrugged without looking at her.

Didn't know he was into soccer? Iris replied.

My stomach did the flutter thing again. It was intensely annoying. *He wants to interview THE Grace Carter. School assignment.*

Ah, right. Come save me from being buried alive in packaged bread products.

26

Iris's wavy hair was up on top of her head, and she wore a short flowered sundress with hightops. She had the usual silver bangles on her left arm, and since her happiness could be gauged on what I thought of as the Bangle Scale (from 0 to 6), and there were currently five hanging from her wrist, it had obviously been a decent morning. She chewed her lip at her phone screen. "Hey," she said without looking up. "Just a sec." She clicked on a few things and then pocketed her phone. "Aasiya's family just found a new apartment, and she asked us if we'd help them move in." Iris and her parents were part of a network that sponsored refugee families. For the last few months, half her time seemed to be spent doing fundraising things for the next family they wanted to bring over. Another chunk of her time was spent answering texts from Aasiya, who came from Somalia last year and was only a few years older than us and had two kids. Iris's parents had helped her husband learn to read English.

"So is the Uppercase in disguise today?" Iris asked.

"Film star camo and her signature give-me-some-privacy force field." I moved to let a stroller past.

"Are you guys still fighting?"

"No."

Someone set off an air gun and everyone looked around. The game wasn't starting for another twenty minutes.

"That thing that happened at Star Club," Iris said. "You know what I mean."

"It's fine. I just don't need to be around her that much. We do our own thing. It's actually pretty healthy." I couldn't meet her eye. Iris had a close relationship with her parents, so by comparison mine was a chronic illness that responded well to treatment. I considered telling her about Palm Springs. If there was one person who shared my dislike of Patricia Forsythe, it was Iris. But suddenly I didn't feel like bashing a family member with someone who would never bash any of hers with me.

5

Before the space obsession, before spelunking and fossils, I'd been a weird little kid with a thing for patterns. Math was just fun little puzzles and a Rubik's Cube was a delightful game of algorithms. I saw repeating patterns in fabrics and sidewalks the way some people see bright colors — they jumped out and announced themselves. I didn't understand how other people missed them.

In Grade 5 I got in trouble for pointing out the way the principal chewed her pinkie finger when she thought no one was watching. It — and she — had been getting more and more ragged for weeks, and this coincided with studying the brain and habits in our class. "You're just like the example in our unit," I told her. It turned out she was getting divorced. My mother was mortified when she got the call from the school.

But I kept observing people, their stuff, their words like they were puzzles. Some people bit their lips, some blinked fast while they were thinking. Charlie pulled on his ears when he was sad. My Grade 7 teacher said "basically" in every third sentence. The old guy across the street did a reconnaissance mission around his perfect front yard at exactly seven every night. People were weird and let more of themselves be seen than they realized. If you knew what to look for.

Mom had two calming habits. She clicked her tongue quietly to herself when she was nervous, and when things got really bad she pulled on her fingers. Slowly and methodically pulling on them one by one, then switching hands.

Once when I was twelve I found her in the kitchen reading something from work and clicking to herself, and I startled her when I said, "What's wrong?"

She leaned on the counter, trying to seem relaxed. "Nothing's wrong, honey. Why would you ask that?"

"You're clicking," I said.

"I'm what?"

I demonstrated.

Her eyes got bigger. People did that when I pointed out their habits.

"It's okay, you don't have to tell me," I said, because I suddenly felt bad. Back then we were still friends, still stepping comfortably into each other's space instead of around it. I didn't want her to think I was studying her.

"I've just got this huge story to prep for." Her lean on the counter turned into more of a sag. "I'll be up all night with it and then tomorrow's the taping ..."

"Can I help?" I asked. I imagined it was something like helping with homework.

She reached over and squeezed my arm. "You're sweet, but no. It'll be okay." She started pulling the fingers on her right hand. "Don't you have a sleepover to go to?" It had been canceled because Leanne had come down with the flu. Mom got to the last finger and clued in. "Oh, right. I'm sorry, Grace. How about you pick a movie tonight? I'll make you popcorn." She hugged me against her, and I could smell her skin. She'd been softer then — less bony. More sweet, with some fragrance — a soap or lotion she used. Thinking about it years later, I figured the scent had disappeared so slowly that I didn't notice it until it was gone, but now the gone-ness of it was stronger than the smell ever was.

*

There she was pulling her fingers again in her nineties-era folding chair, her ball cap low over her face, Jackie O shades on. Watching eight- and nine-year-olds career down the field as if their lives depended on killing the ball.

Iris settled down between me and Mom, tucking her legs under her. In between plays, she chatted about how well Aasiya and her family were managing.

"No, you're right," Mom said to her as I zoned back in. "It's a real challenge to get the community on board sometimes."

"My mom says there was some resistance at the town hall meeting last month. I don't understand how people can be like that. These people have *no home*."

Mom nodded. "But it's hard to change people's views. We see it all the time with comments on stories." A wood-beaded bracelet slipped down her arm as she tugged her cap lower. I'd never noticed that piece of jewelry before. It looked like something Iris would wear. Maybe Mom was trying to recapture her youth.

On my other side, Dad stared out at the field as if trying to figure out all the players' shoe sizes.

"What are you talking about?" I asked Iris.

"Refugee resettlement," Mom said. "ITV has donated a lot to an organization in Kenya. I set up the connection myself."

Iris's eyes widened. "I didn't know you did that."

I leaned back on my hands. It was crazy hot. There was no good reason to be sitting in direct sunlight, even for Charlie's game.

"Did you see that play?" Dad asked, nudging my arm.

"I think I missed it."

"Charlie's on form." He looked over at Mom. "Did you see it, GG?"

The people beside us spilled a bag of chips all over the grass and laughed.

"Darn," Mom said. "I missed it, too."

✳

"I need to pee." Iris nudged me as the ref blew the whistle for halftime.

The women's restroom had a huge line and the men's smelled disgusting, so we walked to the corner of the park with the playground and scouted out the best shrub.

I turned and stood guard as she squatted.

"So, hey," she said from inside the leaves. "I was thinking we could leverage Mylo's connection for a good cause."

I picked a crumb of granola bar off my T-shirt. "I don't follow."

She got up and rustled out of the shrubbery. "I mean, his mother is Sun Ah Kim."

I stared at her. "Yeah, I know she's Korean."

Iris rolled her eyes. "Sun Ah Kim is the director of the Milliner Foundation. Started by that superrich family in Vancouver? And she used to be a politician — my parents hated her party, but whatever." She blinked at me expectantly.

"Okay ...?"

She gave up hiding her contempt. "Seriously, Carter. Your mother was just talking about the Milliners a minute ago. She said Sun Ah Kim's name — they, like, know each other. You were *there*."

"Apparently I wasn't."

"I don't get you sometimes. Your families basically run in the same circles and you didn't make the link? Ugh, come on." She started walking, her canvas bag bouncing on her hip.

I'd spent the past five years putting distance between my mother's life and mine. What did I care about people she knew?

"What I'm saying is, what if we could get Mylo's mom to come to our big refugee fundraiser in the summer and bring all her rich friends?"

"We?"

"Well, since we're all hanging out now, it'd be easier to convince him. Two against one."

"That seems kind of icky. Is that how fundraisers are supposed to work?"

She shook her head. "It won't be icky."

My phone buzzed and we both looked at it.

"Is it him?" she asked.

Running late, his text said. *I'll be there in five. Where are you?*

6

When we got back to my parents' spot to meet Mylo, my mother's chair was empty.

"Dad? Where's Mom?"

He put his hands up, then deflated with a groan, along with half the crowd. "So close *again*."

"Hello? Mom?"

He glanced at me, confused. "Oh, she went to take a call. Someone at work."

"Great. I hope she's not going to spend the rest of the game on the phone."

"It's happened before," he said, turning back to the action.

"Let's go," I said to Iris.

"But Mylo —"

"Can't talk to her if she's not here."

"Are we looking for her or him?"

"I don't know. Maybe we should just go for ice cream and forget everything."

She came around to peer into my face. "Hey, you. What's up?"

I was pissed that Mom had just walked away, I was pissed that now Mylo would show up and we'd have to explain her absence, but it wasn't just that. I was pissed at Dad for being so nonchalant about it, and maybe pissed that Iris could just inveigle her way into Mylo's family so quickly. I was pissed at Grandma for being Grandma. Probably I was pissed at Charlie for making me come to this stupid, sweltering game.

"Hey, I found you," said a voice behind me.

Of course he'd found us. The magnetism was undeniable. My heart rate began to climb.

Iris jumped in before I could fully turn around. "So, Mylo, what are your family's thoughts on refugee resettlement?"

I got to see his puzzled expression, complete with one very attractive raised eyebrow. Something shout-worthy happened on the field, and I managed to turn my face away from his powerful gravity.

"Uh, I think it's a good idea?" he said. "Why?"

"Funny you should ask —"

"My mother's gone to take a call," I said, "so you might have to wait for the interview." His forehead was now lined with confusion and I wanted to touch it.

"That's okay," he said. "There's still a lot of game left."

I shrugged. "She could have a lot of call left. I'm just saying this is how it goes sometimes with her."

"Hey, I saw a good vantage point over there" — Iris pointed through the sea of spectators — "so we can see the game *and* talk business."

"Business?" Mylo asked.

She was already on her way there, so Mylo turned and I followed like one of the orbit-trapped planets at school I'd always made fun of.

She'd climbed up on the wooden box that held equipment for the field and grinned down at us like a kid. "See? Prime viewing."

Mylo climbed up and held out a hand to me, which I thought about not taking but then was clasping, and he pulled me up. Even after he let go I could still feel his warm hand around mine.

"That's my cousin — the kid with the red hair," he was saying to Iris. "He's pathologically obsessed with soccer."

"Are your parents here, too?" Iris asked. I glared at her, but she was looking at the field.

He squinted into the sun. "No. My mom's got this big charity thing."

Iris gave me the side-eye and I glared back. We'd perfected the art of eye-only communication through our nights at Star Club.

"What does your dad do?" I asked, to stop Iris from jumping in.

Mylo stared at the box under our feet. "Literature instructor."

"At the university?" Iris asked.

"The college. He's worked there for, like, ten years." He frowned.

I could see Iris formulating a question. She was good at friendly interrogation but not always tact.

"Maybe my mom could call you tonight?" I said, taking the risk of touching his arm. "If she doesn't come back before the game ends?" We were basically the same height, which was pretty normal for me, being taller than most girls at school. I liked being able to look straight into his face. He was six inches away. There was a faint scar under his lower lip.

"Yeah, sure," he said. "Whatever works."

Iris's phone rang and she groaned when she saw the screen. "My dad's rebuilding my computer and he keeps asking me a million questions." She put the phone to her ear. "Yeah, Dad. Yes ... but I don't need that much storage ... Well, then just use it ... I don't know!"

Everyone around us roared suddenly, and we all looked up to see that Charlie's team had scored.

Mylo grinned at the jubilant parents below us. "This is all Spencer's going to be talking about for days."

"My brother, too," I said.

"Just hang on, Dad, I can't hear you." Iris jumped down from the box and called back, "Don't take off, okay? I'll be two seconds."

"We should take off," I said, and Mylo laughed.

The celebrations stopped and the game started up again.

"Can I ask you something?" he asked.

It was like the volume button got turned down on everything around us. I thought of calming things. The surface of the moon through my telescope, the mountains and canyons of varying gray. "Sure."

"How come GG Carter's your mom and you don't ..." He seemed to be considering the unsaid words.

"Hang out with Sasha Rosenberg and her people? Your people."

His eyebrows knitted together so perfectly. "Not exactly, but ... yeah. I just mean you seem pretty different from your mom. From what I expected."

"But you haven't actually met my mother yet. People think

they know her because she's everywhere, but that's TV. That's makeup."

"So she's not like she seems?"

"Is your mother what she seems?" I didn't know why I asked that. Why I felt suddenly annoyed.

"Uh, actually no." He glanced away. "But maybe no one is."

Even though there was the game for us to be interested in, it started to feel awkward, and I hated that. I'd made it that way and I didn't know why. I really didn't want him to hate me. "I don't mean my mom's some ogre in real life or anything," I said. "It's just a false familiarity, you know?"

He blinked at me. "Yeah."

"I have my own interests. My own life," I said. "I don't care about being seen." I emphasized "seen" with my hands.

"So what *are* your interests?" he asked.

I knew I'd see his right eyebrow raised in question. There it was.

"Astrophysics. Planetary science. Cosmology. Also, crunchy food and jellybeans."

He studied me and I swore my core temperature was rising. "Awesome," he said.

"You?" I asked.

He pulled out his phone. "I posted a few new shots last night." He opened his photos and showed me one of an iridescent green butterfly.

"That's amazing," I said, taking his phone and pretending to be cool that our fingers touched.

"Thanks. But I don't have three hundred butterflies trapped in my room or anything. I'm not a closet lepidopterist."

"A closet what?"

"A butterfly scientist. I love photography and I also have this wicked collection of butterflies from my grandfather."

"Okay, the fact that you know the scientific name is telling me otherwise."

He laughed and I couldn't stop grinning. "My grandfather was one," he said.

"Of course he was," I said.

We looked at each other and the back of my neck started to heat up.

"Hey, kids." Iris scrambled back onto the box. "That was painful but I'm back. What did I miss?"

7

We were on our way to my parents' lawn chairs at the end of the game when my phone rang, which meant it was a parent. I realized I was hoping it was Mom.

The screen said otherwise.

"She had to go on a story," Dad said in my ear.

"She *left*? What the hell? Did someone pick her up?"

On the other end, Charlie was jabbering incoherently in the background. "She got a cab," Dad said. "I guess it's a pressing issue. She said the station needed her right away."

"You talked to her?"

"She texted."

"She couldn't even talk to you about it? Or congratulate Charlie on the game? What is wrong with her?"

"Come on now, Grace."

"No, that's inexcusable, Dad."

He paused on the other end. "You need to give her a break, Gracie. She's under a lot of stress."

Iris and Mylo looked away when I glanced at them.

The crowd was beginning to thin out.

8

I opened my English lit homework to pretend I was working, but then I went online, checked social media, tried Jedi mind tricks on my phone — Iris usually texted at least twice an evening — but it stayed dark and silent.

I spent five minutes trying to compose an appropriate and unlame apology to Mylo for my mother ditching the game and in the end settled on, *Sorry my mom couldn't do your interview. Bailing is kind of her speciality.* Then I felt kind of bad for pushing her under the bus.

I opened the Island TV news site, something I hadn't done in months, scrolled past last night's news segments on Middle East tensions, a crime family caught laundering money and the opening of a new retirement home, and there she was under the *Evening with GG Carter* heading. She was wearing a salmon-colored blazer I hadn't seen before. I'd heard her reporter voice a thousand times, but now something about it made my lungs tighten. She was there and not here. Even when she was physically with us, she was elsewhere. She was always online, always smiling for anyone who clicked on her videos, but who was she really smiling for? Something small and sharp twisted behind my ribs.

Dad knocked on my partially open door. I pulled my laptop closer and brought the novel study sheet up on the screen.

"The bathroom faucet's leaking again." His hair was tufted up on the left side where he habitually combed his fingers through. "So don't use it for a bit, okay? I'm going down to get my tools." Dad fixed things when he was stressed. A year before, during a bad week at work, he'd spent every night tightening the screws around the house.

"Have you heard from her?" I asked.

He stared at the jumbled books on my shelf as if trying to read the titles. "A librarian you are not."

"Very observant. Mom?"

He blinked. "Your mother told Jen that she was traveling to do research for the story. It sounded in-depth, Jen said."

"So her assistant knows more than we do."

He sighed. "I know it's not ideal, but this is the way it goes sometimes. She's with someone from the station."

"Jen said that?"

"Yes." He set his face to calm and fatherly. "She'll call when she's done. Everything's fine. I'll just be under the sink." He pulled the door closed, muttering something about the right-size wrench.

I lay back on my bed, and after a while I heard the clink of the wrench on the tap, the scuffle of feet on the tile, the faint groans that signaled Dad was lying in a position that offended his old back injury.

The click of my door opening startled me out of a pre-sleep drift. Charlie had stuck his head in. "You missed an awesome movie."

"I'm devastated to hear it." I didn't move from my comatose position.

"If you're sleeping, why aren't you actually sleeping?"

"I'm meditating."

"All fixed," Dad called from the bathroom. "You can brush your teeth now, Charles."

"Great game today," I said. "The warm-up clearly helped."

Dad appeared behind him in the doorway.

"When's Mom coming home?" Charlie asked.

"Soon, buddy," Dad said. "I promise, soon."

But there was no word from Mom the next morning, and Dad seemed tired and burned the scrambled eggs. I retreated upstairs again, and when I passed his door, I saw Charlie was deep into *Minecraft*. I cleared my throat, but he didn't respond.

I dragged my brain into my English homework and worked on a report on red giant stars I was doing for extra credit. I went on Jungle and scrolled through my photo feeds. Had a nap during which I dreamed of peeing in the bushes beside the soccer field and kids in *Star Wars* costumes finding me with my pants down.

I woke up to my phone buzzing in my hand.

It was Mylo. *Hey, is your mom still super busy? I don't want to bug her.*

Yeah, she's not even here. When's your assignment due?

Tuesday.

Wow. Bad planning.

Yeah, I know.

Do you have an alternative? I have no idea when she'll be home.

Yeah, my mom knows the premier's assistant, says she can talk to me tomorrow.

Nice.

He didn't reply and I started to audition segues in my head. Texting him was so much easier than having to look at him.

Then he said, *Hey, I'm sorry about what I said at the game.*

What part?

The part about you and Sasha Rosenberg.

It's ok. I can see why you'd wonder. I squeezed my eyes shut for a moment and then typed what was in my head. *I've just spent a long time trying to be different from her.*

Sasha?

No, my mother.

The three dots indicated he was in the process of typing. For a long time.

I got up and checked Jungle, listened for signs of life downstairs.

My phone finally buzzed but his message was unexpectedly short: *I get it. Really.*

*

Dad was at the kitchen counter when I went down for a granola bar pre-dinner snack. He looked up when my bare feet hit the wood floor. "Jen doesn't know where she is."

"You said she got a message from Mom."

"But she doesn't have any idea where GG is now. She's

contacting others at the station to find out if they've heard."

My throat squeezed in on itself. "What are you saying?"

He stared out the sliding glass door. "I don't know what it means. But there's something I can't stop thinking …" He put his phone down. "We've been having a hard time recently. There've been arguments. Nothing that I thought we couldn't work through, but …" He put a hand through his hair. "Maybe she needed time to think. I don't know. I'm sorry you have to find out this way."

Cold crept like liquid nitrogen up my back. I'd heard them argue before but nothing that ever worried me. I thought back to Mom in the en suite, Grandma on the phone, her voice commanding into the space between us: "Tell me you finally got the time off, Grace." Time off to relax, I'd assumed. To get away with Dad. I stared at the floor, the simple repetition of planks across the kitchen. How long had they been having fights? What patterns had I missed — or pattern breaks?

"Gracie?"

I couldn't look at him. "Grandma said she wants us to go to Palm Springs and you two will have a weekend together. She made it sound like you'd have fun. A spa or something."

His exhaled breath was loud in the silent kitchen. "We're hoping to have fun. It's a reconnection trip. We haven't been on vacation, just us, since before Charlie was born." He came over and held my shoulders. "This isn't a permanent thing, Grace. If she needs some time to decompress, it's good that she's taking it. She's been under huge strain — the network's pushing her, and you know she's been working long hours."

It was like everything he said made her more of a stranger

and me more of a jerk. I'd been so mean to her in my mind, so angry about everything, thinking I knew exactly what was going on. Now I wasn't so sure, and it made me feel unattached to reality, bumping into possibilities like sharp corners.

"I'm going to call some of her friends. I bet you anything she's with one of them."

Then I was alone, leaning against the counter in my bare feet, wondering what I even came down for.

9

A reconnection trip. That implied a lack of connection. I was pretty sure you had to have a good connection to have a healthy marriage. Hearing it from him made it real. A dark force over everything. It made the what-ifs grow like popping corn. To avoid it all, I went on Planet Hunters. For the past three years, I'd been one of hundreds of regular people looking at space telescope data that might or might not contain images of transits — exoplanets crossing in front of their stars and leaving evidence with dimming starlight. It was one method of finding undiscovered exoplanets, and anyone could do it, no expertise required. All you needed to do was watch for patterns.

Planet hunting calmed me. I could relax all my muscles, focus on the data, let my eyes work and my brain track. I'd found three exoplanets so far, and one of them — WASP-52h — became the subject of a research paper, and since I was the first person to record its existence I got named an author on the article. That had been last year, in grade ten. I had a copy of the paper in my desk drawer. I'd asked the other authors to sign it before they sent it, which to me was like getting an autograph from a celebrity.

I worked through a data set for a while, and the light outside got golden in that spring evening way. Birds sang. I went through another data set. At eight o'clock I got up for a pee break, dropping out of my astronomy-induced haze back into reality: Mom was still MIA. On the way back from the bathroom I caught the murmuring rise of Dad's voice. I paused outside his bedroom door. The light coming under it bleached my toes.

He was tapping into his phone. Then nothing for a moment.

"Hi, Yasmin, it's Andrew."

I held my breath.

"Yes. I'm looking for GG — has she called you or ... Okay, but today? Uh-huh." Pause. "No, I don't think so. You're right, it is uncharacteristic ... It's three days for missing persons. I know. Okay, thanks. Bye." His phone pinged.

Missing persons? When had he jumped to that?

I turned the door handle, and there he was in the middle of the room, staring at his phone, his face slack.

"What?" I asked. "What is it?"

"I just got a text," he said, unmoving.

"From who?"

"Oh my God," he whispered.

"What?" I grabbed his phone, my heart frozen mid-beat, my lungs deflating.

I'm not coming back. Don't look for me. Goodbye.

10

Everything pressed in around me — the light from the ceiling, the carpet under my feet, the air in the room, stifling and hot.

Dad was pacing, taking deep breaths and talking, but the words weren't reaching me.

I'm not coming back.

I saw that I was still holding the phone, so I dropped it.

Don't look for me. Goodbye.

"No," I said. "That can't be."

"Don't you see, Grace?" He'd stopped across the bed from me. "It can't be her. It must be someone else writing the message. Her phone's been taken, she's not able to reach us —"

"But how do you know that?" I asked, my skin prickling all over like I was covered in tiny insects.

He was staring into the air as he thought. "It said, 'I'm not coming *back.*' Not *home* — back." He scrambled to pick up the phone and check. "She would have written *home* because this is where we are, this is her personal —" He drew both hands up into his hair. "It could be a hostage situation, a ransom thing —" He turned in a circle like he was searching for something.

"But it's just a word, Dad. It's a text." In that moment I wasn't sure I could touch him — not that he'd be violent, but that he'd break somehow, the look on his face scarily unfamiliar. I put a hand out into the space between us, as if I could interrupt the desperation coming off him like energy waves. Anything to bring him back to himself. I needed him. "Just hang on a second. You're sounding kind of crazy —"

"Go to your room, Grace. Please." His face was set suddenly, the wildness disappearing.

"What? Why?"

He pressed his hands together. "You're not in trouble and I'm not angry with you."

I was so relieved to see him back, to see that he saw me, that I nodded. He came closer and put his hands on my shoulders, squeezing like he was holding me together. "I just need to do this alone."

I could only whisper. "What are you going to do?"

"Let's hope Charlie is asleep in his room. I'm calling the police."

∗

I could hear him talking to the cops through my wall as I walked the floor of my room, pacing like he had, but with more obstacles. I covered my ears but being inside the rasp of my breathing was even worse.

Police. Missing person. Hostage. Ransom. How had we gotten here? What was true and what was not?

My phone buzzed and I jumped, knocking my shoulder into the closet door.

It was a photo from Mylo. A close-up of a butterfly wing, yellow, black and orange striped. It was so detailed that it looked like the wing was made of colored dust particles. Underneath he'd texted, *The lepidopterist wanted to show you this.*

It was so beautiful and I was so on the edge of dissolving that I could have cried, but instead I tapped his number and called him.

He picked up after one ring.

"Hi," I said, my voice dry but surprisingly normal sounding. "I'm sorry."

"Why? What's up?"

"I didn't mean to call … I don't normally call anyone, except my parents when they make me, but —"

"I know, me neither. Makes my mom crazy. She's really into decorum and old-school manners. But I think I actually like talking on the phone. Kind of more than texting. Is that weird?"

"No," I said, feeling a strange calmness pull at me. He was oblivious to everything that was pounding inside my head, the police who had been activated, the voice of my father through the wall. This was just a phone call to him. He was living in an alternate universe called Everything Is Normal.

"Because I like hearing another human's voice," he went on. "It sounds different, more … personal than talking in person, kind of. You know?"

I said yes but no sound came out. I wanted to stay in that universe with him.

"Hello?"

My heart started beating in my ears again. "She's missing," I said, the words dropping like stones out of my mouth.

"What?"

"We don't know where she is." I felt my voice slide down to a whisper. "My dad just called the police. He was talking about ..."

"About what?" His voice was in my ear. He was right. It was way better than having to be face to face.

I pressed my phone tight against my head. "Hostage situations and ransom and ... kidnapping, I guess."

Silence. Even Dad in his bedroom had stopped talking.

I strained to listen for sirens or the screech of tires. Would cops show up with lights flashing?

"Holy shit," Mylo said finally. "Is this a joke?"

"I don't think so. My dad doesn't think so."

"I'm kind of speechless right now."

"Yeah, I know —"

"No, this is really ... oh my God."

"I don't know what to believe," I said. "Except that she's *gone*. Something's happened and nothing makes sense."

I could hear him moving around on the other end. "Okay, hold on. Are you at home?"

I sat on my bed and pressed my thumb and index finger against my eyelids. "Yes."

"Are the police coming?"

"I don't know — my dad just talked to them but no one's here yet."

"Can you breathe?"

I exhaled. "I think so."

"Okay, do that. It helps."

I breathed in and out, still listening for sirens. Dad's door opened and shut, and his footfall creaked the floor and then the stairs. I listened for Charlie's door. Nothing.

"Are you still breathing?"

"Yeah."

"Me, too." He exhaled into the phone. "My mom's always trying to get me to do Zen breathing with her. Want to try it?"

"Okay. Yeah."

He told me how — in through the nose, out though the mouth — and we breathed for a minute, until it started to get intense and too silent, and I wanted to say something but I didn't know what. There were too many thoughts in my head for any one to squeeze out.

"How're you doing?" he asked.

"Not great," I whispered.

He cleared his throat. "Your mom's going to be found. She's fricking GG Carter."

"I don't know if that's such a great thing right now," I muttered.

"You don't know what you know yet. No one does."

"Also not great." I closed my eyes against hot tears. At least he couldn't see me. "This is the worst feeling in the world — being paralyzed but wanting to run, search, do something to end the —"

"PWR. Perpetual waiting room."

"What?"

"PWR. Like when you're waiting for someone to come out of heart surgery or something. That stress-worry-waiting combination. Right?"

"Yeah," I said, "that's it. How come you know so much about it?"

He didn't speak for a moment, and I jumped up as lights flashed through my window. It was just a car passing on the road. Everything fell back into darkness.

"I just know of a situation kind of like this. It was a term they used," he said. "But anyway, how's your heart rate?"

"I don't know. Fast? Should I check my pulse?"

"If you want."

"What will that do?"

"It'll distract you."

"Oh. Well, that just feels dumb."

"Want me to talk instead?"

"Yeah, sure."

"About?"

"Whatever you want." I knew he was trying to keep me engaged, that this was something you'd do with a kid who was losing it. My mom had done this when I was little. She'd called it re-centering or something. Calming the brain. It had worked when I was six.

"Can I tell you about the first butterfly larvae my grandfather smuggled into South Korea in the 1960s?"

"That would be so great."

"Okay."

And then I could feel Mylo's voice on my skin — the reverberation of his vocal cords like a thick, soft blanket. I heard about the butterflies and the border guards and the cigar boxes that held tiny chrysalises, but it was really his voice. The up and down, the closeness in my ear, the pauses for breath and then rumbling on.

I lay back on my bed, closed my eyes and breathed.

11

The thing I loved most about telescopes was that they were essentially time machines. They saw the past, what stars and planets and nebulae looked like thousands or billions of years ago. Nothing anyone could see through a telescope was happening in that moment — light could only travel so fast, and because of that we'd never be in the same moment as anything else in the universe. We'd always be looking into the past.

As Mylo talked into my ear, his voice rolling and pitching like a sea made of sound, I thought about how it would be if I could train my telescope on the day of the soccer game, or the week before, when I'd snapped at Mom for not remembering what night I went to Star Club. Or the moment she asked me about a constellation but used the wrong term, and I'd rolled my eyes. I'd see everything differently from this vantage point, but it would also be useless because I couldn't fix those things. It would be like receiving light from a source that had already burned out.

12

A male police officer sat on the love seat in front of the fireplace with a thick laptop on his knee. He had short blond hair and overly tanned skin. The other, a woman, stood at the back of the couch. She was tall with long dark hair pulled back into a smooth ponytail. She had excellent posture. The officers introduced themselves as Constable Baker and Corporal Sanchez. I got the feeling the woman was in charge.

"I'm sure this is very worrying for you," she said. "Given how high profile your mother is, we're getting involved early to try and resolve things as soon as possible. First we'll need you to give us as much detail about the past few days as you can." She gestured to the couch. "Please have a seat. And if you could go with Constable Baker, Mr. Carter."

I watched the male officer get up.

"It's okay," Dad said to me, probably because my mouth was hanging open. "I'll be right through here." He pointed down the hall.

"Why can't you stay?"

"It's protocol, Grace," Corporal Sanchez said. "We question family members separately at first."

A door closed softly. The office, or maybe the garage. My hearing seemed off.

"Okay, so I'd like you to tell me everything you know about this situation." Corporal Sanchez sat down in the old green armchair that Grandma insisted we take after she sold her house and moved all her things into an apartment. It was the least comfortable chair I'd ever sat in and possibly the most expensive. "Anything you think could be useful, going back as far as you need to in the past. I'm here to listen and gather information, so the more you give me, the better. Don't worry about keeping to a timeline at this point."

I stared at her. The room was silent. She smiled. Probably the kind of smile she'd learned to give to people in my position. Not unkind but practiced.

"I don't know where to start," I said.

"You could start with the last time you saw her if you want."

*

An hour later I'd gone through everything from the soccer game to Dad's call to the police station, and my throat was so dry that it hurt.

Corporal Sanchez took notes and nodded occasionally, her right foot tapping the carpet every few seconds. It calmed me a little to see a habit coming out as she listened.

Eventually I ran out of words and sat there rubbing my throat.

She reached beside her and picked up a glass of water. "It's a lot, talking like this, isn't it?"

I took the glass and downed half.

"I'd like to ask some specific questions now. Are you ready?"

"I guess." My legs were cramped from sitting in one position.

"Do you know if anyone else saw your mother when she took the phone call? At the time she left your viewing spot or after that?"

"Probably lots of people," I said, hating the imprecision of that. "It was really crowded. I'm sure half the people there knew her from other soccer games and the rest would have recognized her if she'd been dressed as her TV self. She was wearing a ball cap and sunglasses. Her hair was in a pony-tail. But no, I didn't hear or see anyone else talking to her. I think a lot of the people around us were for the other team. We were talking among ourselves." *And I was beating her up in my head.*

Corporal Sanchez watched me. "We'll do a canvass of the houses around Fletcher Park and speak to the soccer players' families to see if we can get some video footage. That could be really useful."

I stared at her right foot as it tapped the carpet again. She saw me watching it and shifted position.

"Can you tell me more about who your mother is as a person? Her personality, her relationships, her interactions over the past few weeks. Anything that stands out."

There was a simple gold band on Corporal Sanchez's ring finger, no diamond. She kept her nails short and unpainted. No sign of chewing.

"Grace?"

"Yes." I wished I had my phone to check the time — it felt

like midnight but it couldn't be yet. Or maybe it could. My whole body was heavy.

"Do you think you can tell me about her?"

There was a scrap of noise in the hallway — maybe Constable Baker on his radio.

"Do you watch her on TV?" I asked.

Corporal Sanchez spun her pen around her finger. "Yes."

"She's different at home," I said.

"How so?"

I looked out the window, into the blackness that yielded only slightly to the orange beam of the streetlight on the road. "She was always tired here, like she left all her energy at work. But it's been worse in the last year or two. When I was younger she would play with us. We'd do puzzles together or go to the park. She was fun. I remember her being fun sometimes." I rested my head on the back of the couch. "Now she works all the time. She's tired and in five places at once. Sometimes she tries to ask about my day, but there's always something to distract her or make us argue. I miss ..." I couldn't finish the sentence because of the ache in my chest.

Corporal Sanchez wrote something and kept her eyes on me. I was grateful she didn't ask me what I missed. The list would be too long. "You okay to go on?" she asked instead.

I said yes, thinking I might have it under control again. I pulled air into my lungs. "I don't know what else you want," I said. "Her favorite fruit is mango." And for some reason, this caused instant tears to roll down the sides of my face, and I wanted to run up to my room and stuff my head under the covers. I didn't want to be sitting here telling this stranger these things. I wanted Mom to be here; no matter what crap was between us, she was my mother.

Something came through on Corporal Sanchez's radio and she spoke into it, then listened. "We've got a lat/long position on the cell phone," she said, putting the radio on the coffee table. "It's not moving, so that tells us something."

I wiped my face with my sleeves. "What does it tell you?"

"That she's stopped in one spot for now, or that the cell phone was left somewhere."

"Someone could have thrown it out and kept moving, you mean."

"There could be lots of explanations, but it gives us a starting point."

"But if she's been abducted," I said, "they must have taken her phone away."

"Maybe, but we don't know that's what happened yet. We need to be open to all possibilities." Her radio chirped.

"Didn't my dad explain about the text? It said she wasn't coming back. Not home — back. Like this house has no connection for her." She kept watching me and I said, "That's what Dad thinks. That it wasn't her sending it."

"What do you think?"

I stared at her pages of notes. "I don't know what I think. But it doesn't seem in character."

She looked like she wanted to say something, but for the longest time she didn't speak. The heaviness of the last few hours was sinking onto me like a lead blanket and I was okay with the silence. "Sometimes we're presented with surprising perspectives on the people we know," she said finally. "I know I have been."

She must have understood that I didn't get it, because she said, "I'm saying this is a situation where you might learn things about your mother you didn't expect. It's inevitable. Sometimes we're different versions of ourselves with different people."

I closed my eyes and thought of the data set I'd worked through on Planet Hunters a few hours before. Small bumps in the wavy lines that rose at measurable intervals. Evidence of a planet's existence, a whole undiscovered world. Something that had been there orbiting hundreds of light-years away for all this time but that we only discovered now.

"Can you keep going, or do you need a snack break?" Corporal Sanchez asked. "Low blood sugar can make this much harder."

I shook my head slowly. I was thinking about what Dad had told me in the kitchen. What he would be telling the other officer about it. "She and Dad had a fight," I said. "They hadn't resolved things when she disappeared." I rubbed my arms.

Her radio crackled on the coffee table.

"Is that why you separated us?" I asked, panic squeezing my insides. "Are you going to arrest him?"

She looked me in the eye. "We have to deal with the situation from all angles, Grace. At the moment, we're gathering infor-mation. Spousal involvement is not uncommon, so we have to explore it." She put her pen down. "But no, we're not going to arrest anyone right now."

A door opened and closed, and we sat in silence as someone walked into the kitchen, then back out again. They must have been in Dad's office.

"Can you tell me about your mother's habits, her typical activities when she was at home?"

This I could do. I massaged my lower back and counted off the habits in my head. "There are at least three behavior patterns," I said. "Patterns are kind of my thing."

She made a note.

"She clicks her tongue a lot, and there's the finger pulling."

"Finger pulling?"

"When she's distracted or stressed, she pulls on her fingers like this." I demonstrated.

"And she's been doing that a lot?"

"She was doing it a ton at the soccer game. But before that, too. I noticed when she was around the house. Watching a movie with Charlie last week, sitting at the table after dinner — when she was there for dinner."

Corporal Sanchez made more notes.

"And she's gotten really skinny." It felt suddenly wrong to say these things to a stranger, like I was spilling gossip.

"Can you tell me more about that?"

I tugged down the back of my T-shirt. "She's always had a hard time keeping weight on. She told me once that she had to gain weight even to get pregnant. She forgets to eat or something. Fast metabolism. My grandmother's the same." My usual joke was that two out of three Graces got it.

"And this pattern has become more pronounced lately?"

I shrugged. "I haven't been paying attention to her eating habits, but she's been getting thinner."

Corporal Sanchez wrote some more and then glanced up. "And the third thing?"

I suddenly couldn't remember if I'd had a third thing. My mind was a vacuum.

"It's natural to lose your train of thought," she said quietly. "Just give yourself space to think. I can wait."

But the thought that came up was the one I didn't want to talk about: the fight we had after Star Club a few weeks before, the night she was supposed to be there and then totally and completely failed. But what use was an argument like that to this situation?

"Her phone," I said. "She always used to leave it lying around and it would jingle all the time and Charlie or I would yell that so-and-so was calling or whatever and she'd come and answer it." I realized it was actually true — a real third thing even though I'd just grasped at anything to get away from thinking of the fight. "But then a while ago — maybe a few months — she stopped leaving it around the house. We'd always joked that it was like her third kid because it needed constant attention. Maybe she thought it bothered us to hear it all the time. But all I know is recently she's always had it on her. And I never hear it jingle. Maybe she changed the ringtone." I stared at the fake logs in the fireplace. We hadn't turned it on in years, and apparently no one had noticed the thickening layer of dust. "I can't believe I didn't think about her phone until now. That's so stupid of me."

Corporal Sanchez looked up from a full page of notes. "It's not stupid at all. There's no reason to feel guilty."

"I don't feel guilty," I snapped.

"Okay." She rested her pen on the paper. "Tell me more."

"More of what?" But I could see she'd seen something —

a hesitation or a twitch in my face. Maybe she'd been getting things from my body language all this time. Maybe she was better at reading signs than I thought.

"How have you and she been, Grace?"

It was all right there, behind the thin wall I had put up to contain it. "We've been kind of distant, like I said."

"And very recently?"

"More so."

"Because?"

I picked a piece of lint off my sweatpants. "We had a fight."

She waited.

I tucked my legs underneath me. "She misunderstood me and we argued." A headache was forming behind my left eye. "It was at Star Club a few weeks ago. I was exhibiting my photos. She didn't get that being a parent means being present. It's the usual thing with her."

"I see." Corporal Sanchez noted something. Then she asked me if I thought the fight could have contributed to her unusual behavior or her wanting to leave. I said I didn't know. I really didn't. But I was mostly relieved that she hadn't made me go into details. Maybe I wouldn't have to relive that night for someone else like I already did in my own head.

It got later. I rolled the empty water glass between my hands as she asked about Charlie, my feelings about school, our past vacations, whether any of us had seen a therapist. Dad and Constable Baker came back. My throat turned to sandpaper;

I forced myself not to swallow. It was probably one in the morning.

The station manager, Roger, called and Dad passed him to Corporal Sanchez. She walked down the hall as she talked to him, her voice low. Her radio muttered and thudded with static and random voices. Severely tanned Constable Baker talked about doing a video canvass around our street and questioning neighbors. Monitoring our phones.

When Corporal Sanchez came back, she said, "We'll need to speak to you again first thing tomorrow, and a team will come over to examine the house. Plus, we'll have to prepare something for the media. The alert has already gone out, but given how prominent a figure GG is, it will be picked up really fast and there'll be a frenzy." She turned to Dad. "Do you have somewhere you can stay for a few days?"

"Why?" I croaked.

Corporal Sanchez glanced at me and then back at Dad. "It's probably going to get crazy around here and you'll prefer to be elsewhere for a bit. Can we speak in the kitchen, Mr. Carter?"

Sleep pulled at me, but I strained to hear their voices as they walked down the hall. All I got were fragments like "kids" and "privacy." Constable Baker watched me from behind his computer. His eyes were a light blue that didn't match his tan. He had the square jaw of a magazine model.

"So that's it?" I asked, sleep deprivation making me sound kind of unhinged.

Constable Baker closed his laptop. "What's it?"

"You're going home now and we'll have to wait until morning? What about my mother?"

"We've been in touch with our detachment all night. I promise we have as many people working on this as we can. The first few hours of a case like this are the most crucial."

A case like this. The words were cold and hard against my fuzzy brain.

After they left and I dragged myself up the stairs, Dad tucked me in like he used to when I was a kid. He kissed my forehead and I put a hand there after he walked out, like I used to. I must have passed out that way.

13

"Grace, wake up. Gracie, you need to wake up. Now."

Was it a school day? It was bright out, but it felt like the middle of the night to my eyelids.

"Grace, please." Dad's voice was gravelly and low.

"What?" I cracked one eye open.

"You need to pack some clothes, okay? We're going to Marge Wilson's house."

"Marge Wilson? Why? What time is it?"

"Seven-something. The police are here. They need the house."

"Police?" I sat up, unsure what kind of dream this was.

"Yes, honey." Dad looked devastated and I worried that I'd caused it.

Something was nudging me. "Where's —"

"She's still missing, Gracie. They're doing their best — there are teams of people on this. There are three search parties out already. But we need to go, okay?"

It all came back in a cold rush. "Now?"

"Yes. Choose a few days' worth of clothes, get your tooth-brush and come downstairs. They're waiting to search the house."

"Search? For what?" I was still sitting in bed, and I could see the frustration crawling up his face.

"For clues, Grace. They need to look for evidence, for anything that can help them find her. I don't want us to be here." He walked away at that, and I was left to grab my school backpack and stuff clothes into it like we were running away.

∗

Marge's house smelled of the kibble farts her two dachshunds constantly emitted. I sat on the couch while Mozart and Vivaldi disemboweled a toy squirrel on the throw rug. Charlie sat beside them, entranced, but not wanting his hand to be their next victim. Marge had told us they weren't really used to kids, but she didn't take them away. I wondered if it was one of those dog/human relationships where the dogs secretly made all the decisions. Marge and Dad were talking in the kitchen. There was a pocket door between the kitchen and the living room, and it was closed. They talked in tones low enough that I couldn't make anything out over the aggressive growls of the dogs.

"I don't get why Mom hasn't called us," Charlie said then, eyes on the squirrel carnage. He'd started wrinkling his nose again. He'd done it until he was about six, a sign that something was on his mind. I would know he'd wet the bed when he came down to breakfast with his nose twitching like a bunny's.

"You know she sometimes can't get to the phone when she's busy," I said for the third time.

"Do you think they're going to eat it?"

I blinked. "What?"

"That toy. Do you think they're just going to eat it, like it's an actual squirrel?"

Mozart had ripped off a limb and was waving it around in his jaws, chomping as if he might just do that.

"I don't want to know," I said. Cars were going past on the street, but none slowed down or stopped in front of the house like they had at ours. As we'd bundled our things into Dad's trunk, two cars crawled by, the drivers' heads craned, eyes wide, and Dad yelled at us to get in. News traveled fast. I thought about what our front lawn must be like at that moment. And how it would be when we got home.

"Can you do CPR on a dog?"

I closed my eyes. "I don't think so."

"Because that would be so gross. Their breath —"

"Badger."

"No, look — he's totally choking."

I whipped my head around but the dogs were tug-of-warring the rest of the squirrel apart. "Don't freak me out right now," I said.

"It's like watching wolves. With really short legs."

I got up, kibble crumbs pressing into the soles of my feet. I hated this house and I hated being here. Screw them and their stupid pocket door.

*

Later, in the room I was sharing with Charlie, I sat down with my laptop, which I was not supposed to have brought. Dad had taken my phone — for safekeeping, he said — but I knew he was nervous about who I'd text, or who would text me. Every little thing seemed to set his jaw tight.

It seemed like all the news stations in the country were following the story, and they'd found a photo of our house as well as one of Mom and Dad from a few years before, when they went to some gala together. Dad was younger and tanned, and Mom was dewy and smiling and all sequined up. I forced myself not to go on social media — Corporal Sanchez had warned that people might post thoughtless as well as supportive things — but she hadn't said anything about email.

I opened my account, which I really only used for school stuff and occasional things from family members. There was nothing from Iris. She was probably texting me frantically and wondering why I wasn't responding.

I'm at a family friend's house, I wrote. *We're not allowed to be at home because: media. My dad has my phone. I really hope you check this today. It's as awful as it looks on TV. I miss you.*

Charlie shouted something downstairs, and then a dog bellowed his dissent.

I pressed Send and then fell asleep waiting for my laptop to ping.

*

I woke up later to Charlie crawling across the bed, making no effort to be careful.

"What time is it?"

"Seven thirty," he said. "You made a drool patch." He was wearing the baseball pajamas Grandma sent that Christmas. He couldn't care less about baseball.

"Shut up," I said, my neck sore from sleeping off the pillow. My mouth tasted terrible.

"Are you going to sleep in your clothes?"

"Maybe." I rubbed my face and weighed the pros/cons of getting up to brush my teeth.

"Do you still snore?"

"I have never snored."

He gave me a raised eyebrow.

"Shut up, kid."

"Get a vocabulary."

"God." I flopped back onto the pillow, the bed now far too small with him in it. "Just go to sleep."

"Duh. That's what I'm trying to do."

"Is Dad downstairs?"

"Yeah. On the phone."

We lay there in silence, watching the walls. They were papered with pale green ferns.

Then I remembered the email I'd been waiting for. I jumped out of bed and opened the laptop on the top of the dresser.

"What are you doing?" Charlie asked.

I didn't answer him, just watched the screen load and there was a reply from her, the one-line preview saying, *Oh my God, Grace. ARE YOU OKAYY?? I've been trying to reach you but ...* I opened the email and kept reading.

... you weren't answering my texts and I wondered if the cops had taken your phone and maybe what I was saying would be

used as evidence or something?! I can't believe this is happening!!
What do you need? Can I come and bring you food? Moral
support? Am I allowed in? My parents want to write you an email
asking the same thing, so on their behalf: TELL US HOW WE
CAN HELP. I love you, Grace.

I was crying by the second sentence, salty tears rolling into my mouth.

"Hello? What are you doing?" Charlie said behind me, and I wiped my face with my sleeve.

"Nothing. Just checking email. It's fine." I typed a quick reply, promising to get my phone back, promising to find out if she could visit. I pressed Send and squeezed my eyes shut. Breathed through my nose for a three count.

"Do you need Dad?" Charlie asked as I got back into bed.

"No, I'm okay."

"You sure?"

"Yeah, Badger. Let's just go to sleep."

He rummaged under the blanket for a moment, and I thought maybe he was going to throw a disgusting dog toy at me, but he was just untangling his arm from the sheet. He laid it down between us and said, "Can I put my hand in the middle like this?"

"Whatever you want. That's your half of the bed."

He lay still and stared up at the ceiling. "Can you get the light?"

I reached over and switched off the lamp.

We listened to the strange thickness the room had, like it was padded in cotton wool.

I felt with my pinkie in the dark, wrapped it around his.

*

The next morning, Dad left Marge's house after breakfast, saying they needed him at the police station — he just said "station" and then had to clarify which one — so we were alone with Marge and the dogs. After cleaning up the kitchen and fussing over what TV shows she could find for us, she stood beside the couch and said, "Well, guys, I have to get to work. I have a deadline today." Her dyed hair was cut bluntly around her face, and her skin was red with tiny veins all over it.

"You're leaving?" Charlie asked. He'd been acting more subdued, maybe a little more unnerved, than the day before, but he still ate a huge breakfast and had been bothering me incessantly with stupid questions about the dogs.

"No, no," Marge said. "I'm going upstairs. I work from home. But I still have a deadline, so." She looked at me. Her eyes were magnified by her glasses. She was one of my mother's friends I just didn't get. They'd known each other for years, but I couldn't imagine what they had in common. Marge was sort of grandmother age and, judging by the quilts everywhere, very into the fabric arts. "Will you be okay here for a few hours?" she asked. "There's cheese in the fridge and crackers on the counter."

Charlie perked up at that.

"We just ate," I said. "When's my dad coming back?"

Marge rubbed her arms as if she were cold. "I don't know, Grace. He said he'd be a while. The party has a lot of ground to cover."

"Party?"

Mozart and Vivaldi started a new tussle with a knotted sock, and with Charlie's attention diverted, I got up off the couch.

"What party?" I asked again.

Marge sighed. There was a trace of coffee creamer on her upper lip. "The search party he's with. He didn't want to worry you."

"Should I be worried?"

"Not at all, no. He's searching with professionals. If anyone can find her …" She made a strangled sound in her throat, but she might have just been clearing it. "Look, if you need me, I'll be in my bedroom, okay? Working away. You just call."

And she left us with the growling dogs and the TV flashing with a high-speed chase scene Charlie wasn't even watching.

It wasn't hard to find my phone, especially with Charlie and Marge distracted. Dad had hidden it in the top dresser drawer of the guest/storage room that his air mattress had been set up in. I sat in the nest of his unmade sheets and scrolled through Iris's frantic texts, full of capital letters and question marks. There was something from Trina in my physics class: *OMG Grace are you okay!!? What is going on!!?* Then there was a thread from Mylo. It spanned the time I was being questioned by the police to this morning.

> *I just saw the report on the news. How are you doing?*
>
> *Are you okay?? Deep breaths, remember?*
>
> *Just so you know, I won't say anything to anyone. Promise.*
>
> *Hey. I'm kind of getting worried since you're not replying. Should I be?*

The last message was a photo of our school's main hallway, filled with students, lockers being rummaged through. In the middle of the hall, almost at the back, I caught sight of a cop walking away. People's heads were turned to watch him.

Mylo hadn't captioned the photo. It was the last thing he sent, at 8:25 a.m. An hour and a half ago.

I'm okay, I texted. *I haven't had my phone until now. We're holed up at a friend's house while ours is ripped apart by the cops.*

Then I typed, *Now that I have my phone back, I need to hear more about the butterflies.*

I didn't care if that sounded desperate. All I wanted was to hear his voice in my ear, transported there through invisible signals like magic but really by science.

I was about to go downstairs to make sure Charlie hadn't been mauled by the dogs when Mylo replied. *I have a spare period in an hour. I'll call then. Breathe.*

*

"Where are you?" I asked when he called.

"In my mom's car. The only private place at school. Did you get the photo?"

"Yeah. Crazy. Did people freak out?"

"Most people were cool." There was silence for a moment and then he said, "Any news? Have the police questioned you again? They usually do a few rounds."

I crossed my legs. "Is there a cop in your family or something?"

He didn't reply, and I started to wonder if I'd somehow insulted him. Then he said, "No, we had a family member go missing. I'm not really allowed to talk about it. My mom's super protective of the whole thing. Privacy is paramount."

"Sounds just like my mother." As I said it, the trueness of it sank in.

"Yeah, well, I just know what you're going through. Probably way more than most people. It was kind of crazy that you even called me that night. I never fell asleep afterward."

There was something about him saying that, and the comforting roll of his voice in my ear, that made me want to sob with relief. Somehow Mylo McLean and I were Terrible Life Event Twins.

"Are you there?" he asked.

"Yeah, I'm here," I said.

"Should I tell you what happened when the South Korean government raided my grandfather's apartment?"

I lay down on my back on the half-deflated air mattress. "Yes. Please."

14

That evening, Dad sat Charlie and me down on the re-inflated mattress. He'd come home for dinner after more questioning and all that searching, looking like he'd run a marathon. Now he was about the same — thin, slack skinned, pale — but with his face half pulled into parent mode.

Charlie made the air mattress squawk beside me.

"Stop it," I snapped.

"Grace," Dad said.

"It's not our mattress," I said.

"It's all right."

"Can we go home now?" Charlie asked. "Being here sucks."

Dad shushed him. "Yes, we're going home tomorrow after breakfast. But Marge has been incredibly kind to let us stay here, so please be good until we leave, okay?"

"Why did we even come here?" I asked quietly. "Aren't there, like, ten other people we could have stayed with? I've never understood why Marge and Mom are friends anyway."

Dad watched me for a moment too long. "When you were a baby," he said, "your mom had postpartum depression. You might not know that."

I blinked at him, feeling stupid.

"She used to take you to the park to get outside. It was doctor-ordered vitamin D, I think. She met Marge walking her dog in the park. She didn't have Mozart and Vivaldi then. I think it was a Lab or something. They started meeting in the park every day, and it seemed to really help." Dad coughed and reached for the glass on the desk. "Marge's husband was still alive then."

"She never talked about any of that," I said.

But Dad was already leaning toward Charlie, putting a hand on his shoulder. "Look, the point here isn't to talk about Marge. I need to explain some things about what's going to happen when we get home."

"Are there going to be people in the house?" Charlie asked.

"Maybe. But mostly there could be people outside. Reporters. Police. Curious neighbors. I'm not sure what it'll be like."

"Because she's not back yet?"

"Yeah, buddy."

"This is getting crazy, Dad," he said. "Why do so many people know about this?"

Dad glanced at me. "Because everyone's working really hard to bring her home."

"Dad, if she's missing, why can't they do an Amber Alert?"

"That's for kids," I said.

Dad held a hand up in my direction. "Right. Charlie, Amber Alerts are for missing children, but the equivalent has been issued for her."

Charlie brought his knees up to his chest, making me wobble on the air mattress. "So she's actually really lost."

"Yes."

"Like kidnapped?"

"Maybe." Dad looked like he was going to say more, but he just put his hand on Charlie's shoulder and said, "Maybe."

Charlie wrinkled his nose and stared at his socks, his fingers spread across them like fans.

15

The police performed a miracle because there were no reporters or crews at the house when we got there. Just a cop with a guilty expression, like he was some burglar who'd been caught.

The shocking thing was the drift of cellophane-wrapped flowers piled up at the door, and beside it a considerable stack of food containers. I counted them as we got out of the car. Three plastic tubs and four foil trays.

"Isn't this what happens when someone dies?" I asked.

Dad was holding Charlie by the hand. "And when someone has a baby."

"This is what people did when I was born?" Charlie said, rushing toward the stuff, throwing his backpack down so he could examine everything unencumbered.

"Who did this?" I asked.

Dad and I were still standing back, the cop halfway down the driveway, maybe wanting to give us a moment alone with our house.

"Neighbors, friends, I guess." Dad rubbed the back of his head. "People don't know what to do at a time like this. They want to be useful."

"That many flowers isn't useful," I said. "That's an allergic reaction."

"There's three lasagnas," the cop called behind us. He had a deep voice. "A couple more came yesterday, and my colleague put them in your fridge. Hope that's okay."

Dad took a step forward and reached for me to do the same.

Charlie was already into one of the tubs, which evidently contained cookies.

"It's so weird," I whispered. "First we have to leave so cops can take over our house, and now it's like everyone else has taken it over."

16

Everyone I knew had clothing patterns. Charlie wore the same three T-shirts in rotation and always chose the same pair of blue socks as soon as they came out of the laundry basket. Dad liked belts. He'd wear a belt with anything if he could. I thought of it as his version of a shoe habit.

Mom's clothing patterns were categorized in her closet. The evening wear was at the far end, all sequins and lace and satin, several things in plastic dry-cleaner bags. Activewear was a small section at the front, on the left. She went to the gym three times a week, usually at work. Opposite it were her regular work clothes — pantsuits and blazers, blouses and dresses. Pencil skirts and skinny trousers only someone with her figure could pull off. Beside that was weekend wear. I stood in the middle of the closet and breathed in the layers of smells — faint dry-cleaning chemicals, Mom's perfume, the tang of shoe polish. It was amazing how much you could learn about someone from their clothes but also how much you couldn't. What was she thinking as she got dressed the morning she was abducted? Or the morning before that? All the mornings of my life? I felt the jolt of the reality that she wasn't there to ask, that we were picking up the pieces of a mystery. All these clothes were like silent witnesses to something none of us understood.

I ran my hand along the thin shoulders of the hangers until I came to the shirt that stood out the most: a lime green sleeveless buttondown. The back of my neck started prickling. I hadn't seen her wear it since we'd had the fight at Star Club.

I'd been preparing images for the astrophotography exhibition since January, using Claudia's telescope on club nights to get better resolution of the moon's Aristarchus crater. Mom had managed to get out of some media event, a rarity I was hyperaware of. It made me both relieved and nervous. Dad wandered into my room the hour before we were leaving for the show, his lucky belt halfway through its loops, and asked if I was nervous. I knew it wasn't me, it was him. He got nervous for both Charlie and me whenever we did something like this, almost like he was reliving his own piano recitals as a kid. I told him no, it was just an exhibit of photographs and a table of brownies and punch. It wasn't the whole universe. He made a comment about how similar I was to Mom in that way and I shrugged it off. I hadn't thought about us having comparable public speaking skills, and anyway, who knew what I'd feel when I had to start presenting.

I could tell Mom was distracted as soon as we got there. She toured around the planetarium with her arms clasped in front of her, that lime green shirt like a beacon surrounded by navies and dark browns and the silver-gray of photographed moons. And then Claudia cleared her throat for everyone's attention; only about twenty people had shown up, and a chunk of that was my family and Iris's. Mom reached into her purse for something as she ducked behind a couple of tall people. When I glanced over again, I couldn't see her anymore. Claudia called my name and everyone looked at me. Iris gave me a thumbs-up.

My mind went blank for a second. I'd spent the previous night memorizing descriptions for each photo, but now I had nothing. Iris's thumbs were still up. "Hi," I said, and my voice echoed in the still room.

Half in shadow, Dad nodded the tiniest bit.

I blinked at the photo of Tycho crater, blown up to fifty times on the screen. "When Claudia told us we should show our work, none of us wanted to do it," I said. It wasn't part of my rehearsed speech. "We didn't think we were good enough or that anyone would care about our blurry photos. But she wore us down by saying we wouldn't have to do it for months. So we practiced and used the computers here and even had an astrophotographer come and give us tips. And after a while it started to seem like a good idea." Laughter murmured through the room. "So thanks for coming."

Dad was nodding again, but more emphatically.

I looked up at the photo of Tycho and explained what it was. The kind of scope I'd used to get the image. How deep the crater was and what kind of impact might have created it. The next image was of Proxima Centauri, the closest star to us. I explained about the binary star system and about the discovery of an Earthlike planet in its orbit. I hadn't seen any data for it on Planet Hunters, but Claudia had told us when they found it, before the discovery paper came out.

After I clicked off the presentation at my photo of Mars, a dad at the back of the group asked how exoplanets got named.

I told him about what the Kepler Space Telescope did, and Claudia came up and gave a few examples.

As the next exhibitor finished talking about his photos, Mom slipped in the side door and I realized she'd missed the whole thing. In my nervousness, I'd forgotten to look for her again where I'd last seen her.

Things got worse when the brownies and punch were brought out because suddenly GG Carter was there, and everyone who hadn't noticed her before was clamoring to speak to her or eyeing her from behind plastic punch cups. She smiled graciously, her lipstick having worn off, and gave them the answers and compliments they wanted. Charlie horsed around with someone else's little brother, and Dad chatted with Claudia, who kept gesturing excitedly toward my photos. Iris stood beside me and did humorous voiceover for the conversations around us. I heard her voice rising and falling only in my right ear.

Then Mom's phone rang. It was loud enough for the sound to cross the room. She smiled as it rang, clearly trying not to answer it, but just before it went to voicemail — I knew how many rings it took — she ducked her head and stepped out of her circle of fans.

Iris got in my face about something after that, so when Mom tapped me on the shoulder a few minutes later, her face a carefully held together mask of neutrality, I was a little surprised.

"Grace, can you step outside with me for a moment?"

"No, thanks," I said.

"Please. It's important." She had to work to keep from emoting; it had to be something serious.

I shrugged and went, catching Iris's eye just before I turned away, seeing the question on her face.

Once outside, the air cool and damp, Mom crossed her arms over her chest.

"What?" I asked, tense in every limb.

"I just got a call from Melanie Urquhart's mother," she said.

"So?" I had no idea where this could be going. Melanie Urquhart was hilarious but also an insufferable gossip. I rushed to remember if I'd passed her anything that was coming back to bite me.

Mom didn't blink. "Is there anything you want to tell me?"

"About Melanie?"

"About you. Your recent activities. Anything you might have regrets about."

"I think that's called leading the witness," I said, feeling suddenly panicky that there was something I'd done — I just didn't know what it was.

"Grace," Mom said. "I'm serious."

I said nothing, mind racing, but being silent wasn't helping my case.

"Mrs. Urquhart told me you mentioned to Melanie that you did drugs at a party. Is this true?"

I could have exhaled with my whole body. Melanie was a lying, conniving bag of gossip biscuits. "She's full of crap," I said. "I didn't do drugs. I've never done drugs."

"Never?"

She wasn't much closer to belief than when we'd walked out. I ground my teeth. "No, never."

She turned her head away, to the view of the sky beyond the

parking lot, where the stars would be if there wasn't a layer of cloud obscuring them. "I just hope you're being honest with me, Grace. Mrs. Urquhart said police found evidence of several kinds of drugs at a house party and there were several kids involved."

I stared back at her, unwilling to give an inch. "That isn't exactly overwhelming evidence of my involvement, is it? I. Didn't. Do. Anything."

She had the decency to look away, but she didn't look down. She never looked down when we were in public and she had her GG Carter on. "The reality is, in my position, scandals aren't forgiving," she said. "You remember that daughter of the politician in Vancouver?"

"You're not a politician," I said flatly. "You're a TV personality." I left out the journalist part.

She plowed on. "Maybe it's not fair that this family is under a microscope, but that's the way it is. It requires you to be careful of your behavior, which isn't a bad lesson in life, Grace."

I couldn't stop rolling my eyes. "What planet do you live on? We're not under a microscope. I don't have paparazzi following me anywhere. I'm not mobbed at the mall. I don't even go to the mall, but if I did no one would care." Didn't she know we were at Star Club? Not an ideal people-watching spot. I couldn't believe she was doing this on top of walking out on my presentation.

She looked frustrated for the first time. Maybe I'd insulted her view of herself. How like Grandma. "Your father and I have worked hard to keep things that way," she said. "So that you wouldn't notice. Why do you think we chose to live here, not in Vancouver or Toronto? That would be much easier for me — less travel, less hassle. We chose relative privacy for you. For the family. But we are watched, Grace. And if something were to happen, you'd soon realize it."

A wisp of cloud floated through the parked cars in front of us.

"So I'm not allowed to have a life like other teenagers? Or have you assumed since I'm not like you, always socializing and smiling for cameras, that I wouldn't care about partying?"

"Of course you should have a life. That's the whole point of living here."

"But you're telling me not to embarrass you, not to do anything a perfect daughter wouldn't do. Well, that's not me. And it's not you." I pointed a finger at her. "You're pretty far from perfect yourself."

She opened her mouth, hesitated, then said, "This isn't about perfection, Grace. I'm just trying to make a point about how things are."

"But it's ridiculous!" I exploded. "I didn't even do the thing you're accusing me of — it's not how things are!"

"Grace." Her hands had come up as my voice rose, like she was trying to calm a little kid.

"You want to know how things are?" I said. "Things are pretty crappy when your mother leaves your photography exhibition at the exact moment you're up to present. Who does that? Oh, right — you."

She opened her mouth but I wasn't done.

"Was that a work call you got before my presentation? You just had to take it?"

She blinked fast and said nothing.

"Well, thank goodness you answer your phone no matter what. Now you can steer me onto the right path, away from drugs and sex and oblivion. Because you've paid so much attention to the real, important stuff lately. You really get me, don't you? I'm all about the drugs." I reached behind me for the door. "Fuck you."

I walked inside, into the warm murmur of the crowd, the brownie crumbs on the floor and the little brothers sprawled out under the diorama of Jupiter's moons.

17

The room was stuffy and crackled with bursts of radio static. There was a shaggy potted plant by the window. A photo of a kid leaned against one wall — Corporal Sanchez's son, I assumed — and maps and certificates hung on the others. Isabel. She'd shaken Dad's hand and he'd addressed her as Isabel. It made everything seem more serious; being on a first-name basis was for drawn-out processes where people got to know each other.

It was bullshit. It had been two days since we got back into our house and there'd been no new information. I'd let myself believe that by calling us to the station, the cops were getting ready to tell us something — maybe not that they'd found her, but something. What the hell had they been working on all this time? But it became clear when we walked in and Constable Baker greeted Dad and high-fived Charlie, and Corporal Sanchez motioned for me to follow her into her office, that this was just another round of questioning. Which Mylo had foretold, but that didn't make it any better.

"How are you feeling?" she asked from her chair. Her hair was still pulled back tightly, this time in a bun. Maybe there were rules against female officers having their hair down.

"How should I be feeling?" I asked.

She didn't smile so much as open up her face. "This is going to be a lot easier if you help me out. You're here because you want to find your mother, right?"

"Mostly because you summoned us," I said. "Why isn't there any news yet? It's been almost a week since she went missing."

"I know it's frustrating. I wish we had more to tell you —"

"Apparently you have nothing to tell us."

"— But we're working on every lead and I'm confident we'll have more solid details soon —"

"That sounds like a whole lot of zero."

She was good at keeping calm. "We can agree that it's challenging to know so little. But can we also work on nailing down more details while we wait for progress?"

God, she was good at reframing. I couldn't argue with that. I studied the happy face of her possible son. He had dimples. Exceedingly cute kid. "Okay."

She reached under her desk and pulled out a bottle of water. "Want one?"

"You guys really need to start using the tap. You know about the island of plastic in the middle of the Pacific, right?"

She put the bottle on her desk and reached for a flowered mug. "Yes, I do. I actually brought up the water bottles with the captain a few days ago. He's going to see what he can do. In the meantime, I can offer you coffee."

"No, thanks, I'm fine," I said.

She appraised me from her side of the room. "There is one thing I can tell you. We have reason to believe your mother is with someone she knows. This is most often the case and

96

doesn't narrow it down as much as we'd like. But the good thing is we can trace back all leads, all details we find or get from people who know her to find out who and why someone took her."

I swallowed the lump this information created in my throat. Someone she knew. It was worse than if it had been a stranger. "Have you asked the people she works with? There are, like, a hundred people at the TV station. Maybe it was a cameraperson or something. Or a crazed fan."

"We'll be questioning people all week, longer if necessary."

"You mean you don't think you'll find her by the end of this *week*?"

"We're taking it day by day, Grace. As should you." She sat back in her chair. "There are two things I'd like you to tell me about. Your relationship with your dad and that night at the Star Club you mentioned to me."

I stared at her feet, waiting for the tap habit to show up. "Why do you need to know about my dad?"

"It helps round out the picture. Are you close?"

I shrugged. "Closer than I am with my mother."

"Tell me."

I reconsidered my assessment of the potted plant. Shaggy was for harmless hippies. That plant was slightly menacing in its unkemptness. "He and I have always had things to talk about. We cook together sometimes. He tries to get me to do yoga with him. He always has an answer to my questions. He cares."

She wrote something down with a green pen. "What do you two talk about?"

"Lots of things. Science, because he's an ecologist. And 3-D printing, which he thinks is the best thing ever. We talk about what I want to do when I graduate."

"What is that?"

"I want to study astronomy."

Her right foot started tapping, finally. "Sounds like a great goal," she said. "I wanted to be a helicopter pilot when I was in high school, but it never worked out for me. How long has your dad had his business?"

"About five years. Before that he worked for the city."

"And was your mother supportive of your dad starting his own business?"

"I guess. She never said she wasn't."

"And how have things been for the family since he's been a consultant?"

"Fine. Are you asking if my parents fight a lot?"

She looked at me evenly, which meant she now wanted to know.

I kind of wished I'd taken the water bottle. "Dad must have told you about the spa weekend and Charlie and me going to Palm Springs."

"Yes."

"And that they argued before the weekend of the soccer tournament."

"Yes."

"But I don't know what the fight was about or how bad it was." I let the silence stretch out in case she might tell me something. She didn't. "It was kind of shocking when he said they'd been fighting. I never knew it was that bad." I glanced at her. "Was it that bad?"

She looked down to write something and didn't answer.

"You're not going to give me anything?"

She finally met my eye. "You're going to have to ask your father about that. It's up to him."

"Right. Silly me."

She tapped her pen against the paper almost distractedly. "How would you describe your mother's feelings about her work?"

I blinked. A phone rang somewhere outside. "It's pretty much all she does. I mean, she's up late working on stuff and always at the station's beck and call. If you ask my dad he'll tell you how hard she worked for the last promotion."

"Right, but how do you think she *feels* about the work?"

I'd never thought about it, really. I just assumed she worked that hard because she liked the job. How could you get to be a TV celebrity and not actually want to be one? "She loves meeting people, talking about current events. I remember once she told me that learning about people was one of her greatest joys."

"How old were you when she told you that?"

"Ten, I guess."

"So, seven years ago."

"Yeah."

"And she hasn't talked to you about her passions since then?"

"No, but we don't really talk. For all I know she's been chatting to her colleagues about it nonstop."

"Right." She was writing again. "Anything else?"

"No."

"Can you answer a few questions about the night you argued with your mother? At the Star Club?"

I looked away. "Okay."

"Was her behavior normal that night?"

Normal was relative. If missing your daughter's presentation and falsely accusing her of drug use was normal, then sure. "She was typically distracted by phone calls and chatting with people who wanted to shake her hand and get a picture with her. That's all pretty normal."

She was studying me.

I looked out the window at the cedar hedge outside. It took up all the view like a natural blind. What was the point in having a window here? "She was tired, I guess. But she was always tired. Most people don't see it because of her makeup, but I can always tell."

"You say she took a phone call. Do you know who it was from?"

My stomach started to simmer. "The mother of someone from school called her. And I think there might have been a call before that. At least, she left my presentation for some reason and I just assumed. It's typical for her. She didn't deny it when I asked."

"And if there was a first call," Isabel said, "what time do you think it happened?"

"I don't know," I said, trying to recall when we even got there. "Maybe around seven thirty."

She tapped her pen on her knee. "And this was four weeks ago? April seventeenth?"

"Yes."

"And where was your father?"

"Inside the planetarium with my brother." I leaned forward. "Was there another call?"

She didn't blink. "Yes."

My skin went cold. "Do you know who it was?" That evening at Star Club had been lodged in my memory for weeks because of the fight we had, not because of who might have called her. "Can't you check all her calls with a warrant or something?"

"We have the log from the cell phone provider, but the number was a prepaid cell phone."

"And you can't trace that?"

"It's really hard to. In this case, we're not getting anywhere."

I sat back in the chair and rested my head against the wall behind me.

"So if you think of anything that could shed some light on it, let me know."

There was a low buzzing in my ears. Something so small and stupid as that phone call could end up being a huge part of the mystery. It made me slightly nauseated. "Did that number call any other time?"

"Yes."

I stared at the suspiciously shaggy plant, which, for all I knew, was the source of the buzzing sound. "A lot?"

"Yes," she said. "Are you okay to continue?"

I swallowed and the buzzing stopped. "I guess."

18

"Hey," Mylo said when he picked up. His voice had softened in that way your voice does when you become friends with someone — there's an edge that's shaved off by the familiarity.

"Hey," I said.

"You breathing?"

"Yeah. You?"

"So far so good."

"How was school?"

"Mostly boring. Tom Watson hurled at the end of history class, so that was eventful."

"Nasty."

"And Sasha asked about you again. She's actually nice, you know."

"You told her we talk?"

"No, she just asked, like in general, if anyone knew what was happening with the investigation, and how you were doing."

"And you said ..."

"That I knew as much as she knew ... Anyway, people are just curious. In a good way, mostly."

"Mostly? Okay, fine," I said. "Finish telling me about your

grandpa's butterfly collection. You were explaining about when he almost went to jail for smuggling."

∗

There was a knock on my door, but I was half in a dream on my bed and jumped like it had been a gunshot.

"Grace?" Charlie pushed the door open a crack. "Can I come in?"

"What are you doing up?" I asked. "It's after nine."

"It's not like I have school in the morning."

"That won't be forever, though. Okay?"

He looked at me, and I could tell he was trying to decide if going back to school was a good thing in this scenario, if it meant Mom would be coming home. He shuffled across the carpet and flopped down beside me. When he was little he'd gone through a phase of curling up in my bed whenever Mom was away for work. I'd come home to find him cozied like a cat in the blanket, either passed out or mesmerized by some game on his tablet. At bedtime he'd wander in, pajamaed and smelling of toothpaste, and just assume his spot, as if there was no negotiation to be had. He was still young enough, cute enough, that I didn't push it.

"I can't sleep," he said into my blanket.

"Where's Dad?" I asked.

"Inside the internet," he said. "I think Grandma's coming soon."

I hadn't thought about her in days. Which was stupid — her daughter was missing. Plus, this was just the kind of drama she thought she needed to be in the middle of. "Great," I said.

"Dad was talking to her on the phone earlier. I could hear her screeching from across the room."

"Poor Dad."

He flopped onto his back on the bed. "Did Isabel ask you about Mom's friends?"

"Yeah. Did she ask you about her co-workers?"

"And what neighbors she talked to. I told her about Marge and the depression thing Dad said."

"I didn't," I said, wondering if I should have.

He sat up and crossed his legs. "I remembered something."

"What is it?

"I found a note a while ago. She said anything could be important, right?"

"Yeah?"

He reached into his pocket. "I found this piece of paper in a box in the basement." He held out a tattered and softened piece of white paper with faded lines. "I was looking for old Legos. There weren't any other pieces of paper, just this one. I thought maybe it was yours at first."

I opened it carefully and saw three lines in slanted script in now-watery blue ink, each cut off where the paper had been torn. The top one said, "You will never know," the second one said, "if you love" and the third one said, "can't be abandoned." At the bottom, it was signed "Always, F."

"Do you think it's Mom's writing?" he asked.

"No. Hers doesn't lean like that. Plus, her initial isn't *F*."

"I thought about our neighbors," Charlie said. "But no one around here's name starts with *F*."

"Frank Bower."

"Who's that?"

"The guy who cuts Mrs. Emerson's lawn. He's her nephew. But why would he write something like this to Mom? If it was even for her?"

He looked small with his shoulders hunched. "Maybe it's nothing, then. Maybe it's not even anyone's."

My black-hole clock ticked through the silence. It was kind of ridiculous to have a wall clock at all when I had my phone every second of the day, but Charlie had seen it while buying Christmas presents with Mom one year, so that's what I got from him. I loved it.

"You think it's stupid," he said.

"I don't think it's stupid. It just seems kind of random."

He flopped back on the bed. "I hate this."

"Me, too, Badger."

I tucked the note into the pocket of my shorts and lay beside him. We stared at the ceiling together, but Charlie fell asleep first.

19

Dad was in the kitchen unloading the dishwasher when I went down for a glass of water at eleven. Flowers, about half of them bouquets, decorated every surface. It looked like a florist's. We didn't have enough vases, so Dad was using water glasses. A new stack of food containers sat by the fridge.

He was watching me gawk at the flowers. "It's unbelievable. All the money people spent."

I stood at the sink with a glass and let the water run cold.

"You okay?" His skin was gray, like someone who wasn't getting enough oxygen.

"No. You?"

"Same. Did you eat dinner?"

My glass filled to the top and overflowed. "It was hard to choose from the smorgasbord."

"The green bean salad was good."

"I ate some of the hummus."

"I bought that last week."

"Are we only eating condolence food right now?"

He sighed. "Is Charlie in your room?"

"Asleep in my bed."

"Good." He scrubbed his face with one hand. Another stress habit. "Did I tell you Patricia's coming tonight? She found a late flight."

"It's already late."

"There were complications. She won't be here until 1:00 a.m."

"Are you ready?" I asked.

He leaned on the counter. "I know it's not going to be easy having her here, but it's important. She's family."

"It's probably going to be hell, Dad."

"Just another level of it." He closed his eyes. "But she's coming and she wants to help."

"She said that?"

"She basically did. She sounded very worried." He scratched his cheek. "She does love your mother."

I took a sip of water and it ran cold down my throat. "Yeah, but they want to question her, too, right? She probably had to come."

He blew out a long breath.

"Dad?"

"Yeah."

"Are they treating you as a suspect?"

"No, Grace."

"No?"

He closed his eyes. "I'm her husband, so they have to be detailed with me."

"But what about your fight?"

He hesitated. "In the grand scheme of things, what does it mean?"

I couldn't decide if he was asking me or the universe.

"I miss her," he said, then looked away.

I drank half the glass of water, took a breath and drank the rest. Considered telling him about the note Charlie had found that was in my pocket, pressed against my hip.

"You need to get some sleep, Gracie."

"You need to be less parental right now."

He looked up at the ceiling, and I had the urge to hug his shoulders, to really squeeze him.

He swore under his breath.

"What?" I asked.

"I forgot to cancel Charlie's dentist appointment today. Go on up to bed, okay? I'm just going to tidy things a little."

"What, do some flower arranging?"

He stared at a huge bunch of red carnations. "I've never liked these. Don't know why. They always seemed … dishonest, if a flower can have human attributes. They're all … frilly and fake-looking."

"Don't stare at them too long," I said, patting him on the shoulder. "You never know what lies they'll tell you."

He reached up and put his hand on top of mine, holding it there against the muscle and bone. He might have been ready to say something, but he didn't.

20

She was beautiful in her beige interviewing armchair, the lights from above hitting her softly but with precision. Movie-star lighting, as Grandma called it. For the past year the stylist had been flat-ironing her hair, and it hung in a long bob to her shoulders like curtains. Her eyes had lost their tiredness under her full makeup, and they must have put drops in to take away the redness. Her teeth flashed white when she smiled. It was the third time I'd watched her last broadcast, and though I was noticing all these little details about her, nothing new was jumping out. No pattern out of the ordinary, except the things I'd told Isabel.

She talked like she really cared about the guy she was interviewing — her body leaning in and her hands relaxed on her lap. In the middle, he made a joke and she laughed — really laughed. It reminded me of the times we'd play Scrabble on Christmas Eve when I was younger and she'd been present in mind as well as body. She and I crushed it one year, and Dad couldn't understand because he never lost at Scrabble, even when four-year-old Charlie was his so-called partner. Mom couldn't stop laughing at his incredulous face. We teased him about it until New Year's, when we had a rematch and he pounded us.

I sat back in my swivel chair and paused the video. This broadcast was over a week old, the last thing she'd made. What was the use of watching it again? It wasn't reality anymore — it was the glow of a star that was now gone, a parcel of far-traveled light reflected on a telescope's mirrors.

In my bed, Charlie turned over in his sleep. I minimized the window, closed my laptop and crawled under the blanket.

21

I knew Grandma was there in the morning because I could already smell her perfume. Some insanely expensive stuff probably containing the musk of endangered animals. I opened my eyes a crack. Charlie was gone.

I swung my legs over the side of the bed. After my head rush cleared, I tried to determine how there could be perfume assaulting my nostrils. She wouldn't just barge in here while I was sleeping. Would she?

Maybe she had taken Charlie from my bed.

The smell was even stronger in the hallway, so much so that I almost gagged.

"Grace? Are you up?"

I stumbled to the top of the stairs, a hand over my mouth.

She was staring up at me with all her feathers in place: blond-streaked smooth hair skimming a flattering collared blouse, heavy gold necklace with matching bracelet. Well-cut khaki slacks. Red toenails. The stench.

"Is it still strong up there? Your brother managed to spill the entire bottle on the carpet, although what he was doing with it up here, I don't know."

My head was pounding. "Didn't you bother cleaning it up?"

"Of course. It's much better than it was." She held out a hand. "Why don't you come down for some breakfast? My God, you're getting so tall!"

I let her get me a glass of orange juice as I massaged my forehead at the kitchen counter. "Where's Dad?"

"At the police station." She brought the juice and enveloped me in a hug I really didn't want.

"God, that perfume is a biological weapon, Grandma."

"Oh, don't be dramatic." She squeezed me harder for good measure.

"Can't you smell it? Or has it burned out all your olfactory cells?"

She exhaled through her nose, a little ladylike snort that was usually reserved for waiter errors or her online purchases being delayed. "Honestly, Grace, you're as bad as a seventeen-year-old."

"Nice one."

"I do know what teenagers are like."

"Really? Wasn't Mom at boarding school the whole time?"

We both looked away, waiting for the atom bomb of Mom's name to finish detonating.

Her nails ticked on the quartz counter. "Yes, well, I've dealt with enough adolescents in my career as well. Believe me, young lady, there are some pretty snotty seventeen-year-olds in show business." As if somehow that should make me feel worse about my behavior. "Anyway," she said, "let's remember why I came here."

I pushed the juice away. "Where's Charlie?"

"In the garage."

"Why?"

She sighed. "Because he wants to be, I guess. He went in there an hour ago."

"And you haven't checked on him?"

"Grace, what's the matter with you?" She said this with an exasperated smile. "He's not a toddler." Her phone rang — an R&B tune I'd heard on the radio — and she turned to answer it, laughing even before the person on the other end had finished their sentence.

I wanted to yell something into her other ear, but instead I headed for the garage. Maybe the air would only smell of bike tires in there.

I found the place in disarray, boxes opened and the contents strewn about like Christmas morning. Charlie was in the middle of it all, turning in circles with a crazy look on his face.

"What the hell?" I said.

"I thought of something!" he shouted from the chaos.

"You don't have to deafen me. This is a small space." I stepped over a snarl of Christmas lights.

"There's that box of maps somewhere." He turned in a clockwise circle.

"What maps?"

"We used them for art one time. She let me cut out parts and draw things on them."

"Yeah, so?"

He scanned the top shelf of the cupboard he'd demoed, the only part he couldn't reach. "There's a map of Vancouver Island in there and she drew on it."

I tried not to sound impatient. "And?"

He was living inside the idea that had compelled him to tear apart the garage. He didn't even seem to hear me. "There could be clues on there," he muttered. "Places she could be."

"How would an abductor know what's on the map?"

He shrugged, kept eyeing the top shelf.

"You'll need to clean this up before Dad gets home."

He put his hands on his hips, assessing if he could step on the lower shelf or whether a stool was needed.

I closed the door behind me, my stomach suddenly raw and growling. I was about to say something to Grandma about him, but her hunched shoulders, the slight, rhythmic hitch in them, stopped me. She turned suddenly and saw me standing there, her mascara starting to run. "I'm all right, Grace," she said, as if I'd asked. "It's all right."

22

Hey. Check-in time. You doing okay?

I lay on my bed and wished I could teleport myself to Iris's room. *Yeah. Patricia arrived in the night. Like a witch.*

Ugh. Don't let her get you down. And hide the brooms. Unrelatedly, don't go on Jungle.

Why not?

It's a madhouse. Seriously, there are angels and demons on there fighting it out.

I don't know what that means.

I'm protecting you from witnessing intense lunacy. People get stupid when something like this happens. Just be in your cocoon.

I'm not a butterfly.

Moth.

What?

Hasn't Mylo educated you yet? He went on about it at HackAttack.

I just heard the stories of smuggling and intrigue and Korean police.

Butterflies develop in chrysalises and moths develop in cocoons.

But are they just different terms, or actually different structures? Is there mothness to a cocoon or something?

I have no idea. Ask Mylo. Report back.

∗

Earlier, he'd sent a photo of the blue admiral butterfly he'd told me about, its wings a perfect gradation from inky black to electric blue. *Took twenty-nine shots to get this one,* his text said.

Why don't you do anything with these? They're amazing. You should enter contests or something.

Maybe when I leave home. Right now it just makes me feel close to my grandpa. He left me his collection and it kind of feels like he's still here if I get totally focused on his specimens. It's like I'm taking photographs of his actions frozen in time because he mounted and set each insect.

That's amazing. You should do a photo essay about it.

My mom hates that I spend so much time with my camera. She thinks it's affecting my grades.

Is HackAttack your idea or hers?

Kind of both. She thinks it'll make me more employable and I just like hanging out with smart people.

I hesitated, not knowing how to ask the question I wanted to. I imagined him waiting, watching his phone like I did. *Why is your mother so strict?*

The in-progress dots blinked for a long time. *We have kind of a difficult family.*

I wasn't sure that answered the question.

The dots blinked again, then stopped.

I waited a minute but nothing came through. Then I typed, *So what's the deal with chrysalises and cocoons, anyway?*

23

Two days later I was getting out of the shower when a car pulled up outside the house. The engine cut and a door opened and closed.

The doorbell rang. Voices in the living room. Grandma's, Dad's, someone else's, very quiet.

I sat at the top of the stairs and strained to hear what they were saying. I took the stairs one at a time on my butt.

"But it's our first real evidence," the third voice said. Isabel.

I got to my feet and crept down the last few stairs.

"So you know it's the right car? It couldn't be just an abandoned vehicle on someone's land?" Grandma said.

"We're sure. It's a black Honda Civic. The plates have been removed, but we managed to trace it to a used car lot in Ammonite. It's the vehicle GG was abducted in — we have eyewitness accounts of the vehicle. It was twenty-five kilometers from Fletcher Park, which helps focus our search area somewhat. Her fingerprints and those of another person are all over the car."

"Oh my Lord." Grandma again.

I peeked around the wall that hid my view of the living room. Dad was standing with his hands on the back of the couch as if he needed it to keep himself from falling over. He was staring at the tops of the cushions. Grandma came in and out of view, pacing around with a hand to her mouth. I couldn't see Isabel.

"So you can find her now," Dad said. "You have fingerprints. You can match them to the person who took her."

"We're running them through the database now and analyzing the other evidence we recovered from the vehicle."

"It could be soon, then," Dad said. "This is a big step, you said."

"It is a big step, yes." Isabel paused. "But there's still a lot we don't know."

"Like where she is." Grandma's voice had lost all puffiness.

"Yes. There's a good chance her captor took her out of town, but that opens up a pretty huge search field. We have the border, airports and all ferries on alert."

"Andrew."

"Just a minute, Patricia. Isabel, you're saying they could be in the U.S.? Why are you only alerting the border now?"

"We've been in touch with the Canada Border Services Agency since the night she disappeared. Now we have more information to go on. Plus —"

"Andrew."

I looked up from a white stain on the carpet I'd never noticed before, my heart thundering in my ears, to see Grandma watching me from the living room.

*

The police gave a press conference after they found the Honda, and Dad had to be there. I knew exactly what it would be like because I'd seen other devastated people stand in front of the mic, cameras flashing, police officers on either side of them, breaking down as they talked about their missing mother or sister or son. Only this time it was Dad, it was us. How could that be? It felt crazy and agonizingly true, like a dream that you know defies the laws of physics but is happening anyway. We were those people. Our pain and confusion was all over the news, and everyone else was uncomfortable on their couches, glad they weren't us.

The reporters jumped at all possibilities even though the cops still hadn't matched the fingerprints on the car. There was too much juice in the story, too many things unknown, not to make the most out of it. I didn't actually watch the press conference; I found out these things because Iris texted me messages as she was watching it.

God, these people are assholes.

They keep asking insane questions!

Your dad is doing so well.

I think they're going to call it soon.

Like a boxing match.

I'd never thanked Mom for choosing the house where she had, but there was a fair amount of irony to the fact that we lived in the best possible spot for star viewing in the city, and it was all because of her. Thirty kilometers away in the middle of nowhere would have been way better — Claudia had taken us on a few dark sky trips in the last two years, and those skies were insane — but where our house was, on the edge of the forest, at the bottom of a small but steep hill, I could get to a spot that was okay.

A deer trail started between the two properties on our right and traversed the hill for a hundred meters, coming out on the other side in a clearing that overlooked farmland and more forest. Before I got my scope, I'd come here to sit by myself and study the sky with a pair of binoculars I'd stolen from the camping gear bin in the garage. I used to imagine being Charles Messier, finder of over a hundred star clusters and nebulae, peering into the sky centuries before.

The night after the press conference, I had the clearing to myself. Even the deer were asleep. The Big Dipper was spread across the night, its cup tipped down, as if it was about to spill water all over the cosmos.

I unpacked the scope parts from the big backpack I kept them in, fitting the legs into the body. I found a flat spot to position it, checked the glass was clean and adjusted the finder-scope. In a second I found the Whirlpool galaxy, three degrees southwest of the end of the dipper's handle. It was faint and fuzzy, but I'd seen it enough times in high-res photos to know what it really looked like: a swirl of blue-purple with a white center. Millions of stars and planets all circling in a disk like our galaxy, twenty-four million light-years away.

A cool wind blew my hair across my forehead as I peered through the eyepiece.

One night I'd come here with my binoculars — my first telescope on order but delayed — and sat in the clearing for an hour. I picked out the constellations I knew, tracing lines with my eyes. Watched satellites orbit past, the occasional bat flitting across my view. That's when something just clicked: there was nothing but a layer of atmosphere between me and space. My whole life, I realized, I'd been imagining the sky as flat — wallpaper covered with stars. The idea that infinite space is right there — that from where I sat, I was looking *into* it, not *at* it, just like the astronauts on the Space Station were that second — exploded my brain like a supernova. I couldn't unsee it. Every night since, when I'd looked at the night sky, I saw the depth of it, how it went on in all directions, and how we were in it, like a speck of life in the ocean.

I knew I was done for anything else. I had to be among the stars for the rest of my life.

There was a soft rustle in the grass below the clearing — probably a rabbit. I straightened up and stared with my human eyes at the spot where the Whirlpool galaxy was, too faint to see. It was out there even though most of us had no idea.

A scrap of noise — maybe a siren — floated up from below the trees.

Once, a few years before, Mom had stopped by my room on her way out of the house for a flight. I'd been studying the moon and noting landmarks as I found them. She'd leaned down and looked when I offered. I saw her eyelashes almost touching the rim of the eyepiece. "It's so detailed," she said. "This must be a really powerful telescope."

"Not really," I said. "The moon's only 384 000 kilometers away."

She looked at me. "That sounds pretty far."

"But it's kind of nothing. It takes light only about a second to reach us from the moon. It takes over four years for light to reach us from the nearest star."

She tucked her hair behind her ear. As a kid I'd loved watching her do that.

A car outside honked. Her cab.

"I'll be back on Friday and you can tell me more," she said, kissing my hair. "Don't let the moon escape." Then she was gone.

"It can't," I said to the dark room. "It's gravitationally bound to us."

Now, in the night, surrounded by trees and creatures in the dark, the galaxy above me, I couldn't remember if she'd brought it up again when she got back. Since I couldn't remember, probably not.

"Where are you?" I whispered to no one, alone on a dark hillside.

24

I lay on the couch in the TV room waiting for Dad to come home from the police station again. He'd gone three days in a row since the press conference about the Honda. Each time he came home we expected news, progress — something. Each time he came back exhausted and poured himself a cup of the herbal tea that Grandma always had brewing, an air of apology around him.

Charlie had torn himself away from *Minecraft* and was slouched in the beanbag chair that had materialized from the garage at some point. It smelled mildewy and reminded me of slumber parties with elementary school girls I hadn't thought about in years. Grandma had been making noises in the kitchen, but as I flicked the channel to a cooking show where they were boiling lobsters, she appeared in the doorway with a tray of cookies. Actually, a tray loaded with three boxes of cookies. She could carry the boxes in her arms without the tray; it made it seem like she was trying to dress up the cookies somehow. There was a wedge of folded napkins threatening to fall off one corner of the tray.

She stood there stiffly, watching the TV with concern. "They're delicious, but I never like to think about what happens to a lobster before it gets to my plate." She looked around for a place to set down the tray. The coffee table had been pushed under the window so there was an expanse of empty carpet with only the beanbag chair to break it up. Charlie scrambled to his feet and wordlessly grabbed a box from the tray.

"You're welcome," Grandma said.

Charlie mumbled something as he pried the top open. It appeared from the package that the cookies would taste like healthy cardboard.

"Grace?" Grandma offered the tray to me. One box read, "Gluten-free almond bites," and the other, "Flax jewels."

"I'm okay," I said, turning back to the TV. The lobsters were now in the pot.

"I ate my first lobster when I was nineteen," Grandma said, lowering the tray to the carpet. "I was working on my first serious film, this artsy, badly written thing I shouldn't have done. But it was shot in Nova Scotia and there were lots of lobsters."

The cook on TV put a towel-covered hand on the lid of the pot as if to stop the lobsters from climbing up vertical cliffs of stainless steel.

"The director took me out for dinner. A whole bunch of us girls went. He turned out to be a huge misogynist."

I cleared my throat.

"What's a misogynist?" Charlie asked with his mouth full.

"Oh," Grandma said, surprised by her audience. "Right."

I waited.

Charlie chewed and said, "Grandma?"

The TV cook took the lid off the pot and steam erupted into the air.

"It's a man who doesn't like women," Grandma said.

"You mean a man who's gay?" Charlie asked.

I cackled.

"No," Grandma said, cutting a look at me. "A man who doesn't think women are as worthy as men."

"A woman-hater," I said. "Which basically means he was scared of women."

Charlie paused his attack on a new cookie. "Who was?"

"The director." Grandma looked like she regretted coming into the room.

"That's stupid. Why would you work for him?" Charlie asked.

"Because he bought her lobsters," I said.

"He didn't —" Grandma huffed. "It was only the one dinner. One lobster."

"But if he was scared of women," Charlie said, catching on, "it was probably the worst dinner of his life."

I laughed again, unexpectedly buoyed by the gleam in his eye. He'd never stepped into a conversation like this before. We were accomplices. "Yeah, so one dinner was enough," I said. "He probably had to go home and shower to get rid of the scary woman smell."

Charlie snorted.

Grandma stared at me in horror. "What are you teaching him?"

"Oh, come on," I said. "We're joking. Aren't we, Badger? Totally joking. It's called irony."

Charlie nodded. "We're not mis-genicists. Your director was an asshat."

127

25

Bruce and Moira's kitchen smelled like paprika and lemon. They let Iris and me choose dinner from an oil-splattered cookbook that lay on the counter. "Anything you want, really, girls," Moira said, patting my shoulder and leaving us to it. They'd already been on the phone with Dad since I got there, making sure I was okay and not going to lose it, although being with normal people was all I really wanted. Dad had been wandering around the house, apparently feeling useless since he hadn't been needed at the police station in two whole days.

I loved Iris's house. I loved her parents. They were the parents I would have picked from the catalog. Socialists and alternatives and ridiculously intellectual people who burned incense and built their own computers. I knew they were talking in the living room about me, but Iris flipped the pages to the soup section, and I listened to her chatter about which one had too much garlic and which one made her puke once. She had been at my house within fifteen minutes of my message that I needed distraction. I'd never been happier to see her drive up.

Now she moved on to the entrées section and put her finger on one called Three Sisters Burrito. "This is awesome. You like squash, right?"

"Sometimes."

"Maybe tonight?"

"Yeah, I think so."

"You don't have to eat it if you're not hungry, but making food for people gives my parents purpose."

"Along with helping refugees come to Canada."

"Along with that."

"Sure. This one's fine."

She gestured toward the doorway. "We can hang out in my room while the servants prepare it."

"Have you girls chosen?" Bruce and Moira came back into the kitchen as if summoned.

"This one," Iris said. "You guys don't mind if we hang out upstairs for a bit? Grace's feeling a little tired."

"Sure thing," Moira said, smoothing Iris's wavy hair with a casual hand. She was taller than her husband, about the same height as me. "We'll let you know when dinner's ready."

✳

Each wall of Iris's room was a different hue from a complementary color phase she now regretted. I sat on the floor and leaned against the burnt-ocher wall. Iris perched on the exercise ball that doubled as her desk chair, her (four) bangles jingling. She pulled her laptop over and scrolled through a playlist. "Folk rock or acid jazz?"

I stared at her ceiling, which was, mercifully, dove gray. "Contemplative funk."

She bounced appreciatively on the ball, eyes on the screen. "And what kind of distraction do you require? News or board game?"

"Well, I don't feel like Take the Castle."

"Got it. Games are out."

"And no current events."

"Fair enough." She put on some seventies funk band I'd never heard of and bounced lightly. "Okay, don't get mad at me."

"Wow, great introduction. I'm so excited now."

"Yeah, well, I told Zane we could get Sun Ah Kim to the fundraiser."

I stared at the blue-green wall opposite me, making sure I remembered that whole thing right. Zane was Iris's crush in the fundraising group. Sun Ah Kim was ... oh, yeah. Politician-turned-foundation CEO, probably connected to a million rich people. Mylo had mentioned she got to dine on yachts and such.

"It just kind of came out and ..." Iris twisted her skirt in her hands. "I work best under pressure, so it'll just mean we have to get him to convince her. It's going to be fine."

"This is not cool," I said.

"Why not?"

"First off, have you even heard what she's like? Mylo was just telling me how iron-fisted she is."

"Come on. Stalin was iron-fisted."

"She seems like kind of a bitch, Iris."

She cocked her head at me. "Have you met her?"

"No."

"Have you only had secondhand information about her?"

"From her *son*."

"Who's probably not going to give a totally accurate picture. Would you give an accurate picture of your mother?"

We both froze, her question hanging in the air between us. The music jammed on.

"I'm sorry," she muttered. "I didn't mean that. I just meant objectively … It was the wrong example …"

"It's fine. I get it."

The trumpets in the song reached new heights of screechiness. Iris skipped to the next one.

"Listen," I said. "You have no idea if she's interested in something like that, or even if she's available — what connection does her foundation have with refugees?"

Iris put her hands in her lap. "It's not about the foundation. It's about who she knows. She's got access to all the rich people in this town — in the whole province, probably. It's like hitting the jackpot of networking."

I looked up at the calming gray ceiling.

"Are you okay?" she asked.

"I'm still processing," I said.

"Sure." She leaned over and patted my arm. "You take your time. But I need to start talking to Mylo about it pretty soon."

I ground my teeth. "Does this have anything to do with the fact that you have a thing for that guy?"

Her eyes widened a little too much. "What, Zane? No way."

"Is he still broken up with his fiancée?"

"They're totally done. She's moved to Halifax, actually."

"Oh, perfect. You're now in position."

"Shut up." She bounced indignantly on her ball.

"Iris, you've loved him for months. Even though he's twenty-two and almost got married."

"Newly engaged isn't almost married."

"You can't just tell him you're going to deliver a big donor you don't even have."

"But I will!"

"But you're blinded by love!"

"I'm *not* in love."

"And what will the other people in the fundraising group say? Your parents are in it — what do they say?"

"They don't know yet."

I rolled my eyes so hard that it hurt. "Tell me you don't wish you could kiss him. Don't lie."

She crossed her arms over her chest. "That has nothing to do with love. I'm in complete control, thank you very much."

I watched her fidget on the ball. She picked at the skin around her nails when under scrutiny. Like now.

Finally, she put her hands in her lap and looked at me. "Why don't you want me to ask Mylo about this? Are you embarrassed or something?"

There was a clatter below us in the kitchen.

Even though she was edging close enough to the Mylo subject to make me squirm, the second question was what got me. That she would even think I was embarrassed, and that in airing the possibility, she made me wonder if it could be true. "Not a chance," I said. "You're my brilliant best friend and you're going to rule the world one day. Seriously — watch out, unsuspecting male leaders." I got onto my knees and reached over to pull the ball, and her, closer. "You know, I feel like the board game after all."

*

The squash was perfectly cooked and the burritos were delicious. I ate a quarter of mine and implored Moira to wrap the rest in tinfoil, like restaurant takeout, for me to finish later. She brought me a glass dish with three burritos nestled inside, a sprig of cilantro in the middle. "For your family," she said, her voice like a hug.

We were sitting at the table with bowls of vanilla ice cream, having managed to get through the meal without any stilted conversation, when Bruce said, "So how's school been for you this year, Grace?"

Iris made a gasp of disdain.

"What?" Bruce glanced around at everyone.

"It's fine," I said. "It's been okay. Sometimes it's interesting."

"Because my cousin's moving here and he's researching schools for his kids." Bruce looked at Moira as if for confirmation that he was good to continue. She put her hand on top of his. "And obviously we don't have firsthand experience with the system, so I just wanted to check in with our closest soldier in the field." He gave me a wink and I could appreciate his effort.

"It hasn't killed me yet," I said. "But I might do the rest of the year correspondence if ..."

Iris glared at her dad, as if his blunder had just been extra delayed.

"Anyway, I'm not sure," I finished.

He smiled at something behind my head. "Sure. Fair enough."

"Grace, would you like a jar of pickled beets to take home?" Moira rose from her chair and the smell of her soap, herbal mint, wafted past me.

"Sure. Thanks." I put my hands on either side of the burrito container. It was still warm.

26

Dad arrived to pick me up as Iris and I were loading the ice cream bowls into the dishwasher. There were quiet parental exchanges at the front door that I couldn't make out, and then he peered into the kitchen, seeing Iris first, then me. "Hi, you two," he said, like it was a normal day, a normal life. "Ready, Gracie?"

Bruce and Moira stood at the door and offered to supply meals whenever they were needed, computer service if something should ever happen to any of our machines, offers for me to come hang out with Iris, who watched me as if I might object to something. When we finally stepped off the porch, she lunged for me and clutched me into a fierce hug. "I'm sorry," she whispered, but she didn't explain what she was sorry for.

Once we were in the car, Dad's face relaxed into deep-lined exhaustion. I realized how much effort must have gone into the front he just put on. "Your grandmother says you left the house without telling her."

A semi-trailer roared past us, making the car shake.

"No, I didn't," I said. "I called into the kitchen as I went out the door. She answered me."

"She says she didn't hear you."

"That's crap, Dad, I definitely said I was going to Iris's and she could call my cell if she needed me."

He shrugged, and I couldn't tell if he wasn't buying it or was just too tired to care. "Well, did you have a fun time?"

"Yeah, it was good."

"Good is pretty great these days."

"Yeah." I glanced at him. "What did you do?"

He kept his eyes on the road. "Some project work that's due next week. And I had to talk with Constable Baker for a while."

I waited for him to elaborate.

"Nothing new has come up, but they think they're making progress." He stared at the car in front of us.

I picked at a hangnail. "How can you make progress when nothing has changed?"

We drove in silence for a while, the traffic moving around us like everything was fine. People going about their lives.

"You know what I miss right now?" he asked suddenly. "I miss the GG of twenty years ago. It hit me this morning. She was so different back then — the same and yet so different." He stared through the windshield as if his memories were being projected on the other side. "She was infinitely capable. She could have been a trapeze artist and been great at it." It seemed like he was talking to himself. "She had the best laugh when she was young. It sounded like she was almost … made of happiness."

I would have remembered if I'd heard her laugh like that. I massaged my jaw, knowing the reason it was sore was how much I'd been grinding my teeth. "Dad."

I could see he was startled that I'd spoken. "What, Gracie?"

"Why did you guys get married?"

He finally looked over, still surprised.

"I don't mean that you shouldn't have," I said. "Just, what made you love her?" Until the day she disappeared, I hadn't considered that they might not love each other. They argued, sure. They hardly ever saw each other some weeks. But not loving each other hadn't felt like a possibility. Now, with the world cracked open to all kinds of terrible maybes, it seemed stupidly naive to have thought that way.

"You have to understand," he said finally. "People change. Lives change. That's the thing they try to impress upon you in the vows — in sickness and in health, richer or poorer. It all sounds romantic and we've heard it a million times, but after the first few years you start to figure out what it all means."

He hadn't answered my question, really, but I didn't point that out.

"She's still her — Grace Gabrielle who charmed the pants off everyone she met, played the piano so beautifully on a Sunday morning that you thought you'd cry — but parts of her have changed. Gotten lost. It's true of me. I guess of everyone."

"Is it?"

"Everyone our age. You" — he turned his head to look at me — "you have all your options open. Anything you want to be, it's possible. You have no idea how much potential you have when you're young."

"When did she change?" I asked.

He shook his head faintly, remembering, or trying to. "When you think back, it's kind of scary how it goes. Like a glacier. You might not notice it if you're not paying attention, but it has an impact that changes everything eventually. The Stave Glacier on the mainland has been retreating at one hundred meters a year — that adds up to huge changes over a decade." He raked a hand through his hair.

"You're doing the environmental metaphor thing again," I said softly. I wanted to hug him so hard, my dad.

"Oh, right. Sorry."

"It's okay."

"Sometimes it's easier to think about things through natural phenomena, you know?"

"Yeah," I said, because I did.

27

Another week went by without news, and then it was almost June. Charlie started to disappear into *Minecraft*, coming out of his room only to eat and seldom to say anything. I tried to entice him into my room with the promise of letting him sleep in my bed, but he never wandered in. One night I sneaked into his room and watched him breathing under the covers. His hair was all tousled and stuck to his forehead. I felt guilty for something but I didn't know what. When I touched his cheek, he didn't move.

Grandma usually had the TV on late at night, and sometimes I'd hear Dad's voice nearby. They'd stay up flipping channels, and their voices would rise and fall in that hushed way I'd been hearing since I was young enough to remember — adults talking about serious things as quietly as possible. I couldn't make out words, but occasionally I'd hear a disagreement, judging by the abruptness of the sounds and the squeak of the couch as someone got up. In the morning they passed things politely at breakfast, and I could never tell if they liked or disliked each other more or less, Dad looking a little more tired and Grandma wearing the same mask of makeup.

My Jungle page had become bloated with messages since the press conference — notes from people at school, neighbors and strangers. A few people from Star Club left nice comments, and a few classmates wrote "so sorry to hear" messages. Even an interrobang-filled rant from Sasha Rosenberg?!

Then, an email from Ms. Jun, the student adviser, subject: Schoolwork Options. *You've already missed fourteen days*, she wrote, *but with grades as high as yours, if you can keep up with some of the assignments and write exams, you should be okay. Can you meet me to discuss?*

Could I meet to discuss? The idea of stepping onto school grounds was like considering a trip to Bhutan.

What had the principal told everyone? Had there been a carefully crafted email about my situation? School suddenly *was* Bhutan.

I went downstairs, through the empty kitchen and into the backyard. The lawn chairs were still in the middle of the lawn, and Charlie's practice net was slightly off center at the far end, a lonely-looking soccer ball deflated beside it. I flopped onto a chair and stared up at the cloudless sky, just a small chunk of it between the roof and the trees on all sides. Thought about what was out there behind the illusion of that blue: all of space and time.

*

Hey. I asked him this morning.

Iris's text came through as I was working on a French paragraph.

Asked who what?

Mylo. About the fundraiser.

I saved the document and closed my laptop. *And?*

He said he'd ask her.

Okay. Good luck.

Also, we want to jailbreak you from your house soon. We feel you need distraction from outside. Please advise if you are going out of town in the next three days.

Um, no.

Okay. I'll be back in touch. Not about the jailbreak. That will happen when you least expect it.

28

I didn't know what made me google her, but way more hits came up for Marge Wilson than I expected. There was a photo of her husband and her smiling next to the Grand Canyon, he wearing a white visor like a golfer and she with her arms open wide. It was a blog called *Island Heatseekers*, and although I found their names on the caption below the photo, there were no other entries with the two of them. The next hit was a professional site with Marge's business information and a cheesy, posed head-shot with a dappled blue backdrop. She looked younger, her hair a more natural shade of brown. There was something in her eyes that hadn't been there when we were at her house. I wondered about her husband. How he died. I wondered about her and my mother. Their meeting in the park those times when I was little. Had Mom still laughed like happiness cracked open? Probably not with postpartum depression. I tried to picture them on a park bench, a stroller beside them, talking. It was like seeing actors on a movie screen, brightly lit and impersonal. I couldn't imagine what they would say.

*

The next morning, Isabel arrived as Dad and I were clearing the breakfast dishes, the sound of her patrol car alerting us, making us both stop midmotion.

"I have some important information," she said, once seated on the terrible green chair. Her voice was lowered to show the importance. She rotated her ring with her thumb.

"Should we go get Charlie?" I asked.

Isabel frowned. "If he's already distracted, that's probably best. You can decide what to tell him afterward."

Grandma pressed a tissue between her palms.

"The fingerprints on the car belonged to only two people: GG and a man we've now identified. Have you heard of a man called Philip Krause?"

We looked at one another.

"I have no idea who that is," Dad said. "She's never mentioned him." He stared at the wall as he checked the recesses of his memory.

"Of course she didn't mention him," Grandma said beside me. "He's been dead for almost twenty years."

We all stared at her.

Isabel's voice was like glass. "You know something about this man?"

Grandma's eyes wandered the edge of the coffee table. "He moved to Portugal and died in a boating accident. Grace went to university with him. They were friends. I suspected they might have been more, but she didn't tell me so, which wasn't unusual for her."

Isabel got out her pen and paper. "Why didn't you mention him when we originally questioned you?"

Grandma looked around, confused. "Because, well — he's dead. He died in the early 2000s. And I never met him. She told me more about his death — it sounded gruesome — than what he was like when they were friends."

"Do you know the nature of their relationship at university?"

Grandma's expression tightened. "As I said, I thought they might have dated, but she was so private. She didn't tell me anything. There were several men ..."

Isabel looked up from her notes. Her face was stone, not so much from lack of emotion but from concentration. Like she was preparing to study all of us for our reactions. "We have positive identification of Philip Krause's fingerprints on the Honda. We believe he is alive and currently holding your daughter somewhere within four days' drive of here. From what we know, he faked his own death in 2002."

The air seemed to freeze, all of us held in place by the information she'd just released into the living room. But as much as my body couldn't move, my brain was in overdrive. The heat of it radiated out through my skin. He was *alive*? And Mom was with him? "You can't be serious," I said. "That kind of thing doesn't happen in real life." It all seemed nonsensical, like a conspiracy theory someone could easily poke a hole in to disprove.

"I know it sounds unbelievable," Isabel said, "but we have strong evidence. This is a big step forward in the case."

"Oh my God," Grandma choked out. "I can't — *my God*."

Isabel stood. "I know this is a shock, Mrs. Forsythe, but I'll need to question you further. It would be better to get the information at the department."

Grandma looked around, grasping at everything with her

eyes, and I realized that she was not acting for once. Her panic was real and it looked horrible. Her mouth trembled into a grimace and I had to turn away.

"It's all right, Patricia. I can drive you there." Dad had gotten up and was holding a hand out to Grandma.

"If you need a moment, Mrs. Forsythe —"

"No," she said. "No."

Dad's hand was still extended.

"It's okay to —"

"*No!*" She got up jerkily and had to catch herself on the coffee table, her bracelets jingling. "No, no, no."

"Patricia, you have to go —"

Her face was deep red, a color I didn't know it could turn. I wondered if someone should call for paramedics. The image of her being wheeled away on a gurney flashed in my mind.

"Grandma," I said. I was on my feet and I said loudly into her face, "Grandma, it's okay." Which was complete crap. Nothing was remotely okay. I put my hands on her shoulders.

And she trembled for a minute, but when Isabel took her arm, she went with her. Dad grabbed his keys, sent me an appreciative glance, the kind one adult sends to another, and it landed heavily on me.

The door shut behind them and I was alone with the news.

✳

The story they pieced together sounded like a movie of Grandma's: man fakes his death only to come back and claim the woman he's been obsessed with for years.

Except it was real. Philip Krause had moved to Vancouver Island two years before, rented a crappy apartment on the worst street in town, then did some carpentry and moved furniture. The police thought he'd been in contact with Mom for at least a year, maybe more. He had a history of wandering and taking odd jobs, but he also had a reputation as a skilled sculptor. Isabel said he made things out of cedar and Douglas fir. They'd found pieces in his apartment and evidence that he had more somewhere else. She also said he'd been acquitted on extortion charges five years before, and a woman on the other side of the province had briefly had a restraining order against him. Isabel had gone for a no-bullshit approach to relaying the information. Maybe she thought we were strong enough to handle it, but it was a lot more horrifying than flattering.

No one they'd interviewed had heard of him. None of Mom's co-workers. It was hard to even find traces of him in town, except for his apartment. They didn't even know where he worked. The few people they'd found who knew him when he and Mom were at university had also thought he'd died in Portugal. He was a ghost come back to life, only creepier.

I googled him that first night even though I knew I shouldn't. I knew objectively there was nothing wrong with his name, but it was suddenly disgusting. It was weird how two groups of letters could seem toxic to write or think about, as if they might be responsible for vile human behavior. There was nothing on him, of course. The police must have done much more extensive and powerful searches than a quick online query, and they were coming up empty. There was a guy in England who bred sheep, a war veteran in California who'd put all his medals onto an outdated web page. A site for Krause Hydroponics in New Brunswick. A few other hits that weren't even close. Nothing for a guy who'd come back from the dead and kidnapped my mother.

It would have been easier if he had been an actual ghost.

I closed my laptop, fingers trembling as I touched the pile of schoolbooks on my desk. Maybe it was worse knowing things than not knowing them.

Then I was hurling things across the room — books and pens and a box of highlighters. I staggered up and pulled the top row of books off my bookshelf, then the next. They tumbled around my feet, blocking me from taking a step, and I crumpled in a heap, wanting to trample them but unable to actually wreck books. I pressed the sleeve of my shirt to my mouth and screamed until I was light-headed.

29

Being in Iris's car reminded me of nineties movies. Soft navy seats littered with bubblegum wrappers and a mint air freshener on the rearview. She was also fond of old Radiohead and Smashing Pumpkins. It was actually Moira's car but she biked to work, so Iris ended up using it more. It was three days after the news about Philip Krause and she'd shown up randomly, true to her word, just before lunch. Her hair was still damp and the smell of her shampoo mingled with the spearmint.

"We're picking Mylo up," she said as she turned off our street.

My stomach did the flutter thing. It would be the first time we'd all been together since the soccer game, and that was a long time ago. Talking on the phone had somehow made the in-person him even more unsettling to contemplate.

"It was his idea to do this today. He doesn't have a car right now, though, so I'm kind of important to implementation. But he's donating a few of his photos for the fundraiser's silent auction, so it's an easy trade. Not that I wouldn't do more, but, you know." She glanced at me. "And before you ask, his mom is going to come, and apparently she might have a few friends to bring."

I turned the music down a little.

"It's all fine," she went on. "No one feels used. Everyone's glad to help. And Zane's pumped, too. In a totally platonic way." She moved her shoulders to the rhythm of the music.

I touched her arm. She had the palest skin under those freckles. "I'm sorry," I said, but what I really meant was *I love you*. She smiled. "It's okay. And by the way, I brought snacks. There's chips in the trunk, but more importantly, a bag of jelly-beans behind my seat that I'm really hoping you'll help me eat."

I reached back and found the bag, opened it and offered her a handful.

We chewed in silence for a while, except for "Karma Police," and then the song ended.

"So Mylo and I have planned some pretty good distraction activities. You like rock climbing, right?" She tossed two red jellybeans into her mouth. "And I suggested going on that Ferris wheel thing they have at Cranmore now. But did you know Mylo's not good with heights?"

"I had no idea."

"I know, right?" Her phone barked to announce a text and she said, "Can you check that?"

It was Mylo. *I have to bail. Really sorry. My mom's work laptop crashed and she's losing her mind, and maybe her files. Did you get her already?*

I had the urge to text him back, but it was Iris's phone. "He can't come," I told her.

"Oh, crap, really?" She put on the brakes and pulled over. "We had a whole thing planned." She looked at her phone. "Should I text him back?"

I shrugged.

My phone buzzed.

Hey.

I stared at the screen, waiting for more, feeling like part of him was here in the car with us.

Are you at home?

"Is that him?" Iris asked. "What's he saying?"

"Just wondering where I am," I said. *In Iris's car on the way to your house*, I replied.

"What should we do now?" Iris asked, her hands on the wheel. "Mylo had the connection for free rock climbing. The Ferris wheel would work if he's not there, but what do you think?"

I looked up from my phone, where the three dots were in progress. "I don't know. It's your plan."

So you know about the plan, Mylo texted. *I'm so pissed off. Normally my mom's admin person fixes computer problems, but she's away, so it's me. I'm sorry.*

Iris listed off a few options but I couldn't hear her. I was listening to the booming in my ears, waiting for the dots to deliver his next message.

It said, *I wish I was with you.*

"Hello?" Iris said. "Is Mylo writing you a novel?"

"Yeah, kind of," I said, forcing my eyes away from the screen. "He's mad at his mom because she's making him help her. I reiterate my theory that she's horrible."

"Whatever. Maybe she is. I'll tell him we'll check in later to make sure he's still alive." She tapped into her phone.

I typed on mine, *I'm sorry. I wish we could come and save you.*

Then I erased "we" and put "I" and hit Send before Iris did.

She shifted toward me in her seat. "Okay, so which plan B do you like best?"

"You're the jailbreaker. I'm easy." I was still sneaking glances at my phone to see if he'd reply. No in-progress dots.

"How about we run away?" she said.

I reluctantly clicked my phone off. "I don't think that'll solve anything," I said.

"No, like, to Camas Hill. Our Grand Plan. Right?"

A smile stretched across my face, and it felt good to use the muscles. We had this running joke that one day we were going to take a tent, buy some chickens and live on Camas Hill, a local park that had views of the city and also boasted one of the least terrible spots for stargazing. We'd collect eggs and dig up camas bulbs for food. We'd live on the land — we'd *be* the land — in our own little corner of the forest. It was ridiculous and childish but we kept adding to the fantasy — we'd get a goat for milk! Sell wildflowers for money! — and it had become a game of its own. A fiction we chose to believe because it felt so good.

"Yes," I said. "Great plan."

Camas Hill was in the opposite direction, so we doubled back, and Iris put on some new band she'd found, which sounded exactly like three other bands she loved.

I waited for another message from Mylo, but waiting, thinking about it, just made it worse. And then when my phone buzzed I jumped a little. But it was Dad.

I'll be at the station for a bit. Nothing new, just same old details. Call Patricia if you're going to be home late. Love you.

"You okay?" Iris asked.

"Yeah." I put my phone between my knees and massaged my temples. A headache was threatening like a far-off storm.

A woman with two little kids stepped onto the crosswalk ahead of us, and Iris stopped for them.

"It's so messed up," I said.

"What is?"

The woman and the kids reached the other side, and the kids bounded across the grass to the park.

"I keep thinking about him being the person who faked his death and didn't leave a trail for almost twenty years and also being the person who drove her away in that car." I pulled the seat belt away from my collarbone, where it was chafing my skin. "It was easier when we didn't know who he was. Just an unknown entity doing evil things. Now he's a human with a life. And he's the human who stole her. She's with him *right now*." Thinking of it made me shudder.

She didn't say anything for a long time, and I started to wonder if maybe she didn't know what to say about it, like the people on Jungle who were all, "I can't believe it" and "It's just so crazy." But then she took a breath and said, "Sometimes I have to stop myself from thinking about her. You know? Like thinking about the situation even a little bit will make it grow in my consciousness until it's always there, all the time. Like it must be for her." She looked at me and her eyes were bleak. "I know it's way worse for you because she's your mother and I'm just a friend. But I feel like she and I clicked. She was so interested in the work I'm doing and she's got that look she gives you. The one where she's really understanding you. Maybe they teach that in broadcast journalism school. I don't know."

I did know, and it wasn't something taught; it was just her. It was what Dad missed, too. But I hadn't been on the positive side of that look for a long time. The morning of the soccer game, after I'd asked if Mylo could interview her, she'd made me feel skewered with how far into me she looked. Understood to the point of exposure. Otherwise, we'd been avoiding each other's gaze for years. I started reaching for far-flung memories — had I seen Iris and Mom have these moments? Had I missed them? Had she been bonding with Iris because she couldn't with me? My stomach became stone.

"And now she's gone," Iris said beside me, "and it's — what was that thing you said? PWR. I totally get that." She blinked as she stared at the car in front of us. "So I try to think about other stuff. My mom says you should worry about the stuff you can actually control. Because at least I can jailbreak the hell out of *your* situation."

I stared out the window, and the houses and lawns and trees blurred to flashes of color. I tried to think about my breath, but it didn't work.

Neither of us said anything for a long time.

"I hope I didn't say too much," she said, wiping her nose with the back of her hand.

"You didn't," I said, but I thought, *Yes, you said too much. She'd give you that look, not me.* The stone that was my stomach pulled me deeper into the seat. "Everything is too much," I said out loud. "It's impossible to have more muchness than that."

*

We got out of the car on the top of Camas Hill, the small parking lot half full with rental cars, and walked to the first viewing area, where a tourist couple was taking dozens of photos of themselves at different angles.

The breeze sent curls of arbutus bark skittering across the pavement. It lifted Iris's hair into her face. It was usually windy up here. The whole southern tip of Vancouver Island was windy. I liked it, the way the air was rarely still. Something was always moving, which was true of everything — the particles inside us, the planet, rotating and orbiting the sun.

Far below, the trees of the park gave way to fields and houses and roads. We'd found Iris's house once, with my binoculars. Mine was on the other side of the hill and behind another, smaller one. In the distance, the edge of the land broke off into the Salish Sea, which glinted in the sun.

"I love this," Iris said beside me. "We should totally homestead here. How are you fixed for next week?"

"My schedule's pretty open," I said.

"Cool. I can shift some things around. My dad knows a guy with chickens and sheep. What do you think of sheep?"

"They're woolly."

"But as homestead animals. I mean, we could sell the wool, right?"

"Do you know how to shear sheep?"

"I've watched a few videos. Maybe we could contract that part out."

"Invite a professional sheep shearer to our homestead, thereby revealing our location?"

"We wouldn't be hiding."

"Yeah, we would. This is city land. Homesteading must be illegal."

She held up a finger. "Ah, but you have not suspended your disbelief enough. You have to *be* the Plan. This whole thing hangs on your commitment to believe."

The tourist couple packed away their camera, smiled at us and walked back to their car.

I wanted to believe in the nonsense. It had been a fantasy for so long that it sometimes felt like a possibility. But belief was a tricky thing. I could believe my mother was going to be found, but that didn't make it a certainty in the laws of the universe.

"Come on, let's walk to the top," Iris said, grabbing my hand and leading me back across the parking lot.

We took the winding path that circled up the peak of the hill, to a concrete ring of benches that had been so grafittied through the years that the words and symbols blended together — the faded and the fresh — to create a kind of texture on top of the original white paint. On the south-facing side was the plaque commemorating Anna-Sophia Bumber-Lightfoot, a name etched into my memory from all the times as a kid when I'd made Dad read it out so I could die laughing. Mom would stand there worrying that one of Anna-Sophia's relatives might walk by and be insulted, but still I laughed. I didn't think Anna-Sophia would mind. I imagined her as a nice person with a ridiculous name. The last time we came up here as a family, the summer I was fourteen, Mom took my picture next to the plaque. "So you can have your giggles with her name anytime you want," she said. I'd been pissed off. She felt more comfortable if I giggled about Anna-Sophia in my room rather than on the top of her favorite mountain, in public.

Iris stepped up into the circle of the seats and looked east, toward the mainland.

I hadn't thought about Anna-Sophia and the plaque — or the photograph still pinned to my wall at home — in months. It all seemed different now. I'd always been angry that Mom would try to save herself embarrassment, and maybe that was still true, but now her taking the photo and printing it out for me at home felt somehow generous. Maybe she'd been trying to catch my gaze and I never knew it.

"Okay," I said. "So how would we get water at our homestead? And where the hell would we build an outhouse?"

30

I slipped in the front door while everyone was getting dinner on the table. I really wanted a shower, but Dad saw me as he passed by with a stack of plates.

"Hey, Gracie," he called. "How was your outing?"

"Fine," I said, trying for neutral but hitting weary. At least both were appropriate.

"We're just serving up another lasagna. Hope you're not sick of them yet."

I bent to untie my shoes, doing each one slowly.

Dad was suddenly beside me as I straightened up. "Your grandmother's still fragile, but she's agreed to eat with us," he murmured.

"And you're telling me this because …?"

"We need to take it easy on her. Charlie, too. It took some persuading to get him off his computer. Have you seen what he's doing on *Minecraft*?"

I shoved my shoes in the closet on top of Charlie's soccer cleats. "No."

"He's built all these towers. The detail … I'm thinking of setting a daily limit, making him get outside." I could see his thoughts churning behind his eyes. There was something manic about his tired face, if those two things could go together.

"Can you go say hi at least?" he said. "I have to get something in the garage. Keep things light until I get back?"

Charlie was already sitting at the table with a carrot stick, a trick Mom used to keep him from getting hangry before dinner and to get him to ingest a vegetable. He looked up at me when I came in, his mouth full of macerated carrot. "Where have you been?"

"With Iris."

"Where do you keep those hot pot things?" Grandma said behind me.

"Hot pot?" Charlie asked, spraying carrot bits on the table.

"For taking hot things out of the oven."

"Oven mitts?" I suggested, moving around to open the low drawer where they were kept.

"Yes, oven mitts," Grandma said. "This is why I get meal delivery." She took the mitts from me, her eyes flitting to meet mine for a second, and then she turned to open the oven door. "Does this look done?"

The lasagna was dark brown on top and some of the sauce had bubbled over the side of the pan, burning itself onto the floor of the oven.

"Yeah, it's done," I said, the smell of yet another heavy pasta dish turning my stomach.

"I think this one's pesto," she said, her voice strained from the weight of the lasagna, which she plopped on the countertop, oblivious to the fact that normal people don't put hot things directly on the surface. "It looks almost burned," she said.

"Don't you think?"

"Very burned," I said, slipping a trivet underneath the pan.

"The lighting in that oven is deceiving."

"What, like in a changeroom?"

She frowned at me.

"You could scrape that layer off," I said.

"Scrape?" She looked repulsed.

"I hate pesto," Charlie called.

Grandma and I blinked at each other.

"I'll get the bread," I said, "if you get the peanut butter."

We were sitting at the table completing a tall stack of peanut butter sandwiches when Dad walked in with a box marked light bulbs.

"We're having a mutiny," Charlie said. "Peanut butter sandwiches."

Dad looked at me and Grandma.

"You don't care, Dad," I said. "You hate the thought of another night of baked pasta, admit it."

"Well, okay, but it just seems wrong to waste it." Dad put the box on the floor. "That one was from Lorraine Prinze."

"Too bad, so sad, Lorraine," Charlie sang. "It's peanut butter for us." He swung the stump of his carrot for a flourish.

Grandma's shoulders were shuddering beside me, and for a second I thought she was crying.

"Patricia?" Dad took a step toward the table.

Grandma's giggles turned to laughter and then Charlie was in, snorting at her as she pressed the corners of her eyes.

Dad was clearly bewildered.

"It's all good," I told him. "Lasagna therapy."

31

How was the adventure? Wish I could have been there.

Good. We hung out on Camas Hill. Ate too much sugar.

I haven't been up there in so long. Used to fly kites at the top when I was little. There will have to be another jailbreak event. One that I can actually be at.

Talk to Iris. She seems to think they should be frequent occurrences. I swung around on my swivel chair as I typed. *How did it go with your mom's computer?*

It died. She needs a new one, but I managed to retrieve the stuff on the hard drive. She was super grateful, though. I think I might be getting a car for my birthday.

Is your dad not good with computers? I couldn't remember him mentioning one. Or had he?

The in-progress dots blinked for a while and then: *He doesn't live with us.*

I didn't know how to respond, so I said, *Oh, right.* Had Iris said anything about his parents being divorced? I felt bad but didn't know how to fix it. So I texted, *Hey, I'm coming to school tomorrow.*

You're coming back?

No, just to talk to Mr. Shand and Ms. Jun.

Will I see you?

That was an odd question. Was it "Can I see you?" Or "Will you be around to be seen?" Or "Do you want me to see you?"

The meeting's at 10.

I have history until 10:30.

I waited while the dots danced.

I'll check in to see if you're still there, okay?

Okay.

32

Dad smelled like he was going to a meeting as he drove us the ten minutes to school. He'd combed his hair as well, and his shirt looked extra pressed. He was far too handsome to be driving me to school to see Ms. Jun.

"Are you going to a work meeting after this?" I asked.

He looked surprised. "No. Why?"

"You're just so ... dapper."

That got me one of his self-conscious smiles. The kind where I could almost see him as a little boy who received a compliment. "I just thought I should pull myself together for once. When you work from home, you do a lot with your sweatpants on. Add on everything that's happened and it's pretty easy to end up in the grocery store in your pajamas."

"Have you?"

"Luckily, no." He stopped so two kids on bikes could cross the street.

"How's work going?" I asked.

"Things are calm right now," he said. "The city's not barking for the report I owe them next week."

"Can't you take time off?"

"Not really. Consulting doesn't work that way."

We didn't speak as the traffic inched past a construction zone, men in bright vests and hard hats drilling huge chunks out of the road.

Then he said, "I want you to know how proud I am of you."

A wave of emotion was sitting there, waiting to crash into me. I watched the neon workers with fake interest.

"You okay, Gracie?"

The flag person looked at our car with the glazed eyes of someone who'd been up since 4:00 a.m. Another drill whined behind us.

"Sometimes I wonder what she's doing this second," I said.

He watched the road.

"Maybe she's wondering about us," I said. "Imagining us in the car right now."

"I try not to think about that too much."

"Why?"

The cars ahead sped back up to normal and we cruised past the mall, the lot already half full with weekday shoppers.

He still hadn't responded, so I said, "Dad?"

"When your mother would go on longer assignments, we used to play that game."

"What game?"

"We'd guess what the other was doing, and then the next time we talked on the phone, we'd find out if we'd been right. My success rate was about forty percent."

A woman with a gaggle of preschool kids attached to a rope plodded down the sidewalk.

"So what do you think about?" I asked.

He turned down the road that ended at the high school. The trees swayed in the wind. "I remember the good things and try to focus on that. I spent too much time getting really dark after she first disappeared, Grace. What good does that do?"

"Have you heard of the Perpetual Waiting Room?" I asked, knowing he hadn't.

He glanced at me with a questioning smile. He really was handsome. I'd forgotten to notice.

"That feeling of helplessness," I said. "Not being able to do anything but wait and let your mind torture you. Like if you were waiting for someone to come out of surgery. PWR."

"Yeah, well, that's it." He pulled into the parking lot and took a spot beside a camper van. "But maybe we play a different game." He turned off the engine and we sat there. "Maybe we play the moment-to-moment game. Just focus on getting through what's next."

While I'd been gone, someone had carefully explained their feelings about high school on the side of the gym. **RDSS SUCKS** was splayed in bright purple ropy letters halfway between the gym doors and the corner of the building. I admired the penmanship — spray-can-manship — for a long time, soothed by the white-noise chatter of students walking to class, the twitter of birds in the Garry oak tree behind me. I took a step and my sandal crunched through dry leaves.

Dad and I had sat with Ms. Jun and the principal for fifteen minutes before they let me go. We'd gone over the details of the arrangement — I would complete assignments my teachers sent me and show up for exams on exam days. Mr. Shand made awkward comments about the investigation, clearly hoping for a tidbit, but Dad gave him nothing. Ms. Jun watched me with her usual compassion, and when I asked if I could talk to my physics teacher about homework he'd already sent, she was the first to catch my eye, saying, "Of course. We've gone over everything here, right, Herman?"

Now I crunched around the back of the gym, relieved at the birds and the quiet, relieved, too, that the bell wouldn't ring for another sixty seconds so I could make it to Mr. Ardavan's physics class with minimal attention.

My phone buzzed.

I see you.

I spun around, but it was just trees. Just birds.

That's super creepy, I replied. *Where are you?*

By the gym door. Hi.

I looked.

He waved.

By the time he'd walked over to me, I could feel my pulse beating in my throat. He was more beautiful. Those eyebrows were more magnificent. His gravity had been upgraded.

"Sorry for the stalkerish tone."

"Apology accepted. Aren't you supposed to still be in class? It's not ten thirty yet."

"I'm supposed to be in the bathroom." He grinned at me, then glanced away.

A voice called something unintelligible around the other side of the gym.

"Are you here by yourself?" he asked.

"As opposed to with my security detail?"

"Yeah, no, I mean, is it okay for you to just walk around and maybe run into people who'll be kind of shocked to see you here?" He scratched the back of his neck. I'd seen him do that in class when he had to stand up front and talk.

What had people been saying? "My dad's waiting for me," I said. "I'm trying to get to Mr. Ardavan's room before the bell goes."

He stepped forward. "Because I was kind of hoping we could —"

"Where the hell is McLean?" It was Trent's gravelly voice. "Hey, Tyler — have you seen McLean? He skipped out of history."

"Shit." Mylo ducked his head and pulled me back behind a spindly salal bush that didn't really offer cover. "Are you sure this is a good idea?"

"You being seen with me? The jury's still out."

He squinted through the leaves. "It's Trent. I've got to go. He's your worst nightmare in this situation."

"Why —"

"Boo!" said a voice at my other ear, and I yelped, falling into Mylo, who collapsed onto the dirt.

"What the hell, Trent!" Mylo yelled. "You're psycho!"

"What is *she* doing here, man?" Trent was leaning over us, his square chin making the leering look on his face that much leerier. "And why are you hiding behind a freaking bush?"

"From you, you idiot!" Mylo scrambled up and helped me to my feet.

"Seriously?" He appeared to be gauging Mylo's level of concern. "I'm harmless. Super chill. I just came out to find you, dude, because Mr. Lockheed thinks you're skipping class. I covered for you." He lifted his hands in front of him. "But hey, I don't have to do that."

"Okay, thanks. I appreciate it. I'll be right there."

Trent cocked his head and didn't move.

"Really. Go." Mylo brushed off his jeans.

Trent clicked his jaw. "Are you worried I'm going to get on the PA system and announce her presence or something?"

"No, it's just —"

"I'm right here," I said, waving my hand in Trent's face. "You can address me directly."

He blinked at me. "Yeah, well —"

"I need you not to say anything to your friends about me being here," I told him. "I'm finishing the year via correspondence and I just came for a meeting and now I'm going home. It's better to keep the rumors to a minimum, okay? Can you do that?"

Mylo pointed his finger at me and raised his eyebrows at Trent.

"I just need to talk to Mylo about some French homework," I went on. "It'll be quick. Can you tell Mr. Lockheed he'll be right there?"

"Tell him my calf seized up again and I'm stretching it out," Mylo added.

"Fine, yeah. Whatever." Trent backed away and mumbled something that sounded like "see you later." Then he was gone.

Mylo couldn't keep his face straight. "That was awesome. You told him."

"He needs telling," I muttered. "Why do you hang out with him?"

He paused, the grin slipping off his face. "He's fun to be around. Most of the time. Except for sometimes." He picked a twig out of his hair.

"What have people been saying?" I asked quietly. "About ... my situation?"

He studied the ground and bunched up his eyebrows. "There are lots of theories. Some worse than others. Trent hasn't been grinding the gossip mill, if that's what you're asking. He's more of a consumer than a producer."

"That's not what I meant."

It was getting so hot out that the smell of baked dirt filled the air.

"It's the worst on social media. At school people mostly keep talking about who the abductor is. And if he was an old boyfriend or something. There're rumors that the guy is a TV exec and they've run off to Europe together. Or that your mom's connected to the Mafia."

"And?" I asked. "Tell me it all."

He looked more uncomfortable than I'd ever seen him. "There's one really ridiculous one ..."

"About?"

He grimaced. "No one believes it. You know how people just say crazy things to get a reaction."

I waited, knowing someone could come around the corner any moment but unable to let this go.

"That the reason you're not at school is because you were involved in the abduction and are under house arrest or something."

I closed my eyes. Did people think I hated her? Had they assumed because I was nothing like her that I was out for her destruction, like some jealous character in a movie?

"It's so stupid it's almost funny," he muttered.

"Almost."

"They're assholes. I'm sorry. Can we stop now?"

"Yeah."

"Are you okay?"

"Yeah."

He touched my shoulder so gently it made me ache. "I have to go."

"Yeah. You go."

"I'll call you later? You're good?"

"Sure."

The sun was hitting an empty candy wrapper on the concrete path, making it glow with reflected light.

He leaned in close, so close I thought he was going to kiss my cheek. I could hear the pounding of my blood in my ears. "One breath at a time, right?" he said against my skin.

33

Dad's cell was ringing and he wasn't picking up. I'd been finishing an assignment to email to a teacher, and the fact that it took a million rings for Dad's phone to go to voicemail was driving me crazy. Then a moment later it started ringing again.

I went into their bedroom and found it on the end of the bed, flashing as it rang. The screen said Isabel Sanchez. I took a breath and swiped right. "Hello?"

"Grace? Is that you?"

Mom.

Everything froze. I couldn't breathe.

"Hello, is that Grace?"

No. It wasn't Mom. It was Isabel, like the display said. Movement came flooding back into everything — my circulatory system, the air, the spin of the planet. I hadn't heard Isabel on the phone before. Her voice was lower, more hushed when traveling by cell-phone tower. More like Mom's.

"Is anyone there?" she asked.

"Yes," I said, clearing my throat. "It's me. It's Grace."

"Are you okay?" she asked.

"Fine. I just ... My dad's somewhere ... I can find him for

175

you —" Holding back from the crying was making it hard to speak, the truth/untruth of that moment hitting me like a physical impact.

"We've made another connection in the case and I was calling to find out a good time to come over. It's a small detail, but I want to keep you all informed and find out if it means anything to any of you."

I sat down on the bed. "How small is small?" Did that mean it was worth us freaking out over or not?

"All information is useful."

I closed my eyes. "Please stop pointing out the obvious."

"I'm sorry?"

"If it's worth telling us, it's not small. If it's something new, it's big. To us. Everything you tell us is another projectile we get hit with."

"Yes," she said, three kilometers away, in her office. "You're right. It must be just as hard every time I bring you new details. Are you doing okay, Grace?"

I didn't know how to answer that because there were multiple answers. It wasn't the yes/no question it appeared to be.

She didn't seem to need an answer, though, because then she said, "Is it okay if I come over in twenty minutes?"

I found Dad before she arrived, and for some reason Charlie was out of his cave and interacting with the world, which was ironically not what Dad wanted at that moment. But there he was, drinking a glass of orange juice, when Isabel walked into the kitchen. It wasn't like we could just shoo him back upstairs.

"What's going on?" Charlie asked, his eyes already lit with the question he wanted to ask next: *Did you find her?*

"We're still working really hard," Isabel said, turning her radio down as it squawked. "I'm just bringing you a little update on something we already know." She looked at Dad and he motioned to the dining table, which still had breakfast crumbs on it. Must have been Grandma's turn to clean up.

"Where's Patricia?" Isabel asked.

"Out," Dad said. "Some therapy with rocks."

We each took a chair and waited. Dad eyed Charlie, probably wondering if he'd be able to handle whatever was coming.

"You'll remember what I told you about Philip Krause," Isabel said. "Well, he's also used the name Felipe, both in Portugal and occasionally here in Canada. Mostly informal situations, not on legal documents in this country, but it's given us a wider field to search in terms of his activities and locations of residence."

"Felipe," Dad said.

"The Portuguese form of Philip," Isabel said. "It appears to be the name he was given at birth, in Portugal."

Charlie was turning his half-full orange juice glass around in circles just like Mom hated him doing because he often tipped it over. No one seemed to care now.

"I wanted to tell you this in case it rang any bells," Isabel was saying. "As always, connections can sometimes come out of —"

"Wait," I said, realizing I'd put my hand up like I was in a classroom. "Just hang on."

"What is it?" Dad asked, his voice tight.

"Yeah!" Charlie said beside me, wide-eyed. "My note!"

I ran up the stairs and flew into my room, throwing clothes around like a crazy person until I found my shorts. Thank God I'd lost them under a pile of other stuff and they hadn't been washed. I reached into the pocket and pulled out the scrap of paper. When I turned around, all three of them were standing in my doorway.

*

"But where was it? How could she have forgotten something like this?"

I could hear Grandma pacing the kitchen as I started down the stairs that night. I paused three stairs down to listen.

"It's not her fault," Dad was saying quietly. "And they said it wouldn't have changed much in the investigation — it hasn't told them anything else conclusive."

"But it's his handwriting. They have all kinds of techniques these days. What if it tells us where she is?"

"How can a few fragments do that?"

"You're not a detective, Andrew! I just —" She growled, a sound I'd never heard her make. When she spoke again, her voice was strangled. "It's like being teased. Here's another clue that this psychopath had plans all along. That he wrote things to her. It's sick. And if it can't tell us anything … I just don't know how we're supposed to stand it."

"Would you rather not know?" Dad asked.

She sobbed. "No, of course not."

"Then we wait. PWR."

There was a pause.

"What's PWR?" she asked.

I crept back up the stairs.

34

I couldn't avoid Grandma that night. I was filling a glass at the sink as she swished into the kitchen in her fluffy white slippers. Her hair was in some kind of treatment, wrapped in a plastic bag. She looked older in the face than I'd ever seen her.

"Goodnight, honey," she said dully.

I took a long drink of water.

She pulled open the utensil drawer, stared at everything, then closed it again. "Isn't there an elastic band anywhere?"

"Other end of the counter. Second drawer down."

"Thanks."

"I heard you earlier," I said. There was no point in being mad right now. I'd spent time rehearsing cutting remarks, but now that she was here, looking so pathetic and tired, I didn't have the energy.

She had paused on her way across the room. "Oh?"

"I didn't hide the note," I said.

"I know you didn't," she said, inspecting her painted nails. "Of course it was a mistake."

"You really thought I'd do that?" There was more hurt in my voice than I intended.

If she heard it, she didn't show it, and for some reason I was grateful. She slowly opened the right drawer and started to untangle an elastic. "No, I didn't think you'd do that. Not knowing is making us all uneasy. We try to find truth in places where there isn't any." She finally looked at me, her eyes wrinkled and unpretentious. "You sleep well," she said, turning away.

"Grandma?"

"Yes?"

I swallowed. "Isn't it weird that she kept the note?"

She blinked several times, the elastic taut between her stretched fingers. "It was ripped up. Maybe she didn't even know she had that tiny piece. She obviously meant to destroy it."

"But what if that's wrong? What if she ripped it up but kept the pieces or something?" I swallowed again, this time my throat going dry. "What if she wrote him back?"

Grandma's eyes narrowed. "There is absolutely no evidence of that. Isabel would have told us if there were."

"But you said they might have dated. What if her feelings for him —"

"Have the police said this is a possibility? I'm pretty sure they work with actual, hard evidence, not a bunch of crazy what-ifs. I'm going to trust they know what they're doing." She clenched the elastic in her hand. "Now, it's late and we both need to get to bed." And she walked away without saying goodnight, her shuffling slippers loud against the floor.

The house settled back into silence. I stared at my empty water glass, then slowly went up to my room.

But I couldn't stop thinking about her argument. About how people were more content to believe the things that kept them feeling safe and comfortable than to challenge their own worldview. Like early astronomers imprisoned and killed for defying the beliefs of their time. Grandma's logic was false. It wasn't about whether the police knew what they were doing or not. I could trust them *and* believe there were explanations they hadn't found yet.

And Grandma's distrust of what-ifs. The foundation of the scientific method. Of hypothesis. Of questioning whether Earth was the center of the universe. And I was pretty sure what-ifs were also important to a detective solving a case.

35

Marge's door opened into a chorus of yaps so loud that I wanted to cover my ears. I didn't know how she could live with it. "Get down, you fools," she told the dogs, using her foot as a dog barricade. "Honestly."

The house had that familiar stale-kibble smell, the TV showing a tropical destination with white-sand beaches. There was a glass of wine on the sideboard, which Marge picked up after she closed the door.

"I didn't mean to interrupt," I said. I hadn't called first. I'd taken Dad's car for a drive and ended up here, as if by coincidence or luck, though neither was really true.

"Nothing to interrupt," she said, shooing the dogs into the kitchen, where their claws ticked on the tile floor. "Do you want a drink?"

She gave me a glass of apple juice, the kind that came in frozen tubes and tasted like candy rather than apples. I sipped it as Mozart and Vivaldi came over and snuffled around my feet.

"Is everything okay?" Her hair was darker than last time, the red less aggressive. Her eyes had that pulled-down look that made her appear permanently sad. Mom would have makeup to help with that.

Suddenly I didn't know why I'd come here. I hated this house. I didn't know Marge. I stared at the closed front door.

She saw my panic because she put her wineglass down and said, "Grace, tell me if something's wrong."

I almost laughed. "There are so many shades of wrong right now that it's not funny."

She didn't seem to react. The dogs waddled away, bored.

"I need to know if Mom told you about Philip Krause."

"As I told the police, she never mentioned him to me. I had no idea who he was until they questioned me about it." She picked up her wineglass and took a sip.

Being here suddenly had way more gravity. I took a breath. "No hints about a past boyfriend? Someone she couldn't forget? Or someone she'd recently gotten in touch with?"

She seemed confused. "Has something changed in the investigation?"

I told her about the note — decided not to mention the new theory that Grandma had railed against — as my heart jolted under my ribs.

She stood for a long moment and stared into the air.

In the kitchen, a dog made loud slurping sounds.

"I'm sorry. She never mentioned him," she said finally. "I had no idea."

I didn't believe her, or maybe I wanted not to believe her. I'd come all this way and I was breathing in kibble-air and I didn't want to leave with nothing. "You're sure?" I asked.

Her face had hardened slightly. "Of course I'm sure. I would have remembered."

I looked away, to the dogs making themselves comfortable on the couch they weren't allowed on. The reality was that Marge knew Mom better than I did. Or at least a side of her. They'd had personal conversations for years — Marge could actually feel disappointed that Mom never told her about Philip Krause. I shouldn't feel that way because it never would have happened. I'd never be able to gather all the pieces of my mother that were contained in her relationships with other people. How could anyone — me or Dad or the cops — ever find them all?

Marge cleared her throat. "Your mother was a huge support to me when my husband died. I couldn't have gotten through it without her. We've always been sort of indebted to each other for things like that."

"Things like her postpartum depression?" I asked.

Marge fluffed her hair. "That was the lowest I've ever seen her. She told you about it?"

The sweetness of the apple juice made my teeth ache. I set the glass on the bookshelf. "No, my dad did."

"What did he say?"

"Not much."

"Well," she said and picked up her wineglass again.

I had the feeling she made a habit of drinking alone. Not in an alcoholic way, necessarily, but in a lonely way.

"I remember we were walking in the park," she said. "She was pushing you in the stroller, trying to explain how it felt to be so sad. I had my old Labrador then. Whenever you screamed he'd crouch beside the stroller and wait for directions." She took a sip of wine and swallowed slowly.

One of the dogs started snoring.

"Anyway, do you know what she said?" she asked.

"No."

"She said she didn't think she could be the mother you deserved. That even though she'd read books before you were born and talked to other parents, she felt like half a person, still under construction. Not ready to shape a new life, I guess."

"Was it the depression talking?" I asked after a moment of waiting for her to continue.

"Maybe. But maybe not. I can understand that fear. Reaching adulthood isn't equal to enlightenment, by any stretch."

"Do you think she still feels that way?"

Marge wrapped an arm around her middle. "I can't say for sure, Grace. She hasn't talked about that in years." She blinked at the painting on the wall, a red wooden bridge over a stream. "But I have wondered how contented she is as a person. How fulfilled she feels."

"Fulfilled by what?" I asked.

Marge shrugged. "Everything. Her life, her work. For someone so dedicated to her job, working those long hours, she's sure consumed by it."

"But she was the one asking for promotions — if she didn't want them, why did she take them?"

"I don't know, Grace. She's never said she hated her work. It's just a question that came to mind. You know what this investigation is like — they have you questioning everything."

Mozart snuggled closer to Vivaldi on the couch.

"Anyway," Marge said, patting her hair, "what I do know is one of her biggest regrets is not being closer to you."

My eyes started to sting. "There hasn't been anything stopping her." But that didn't feel as true as it had a month ago.

"You don't know. I don't know, really." She sighed. "Obviously there are things about your mother none of us know."

36

Iris and I were in her bedroom after another delicious Bruce and Moira dinner. The Take the Castle board game we'd started weeks ago was still ongoing, partly because it was such a crazy detailed game that it took forever to make a single move, and because of its medieval and strategic complexity, we had to take regular breaks. I was starting to wonder why we were still playing. There was a very slim chance the castle would ever be taken.

Iris looked at me over the board. "Zane asked me to go for coffee."

I put down the game rules I was consulting. "What? When?"

"Yesterday. He wants to talk about university or something."

"And?"

She shrugged. "And what? He thinks I should go to UBC for IT. Apparently he sees brilliance in my tech abilities." She inspected the game pieces she'd moved into the castle's moat.

"And you're telling me this because …"

"I don't know." She sat back against the wall. "Because you're my best friend, I guess."

"And … I'm also proud of your tech abilities," I said,

purposely avoiding our previous argument about Zane. "I think it's a good idea."

She stared at the game board.

"You okay?" I asked.

"Your army's not going to make it across the field, you know."

I considered my lackluster troops, spread out over the green part of the board. "I just don't know how to get them in shape. They'd rather spend their time drinking and carousing than training for battle, you know?"

"That's not in the game."

"What's not?"

"There's no drinking or carousing in the game. It's strategy and problem solving."

"Drinking and carousing are a huge problem and a terrible strategy."

"See, my army's already taking the moat."

"That's one small unit. I doubt they can all do it."

"No wonder you can't command your army — you're all pessimism."

"I should just go home to my country estate and work my vassals harder."

"That sounds just like you."

I moved one of my units onto higher ground, which was not actually higher because the board was flat.

"Finally she makes a decisive move," Iris said.

"Did you know Mylo's mom will only pay for his university tuition if he studies things she approves of?"

Her hands were clenched under her chin as she stared at the board. "Hmmm."

"Isn't that ridiculous?"

"It's positively medieval."

"I'm serious," I said. "It's a dictatorship. 'Be what I want or you're cut off.'"

"I guess he could always pay his own way, though, right?"

"Yeah, but …"

"He told me he was saving money from his landscaping job to pay for school."

I straightened my legs and stretched. "She just seems super mean and controlling. He hardly ever talks about her in a positive way."

Iris was watching me.

"What?"

"Oh, nothing."

"Don't 'oh, nothing' me. What?"

She sighed.

It seemed there was something I was supposed to be getting.

"I agree with you that she seems controlling," she said. "It's kind of unnecessary that —"

"Thank you."

"But his parents are separated or divorced or whatever. Who knows what's actually going on. I'm not saying she's right. It's just, you know." She waved her hands around to somehow drive her point home.

My shoulders were tight, like I'd been living with them hunched up. Something about her argument bothered me. "You sure you're not just defending her because you want her to love your fundraiser?"

She was annoyed. It didn't happen often, but when she

looked at me like that, I felt horrible. I studied a random sock sneaking out from under her bed.

She leaned back against the wall with a thud. "Are we leaving the castle-storming for another day?"

"Yeah, I guess." I folded the game rules and took a photo of the board so we'd know where to start next time.

She stretched out her leg and kicked me in the knee.

"Ow," I said.

She rolled her eyes, scooping up the game pieces. "You're so full of it. That didn't hurt."

"Malicious intent," I said.

"That's what you get for being so irritating."

"Okay, okay. I'm sorry. Are we done doing battle?"

She got up and put the lid on the game box. "Yeah. I think so."

"Geez. Thank you." I looked up at her and she looked down at me.

Moira called something to Bruce downstairs.

"There's probably dessert in the kitchen," Iris said, reaching out a hand to pull me up. "Should we go?"

"Yeah," I said. "We should."

37

The next morning, I woke up to a text from Mylo.

Had a rough night. Can we go somewhere?

I rolled onto my stomach and replied, *1. That sounds ominous. And 2. Is this a jailbreak? Should I alert Iris?*

First, I'm okay. Rough nights are kind of the norm for me.

I watched the in-progress dots.

And second, I need this to just be us. Is that okay? You're kind of the only person who can know. But give your dad my number if you want.

Now I really wasn't sure what to say.

Can I pick you up in an hour?

I rolled onto my back and thought about breathing.

Please?

Okay.

*

Ammonite was a small town spread along the highway forty minutes from our house. It was touristy for its colorful, quaint old buildings and planters spilling over with summer flowers. I hadn't been there in over a year; the last time was when Mom entertained an old broadcasting friend, and Charlie and I were dragged along to shuffle behind them up Ammonite's main street as they perused the shop windows and exclaimed about the snapdragons and daisies.

Mylo pulled off the road beside the community park where kids were playing baseball with their dads and a couple of tweens sat on the swings and dragged their feet through the wood chips. There was an artistic play structure made of driftwood behind them where someone had piled wood chips on the bottom of the tree-trunk slide.

He hadn't wanted to talk much on the drive, and I was almost jittery with all the possibilities I'd floated in my head. I pretended interest in the park as I waited for him to speak.

"Over there," he said.

"Over where?"

He pointed to a bench that looked over the field. He unclipped his seat belt. "Come on."

*

"Is this where you break the suspense for me?" I asked as we sat down.

The kids were horrible at catching the baseballs.

He watched them for a moment, then took a breath. "This is the last place I saw my dad."

I stared at him. "He left you and your mom."

"Yeah. Kind of. But literally."

I waited for more, but he seemed to be waiting for something, too. "I don't understand," I said.

"Five years ago next month, he and I sat here and he acted as if everything was normal, even though I sensed something was up — he'd been acting weird for a month or so — and then he walked around the corner to get something in the car, and I waited and he never came back." His eyes were focused on a crumpled coffee cup lying in the grass in front of us. "My mom's assistant had to come and get me because my mom was out of town and I was twelve and I had no way to get home."

I watched him pick at the skin around his fingernails. I didn't remember them being a mess before.

He exhaled through his mouth. "No one knew where he'd gone — he just disappeared. The police searched but came up empty. They said maybe he had walked out on us and gone overseas. He has relatives in Scotland." He coughed and wiped the back of his hand across his mouth. "But then someone found him a year later."

"Someone?" I asked.

"A social worker at a homeless shelter in Vancouver." He lowered his head to stare at the ground, where an ant was toiling along with a piece of leaf.

"So he was alive?"

He nodded.

"He was staying at the shelter?"

"No, he wasn't. He was on the street."

One of the kids finally caught a baseball cleanly.

"The social worker saw him on the street," I said.

His eyes snapped over to me for a second. "He was *living* on the street."

"He was homeless?" I couldn't scrub the disbelief from my voice. "Is he *still* homeless?"

Instead of answering, he leaned forward, his elbows resting on his knees.

"Wait," I said, something surfacing in the back of my mind. "When you told me about the PWR, the person who went missing ... were you talking about your *dad*?"

"But it's because I know how you feel, right?" His face was so unguarded that I didn't know how to look at him. The pain there was sharp. "No one else understands what it feels like to have a parent just ... gone."

"But, Mylo," I said slowly. "It's kind of different ..."

"Yeah, maybe," he said. "Your mom's a celebrity and everything's been out in public and my dad was just a community college teacher and it's all covered up. But how many people are going to understand what it feels like?"

"But why keep it such a secret? Why can't your mom tell someone — her family? Friends? Someone? It's been five years."

He picked at a scab on his thumb. "My mother's M.O. is silence and secrecy. She's scared this will affect her business connections, her reputation. Last night we had a huge fight, and she said my dad was just like her dad. I think she actually hates them both."

"Your grandfather, the butterfly smuggler? How is that possible?"

Mylo stared across the field at something, but I couldn't tell what. "He was a dreamer. He couldn't hold down a job, got obsessed with his collection and let my grandmother raise the kids basically on her own. He was an expert in butterfly anatomy, but he kind of couldn't function as a person. My mom never forgave him. She made me swear not to tell anyone, even after my dad was spotted on the street." He rubbed both hands over his face. "I haven't really wanted to tell anyone at school because it's such a crazy story anyway, but then you called me ..."

"Wow, you knew exactly what to say." We both stared into the distance and listened to the shouts of kids and barks of dogs.

It did seem crazy and unbelievable. And heartbreaking. I could imagine someone like Trent being unable to summon the necessary gravitas.

"Have you tried to find him? Since he was spotted?"

He sat back on the bench. "Mom hired a private investigator to find him. Apparently when homeless people don't want to be found, they're really good at hiding. And for all we know, he could be in Toronto."

The dads on the field called out to the kids that baseball practice was over. Sounds of disappointment ensued.

"This park has changed," he said. "I've been coming here for five years, stupidly hoping he would be here, that I could step into the past or something and find him like nothing had happened." He massaged the spot below his ear where his jaw ended. "There used to be more swings, but they were super old and sketchy. And the play area's been completely redone. It used to be metal and the slide was really steep. Now it's that wood thing. I was here when the guys were putting down the new wood chips." He looked at me and then started picking his fingernails again. "I guess I want you to get me," he said. "Since we've both got this screwed-up situation to live through. I've been thinking we could be our own support group. You know?"

I reached over and touched his hand. He turned it palm up and I pressed mine onto it, our fingers threading and curling together. There was a zing up my spine, but mostly it just felt warm with the sun hitting us and our billions of atoms humming inside us. He could sit in my PWR with me because we actually shared the waiting room. We were sitting against the same wall, staring at the same old magazines, waiting for different people to come through the door.

38

So I'm planning the next jailbreak, Iris texted. Just want to give you a heads-up. Be prepared … one night this week.

Any night in particular?

I can't say. It needs to be a surprise.

Is it Thursday night? Are we going to Star Club??

The in-progress dots blinked. Okay, you're not allowed to guess these things anymore.

You're not very original. Star Club is always Thursday nights.

But you haven't been in a while. And I figured it would be too obvious, so you'd think it would be something way more exciting. Which it is. Anyway, I give up. Mylo's coming, BTW. I assured him we wouldn't make him feel stupid for not knowing if Pluto is a planet or not.

You talked to him?

I saw him at HackAttack last night.

Was he okay?

Yeah. He seemed kind of chipper, actually. Why?

39

Dad adjusted the stereo until he found a suitably hillbilly banjo tune.

I'd agreed to come along partly to get out of the house but mostly because I was getting the feeling that Dad needed less time on his own.

"This guy gives me no notice on the work he wants done and now I have to drive across town to pick up his flash drive," Dad grumbled.

I rolled down the window because the A/C was broken. "You should fire him."

"I'm a consultant. He'd be the one firing me."

"But he sounds like a piece of work. Why do you take that crap from him?"

Dad backed down the driveway. "Because he's a client and that's the way it goes. Plus, he's not a bad guy. He's just a grumpy person to work for."

On the stereo, the banjo went into an elaborate solo.

"It's nice that you're here," he said as we pulled onto the street.

I studied him as he drove: the light brown hairs on his arms, the slight slackness of the skin around his jaw. He'd probably have jowls when he got older, like his dad had. Something about that was disturbing and comforting at the same time.

"Do you want to stop for ice cream on the way home?" he asked.

"That's okay," I said. "I'm not ten anymore."

"I didn't know there was an age limit to ice cream enjoyment."

"It just doesn't have to be a bribe. I came because I wanted to."

He cleared his throat but didn't say anything.

"Are you sleeping okay?" I asked.

"Not badly. It could be worse."

"What does that mean?"

"It means at the beginning I slept about two hours a night."

"And now?"

He squinted at the road. "Now it's about four."

"That's not great, Dad."

"I never said it was great."

"And you're still working all the time."

"Can't do much about that."

"I know, but ..."

"You don't have to check up on me, Grace." He patted my arm. "I'm okay."

"That's what a lot of people who aren't okay say. That's what I say when people ask me."

"And you're not? Okay?"

I snorted.

"Fine, so we're a different level of okay, a level unknown to fully functioning okay people."

"Okay to that."

We were driving through a neighborhood filled with 1970s split-levels in browns and dark greens. Our babysitter when I was little, before Charlie was born, lived here.

Two kids walking a huge white dog wandered into the park on our left.

"Why is she such a mystery to everyone?" I asked. The sun was beating down on my right arm and I hadn't put on sunscreen.

"What?"

"Mom," I said. "Why doesn't anyone know what was going on with her?"

"I don't know."

"Don't you?"

He looked torn, as he often did now, but I couldn't tell what thoughts were tearing him. "How can we know what's going on with anyone?" he asked quietly. Then he said, "She's one of the most complicated people I know."

"Why?"

He hesitated, then pulled over as a fire truck screamed past us and turned left down the next street. "Did you know she's always had a fear of snakes?"

"No."

"When she was twenty, she got a snake to get over the phobia."

"Seriously?" I couldn't imagine her doing something like that. A snake?

"She took it back to the pet store after two weeks."

"Because she was too freaked out?"

"Yeah."

"Why would she even get a snake?" I asked.

He shrugged. "Because she was brave."

"It doesn't sound very brave if she had to take it back."

"Even though it didn't work out, it was pretty courageous to face her fear."

"I guess," I said.

"She was so spontaneous. God, the trouble we got into when we first started dating." He let his face relax a little, and the lines on his forehead smoothed out.

"What was she like then?" I asked.

He slowed down for a traffic light. "She had a perm."

"No."

"Honest. It was the hottest thing to have."

"But there are no photos of it."

He winked at me. "For a reason."

"Oh my God, she destroyed the evidence?"

He smiled and it looked so nice. It was so nice, too, to find out something simple and embarrassing about her. I wanted more.

"She was excited then, Grace. About life, her work, about what she could do with it. She had all these goals and missions and she had endless energy, which was useful when she worked fifteen-hour days."

"Was she in journalism then?"

He turned right onto a side street. "She'd just been promoted to reporter. Before I met her, she was an assistant for some TV guy. I think Patricia got her that job."

"Sounds like Grandma."

"But GG wanted to travel overseas and make documentaries,

to report on war — all kinds of dangerous things you can imagine made Patricia terrified."

"Did Mom ever do those things?"

"No, she got promoted to news anchor too quickly. But she wanted me to follow my passion. She persuaded me to apply for my environmental science program on our second date. I probably would have applied to medical school for her if she'd suggested it."

I stared out the window with a sudden sinking feeling. Where had that person gone?

*

Dad parked outside Pierce Labs Inc., and I sat with the windows down, baking in the sun, while he ran in.

Had something happened after I was born — the PPD maybe? How could she be such a different person from the one Dad had described? She sounded so unlike Mom. I felt cheated. Like I was mourning someone I had never met.

We were quieter on the way home, letting the jazz station I'd found fill the car with sound.

"I think we can work it out, you know, Grace," he said when we were a few streets from home.

"Work what out?" I asked.

"Your mother and me. One thing this abduction has made me realize is that you can move through anything if you want to badly enough. Whatever problems we had — we can work them out. I know we can."

Maybe he meant it to sound reassuring, but I dug my

fingernails into my palms. Who knew what was going to happen, least of all him? No one knew if she'd come back or if she'd want to fix things like he did. They'd argued right before she disappeared, and now with the note and the what-ifs that kept multiplying ... If I'd been naive about the world before, I was awake now. You couldn't count on everyone to be who you thought they were.

40

Mylo had already taken shotgun in Moira's car, so I got in the back, beside Iris's ever-present canvas bag and metal water bottle.

"Did you know Mylo hates the Tigers? It's a wonder I let him into the car." Iris turned out of our driveway, all six bangles jingling merrily.

"I just find Jake Townsend kind of whiny," Mylo said. "He writes good songs — it's a shame about the voice."

"But it's the *Tigers*." Iris threw her hands up.

Mylo grabbed the wheel for her.

"I can see how you think he's whiny," I said, shifting Iris's stuff so I could sit in the middle seat.

"Where's your seat belt, missus? Don't make me stop this car."

I clipped it. "It's never really bothered me that he sounds like a strangled cat sometimes."

"I'm sorry, it's not clear whose side you're on," Iris said.

"I'm Switzerland."

Iris grumbled something about neutrality and the easy way out.

Mylo lowered his window. "Hey, can I get a primer on the kinds of things I'm supposed to know before we get to Space Wizard Camp?"

"That's offensive." Iris slapped him on the shoulder. "Grace wouldn't call it Hacker Wizard Camp, Mr. Coder."

"I certainly would not," I confirmed.

"Fair enough," he said, "but can you give me some quick facts anyway? Grace?" He twisted around and caught my eye. Bunched up his eyebrows at me. I got the feeling he wanted to reach out his hand. Or maybe it was that I wanted to touch him.

"Okay, fine," Iris said. "Where does your knowledge end?"

"Uh, at the edge of the solar system, maybe?"

"So beyond Neptune is the Kuiper Belt," I said, "which is basically a donut-shaped field of objects smaller than a planet, so lots of comets and icy objects that move in really huge and weird orbits. And beyond that is the Oort Cloud, which either is or isn't part of our solar system depending on who you talk to, but it has even more commets, and way longer range ones. And then there's interstellar space, which is mind-meltingly big."

Mylo looked over at Iris. "I'm totally not going to remember those names."

"It's okay, the newbie quiz is pretty easy," Iris said.

"She's kidding," I said.

"And what's the deal with black holes?"

"Define 'deal,'" Iris said.

"Okay, wrong question. Uh, where could I find one?"

Iris sighed. "*God*, I love black holes, don't you, Grace?"

"They're really common — there might be tons of them around the galaxy. But there's a well-known supermassive black hole in the center of the Milky Way and we've actually seen images of it," I said. "It's pulling everything close to it as we speak."

"I thought they were invisible."

"They are. But because their gravity is so strong, stars orbit them just like we orbit the sun. If you look at those orbits, you see the stars must be circling something really massive and dense. You can study black holes by studying what happens to the matter close to them."

"Are we going to get sucked into it?"

"No way. We're really far from the center of the galaxy. Like, twenty-five thousand light-years away."

"So, basically, we're safe?"

"Completely safe from that black hole," I said. "But we could totally get hit by an asteroid like the dinosaurs did or obliterated by a gamma ray burst from a way closer source, so I think seeing black holes as cosmic death-eaters is kind of dumb. There are way worse things that could happen."

Mylo blinked at me, then turned back around. "Awesome. I feel super uplifted now."

"But those things are pretty unlikely on the scale of a human life," I said. "In the grand scheme of things, eighty years is nothing, right? Think about all the thousands of generations of dinosaurs that lived totally normal lives before the asteroid hit the planet. We focus on that one moment, but really there were *millions* of years before it that were all systems go."

"So you're saying we'll probably get out of this okay, but maybe our eight-times-great-grandkids won't be so lucky?"

"Well, actually, no," Iris said. "No one's getting out of this okay. We all get to be stardust again. Until they figure out immortality."

He stared out the windshield. "So is the point of astronomy to make you feel depressed and insignificant?"

I leaned forward, my knees scrunched against both front seats. "The point is to ask questions about the universe, probably forever, which is so awesome. Being curious keeps you grounded and being grounded helps you fly."

Iris laughed. "You totally stole that from Claudia!"

"Yup. Totally," I said, sitting back against the seat.

"Totally," Mylo murmured, staring out the window.

*

We got the last spot in the parking lot, which was usually half-empty on Star Club nights, and I was about to comment on it when Iris jumped out of the car and ran over to Claudia, who was walking with someone toward the planetarium.

Mylo got out and opened my door for me, which was unexpected and quite charming.

"What's with her?" I asked as I got out.

"She's just micromanaging. Have you noticed she does that?" He slid his hand into mine and I forgot to take a breath.

Iris was deep in conversation with Claudia and someone who might have been her husband.

I found a breath and asked, "What thing is she micromanaging?"

His hand squeezed mine and then let go. "The guest speaker."

Iris bounded back to us, her face bright and her hair waving behind her. "It's going to be *so amazing*."

"What is?" I looked at Mylo, then Iris. "Is Carolyn Porco

here or something?"

"Better!" She was jumping up and down. "It's Elizabeth Tasker! Via Skype from Tokyo!"

At the other end of the parking lot, Claudia was carrying a box through the planetarium's front doors.

Elizabeth Tasker, the exoplanet expert. The astrophysicist Iris had interviewed, the astrophysicist I'd always wanted to meet.

"And — and!" Iris had grabbed my arm and it was jumping up and down with her. "She was super impressed about the exoplanets you found!"

Mylo was staring at me with a half smile. Iris was fizzing like a shaken soda can.

"How did you ...?" I asked her.

"Amazing, right?" She exhaled. "I knew this would blow you away!"

She was hugging me and I was hugging her, and because it was just before the summer solstice, the sun was a few hours from setting and the sky was that deep, clear evening blue. But the stars, their exoplanets, all the comets and asteroids were out there, beyond our atmosphere. Thousands of black holes were doing their thing around the galaxy at that very second.

$$*$$

We sat near the front, where Claudia had saved us seats, and then the lights went down and the screen went black and then there was Elizabeth Tasker, sitting in an office somewhere, books on her left and a plant on her right, her blond hair pulled back. I'd always liked that she seemed like a real person, not some serious scientist who wrote serious research papers and studied all the incomprehensible things. She was funny. I'd seen videos of her talks. Her book, *The Planet Factory*, was the kind of thing I could get lost in because it had the science and the jokes. It felt like she was writing for people like me.

Mylo sat beside me and his arm pressed against mine, it felt like on purpose. "She's a real hero to you?"

"Yeah. I'm kind of excited-nervous."

"Yeah, I know that feeling."

I looked over but he was watching the screen.

Elizabeth smiled and said, "So I'm going to start with the small — how I got into science and astrophysics in particular — and then move to the big — namely the solar system and beyond, to other systems that have exoplanets and stars and some of the most unbelievably weird objects you could ever imagine. Does that sound all right?"

The room murmured.

Elizabeth grinned. "That sounds positive." She launched into her childhood in England and how her dad took her to the London Planetarium when she was nine and got her a giant poster of Saturn that she kept on her wall until she left home. And how her mother was a science writer and edited her first essays about space. How her mother was so proud of the space trivia she spouted at family gatherings when everyone else got tired of it.

It sounded amazing. It sounded the way it should be — the way I so badly wanted it. If I could trade mother situations, especially right now, I'd do it with her.

I felt Mylo's fingers on mine.

"You okay?" he whispered in my ear.

"Yeah." I leaned into his shoulder. "You?"

His breath was warm on my skin. "Totally not feeling depressed and insignificant."

"No?"

"No way. Curiosity keeps you grounded and being grounded helps you fly."

And we giggled silently in the dark as Elizabeth Tasker explained the beauty of the TRAPPIST-1 exoplanets.

*

Iris's text came through just as I was falling asleep. *Wasn't that the BEST?*

That was totally the best. You're the best.

I kind of am. But you're the best at space. Did you see Elizabeth Tasker's face when you told her about your exoplanet research paper?

Yeah. That was cool. I got under the blanket so my phone lit the space like a lantern in a cave.

She was really impressed, Iris replied. *I don't think she asks just anyone to become email buddies.*

She didn't ask to become email buddies.

Basically, she did.

I had broken into several spontaneous grins since getting home. And also spontaneous tears. It was all so much. *Thank you,* I typed back.

You're welcome.

You're the brightest star in my universe.

Love you, too.

41

As another, hotter heat wave was beating down on the city, Mylo texted a photo of a lake. *Can I pick you up? 30 mins?*

Birds chirped in the trees outside, and somewhere downstairs I could hear the thuds and grunts of Dad trying to install a mini air-conditioning unit.

My phone rang. "It's called Constance Pond," he said. "It's on private land, so there won't be lots of people — the owners are family friends. We won't get run off or anything."

"Sounds charming."

"So can I pick you up? Please? This is my way of feeling part of the universe."

*

The lake's name was accurate — it was more of a pond. About the size of our local swimming pool. Cottonwood trees rose up on three sides of the water, shading us and acting as a screen from everything else — the gravel road Mylo parked the car on, the red rooftop of the house nearby that he said was his mother's friend's, the possibility of an outside world. He stood beside me in his T-shirt and swim trunks, his tanned legs stretching down to flip-flops hidden by the grass.

"You've been here a lot?" I asked.

He squatted by the edge of the pond, bouncing on the balls of his feet, surveying the surface as if he could read something on it. "Yeah. Every summer for a long time. My dad used to bring me here." His hair ruffled in the breeze. "He'd float in the middle in a big inner tube and read a newspaper. We'd spend all day here, just doing nothing. He'd skip stones across the water all the way to the other side. It was the best." He looked lost in the memory, and for a second he was just an overgrown boy, towel slung around his neck, reaching down to test how cold the water was. He stood up and unwound the towel. Pulled the T-shirt over his head in one smooth movement, and underneath was skin that assaulted my eyes with its smoothness. He raised his arms and dived in, entering the water with a splash that shattered the silence around us. He came up in the middle and shook his head like a dog, the spray scattering across the surface.

"How is it?" I called.

His eyes followed a single green leaf, curved like a little boat, that floated by his shoulder. He poked at it with a finger. "It's perfect."

I dropped the towel into the ankle-high grass and weeds and pulled my sundress over my head.

We treaded water side by side in the middle and I pretended not to feel the slimy tickle of a weed on my foot. He kept glancing at me under water-rumpled eyebrows. It felt like something wanted to be said, that the intimacy of swimming in this little pond required a caption. But I didn't have one.

I swam to the far side and knew he was watching me, that there was something intense about this place, or maybe it was that something intense had developed since we were last together. I wasn't sure how to address it, if I even should. Did I really know what he was feeling? The cottonwood trees above us shivered and a bird flew across the blue. I scrambled out on the far side, into the heat, my wet feet catching on the scratchy weeds, and walked back around as he did a few laps of front crawl.

From my towel I watched him get out and stand at the edge of the water and drip, his back to me. I didn't think I could stand the ache I felt, digging into me like a curled fist. It was his beauty, his sadness. It was this place, his stories. How much I understood the part of him that was stuck in PWR.

I thought about times Mom had taken us to the beach when I was little and Charlie was a baby. He'd always eat the sand and she'd stick her pinkie into his mouth to get it out. She'd hold my hand and we'd jump over the rushing waves together. Suddenly I could hear her laugh, that full, loud laugh that must have been what Dad was describing. I could hear the seagulls shrieking overhead and the water roaring in and Mom's laugh in my ear. I knew it had happened, but it felt more like a description of a real moment. A greeting card of someone else's family. One I couldn't actually live in.

He lay down on his back next to me, staring up at the sky. "Sometimes he'd recite poetry to me and I'd pretend I cared."

"Your dad?" I crossed my legs, watching a bead of water run down over his ribs.

"I can't remember any of it now. I wasn't really paying attention. Why would I? It was fricking poetry." His eyes tracked across the sky. "But now it feels like I should have. Like maybe there was meaning in it, the way he cared so much about those words."

A raven croaked in a tree somewhere, making everything much too atmospheric.

I tucked my wet hair behind my ears. "What would you say to him if you could?"

He didn't answer. He stared up at the sky and then rubbed his hands over his face, wiping his eyes with his thumbs as if there was still pond water on his eyelashes. "I'd ask him why. Why he left and if he regretted it." He sighed and his eyes filled and spilled over, tiny streams running down into the grass. He didn't wipe them away.

I pressed my palm to his chest, felt his heartbeat steady beneath his ribs. My own cheeks were wet.

He rolled onto his side and I lay down facing him, our foreheads touching. He reached an arm around me and pulled me in.

"What would you ask?" he whispered.

"The same," I said, my mouth salty.

We lay like that for a long time, until our faces dried in the heat, and then he touched my cheek and softly kissed me. I kissed him back. We kissed each other and the planet rotated at 327 meters per second.

42

Hey, you up? Iris didn't go to bed until late — hence the morning sleep-ins — and I was often asleep when her late-night texts came through. But after Constance Pond I was too wired to do anything restful. Whatever had happened between me and Mylo and the cosmos had come home with me, and my heart still jammed against my ribs every time I thought about it.

Yeah, I'm up.

Zane told me he's not getting back together with his fiancée.

I started typing, then erased the words, then typed again. *Okay ...?*

And he said he likes me. For real.

Was this a text?

No. He gave me flowers. A flower. And an iced latte.

Aw.

What should I do?

What do you mean? You know you want this.

But you don't think I should.

I think you're going to do what you really want to do. No matter what I say. So do it. I thought about telling her I had news, too. Mylo, Constance Pond, the way he'd let me see him and how we'd kissed. But I didn't. It felt too personal. Too exposing somehow. Like the image I'd seen once of a baby born with its heart beating on the outside of its chest.

*

Hi, his message said.

Hi.

Are you feeling okay about what happened?

At the pond? Yes. Very okay. Are you?

Very okay. I wasn't sure if you'd be weirded out by me being so emotional. I don't usually cry in front of people. Definitely not girls I like.

I'm a girl you like?

You're THE girl I like.

...

What are you doing?

Focusing on my breathing.

Me, too.

43

I smelled Grandma before I heard her, perfume filling my room like invisible smoke.

"What's that?" she asked over my shoulder, concern in her voice, like the image of the Crab Nebula was a photo of someone's cancer.

"Star explosion leftovers," I said.

"Oh," she said, quiet behind me for a moment.

I glanced back in my periphery, expecting her to be checking her nails or something, but she seemed to be staring at my screen.

"And is this one of the things you wrote about in that article?"

I swiveled in my chair so I could fully see her. "What article?"

"The one you wrote with the other scientists — your dad told me about it." She looked a little out of her depth, which she was, but in a way that was endearing.

"The exoplanet paper?"

"That sounds like it."

"No, that was about a single planet I found. You can't actually see the planet because of its distance from us — we only know it's there because of how it passes in front of its star and dims the light we see." I pointed behind me to the laptop screen. "This photo is of a cloud of dust and gases. Totally not the same thing, totally different part of the universe."

She studied the photo, then me. "I see."

Part of me was amazed that we were still having a conversation about space, and another part was skeptical as to why. "I told you about the exoplanet paper," I said. "Two years ago."

She huffed a little. "Well, there's been a lot going on in the last two years. At any rate, I'm impressed to hear your name is up there with such distinguished company." She smiled and I saw she was trying. It wasn't an act, at least not the core of it, even though it still sounded like she cared most about my name's proximity to the researchers', like we'd all shared top billing on a movie's credits.

"Thanks," I said, turning back to my laptop, unsure how long she'd be there.

"So I was thinking," she said. Dramatic pause.

Now I felt split again between slight affection toward her and feeling pissed off that all the exoplanet talk had been a warm-up for what she really wanted. "What?" I said, staring at the screen, which now showed an artist's rendition of a supernova.

"You and I should go to a movie," she said.

The pissed-off part of me won. "And why is that?" I asked.

"Well, I've noticed you haven't even talked about being done school for the summer. Shouldn't you be out celebrating or something?"

I shut my laptop. "Is that what normal teenagers do, in your experience?"

She took a step back, maybe because I'd been a little rougher with the laptop than I intended.

"I just mean you've been cooped up in here for a while now and maybe some time out, doing something fun, would do you good. It always does me good."

I tried hard to retain some of the warmth I'd just felt for her. "I do have fun. I just don't tell you about it."

"Well, I know. Grace was the same, but —"

"Grandma, when have we ever gone to a movie together?"

"Isn't it high time!"

I stood up and she had to take another step back. "What makes you think I'd want to?"

She frowned a little, and the lines that were normally obscured by makeup created creases in her skin. "I was hoping you'd ..."

I leaned against the desk. "I'd what?"

She touched her collarbone, prominent like Mom's, but not as exaggerated. "Give it a chance. It's an opportunity for us to talk, Grace. About whatever you want. I wasn't lying when I said how proud I was of your research. It's incomprehensible to me, but it's still remarkable."

"And you want to hear me go on about it in the enclosed space of the car, where you can't escape?"

"Yes, I do," she said. "Honestly."

I stared at her. Then I grabbed the denim shirt off my bed. "And you're saying we go right now?"

Her face opened up. "Well, there are a few films playing around seven. I checked the times."

I put my phone in my pocket. "Okay."

"Okay?"

"I'll go with you."

"You will? That's wonderful, Grace. I'll just go tell your father we're going out."

I wondered if he'd suggested it or whether it had been her idea. "But I need to make a deal with you," I said as she turned to go. "I'm only coming if you tell me some things about Mom while we're out."

*

It was the movie theater we never went to because the other one had better seats and an arcade next door that Charlie liked. This theater smelled like stale popcorn and the concession workers looked totally unimpressed.

Grandma adjusted her hair and walked toward the acne-afflicted guy at the kiosk.

"This movie was filmed at the lot right next to where I was filming last year," she said loud enough for me and the acne guy, and possibly the cashiers, to hear.

I didn't say anything.

"I was visiting a friend who was playing the lead when they were setting up for one of the chase scenes with the explosions." She smiled conspiratorially, as if I'd care. "But I don't want to give anything away."

The guy was watching her with an eyebrow raised, assessing if she was worth the trouble.

On the drive over, she'd asked me the kind of question a grown-up asks when trying to get a teenager to talk: "What do you love so much about astrology?" Except that astrology was not science, it was horoscopes in the newspaper. Astronomy was science. That was my initial response. Then she asked me to explain astronomy. I told her about the Lick Observatory, my go-to origin story for anyone who didn't know me or my obsession. She listened, or acted like she was listening, and I went on about the first things I'd seen through my telescope. And it was kind of sad because some of that stuff she'd heard before. Back when I was a super-enthusiastic fourteen-year-old space geek, I'd talk to anyone about it, and there had been some phone conversations and Christmas moments that involved me giving a lot more information than Grandma would ever need or want. My interest-detector had improved since then.

The kiosk guy handed us our ticket stubs, and we walked toward theater number six.

"I have to pee," I said at the last minute, wanting at least a few minutes away from her and her accompanying perfume cloud.

"Sure, honey. I'll get some good seats. Don't get lost!"

In the stall I texted Iris, who knew I was out with Grandma.

This was a bad idea.

A fight already?

No. Just sucks.

All you have to do is sit next to her and watch the movie.

It's not even one I'd choose.

Chin up, Eeyore.

Screw you, Pooh.

*

"Oh, there you are," Grandma said, flashing her teeth at me as I inched down the row to my seat. "I was worried you'd gone into the wrong theater."

"I can remember a single-digit number pretty well," I said.

She appeared not to have heard me and pulled out her phone, where a message was waiting. From my vantage point I could just make out the name Kyle Feronzi. Her manager or something. I'd heard her say his name into her phone on numerous occasions around the house. *Yes, of course, Kyle. Sure I can, Kyle! Don't be so cynical, Kyle, it'll be fine.*

Now she typed a reply to him.

I pretended to look at my phone but tried to see her screen.

"He's so pessimistic," she said with a chuckle.

"Who?" I asked, knowing she wanted me to.

"My publicist. His wife just left him and he's having a hard time adjusting."

I stared up at the ceiling. "Doesn't your wife leaving you kind of predispose you to pessimism?"

"Oh, he's pessimistic as a personality. It's not the wife who did that." She kept typing.

"So why did you mention that part?"

She looked over at me. "His wife has been spending him dry for years and sleeping with who knows how many men. They had a complicated agreement where he couldn't ask for a divorce without basically losing everything he owned. She finally set him free and before I came up here we celebrated with champagne."

I stared down at my phone's black screen. "So then why is he —"

"He's like the rest of us, only more so." She put hers away as the lights above us started to dim. "He wonders who'll love him. He's terrified he'll be alone forever. He lives too much in his thoughts instead of in here." She pointed to her chest.

The theater went dark and we entered Big-Screen Commercial Land.

Grandma patted my arm briefly and I was filled with an electrical storm of conflicting feelings. I still didn't want to be here, and I also wanted her to keep her hand on me. She'd just said something kind of deep, something unexpected, and I was still trying to figure it out. My throat got tight as the dog on the screen brought his owner a Coke.

"What did you think?" she asked as I started the Ford's engine two hours later, my brain half melted in my skull from all the terrible dialogue and predictable everything else.

"Not my kind of movie," I said.

"No? I thought the servant storyline was quite original. The way they had him doubling as a spy."

I turned out of the parking lot. "I generally don't like it when the female characters need a man to save them."

"But she ran out of the burning building."

"Because her boyfriend went inside and held up the doorway for her, and then he died a hero."

She muttered something about being hard to please.

"My turn," I said.

"Your turn?"

The neon sign of a greasy diner flashed across the front of the car.

"What did Mom want to be when she was growing up?"

She opened her purse and got out a tin of mints, holding them out to me. "Want one?"

"No, thanks."

She popped one and looked out the window. "Did you know she almost didn't finish high school?"

"What?" I stared at her, then remembered I was driving.

"She was completely scattered in her last year — wanted to do a million things and couldn't even focus on three. One day it was fashion school, next it was charity work, then learning to make croissants or something. She had enthusiasm, but the girl couldn't decide where to put her energy." Grandma got out her lipstick and applied it, maybe forgetting that we were heading home to a quiet house. "She failed two subjects in Grade 12 because she was so distracted. Maybe it was boys, too — I never found out. I shouldn't have sent her to a coed school."

"She failed?" I was shocked. How could that have happened? This was not the Mom I knew or that anyone had talked about. I remembered what Marge had said when I went to her house. There were things no one knew. Except Grandma, apparently. "She never really talked about high school at all," I said, "but failing subjects …"

"Oh, it was very hush-hush. She was ashamed. She lied to her friends about it — I lied, too. It was the last time she failed anything, though. It was the lesson she needed."

"You said she almost didn't finish."

Grandma growled out a derisive laugh. "The principal was a

fan of *Sunbathers*, the show I was doing at the time. I got her a walk-on role, and she fudged the grades."

My mouth was open. "No way."

She shrugged. "There are advantages to play."

I stared at the oncoming traffic. "Oh my God."

"Grace muddled around for a year or so before she decided on a university, but by then she'd whittled it down to some sociology program overseas or an internship in broadcasting. And thank goodness she made the choice she did."

"Why did you tell me about the fake grades if it's such a secret?" I asked.

Grandma clasped her hands together on her lap. "I guess I was assuming you could keep it to yourself. If it got out it could make a stink with the media. Your mother would be mortified."

I couldn't quite figure out her motive. "Shouldn't she be the one to tell me all this?"

She looked unrepentant. "Yes, maybe. But she's not here, is she? And you asked. We had a deal, right?" She ran her fingers along the strap of her purse and watched the street. Was she trying to get my trust by telling me something unexpected? Did she think I would thank her for it? Should I? "You wanted to know about her. I thought this would be a key piece of information for you. Isn't it interesting to think about who she was when she was your age?"

"Yeah, but ..."

"And that's what you're wanting, isn't it? To know more about her when she was young?"

But this wasn't quite what I had in mind. I felt like I needed to defend Mom, like the seventeen-year-old her needed an ally here, but what good would that do against Grandma? "But she chose journalism," I said finally. "She went to Ryerson."

Grandma sighed. "And was a natural, as you know. To so many people it was the perfect fit — she finally realized her innate talent. It was a huge relief."

I wondered how Mom had actually felt about journalism. Kind of like how Mylo felt about computer science. I changed lanes. "Are you sure it wasn't your relief?"

"What?"

There was no point in picking this fight. I should drop it.

"Of course I was relieved. She'd been adrift. She was finally able to focus on something meaningful and permanent."

"Right," I said through gritted teeth. "Of course." I pressed the radio on, classical music filling the car. I had never missed my mother so much in my life, but not the one I'd known. I missed the one I was getting glimpses of, that I'd never even known existed.

44

I stood outside Charlie's room with a glass of lemonade. I'd just knocked and got a grunt in reply. Instead of walking away, I pushed the door open.

"I didn't say come in," he said without turning around.

His screen was filled with a brown brick wall cut with thin windows. At the top I could make out a bit of blue sky.

"Is that a castle?"

"Yeah, so?"

"Just wondering, Badger."

"You can stop calling me that."

"What? Why?" I came around to try and see his face. I half expected tears but his eyes were dry.

"I just don't want you to anymore. It's not flattering."

I shrugged. "Okay, but ..."

"Dad tried to kick me off *Minecraft*."

"I know." I was still holding the lemonade.

He took his hand off the mouse and turned his head. "Why didn't you say something to him?"

"What was I supposed to say?"

"That I can play if I want. It's not like any of you are doing much with your time."

"Charlie, I just brought you some lemonade." I put the glass on the side table. "Then I'm going out to kick the soccer ball in the yard."

He picked up the glass and wrinkled his nose. "Yeah, right."

"You can watch from your window. Maybe you'll want to join me."

"Maybe not."

I found Charlie's ball in the garage, opened the patio door and threw it down the lawn. Someone had put the goal away, and the grass was fading to its summer gold. Dad preferred letting it dry out for both ecological and maintenance reasons. The crisp blades pricked the soles of my feet as I walked after the ball.

"See, Badger?" I shouted up at his empty window. "Here I am. Ready to play. Enjoying the fresh air and summer sun. Just kicking the ball."

Nothing.

"Charlie, come on. Help me out. Just five minutes. I helped you warm up, remember?"

Nothing moved behind the square of glass.

I sat down with the ball between my feet. Listened to the neighbors' sprinklers hiss and tick.

45

I'd found the exhibit by accident, while searching for something else. Some art gallery on the other side of town was hosting a nature photographer who also happened to be an entomologist. Her focus was butterflies. The show started that week.

"So are you free tomorrow night?" I asked when Mylo picked up.

"For what?"

"A jailbreak."

"I thought Iris and I handled that."

"This is for you."

"Me? I don't need jailbreaking."

"Uh, yeah, you do. Big time. So are you free? At 7:00 p.m., say?"

"I guess."

"There will be penalties for bailing. And no 'my mom won't let me' excuse will be accepted."

"Can you tell me anything about this event?"

"Nope. Nothing. Just be ready."

"Wow. Suspenseful."

"Yup. It's fun being the jailbreaker."

*

Bruce drove us because Dad was busy with another deadline and neither Iris nor I could score a car for ourselves. We both sat in the back so Iris, whose bottom five inches of hair had been dyed pink, could tear open the bag of pretzels she'd brought and share with me. She wore five bangles and a mood ring and occasionally held the bag out for her dad, who kept smiling at me in the rearview mirror.

"This is going to be so great. Right?" Iris said.

"So great," I said.

"I can't believe you just stumbled upon this photography show. You're amazing. Mylo's going to freak out."

"I know."

"I hear he's very talented," Bruce said.

"Did I show you the one he took of the orange butterfly?" Iris asked him.

"The mourning cloak?" I said.

She looked at me. "You know the name? How much research *have* you done?"

I shrugged. "He told me, I guess. It's a cool name."

"What time do you want me to come back to get you?" Bruce asked. "I'll be half an hour at the gym, and if you need longer I can just go to a coffee shop to consume the calories I burned."

"I'll text you," Iris said. "This is his house."

Mylo got into the passenger seat and put his hand out to Bruce. "Hello again, sir."

"It's Bruce, not sir," Bruce said. "But when I was younger,

people called me the Bruce Boss because I was really into Bruce Springsteen."

"*Dad.*" Iris threw a pretzel at him but hit the windshield.

"No littering in my car, please. Don't make me bring out the Bruce Boss."

"Uh, Bruce is fine for me," Mylo said as we started up the road.

Bruce inclined his head. "Just as well."

Mylo twisted around and gave us a smile that made my insides go squirmy. We hadn't been face-to-face since Constance Pond, and it was really hard not to feel all the things. "Being the jailbreakee is awesome," he said. "Can we do this on a rotating schedule?"

Iris offered him the pretzel bag.

"So can you tell me what's happening now?" he asked as he crunched.

"Nope," I said, wishing I could touch him.

"You're not allowed to guess, either," Iris said. "No hints, Dad."

Bruce splayed his fingers out on the steering wheel. "I'm just the cabbie."

*

The gallery was in a converted warehouse beside a bunch of other old warehouses that still looked warehousey. There were five cars parked out front and a sandwich board by the door that said, "Ashanti Donkor: Exploring Wings."

"Oh my God, is this what I think it is?" Mylo said. His eyebrows were halfway up his forehead.

"Do you know her?" I asked.

He stared at the name on the board. "I think I've seen her stuff online."

"She's from Toronto," Iris said beside me. "I googled her."

We all stood there for a moment, watching two men walk into the gallery.

"You guys," Mylo said. His eyes were everywhere. I couldn't tell what he was thinking.

"What?" I asked.

He pushed his hair off his forehead. "I'm kind of nervous."

"That's so cute," Iris said.

"Why are you nervous?" I asked him. His shoulder was touching mine.

"I don't know," he said. "Let's go in."

✳

The exhibition took up two small rooms, and there were about ten people already walking around. Some photos were like Mylo's, tightly focused on the grains that covered the wing, and others were a full set of wings, the colors and lines radiating out past the edges. One was focused solely on the head, with its bulging eyes and furry covering and tongue curled up like a roll of candy tape. They were amazing. There was simple, focused genius in them. Each photo had a card under it with the species, date taken and a note about where and how the butterfly lived. I never knew there were so many different kinds with so many variations. It was like my knowledge of butterflies ended at monarchs and swallowtails and there was this whole world of others out there.

Mylo wandered off to a far corner to stare at an image with blues and purples so bright that they made my eyes water.

I watched him for a moment, until Iris caught my arm and squeezed it. "Hey," she said. "This is pretty awesome. Good work."

"Yeah. And I feel like a grown-up here. Look at all the creative-type adults. I should be wearing artfully mismatched socks or something."

"Do you think Mylo likes you?" Iris asked in my ear.

Everything stopped around us.

"Uh," I said, feeling my heart galloping in my chest. I could tell her. Why couldn't I tell her? This could be the right time.

"I just get a vibe, you know? What do you think?" She was watching me.

"I don't know," I said, knowing that was a stupid way to start a confession, or whatever I knew I should be saying. "I haven't ..."

"Thought about it? Come on." She rolled her eyes. "He's supercute, plus you guys have that other thing in common."

I almost couldn't breathe. "What thing?" I whispered.

She looked uncomfortable and my brain started screaming: What has he told her? What part of his big family secret isn't secret? "I'm sorry, I shouldn't have started this," she said. "It's not okay to — "

I lowered my head and spoke into her face, unable to handle the suspense. "What *thing*?"

She swallowed. "I just meant you both argue with your moms. That's what we talked about at my house last time, right?" She picked at the corner of a fingernail. "I shouldn't have gone there."

My breath came out in a rush as I deflated. "Oh, yeah. Right."

"Are you okay?" she asked, eyes on mine.

"I'm okay," I said, smoothing my hair back. "I'm fine."

I walked around for another five minutes on my own when she went back in the other room, and then Mylo came up beside me and nudged my shoulder. "This is one of the coolest things anyone's ever done for me."

I looked at him. "You're welcome."

"Seriously. I think it might be life changing."

I couldn't stop myself. I kissed his cheek.

"Iris wants to know if you want to check out the gift shop," he said.

I glanced around. "There's a gift shop?"

He led me through the second room to the entrance and on the other side of it was an alcove stuffed with ceramic pieces, watercolor prints and photographs in plastic sleeves. Iris was digging through a basket of silk scarves.

A gray-haired woman in a brown dress was smiling at us from behind a small desk. "How'd you like the photographs?"

"Amazing," Iris and I said together.

"Is Ashanti Donkor here?" Mylo asked her.

They started an excited conversation about the artist and the art and the butterflies, and I stepped into the alcove with Iris. I needed to figure out what to say about Mylo. It felt too important to mess up.

But then a display of bracelets caught my eye. Wooden beaded bracelets that hung from a wooden T stand. They were pretty and smelled amazing and seemed weirdly familiar. I pulled one off and read the tag. Coast Cedar Designs.

"Those are pretty," Iris said over my shoulder.

Something cold was creeping up my spine. "There's something about them," I said.

She took a closer look.

"Does it feel familiar to you?" I asked, my voice steady but my insides shaking.

"Uh, should it be?" She wrinkled her forehead. "The name is kind of generic …" She was staring into the distance.

I looked, too. At the doors leading outside, the parking lot beyond. There was a reason it felt like my whole body was buzzing with electricity.

"Wait. Philip Krause is a wood sculptor, right?" she whispered.

I squeezed my eyes shut and tried to recall the memory that was bumping up against the back of my brain. Where had I seen this before?

"There's no other information on the tag," Iris said beside me. She took it to the gray-haired woman. "Where are these from?"

"Oh, they're made by a local guy," she said. "He specializes in art using coastal wood. Apparently he's done some sculptures around town as well. I can look up his information, if you like. I'm new here, so I don't know about all this stuff yet, I'm afraid."

"What is it?" Mylo asked.

"I'm not sure," I said, but then I was. The soccer game. I could picture the bracelet she was wearing that day. I remembered thinking it was unusual for her. Something I should have noted to Isabel when she asked about unusual details, but it had slipped down some crack in my memory. I felt the deep tug of dread, the kind that's made heavier by guilt. How could I have forgotten? It was a bracelet just like this.

46

Isabel got to our house an hour later with Constable Baker, in a not-so-funny replay of the night Dad first called them. She sat in the living room with Grandma, quietly going over a list of questions. Grandma's voice was hushed for once, but there was an edge to it. She clutched her hands together in her lap. Isabel had placed the bracelet on the coffee table between them, and it sat there radiating the unknown. I could feel it from the kitchen.

Iris had bought it from the gray-haired woman because I couldn't. She'd found Isabel's number in my phone and held my hand as I called. The drive home was a blur. Mylo must have said goodbye, Iris must have talked to me. I could vaguely recall her sitting beside me in the backseat. The existence of the bracelet didn't change anything — if it was him, we knew he was a wood sculptor, that he had a connection to Mom, that he'd been in touch with her for months. All those things were old news, but it changed everything anyway.

It pointed at the theory that had been orbiting in my mind for weeks, the one that I hadn't looked directly at, like the sun during an eclipse, for fear it would do permanent damage. But now I couldn't avoid it: maybe she went willingly with Philip

Krause. Maybe she planned to go. Maybe she wanted to. There didn't seem to be a better explanation for why she would wear his bracelet.

Charlie sat beside me on a stool at the kitchen counter and kicked the wall, which would normally have gotten him in trouble, but no one said anything. I couldn't tell if the expression on his face was from being pissed off that no one was paying attention or from wanting everyone to go away. Sitting beside him was somehow calming. It reminded me that we were both in the same awful boat, minus the details I knew but he didn't. But really, we were both shaken and scared and confused. And having him there, kicking a steady beat, was everything I needed, almost.

I pulled out the old mind-calming trick I'd devised for pretest nerves: reciting the names of as many moons in the solar system as I could. I'd once found a video online of a guy who'd turned them into a song to the tune of "It's the End of the World as We Know It" and it was hugely satisfying to mentally mumble through it.

Charlie wiped his nose with his shirtsleeve and kicked some more.

Europa, Eurydome, Ganymede, Harpalyke, Hegemone …

Someone had brought out a few bags of snacks and left them on the counter. I reached for one. "Popcorn?" I asked.

He shook his head.

I opened the bag anyway.

He eyed it but kept kicking.

"Did you get back on *Minecraft* after Dad banned you?"

He nodded.

I felt glad for him. At least he had something to focus on, even if it was on the computer.

"How's your fortress coming along?"

He shrugged.

"Does that mean good? Terrible? How about two shrugs for disaster and one for awesome."

He cracked a smile and shrugged once.

"How many rooms does it have? Five? Six? Nod if it's more."

He nodded.

"Seven."

He nodded more.

"Ten. Seventy-five."

He violently shook his head.

"Okay, eleven."

He smiled.

"Wow, that's a lot of rooms, Badger."

He reached for the popcorn and scooped up a handful.

I patted his back, wanting to hug him or something, but worrying he might not like that.

"Grace, can I talk to you?" Isabel stood behind me. She gestured for me to follow her into the living room.

Charlie looked at me, paused mid chew.

"You want to go watch TV with Grandma?" I asked him. "I'm sure she'll let you watch whatever you want."

He blinked at me and I saw how unnerved he was, how his kicking and silence were really gnawing fear.

I put my hands on his cheeks and kissed his forehead before he could pull away. "It's going to be okay, Badger. Go with Grandma. Okay?"

"Okay," he whispered, grabbing the bag of popcorn and holding it to his chest.

∗

I sat on the couch and Isabel took the love seat. The bracelet filled the entire space between us with its magnetic field of questions. I tried to breathe normally but suddenly my lungs wouldn't expand to their normal size.

She spun her ring around her finger. "We're working on verifying the link now, but there are a few likely scenarios if this bracelet was made by Philip Krause. You've probably thought about them yourself."

"Isn't there just one likely scenario?"

She raised an eyebrow. "And what is that?"

I felt like a kid being led to give the answer everyone already knew. "You seriously think there's a better explanation than the fact that she went with him? That all along this wasn't an abduction but a ... a chance to run away?"

She calmly put her hand out, gesturing for me to keep my voice down. "That's been a consideration from the beginning, but that doesn't mean it's the only possibility."

"A consideration from the beginning?" I felt weighed down, like there were twice the normal g-forces on my body. "You never said anything."

"Because it wasn't the biggest potential then, and I still think —"

"But can't you see how it looks? She was angry with my dad, she was in touch with this guy for months — maybe years

— and now we find out she wore his jewelry? It seems pretty obvious to me."

Her eyes snapped to mine. "You're right that this is a strong theory. Several things point toward this kind of explanation."

"It's *all* pointing toward this explanation!" I had raised myself half-off the couch without noticing.

She waited, her face composed, for me to sit again. She did this kind of thing all the time. I wondered how many other families she'd sat with, how many other people in crisis she'd spoken to. I wasn't prepared for her composure. "I agree with your reasoning," she said slowly.

"But," I muttered.

"But I happen to think there's a different explanation, or at least more nuance to the story." She leaned forward so her forearms rested on her knees. "I have no hard evidence to base my hunch on, but I believe it's not as simple as it might appear. The descriptions of your mother and Philip Krause that have emerged from all the interviews we've done ... they paint pictures with some contradictions."

"What do you mean?" I thought about Marge's statement, which had become a meme in my head: *There are things about your mother none of us know.* The feeling I'd had in the car, coming home from the movie with Grandma.

Isabel straightened her back. "I mean I'm trying to think thoughtfully about this situation. I've been asking myself a lot of questions. What if Krause was threatening GG? She's a public figure. He was accused of extortion five years ago. If she were afraid enough, she might leave with him and maybe not even try to escape. She may not have felt she could throw out gifts from him — he might be unpredictable or controlling. I've seen cases where people make choices their loved ones would never expect because of these kinds of relationships. The bracelet could be part of a much more complicated interaction than it appears."

I stared at a tiny hole in my leggings, just above my right knee. I didn't want to think about a whole new scenario. Maybe I should be more open-minded, but this time I didn't want to think about other options. The one I had was complicated enough.

Down the hallway, I saw Grandma walk into the kitchen, her blouse floating behind her.

A weird feeling, like déjà vu, came over me.

"Fine," I said, pulling on the fabric until the hole stretched to double the size.

"Fine what?" Isabel asked.

"That's a plausible theory," I said. "And we're all entitled to them."

47

"What happened?" Mylo asked as I lay on my bed, my phone pressed to my ear. I hadn't talked to him since we found the bracelet at the art gallery and I knew I owed him a call, but for some reason I kept delaying it. Maybe I was ashamed of how out of it I'd been. Or maybe it was that my mother's story — my story — kept getting more and more convoluted and no less resolved. Thinking about all the layers was getting exhausting.

"Isabel came over and told us her grand theory."

"Which is?"

"That it's complicated. That we can't be sure of anything. That my mom may have been threatened into going with him or something."

"Really?"

"I don't know."

"Okay ..."

"I just — can we talk about something else, please? I'm sorry, I can't think about it anymore. Not tonight. It's too much."

He hesitated. "Sure. No problem."

I rolled onto my stomach. "Are you okay?"

"Yeah. My mom and I had another fight, but it's all right."

"What was it about?"

"She doesn't think I should spend my time starting a photography club at school next year. I would be better off using that time to study for exams and get into a prestigious university."

"Who won?"

"Won what?"

"The fight."

He hesitated. "I don't know. Maybe no one. It's obviously not over."

I watched my black-hole clock tick past nine thirty. "I think you should do the photography club," I said. "Don't let her ideas kill yours. It's your life."

"Yeah, maybe. It's hard when it's just us. She does a lot for me, actually. I know she really cares, even though it doesn't seem like it. She just can't see me. You know?"

I buried my face in my pillow. I knew.

"Are you there?" he asked.

"Yeah," I said. "I'm here."

48

Two days later, Grandma walked into the laundry room as I was searching for my favorite skirt. I was planning to wear it to Iris's fundraiser, if it would let itself be found.

"Did your father tell you I was coming tonight?" she asked.

"Coming?" I echoed, unsure what she meant, until the reality of "tonight" clicked in my brain. Oh, no. "To the fundraiser?"

She appeared vaguely annoyed at my tone. "Your friend Iris asked me."

"She did? When have you even talked?"

Now she looked dramatically at the ceiling, the whites of her eyes contrasting with her black eyeliner and mascara. "The other day when she dropped you back home. She ate five of the cookies I bought. Remember? Anyway, she asked if I knew anyone who might be able to donate. As it happens, I have a friend who'd be a great resource."

I reached into the dryer and pulled out one of Charlie's shirts. "An actor?"

"No, a producer. Documentaries. Anyway, I also wanted to give you this." She held out a small black box. The kind men gave to women in movies.

"No, I won't marry you."

She laughed and the air in the room lost some of its density.

I took the box and opened the lid. Inside was a gold chain with a teardrop diamond pendant. It looked expensive. "Is this yours?" I asked.

"Yes. I wore it to my first big movie premiere. It always reminds me of those early years."

I assumed that was a positive association, although I couldn't tell by the wistful look on her face. I closed the box and put it on top of the washing machine. "Thank you, but I'm not sure it'll go with my outfit. I'm not really —"

"What are you wearing?"

I finally found the skirt, a little rumpled from the dryer but otherwise presentable. I shook it out and held it up.

"Oh God, no," she said, reaching out and then deciding not to touch it. "You must have something else. Something better quality?"

I lowered my arms. "This isn't a red-carpet thing, Grandma. There won't be any tiaras. This is totally fine."

She closed her eyes and I prepared for a sermon. The intensity of her speeches could be gauged by the length of the eye-closing at the beginning of them. "Here's the thing about presentation," she began, stepping fully into the small room so that her perfume got caught in every corner and concentrated right where we were standing. "How we present ourselves, the effort we make, is really a reflection of the respect we have for others."

I chewed the inside of my lip and tried not to draw blood.

"When we take care to look good, it communicates who we are. It's as important as what we say."

"Maybe in movies," I said, turning back to the laundry.

"In real life, Grace. Your mother is keenly aware of this. It's why she's always so put together."

I had a vision of Mom standing in the doorway of my room the morning of the soccer game. Thin and pale in her dressing gown. Asking me to help her with Charlie so she could get some sleep. Her face had been so tired and I couldn't remember if I'd said anything nice to her. Maybe it was *not* being put together that showed who a person was. I shoved the skirt under my armpit. "I just don't agree," I said. Waited for her to huff about my stubbornness.

"Grace." She picked up the black box again and her eyes held me with a softness I wasn't expecting. "I want to give you this because I happen to have a lot of respect for you."

I didn't say anything. I wasn't sure what I could say.

"We may not see eye to eye on many things, but I know how intelligent and driven you are, and how well you're handling the stresses of everything. It's not easy for us adults, and look at you." She held out the box. "I wouldn't have been able to get through this at seventeen the way you are right now."

I stared at her outstretched hand. She'd painted her nails pale pink yesterday. And she'd just made my insides feel like they were crumbling.

She stepped forward and wrapped me in her perfume and held me.

"Thanks," I whispered.

"You're welcome." She pulled back and put the box in my hand. "And can I suggest one thing?"

My skirt was still bunched up under my arm.

"I have a lavender top that would fit you nicely. It would go really well with that long white skirt I saw in your closet. Would you at least try it on?"

And even though it seemed like I'd stepped into another dimension in which my grandmother understood me and lent me clothes, I found that both those things were happening in real life. And for the moment they were kind of working.

49

I hadn't thought about how it would look, or how I would feel, being in the ballroom of a fancy hotel, surrounded by tables with red and gold centerpieces and soft lights and people in nice clothes, Iraqi music playing over the speakers. I'd thought about it on a basic level — the level where I felt happy to be there for Iris and proud of what she was doing and curious to see what kind of appetizers there would be. But I wasn't prepared for how much it would remind me of my mother.

Which was stupid, once the wave of significance washed over me, because of course it reminded me of her. This was what she did, where she spent her time. Where she probably would be if she hadn't disappeared. She would have brought in huge donors for Iris's refugee resettlement group. I hadn't thought about it until that moment, as I stared up at the strings of fairy lights hung from the ceiling like softly glowing stars. She and Dad had made a decision not to have Charlie and me attend her big events, to shield us from the media and flashy everything. It was why we didn't live in Toronto or Vancouver.

I turned in a circle and the fairy lights blurred the way they used to when I was little, spinning in front of the Christmas tree. Mom would have been excited for this fundraiser. I might have known that before because I sort of knew what organizations she liked to support, but now I knew more. I knew that she and Iris talked about this stuff, that Mom had been interested in social science at university — Grandma had said she'd had a program picked out. I knew from Dad that she was once as enthusiastic about life as she always appeared to be on TV. I wondered what it would be like to be here with her — the her of all those things.

The lights shone, people laughed and glasses tinked as they were touched to each other, and it all made me feel so alone. Motherless.

Grandma clicked her tongue beside me. "Well, isn't this nice. Iris has done a lovely job. Is she here yet?"

"Somewhere."

She'd texted me to meet by the stage but there was no sign of her. Or Mylo.

"I'm going to see if Danielle is here yet," Grandma said. "Will you be all right?"

"Danielle?"

"My friend, the producer. Danielle Lafontaine."

I thought that maybe I wouldn't be all right without her. How had I suddenly developed a dependence on her being here? "Yes, I'm fine," I said. "No problem."

I watched people mill around and sip drinks while the few kids in attendance tried to sneak under the tablecloths.

My bag buzzed.

Iris. *Where are you?*

Waiting for you. Everything okay?

Be right there.

I waited but she didn't come. I started to feel like the only person without someone to talk to. This was why I was going to be a space scientist: I wouldn't have to do parties. I wandered over to the silent-auction table, where I immediately recognized Mylo's photos. The one of the mourning cloak butterfly that I loved and two others I hadn't seen before. I got out my phone to text him.

Just as I was about to start typing, a familiar-looking guy walked by. Blond chin-length hair, square jaw. Zane. I'd only seen him in Iris's photos but I knew it was him. He was on the phone. I stepped after him, thinking he'd lead me to Iris.

"I know, Abby, but I can't right now," he said into his phone. He ducked his head and said something I couldn't hear.

Abby. Had Iris mentioned the ex-fiancée's name? I kept following him.

"I know, I know. I made a big mistake, too. I promise. Tomorrow, okay? I'll call you tomorrow." He hung up the phone and turned around.

I pretended to be looking for something in my bag, my heart racing as he walked past me.

∗

"There you are!" Iris found me by the appetizer table, which was filled with platters of dates, fruit and little meat pastry things. I'd discovered a kind of cheese I wanted to eat all night. The calories seemed to calm my rushing thoughts.

"Sorry, my mom needed me for something," she said in a

rush. "Did you see the chocolate fountain? It's amazing." She was gorgeous, her half-pink hair up in soft waves on top of her head. She wore a dark purple dress that skimmed her knees and made her freckles stand out in the best way. I loved her so much, and I was so unsure what to do about Zane that it made me slightly nauseated.

"You look great," she said, hugging me. "Where did you get that top?"

"A very unlikely source," I said, taking one more piece of cheese because I couldn't stop.

"Did you see Zane? I can't find him anywhere." She scanned the room.

I swallowed.

"I saw Patricia with some important-looking people by the door," she said, nibbling a date.

I took a sip of water. "That sounds like her."

She turned to me, putting a hand on my arm. Six bangles. "Zane seemed really nervous earlier. I kissed him in the hallway, but I think he might be overwhelmed or something. I hope he's okay."

"Iris," I said.

The people on the other side of the cheese tray broke into roaring laughter at something.

"We might be moving too fast," Iris said, half to herself. "We agreed to take it slow, but it's so hard when —"

"Grace?"

I turned and there was Mylo, wearing a white button-down shirt, his hair styled back, his eyebrows making me forget what I should say. Beside him was a black-haired woman who shared his features but not his height. She smiled up at me and held out her hand. Sun Ah Kim.

"This is my mom," Mylo said. "Mom, this is Grace Carter."

*

It turned out that she had the same taste in cheese as me. We were still by the appetizers and both kept reaching for the same kind. She turned to me and said, "Mylo tells me you're already taking university courses in astronomy."

"Not really," I said. "I got invited to sit in on a lecture, but that's just a one-time thing."

"But you've already written a research paper, is that right?"

I took a bunch of grapes from the cheese tray, just for variety. "I was named a co-author because I helped discover an exoplanet."

She smiled at me and it felt warm. There was a glowy-ness to her that reminded me of Mom. "Those are quite the accomplishments. You sound very gifted."

"Definitely not gifted —"

"She is," Mylo said, suddenly beside me.

"I've just been a geek about space since I was thirteen. Obsession helps you get smart fast."

"Yup," Mylo said, his mouth full of pastry. "Ask her about black holes and gamma-ray bursts."

We stood by the table as the band played and people milled about. Sun Ah asked me about school and what university I wanted to get into. Sometimes someone caught her eye and she waved them a quick hello; she obviously knew quite a few people here. She held her hands clasped in front of her and smiled a lot, her earrings sparkling in the light. She wasn't what I expected.

Iris had gone to help with something and then Mylo excused himself to find the bathroom, so I was alone with her, looking around for Grandma, who still hadn't reappeared. I reached for definitely my last piece of cheese. She stepped closer and put her hand on my elbow. "I've never seen Mylo like this, you know."

I gulped. "Like what?"

"He talks about you all the time. He seems happier … I thought when he found a serious relationship he'd be distracted from everything. And sometimes he is, don't get me wrong." She laughed. "But he's also more focused. He seems … more like the old him."

I was briefly blindsided by the "serious relationship" part, but then I registered what she'd said after that. "What do you mean 'the old him'?" I asked.

She smiled and there was a hint of sadness in it, the way Mom would smile at fans with the barest trace of exhaustion that I could always see. That's how I understood what Sun Ah meant, even though Mylo had told me she didn't know I knew about her missing husband. She meant the Mylo before his dad left. "Oh, he's just changed in the last few years, as I'm sure you have," she said, looking across the room. "Being a teenager does that."

"Yeah," I said. "Of course."

She nodded and ate a piece of cheese.

The absence of Mom felt heavy again, and I could tell Sun Ah was deciding what to say. Or not say. It wasn't as simple as the usual condolences people gave me; she had a missing person, too.

She picked up her wineglass from the table and pointed across the room, where Mylo was walking out of a doorway. "And I must say, I'm glad he's spending time with someone so focused on her future. You are a good influence." She took a sip of wine. "He needs that. Some of those boys he hangs around with will end up working at a gas station, no doubt."

That made me want say something flattering about Trent, which was almost impossible, so I said how much I respected gas station attendants and waited for Mylo to get to us, and he said, "Did you see the chocolate fountain?"

His mom laughed. "You kids go have fun. I'm going to peruse the silent auction."

As we walked away, Mylo kept glancing behind us.

"What is it?" I asked.

"My photos," he said.

"What about them?"

He put his hand on my back and guided me around a table. "She doesn't know I donated them. I kind of told her I wasn't into it anymore."

I stopped walking. "Why?"

He grimaced. "To make her stop nagging me. It was what she wanted to hear."

"But you knew she was coming. What about when she sees them over there?"

He scratched the back of his neck, his signature nervous move. "I didn't really think ahead when I said it. I guess I hoped she wouldn't want to lecture me in public."

"I don't know," I said, "she seemed pretty nice to me. I was expecting —"

He was watching me. "Expecting what?"

I picked at the hem of my loaned lavender shirt.

"I'm surprised you're not diving into the chocolate fountain, honey."

I turned and Grandma was standing behind me, her lipstick refreshed. "And that pendant looks lovely on you, by the way. Just perfect." She came around and held out her hand to Mylo. "I'm Patricia Forsythe. Grace's grandmother. You are …?"

Mylo shook her hand. "I'm Mylo McLean. Grace and I —"

"Oh, yes, you're the one," Grandma said, patting his arm.

I held my breath for supreme embarrassment.

"Your mother works for the Milliner Foundation, right?"

"Yeah. Do you know her?"

"Not personally, but I remember when she was in politics, and a friend of mine just told me Sun Ah Kim's son was here." She smiled at us both. "I'm so glad to meet the reason Grace has been on her phone all waking hours."

I squeezed my eyes shut. "Ugh, Grandma, that's not true."

"Hey, wait," Mylo said. "Are you … on TV or something?"

"Movies mostly." Grandma was smiling at him when I opened my eyes. "My last film was —"

"That one with the gorilla suit?"

"Yes, *Flash Flood*." She touched her necklace. "Did you see it?"

"No, I just remember the gorilla suit from the trailer." His eyes were wide and he turned to me. "How come you never told me *your grandmother was an actress?*"

I shrugged. "Is it necessary information?" I hadn't talked to him about Grandma at all; it hadn't entered into our conversations. Iris was the one I vented to about her. It had been nice to just have what Mylo and I had without the complication of Grandma.

He was gawking at me, a face that would have made me laugh if I hadn't seen his mother bearing down on him with a serious look on her face.

"Uh, watch out," I muttered, just before she got to us.

"Oh, hello, Sun Ah, I'm Patricia Forsythe," Grandma said, her hand out again. "I've just been introduced to Mylo here."

His mom shook her hand and gave the same kind of smile my mother — or Grandma, for that matter — would have given when pressed into duty while pissed off. "Nice to meet you, Patricia. I just need to steal my son away for a moment. You don't mind, do you, Grace?"

Mylo furrowed his eyebrows at me as he turned away.

After they were gone, Grandma took my arm and steered me toward the chocolate fountain. The music had been turned down, and something was being set up in front of the giant screen by the stage.

"How are you doing?" she asked me.

"Okay," I said. "Did you find your friend?"

"Danielle? Yes, I'll have to introduce you. She's fantastic. She knew your mother when she was starting out in journalism."

I looked at the piles of strawberries, grapes, banana and mango slices. The tiny silver forks in a basket beside them. Mom would have loved the mangoes.

Grandma took a grape and patted my shoulder.

Someone behind us said something about a presentation starting.

"Where's Iris?" Grandma asked.

"There." I pointed at the screen, which now had the words "Dates and Roses: An Iraqi Family Fundraiser" projected on it. Iris stood in front of it, helping Zane get the microphone adjusted. She was smiling at him, saying something into his ear, and he was shaking his head in reply.

I had to tell her. It was horrible watching it happen in front of me and doing nothing. "Excuse me," I said to Grandma.

A large crowd was gathering by the screen and the mic had been prepped. Zane stood behind it nervously, and I realized he was the one giving the speech. Iris squeezed his hand and stepped away. I sneaked through the crowd and found her on the other side, beside Bruce and Moira, who saw me and held out their arms. "Grace!" they whispered. "We wondered when we'd see you!"

I hugged them back and tried not to sound breathless, even though it felt like my lungs were being pressed in.

"Zane's super nervous," Iris said into my ear, clutching my hand. "I'm nervous for him."

I didn't know what to do. I couldn't drag her away from his speech, but watching her watch it was killing me. And looking at him made me want to pick up one of the serving forks and stab him.

"It's truly an honor to work with all the amazing people in this fundraising group," Zane was saying. "Everyone's worked so hard, and we're within reach of our goal of twenty-thousand dollars, which would mean the family of five we're sponsoring could start their journey to Canada. So far we've raised twelve thousand, and by the end of tonight, we could be at our target, thanks to you."

Iris sighed beside me.

I ground my teeth.

"We've learned a lot about Iraqi culture and history over the past few months, and Iris Falino and I put together a slideshow of some of the highlights for you. Give everyone a wave, Iris."

Iris blushed and waved at the crowd, and when Zane started talking again, she whispered, "He was just nervous. I was worried he was angry at me or something, but look at him — he's loosening up. He gets jittery before something like this, clearly."

My stomach dropped. "Hey," I said. "Can we go outside for a moment? I need some air."

I did actually need it. The room had started to feel hot and stuffy and all the applause was making my ears ring. I knew she thought I was having some kind of panic attack — why else would I make her leave the presentation her new boyfriend was making? But she did leave. She came with me and held my hand, and I felt horrible for what I'd brought her out into the foyer to say.

Some of her hair had slipped down and was hanging beside her face. I reached out to tuck it back.

"Are you okay?" she asked. "Do you need water?"

"No," I said. "I'm fine."

She glanced back into the ballroom. The foyer was empty except for us.

"Hey, do you know the name of Zane's ex-fiancée?" I asked.

"Yeah, it's Abby. Why?"

I looked at the chandelier above us, all sparkly and dangling.

"What is it?" She was peering into my face. "Grace."

"I overheard him talking on the phone an hour ago." I couldn't meet her eyes. "To Abby."

A kid rushed out of the ballroom, giggling, and then back in again.

"He was apologizing or something," I went on. "He said he'd made a mistake. And that he'd call her tomorrow." I tried to breathe normally but my palpitations made it impossible. "I wanted to give him the benefit of the doubt — maybe he meant something else, something stupid and small. People can be friends with their exes, right? Maybe. But I just thought you should know." I gulped air and finally looked at her.

She was staring at the floor.

I touched her shoulder. "It's the wrong time to talk about this. I'm sorry — this is your big night. I shouldn't have said anything."

"No, you should have." She squeezed her eyes closed. "You're sure it was her?"

"He said her name. And said, 'I made a big mistake, too.'" I ground my teeth and watched her.

She looked ready to speak, but for the longest moment she didn't. The loose hair had fallen back around her face. "He said they weren't talking at all." She hugged her arms against her. "He said he didn't want to talk to her again. That she was psycho."

"Shit. I'm sorry."

She let out a bitter laugh. "Seriously? Is this really what's happening?"

"I know," I said, trying to pull her closer, but she kept her feet planted.

"And you warned me," she said.

"Well, not really. I didn't know. I was just ..." I wasn't sure what to say. I still felt horrible for dropping this on her. The urge had been so strong, but now, seeing the impact, it seemed like maybe I'd done it to get it off my chest, not to help her.

She pressed her fingers against the inside corners of her eyes. "Oh my God. The slide show's almost over. My parents ... my makeup." She sniffed and cleared her throat.

"Iris," I said.

"Yes."

I really wanted to hug her. "Don't go back in if you're not okay."

She shook her head and her hair swayed around her face. "I'm not okay. I'm battle-ready. Boys suck."

"Totally."

She cleared her throat again and swallowed.

"What do you need?" I asked.

She wiped the corners of her eyes with her pinkies and her bracelets jingled. "Nothing. Maybe some girl-pretzel-jellybean time if we're not too late tonight. You could sleep over?"

"Yes, for sure," I said, squeezing her arm, feeling relief that I could help at last. "I'll ask my dad."

She sighed. Reached up her arm, pulled her bangles off and stuffed them in the pocket of her dress. "God, these are super annoying right now."

A moment later the crowd broke into the kind of loud applause that signaled the end of the presentation, and Iris walked away from me, back inside the ballroom.

I stood at the doorway and watched everyone milling around,

the rumble of hundreds of voices filling my head. The figures blurred together into an unfocused mass, like bees moving in a hive. This evening wasn't supposed to go like this.

Someone was waving at me. I snapped back into focus. Mylo.

"How did it go with your mom?" I asked as he led me away from the busyness to the corner behind the silent-auction tables. A new band had come out and was playing an upbeat song with a lot of banjo. It was a relief to think about another drama and block out Iris's for a moment.

"It was … okay," he said, his face close to mine.

I could feel the heat radiating from his skin. I wanted to kiss him so badly.

"Actually, I think you might have done something to her," he said.

"What?"

His eyebrows pushed together. "I mean, she was initially kind of pissed that I lied to her, but then she started asking questions about the photos and what I wanted, and in the end she didn't tell me to stop doing it. She just kind of … accepted it." He seemed amazed by what he was saying.

"What do I have to do with that?"

He touched my hair, which I didn't usually wear down. "I don't know, but I think she likes you. Maybe you shifted her somehow."

"This is the strangest night ever. Seriously."

He was looking into my eyes the way he had at Constance Pond, like he didn't want to break the connection. "I know." He leaned in and his lips touched mine so softly that an electric pulse shot through my body.

I was about to sink deeper into it when a voice behind me said, "Uh, *what*?"

We let go of each other in a nanosecond.

Iris stepped closer. "Oh my God." She didn't sound mad, exactly. More tired and over everything, which made me feel worse. "Seriously? And now a fundraiser hookup?"

Mylo backed into one of the auction tables, making it shudder.

"I'm sorry," I said, the first pathetic words to fall out of my mouth.

"Uh, yeah," Mylo mumbled. "We didn't know ..." He looked at me.

"Didn't know what?" she asked, her face flushing, or maybe it had already been pink.

"That ... it would be a big deal?" Mylo said, not making it better.

Her face went from weary to annoyed. Then to pissed off. "Oh, so you just make out with random people when you feel like it?" She crossed her arms over her chest.

"I ..." I hung my head. This was bad. "This whole thing is messed up. I'm so sorry about Zane, and then —"

"Is Zane the guy who did the presentation?" Mylo asked.

She snorted. "You didn't even fill him in on the drama?" She stepped closer. "He's a lying asshole. He just told me that he's probably getting back together with his ex." She threw up her hands. "Really? When does this happen? Oh, I guess at the same time your two friends decide they need to suck face." She stared at me. "Or wait. Is this not a new thing?"

I couldn't meet her eye.

"The art gallery," she said. "When I asked you."

I nodded. "I'm sorry."

She paused for a moment, her mouth half-open, her eyes on something behind our heads.

I could see the hurt expanding in her, but I couldn't think of the right thing to say.

Then she said, "Okay, fine. You do this. I don't understand why no one is telling me the truth around here, but I have funds to raise, so you'll have to excuse me."

"Crap," Mylo whispered when she was gone. "Is she actually mad? I can't tell for sure."

"She's mad." I sank down onto the floor and resisted the urge to take off my heels. How could things have gone so badly in such a short time? I looked out across the ballroom at the people dancing and talking and drinking and the fairy lights twinkling and Grandma there in her navy-blue dress, laughing with someone by the stage. Someone came up and started gathering the silent-auction bidding papers, glancing awkwardly at me.

"What did she mean about Zane?" Mylo had kneeled down beside me. "Is that the guy who gave the speech?"

"Yeah."

"Were they going out or something?"

"Apparently not."

He gazed at the milling crowd. "I don't understand."

My phone buzzed in my purse. *Can't do sleepover tonight. Busy.*

I closed my eyes and the frenetic music swirled around us.

50

The next morning I sent Iris a text. *Please don't be mad at me. Well, be mad because I deserve it, but don't stop being my friend. Please? I'm sorry.*

I didn't hear back, so I went downstairs for breakfast. Stared at my phone as I ate my cereal. I felt emotionally hung over and not sure how to fix it. How mad was she? I could still see her face, the disappointment or something worse as she looked at Mylo and me. Like the orbit of our group had shifted and one of us had been ejected. Except it wasn't true.

I called her and left a voicemail.

Maybe she was dealing with Zane. Maybe more had happened after she walked away at the fundraiser. I wished I knew.

I finished my cereal and took the bowl to the sink.

My phone buzzed and I leaped over to check it.

It was Grandma. *I'm at the health food store getting wheatgrass. Need anything?*

That afternoon, Mylo and I walked to get iced coffees near his house, and we passed the ice cream parlor where he'd gone supernova on me and where Iris had been so happy that we could all be friends. We didn't hold hands or anything as we walked and I couldn't make myself look directly into the window, but the smell of waffle cones and chocolate sauce was assaulting and once we passed it, Mylo said, "Well, *that* was awkward."

I took a deep breath of the vinyl-scented air from the carpet store we stood beside. "Not going in for ice cream?"

He bumped my shoulder with his. "Yeah, but also, that's Iris's favorite place, right?"

I kept walking, keeping my eyes on the coffee shop at the end of the block, a place that was neutral and wouldn't remind me of anything except maybe my dad's loathing for dark roast.

"She's a really cool person," he said quietly enough that it might have been to himself. "Super-smart and super-resourceful. I'm kind of surprised she hasn't gotten over this yet."

I felt the littlest bit pissed off. What right did he have to say that? She was hurt and angry and who knew what else. But I knew I'd had the same thought.

Ahead of us, a blonde woman walked with her arm around the shoulders of a boy with the same color hair. From behind, they were just like Mom and Charlie, if he'd been a few years older. The woman had longer hair and bigger hips, but she wore something my mother might wear. The boy wore shorts I could imagine a ten-year-old Charlie wearing. Which made it almost impossible not to see them as future Mom and Charlie — the her she could be and the him he'd grow into. If only she'd come back to us. Maybe everything was falling apart because she was gone. Maybe the fabric of the universe was held together by my mother and it was slowly tearing, like old, worn-out cloth.

"Are you okay?" Mylo asked beside me, watching me with concern.

I blinked a few times and the woman and boy turned the corner and were gone. "Yes, I'm okay. It's just —"

"Tough?" he finished for me. He took my hand, lacing his fingers through mine. "I know."

51

I called Isabel in the morning, desperate, if not to have her tell me they'd found a big lead, then to just hear her voice, to be reminded that they were still looking. She'd always been one of the most positive people about the whole thing, and I had a feeling I'd been kind of rude to her on occasion.

"Grace," she said when she picked up. "How are you?"

"Terrible," I said, "but not for reasons related to my mother. Well, maybe indirectly."

"Okay. So do you want to talk about it?"

I realized she was asking why I was calling.

"I just wanted to … speak to you," I said. "It feels like there hasn't been any news with the case and it's been so long."

"I know," she said. "We've been doing some time-intensive research and it can feel like nothing's happening."

"But things *are* happening?" I said, trying to preempt her next statement.

"You bet. Just glacially at this moment. Little details will add up soon."

A numb hopelessness settled on me, or maybe it had been there for a while and I'd only just noticed it. It felt strange that

I couldn't feel the air on my skin, but had I ever been able to?

"How about I call you tomorrow?" Isabel said into my ear. "Just to check in and see how you are."

"Yeah, that would be good."

The leaves on the tree outside my window rustled in the wind.

"It's a phone date," she said. "You take care until then, okay"

＊

Grandma was attempting to make a salad when I came down into the kitchen. Her tablet was propped against the fruit bowl and there were vegetables and their peelings everywhere.

"This looks dangerous," I said, picking up a long strand of carrot skin.

"It can't be that hard, I thought. It's lunch. It's a salad." She checked something on the screen. "But there are an awful lot of ingredients. And they all need preparing in some way. Hand me that knife."

I reached for the knife she was pointing to, the one Dad used to cut big hard things, like potatoes, and passed it to her. "I think this is the wrong tool."

"It cuts," she said, wielding it in a way that made me cringe.

"Can I help?" I asked.

She passed it back to me. I put it down and got the paring knife.

She focused on tearing the lettuce, a job where she couldn't cut herself, and I cut the cucumber.

"Have you been to a place called Ammonite?" she asked, rinsing her hands in the sink.

"Yeah, it's not far up the highway. Why?"

"There was a thing on TV about it earlier. It's got such pretty hanging baskets."

"Yeah, Mom was always going on about them." I felt the usual sting at remembering something about her, but this time I didn't tense up. I just kept chopping. The feeling melted away. I wondered if I was getting used to how things were.

"Well, I was thinking of going out there sometime. I haven't done any sightseeing, and I've been here for weeks."

"Grandma, this isn't a vacation."

"You're telling me." She snorted. "Anyway, I think I might take Charlie next week. What do you think?"

"Good luck getting him to agree."

"Oh, I won't tell him we're going there. I'll say I found a *Minecraft* conference or something."

I dumped the chopped cucumber into the bowl with the lettuce. "You can't do that. How would you explain when you got to Ammonite and there was no *Minecraft*?"

She shrugged. "I'll think of something. The important part is getting him out of the house. That's worth a lie and a little anger."

I leaned on the counter. "Do you always do things this way? Pushing people's buttons and causing drama?"

She laughed. "I guess it's my way of making things happen. It's worked so far. Or at least as often as I needed it to."

*

An hour later, as I was going back upstairs after lunch, Isabel's name showed up on my buzzing phone.

"Are you at home?" she asked instead of saying hello.

"Yes," I said, already breathless. "Is everything okay?"

"Actually, we've just found something that could be a break-through."

"You're kidding," I said.

"I'm going to come over in an hour, as soon as our guy gets back to me with a few more details, but we've found a warehouse with a lot of driftwood in it — stacks of logs and branches — and we suspect it belongs to Philip Krause. Wood for carving and such. The owner of the warehouse doesn't know anything and he lives out of town, so there must be a deal between some of the people who store things in it. Like subletting an apartment. Plus, Krause has been using aliases since he's been back in the country."

"So how can you know for sure?" I asked, my mouth dry.

"We're figuring that out now. Everyone's cooperating. This could really help, if it's true."

I exhaled. "Okay. Thank you."

"I'll be by soon."

But then as I was waiting for my toast to pop out of the toaster, even though eating wasn't something I actually felt like doing, a thought slid half-formed into my brain and I grabbed my phone. Ammonite. When Mylo and I had been there, we'd watched kids playing on a wooden playground. Had it been made of driftwood? Or was I imagining it?

The playground in Ammonite. What's it made of?

Wood. Why?

Is it driftwood? My fingers were sweaty on the screen.

Yeah, I think so. There's a tree trunk and a few branches for railings. Why??

I felt a little like puking. *I need to go there. Now.*

Can I come?

I'll pick you up.

52

A group of summer camp kids had infested the playground when we got there, sliding and swinging and screaming in identical orange T-shirts. A bored and texting camp counselor sat on a bench beside the driftwood play structure and didn't even look up when I came into her periphery.

I stepped into the wood chips and waded through the melee of orange bodies. A kid went down the tree-trunk slide with a squeal and I lunged out of the way. The bottom of the structure was the base of a huge tree, like the upended ones I'd seen in the forest before, blown over in high winds. It was fixed to the ground upside down, so its roots radiated up from the base like branches, and kids climbed between them and sat on them like twittering birds. A ladder made of rough-cut wood went up one side to a platform made of more driftwood, varnished and smooth like caramel pouring off one corner into the slide. It was kind of amazing.

"Do you think he made it?" Mylo said, crouching beside me. "How will we know?"

"Excuse me," a boy said on my right. "I need to get in there." He pushed past me and wriggled between two roots.

"I don't know," I said to Mylo. "I guess we keep looking."

"It's not like you can trace the origin of wood."

"Maybe you can."

He got on all fours and peered under the reaching branches. "How?"

A kid raced past us, clipping me in the shoulder without apology.

"There are always signatures," I murmured, rubbing my shoulder. "Like in space, you can usually figure out what an object is if you study its composition, how light interacts with it. Its specific characteristics."

"Coming through!" a girl yelled at us, pushing between us and up onto the trunk.

I crawled along the base, my knees digging into the wood chips.

"This seems kind of dangerous," Mylo muttered behind me. "We're going to get pummeled."

I came around to the other side of the trunk, where a large branch — really a root — curved up toward the sky. Below it, at the very base, was a depression in the trunk that folded in toward the middle. I lay on my stomach and peered into the small wooden cave it made.

"Grace? You're going to get stepped on. I can't keep these hooligans away for long."

"Just a second," I said, getting out my phone and turning on the flashlight. I shone it into the dark, focused the beam, and the sight of the curling lines — letters — shocked the breath out of me. I held the light on it. "Holy shit," I said. "Mylo." My skin started to crawl. My mind got so still that it felt like the orange blurs around me were moving extra fast.

"She said 'holy shit'!" a boy yelled from somewhere.

"What?" Mylo was on the ground beside me. "What is it?"

I shone the light on the letters, separated by a fat heart, etched carefully, expertly into the wood in a place that could only have been marked before the trunk was placed into the playground. Probably by the person who made it. An *F* and two *G*s.

53

And then it happened all at once — they connected the drift-wood play frame to Krause's alias, which was used at the warehouse, and the next day we were told someone fitting Philip Krause's description had recently been seen in a tiny fishing village on the west coast of Vancouver Island that was famous for white beaches and huge drift logs. The wood in the warehouse could reasonably have come from there, but the police had enough leads that they felt confident. Coast guard and hired boats scoured the shoreline. Officers went door to door asking for information. Dad called Isabel every few hours, but there was no word yet, no word yet. Close, she told us. They were so close.

We did stupid nothing things. Charlie sat unchastized at his computer for hours and spent the rest of the time sleeping. I restacked magazines, flipped channels and picked stickers off old binders. We were told not to tell anyone what was happening for fear it would get leaked, so I didn't text Iris every ten minutes like I wanted to, even though I didn't know if she'd answer. I told Mylo the police were checking some things out and that I'd update him, then put my phone in a drawer.

I tried to make the time go faster by looking for exoplanets, but even Planet Hunters was too much — or too little. My brain was caught in some in-between place. Dad worked, or pretended to work, and was sometimes staring at the wall when I walked past his office. Grandma sat on the couch watching bad TV and scrolling through her phone. Sometimes I'd hear her talking quietly to Kyle, her publicist. A few times we'd be in the same room together and she'd give me a hug for no reason — as if there was no reason *not* to. Which was reason enough for me.

Then my phone rang as I was pretending to look through a Star Club newsletter on my laptop.

"Grace, is your dad there?" Isabel asked right away. "He didn't answer his phone."

The words sounded rushed, and I was instantly tingling. "He's in the shower."

"Is your grandmother there?"

"Yes. On the couch probably. Is it … Did you …?"

"I'm coming over right now. We found their boat, Grace — in a tiny bay in the middle of nowhere. We found her. Your mother's okay."

"She — What?" I dropped the phone onto the tile floor. "What?" I said again into the empty kitchen. Then I yelled for everyone at the top of my lungs.

54

The drive up the Island was the longest drive of my life. In reality it took three hours, but it took three days in the time warp inside the car. An eternity during which a list of questions looped in my brain: Would she be the same? Would she be traumatized? Would she want to see us? Would she look different? Was she hurt? What would she say to us? What would I say to her?

The police hadn't given us much except that she was okay. She was talking and asking about us and waiting in a tiny fishing village with round-the-clock care. Philip Krause had been arrested on the boat they'd been living on. That was all we knew.

Charlie talked nonstop as we drove, but his noise didn't resolve into words I could understand. Dad's voice rumbled in reply, Grandma's hushed voice made calming sounds. It had been the four of us, this strange team against the unknown of the abduction, for so long. Now, twenty-one hours after I answered Isabel's call, it felt like we were somehow disbanding, moving to separate corners to process what was happening. To reckon with the questions in our heads.

What was the right thing to say when I saw her? How would it feel to see her? Who would speak first? What would she be like?

The landscape flew by outside the window, and the clouds rolled in front of the sun. Tall trees closed in on the highway as we got farther north. I'd never been this far up the Island before.

It was shocking to think she'd been this distance away all this time. Now there was a location. A line could be drawn from our house to that boat, like a piece of yarn connecting two points pinned in place on a map.

Dad said something to Charlie, and Charlie said something back.

The road ahead wound sharply through the forest.

I tried to imagine her, safe now, with people who were helping her. Waiting for us. Mom.

The blur of light through the thick trees made me dizzy.

Who was she now?

Who were we?

55

The Port Melandron health unit was an old single-story building surrounded by reaching cedars and hemlocks, its parking lot strewn with branches from a storm that had just come through. Because Fortune Bay was so small, they'd transported Mom here yesterday and doctors had been sent up with the police — Dad said there was a whole team, though they were trying to keep everything quiet, even here.

Charlie gripped the shoulder straps of the backpack he insisted on wearing as we walked through the sliding-glass doors into the entryway, where a female police officer with short brown hair stood, apparently waiting for us.

"I'm Constable Freisen. Beth," she said, holding a hand out to Dad. "I'm the Family Liaison Officer, here to help and answer your questions."

I guessed they must go straight to first names when they were liaising with distraught families.

"More police?" Charlie muttered as we followed Beth down the corridor, past closed rooms with charts outside them and open offices with people at desks who watched us go by.

A man wearing a white shirt and blue lanyard with a hospital tag held his hand out to Dad. "Hello, I'm Mandeep Bansal, GG's psychiatrist."

"You're the one she's been seeing for a while," Grandma said. She was holding Charlie's hand.

Dr. Bansal inclined his head. "I've worked with her for a few years, yes. Corporal Sanchez asked me to come up."

"Where is she? I need to see her *now*." Charlie peered around Dr. Bansal, wrinkling his nose, but didn't move from his spot in the middle of the hallway.

"Of course you do. She's requested you to all come in together."

"Is she in there?"

"She's just down the hall." Dr. Bansal looked at us all in turn. "All right, Andrew? Patricia? Grace?"

Dad cleared his throat, turning to me and grabbing my hand, which was halfway to his anyway. "Ready?"

MIZAR and ALCOR

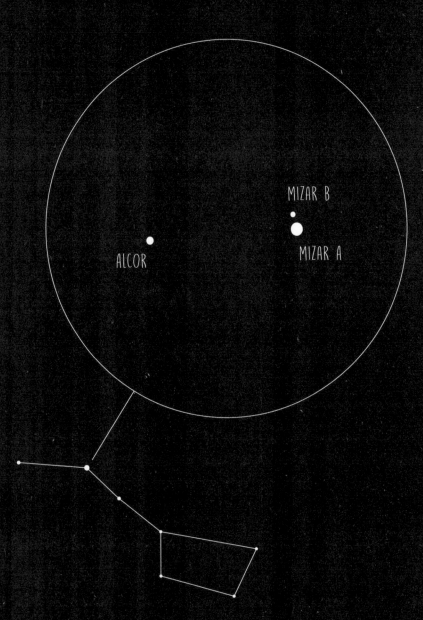

PART TWO

56

I don't know how to look at her, so I do it in stages. The wall behind the bed is pale yellow. Machines flank her, and a line runs into her arm, taped in place. Her legs are under a blue blanket. Her skin is pale, almost translucent where the blue veins show through. Her collarbones push out like someone famine-starved. And her eyes. They are hers but not hers. They are old and tired, dark with something I don't recognize. They flicker from one person to the other, a smile lifting her cheeks, but only barely reaching her eyes. This is not a smile I've seen from her. This is the smile of someone who knows what being broken feels like.

Charlie climbs onto her lap, and her thin arms clutch him. There is a howling sound, and I can't tell if it's her or him. There are tears. Dad and Grandma crowd around. They don't know how to touch her.

I turn away. I don't know how to look at her.

"Grace." Her voice is the same, but flimsier, like it could be blown away in the slightest breeze. "Grace, come here."

I go. I stand beside her and my eyes spill over. She puts her cool fingers on me. "There you are, my girl. I've missed you so much."

I can't keep my knees from buckling, so I kneel on the floor while she strokes my hair. People are talking around us — the room is full of noise — but I put my forehead against the edge of the mattress and feel her hand moving against my skull. It's a slow, steady rhythm and I can almost imagine myself back to being five, snuggling in bed, wanting to prolong bedtime. Her touch was the same. I'm in my five-year-old body somehow, resting against her, impossibly tired but resisting sleep. Wanting to feel her hand on my head forever. Knowing it was always meant to be there.

*

Later, when Beth the liaison officer signals that Mom's had enough interaction for now, we're shepherded out into the hall again and told there's a motel room reserved for us if we want to wait there. We may or may not need to stay the night. It depends on Mom's status, if she's well enough to travel right away.

"Is she sick?" Charlie asks accusingly. "Like, does she have a disease?"

Beth glances at Dad and then back at Charlie. "She doesn't have a disease. She's remarkably healthy, considering. But she's underweight and exhausted, and she's not feeling great up here." She taps her head. "We need to make sure she's recovered enough to get into the car with you."

Charlie obviously thinks that's ridiculous. "But she knows our car. She was so happy to see us. Why would she want to stay here?"

Dad bends down. "She's got a team of doctors and nurses

here to take care of her. She won't have that for the drive home. They're just looking out for her, Charlie. This is what they do."

He is unconvinced.

Outside the window, a bald eagle floats by with something in its talons. I walk closer, but it's already disappeared behind a tree.

"They're all over the place up here," Beth says behind me. "Like crows, almost. Why don't you go down to the beach for a bit? Get some fresh air?"

"Yes, all right," Dad says. "That sounds like a good idea. Patricia?"

I turn back and see Grandma blotting her eyes with a tissue, her mascara smudged at the corners. "I think I'll rest in the motel room," she says. "You all go."

"You sure?"

"Yes, go. I'll be fine."

I walk to her then and put my arms around her. She pats my shoulder. "It's hard, isn't it?" she whispers into my ear.

57

Down on the beach, the air is cool and salty and funky with dead seaweed. There are driftwood logs and branches everywhere, but we all pretend that's not super creepy, knowing what we do about Philip Krause's sculpting. The ocean washes the fine gray sand and tiny smooth stones on the shore, and out on the horizon the sky is almost the same blue as the water.

Charlie tosses rocks around and wanders down the waterline, his blond hair rising up in the wind.

Seagulls shriek and circle.

"It's a miracle," Dad says. He's leaning against a huge log, looking out at the water.

"Is it?" I ask. I want to sit beside him, but my legs feel restless. I walk in nonsensical circles around him.

"Life, I mean. Just — all this. This beach, this ocean, the forest behind us. It's teeming with life. Hundreds of species. All doing their thing as we sit here, too big to notice."

"You're noticing."

He picks up a white shell that was nestled in a crack in the log. "Yeah, and now you are, too."

Charlie goes to the edge of the water barefoot and sticks his toes in.

"I try to notice things," I say. "But a telescope only works for faraway objects."

He's watching me. "You're amazing, Grace." The old affectionate joke he hasn't said in a long time. It's nice to hear it again.

We listen to the rush and draw of the ocean.

"Were you shocked?" I ask after a while.

"When I saw her?"

"Yeah."

He pulls himself up onto the log so his legs dangle. "I knew she'd look different. That she'd be tired. But yes. I was shocked." He pats the log. "Come sit with me."

I go over and lean beside him. Some kind of seabird is diving in the water and coming up empty. Up to his knees, Charlie's watching it, too.

"I feel ... I don't know," I say.

"For all the time I spent thinking about what it would be like to have her back, to get back to our lives, I didn't really consider how this part would go."

"Yeah," I say.

Charlie rushes out of the water with something in his hand. "Look! Look what I found!"

A wave of love for my brother crashes over me. His pants are rolled up to the knees but soaked to the thighs. He reaches us and holds out a lump of see-through jelly.

"What is it?" Dad asks.

"It's a jellyfish. We saw them on a field trip last year," Charlie says. "I think it's a moon jelly." He holds it out to me. "Touch it — it's so cool."

"Won't it sting?"

"No, it's dead. And they don't sting on this smooth part." He runs his finger along the jelly lump.

"Why's it called a moon jelly?" Dad asks.

Charlie shrugs. "I don't know. Maybe it comes out on the full moon or something." He looks up at me. "Right, Grace?"

"Yeah, maybe." I poke the jellyfish and it jiggles in his hand.

Moon jelly.

Charlie marches to the water and throws his catch back in.

Dad rubs my back. "There it is — the universality of life."

I lean against him.

A jellyfish named after the moon.

*

As we're walking back up from the beach, Dad's phone rings.

Charlie and I wait at the top of the stairs, watching the seagulls ride the wind.

Dad's silent, listening for a long time before he speaks, and when he does, his voice is low. He turns toward the sea and I can't hear him.

Charlie brushes sand off his legs and it gets into my shoes.

"How was the beach?" says a voice behind us.

I turn and see Dr. Bansal, his hands folded in front of him.

"Fine," I say, a thread of uncertainty weaving through my thoughts. "Is everything okay?"

Dr. Bansal nods slowly, in a way that doesn't necessarily mean an affirmative.

Charlie goes down to Dad, and I wonder if there's a link between the phone call and Mom's therapist being here right now.

I let out a breath and inhale salty air.

"The west coast of Vancouver Island is one of my favorite places," he says. "My wife and I had our honeymoon in Tofino."

Charlie hops up to the top of the stairs.

Dad reaches us and grips my shoulder. The look he and Dr. Bansal exchange makes me sure there's something more going on.

"What?" I ask them both. "What is it?"

"Charlie, have you seen the deer antlers over here?" Dr. Bansal asks, pointing behind him.

When we're alone, Dad looks at me for a moment, his hair blowing into his eyes. He hasn't had a haircut in months. "It's not ..."

A seagull cries just above our heads.

"Just tell me, Dad."

He squints at me. "That was Beth on the phone. Philip Krause has committed suicide in police custody."

The wind whips up suddenly, then falls. It should shock me, this news, but I'm just relieved it's not Mom. And that the monster who kept her on a tiny fishing boat all this time is gone. Another eagle, or maybe the same one, lands in a tall cedar at the end of the beach. It starts to actually feel if not good, then right. "And Dr. Bansal knows."

"Yes."

"Why did Beth call you if Dr. Bansal came down to talk to you?"

He watches the next wave come in. "Well, your mother found out."

"Okay. And?"

Dad looks down at his phone, then back at me. "She's pretty upset. She wants to see his body."

58

We are sent to the motel room, which must have been last decorated when it was built in the seventies. Charlie pushes open the orange door and calls for Grandma, but the room is empty.

Dad goes into the bathroom, as if she might be hiding in there, and Charlie flops onto the nearest bed.

"Maybe she went for a walk," Dad says.

I can tell he wants to go back to the health unit, that he didn't like being banished. None of us did. Dr. Bansal said he'd call when we could see her again, but the way he and Dad spoke quietly to each other while Beth distracted us with photos of eagles on her phone made me sure he had tried to make a case for staying. "Should we go look for Grandma?" I ask. "The last thing we need is for her to get lost."

"I'll go with you!" Charlie jumps up.

"No," Dad says, peering out the window now. "We need to stay here for a bit. Dr. Bansal said there may be a reporter already aware of your mom's rescue. They've had a few calls at the health unit. I don't want you walking around unnecessarily."

"Are you going to go?" Charlie asks.

"No, not right now."

The feeling we had on the beach, the peace that settled on us as we sat on the log, is gone. The motel room has thick, dark curtains that block most of the light, and the brass bedside lamps are not very bright. It feels like a seventies dungeon.

I thread my arm around his and lean against him.

He rubs my hand. "I'm going to lie down for a while. It was an early morning."

"Me, too." Charlie climbs on top of the quilt.

I can't imagine getting into one of these beds. They look as old as the room.

As Dad and Charlie settle down together, I get out my phone and check for cell reception again. Dad said there wasn't much out here, but that there was sometimes a signal near the motel. Not right now, apparently.

The mustard walls press in, and I rub my face with my hands. I miss Mylo. I miss his hands on my skin and his ridiculously animated eyebrows. But it's thinking about Iris that makes me want to cry.

So I shake my limbs out and pace around the room, mentally avoiding the thought of my best friend.

Dad's and Charlie's breathing has evened out, and they're curled up together like hibernating bears. I watch them for a moment, then open the door as quietly as possible, just to see what's out there.

Then I step out to have a better view.

No cars on the road. Across from the motel is the Landlubber Pub, and next to that is the post office/general store/ATM. An old man walks slowly down the sidewalk. The sun glints off the sea in the distance, and more seagulls glide in the air.

The boys won't wake up for hours if no one disturbs them.

I close the door behind me and walk in the direction of the health unit. Someone has to find out where Grandma is.

59

I walk though the glass doors and the place is empty. Tensely silent.

A male nurse walks out of an office and sees me. "Can I help you?"

"No," I say. "I'm just ... looking for my grandmother."

"Is she here for treatment?"

I look at the floor.

"Oh, wait. Are you GG Carter's daughter?" He recognizes me with a tinge of alarm.

"Yeah. My grandmother was supposed to be at the motel, but —"

I'm cut off by a shout, muffled by a door and the length of the hallway, but it starts my heart pounding. Was it Mom?

"I think you should go back there," the nurse says. "To the motel, I mean. There's a delicate situation happening right now." He glances down the hall.

"Is it my mother?" I hug my arms against me. "What's going on?"

He's about to say something when a door opens and two people come out. One looks like Beth and the other is Grandma.

A painful shout escapes from the door before someone shuts it.

I start running before he can stop me.

Grandma sees me and grimaces, her face red and blotchy. She holds her arms out and I run into them, but there's no perfume there to envelop me, just the disinfectant smell of the floor. "You shouldn't have come," she mutters into my hair. "They've kicked me out anyway."

"What's going on?" I ask, trying to see past her, but none of the doors have windows.

"Let's get you both outside," Beth says, "into the fresh air."

"That's what you said last time," I say under my breath.

Grandma takes my hand and I feel that she's shaking, her eyes moving around the hallway.

Once outside, we stop by the side of the building, near the deer antlers that Dr. Bansal showed Charlie. There are cigarette butts around, so this must be the smoke break spot. How ironic.

"It's so hard when a loved one is dealing with trauma," Beth says in her liaison officer voice. "Family often don't know what to do. There's no manual, right?"

"Isn't that why that psychiatrist is here?" Grandma says.

"Where is Dr. Bansal?" I ask.

"In with your mother." She dabs at the corner of her eye with a tissue.

I want to ask her to tell me everything but not with Beth here.

We stare out to sea for a while, maybe united in the hope that if we appear calm, Beth will leave.

After a while, she clears her throat. "Would you like someone to walk you down to the motel?"

"No, thanks," Grandma says. "We'll be fine."

Beth clasps her hands in front of her.

Grandma squeezes my arm.

"I really enjoyed you in *Flash Flood*," Beth says. "I don't get to see a movie very often, but I did see that one. You were great."

"Thank you," Grandma says with more feeling than I would have mustered. "I appreciate that."

When she's gone, Grandma leans against the building and closes her eyes. "This is a nightmare."

"What happened?"

She pushes off the wall and starts to walk. "Come on. We'd better get going."

"Why did you come back here?"

"I couldn't stay in that horrible motel room. Plus, I wanted to see her. Isn't that normal?" She asks as if I were someone outside the situation, someone who hasn't had the exact same urge.

We walk past the beach access and keep going, the smell of salt wafting up. And maybe something dead, too. I can never tell if it's just the way the beach smells or if things are decomposing under the logs.

"They're going to let her see him," she says, startling me from my thoughts.

"Him?" My whole body tenses. "Today?"

"I don't know when. That's what the fuss was about. She was beside herself when they said no. They were going to take the body back to the city for whatever it is they have to do, but she begged —" Grandma puts her hands against her mouth.

I don't know what to say. Maybe something to stop her from telling me more, or maybe something to keep it coming. I can't decide which is worse.

"They had to sedate her. Dr. Bansal said it was for the best." Grandma clears her throat and starts walking again. "He says this could be the closure she needs."

"For the best? She begged to see her dead abductor's body and it's for the best?" My voice sounds foreign to me, and then I realize it's cracking, like something dried out in the sun.

Grandma sighs. "What can we do? They're in charge. He's a professional."

"But why does she need to see the body?"

We've reached the ramp of the post office/general store/ ATM. Across the street and down a little is the motel. Our room's curtains are still closed.

"I don't know," Grandma says. "But the medical professionals seem to think it's going to be okay."

I'm suddenly so tired. Dad was right — we didn't think about all the possible scenarios that could play out here. We were just focused on having her home. As if she'd just be her again. Ours.

60

We finally leave Port Melandron the next afternoon with an entourage that includes a police car and Dr. Bansal in his BMW. Mom is bundled into the front seat with a blanket — apparently she's so thin now that she can't keep her body temperature stable — and Grandma's squished between Charlie and me in the back. We were all offered a seat in another car, but none of us took it.

No one talks as we drive onto the highway and away from a village I'll always think about as the place where Mom came back to us. The place where the nightmare was supposed to end but actually morphed into something else.

"Are you cold?" Dad murmurs to her in the front. "I can turn on the heat."

It's not superhot out, but it's still August.

"I'm fine," she says.

"Are you hungry?" he asks.

"I am," Charlie says.

Grandma shushes him.

"I think there's a granola bar in the glove compartment. Otherwise there are some cookies in the trunk. I can pull over."

Mom shudders under her blanket. "No, thanks."

"Dr. Bansal said to keep your blood sugar stable."

"I know."

We pass a sign that tells us we're 280 kilometers from home.

"Hey," Charlie says. "Let's make a list of all the things we want to show Mom when we get home."

There's a small silence and then Dad says, "GG?"

"I'd love to hear," Mom says, craning her neck to look at Charlie.

"I'll go first," he says. "My epic *Minecraft*. Your turn, Dad."

"The huge mess that is my office, which is messier than it's ever been. Ever. If that's possible."

Mom reaches out and touches his arm. "I think it's technically possible, although after a certain point you stop noticing the increased messiness."

"You know that from experience?"

"From experiencing your mess," she says.

"Right." He smiles at her.

It's a warm moment that feels just normal and *us*. Banter. Mom and Dad. The whole family piled in the car, going somewhere.

"Patricia?" Dad says.

"Well, I've been getting pretty good at making salads," Grandma says. "I can show off my knife skills."

I cough.

"It's true," she says. "I know you're all skeptics, but I watched a dozen videos on using knives, and I can segment an orange better than you can, I bet."

"What's 'segment an orange'?" Charlie asks.

314

"I'll show you when we get home."

"We can't wait, Patricia," Dad says, and Mom smiles at him.

"Okay, your turn, Grace," Grandma says, patting my knee.

I watch the land whip by outside the window. What do I have to show her? "I don't know," I say.

"Come on," Charlie says. "Haven't you found a new star or something?"

"Not lately."

"Well, what about the picture of the gas ball you were showing me the other day?" Grandma says.

Charlie breaks into obnoxious laughter. "Gas ball!"

"Nebula," I say. "I didn't take the image or anything."

"But still —"

"It's okay, Grace," Mom says from the front seat. "You don't have to tell us now. We'll have time." She twists carefully to try to catch my eye. "Okay? I promise."

"Okay," I say, as Charlie finally runs out of fuel and sighs against the window. I spend the next thirty minutes thinking about all the things I want her to know and which ones I could actually express.

61

We don't go home but drive straight to Marge's, which is apparently the safest place in the universe for anyone evading the press.

Half an hour outside the city, Dad got a call from Isabel that the media had fully gotten wind of the story and were camped out at the house and at ITV. Mom had fallen asleep with her head against the window, so Dad whispered this news to us after getting off the phone. We drove the rest of the way in silence, probably all watching for anyone who might be a reporter looking for us.

Now Mozart and Vivaldi bark and dance behind the frosted glass beside the front door like sausage-shaped Rottweilers as we wait for Dad to get the key out. Marge is out and won't be home until late.

Mom, who woke up as we pulled into the driveway, moves slowly and still looks pale. She steps through the doorway with Charlie holding on to the back of her shirt like a baby elephant. The dogs set off a series of firecracker barks from somewhere in the house.

Dad's watching me with the keys in his hand. "You coming, Gracie?"

I step inside.

Mozart and Vivaldi snuffle us and waddle around the kitchen on their stubby legs. Marge has left a note that says she's left cheese cut up on a tray in the fridge and a box of crackers on the counter — apparently her go-to guest food — along with a bottle of fake champagne.

"They're the most annoying dogs ever," Charlie says to Mom.

"GG, I'll just put your bag in the guest bedroom," Dad calls from the hallway.

"You loved the dogs when we were here last time," I say to Charlie.

He rolls his eyes. Since when does he roll his eyes? "No, I didn't."

"Yes, you did. You practically wanted them to sleep in the bed with us."

"I did not."

Mom lowers herself onto the floor and the dogs come over and attack her with their noses. "I remember when Marge got them. They were the cutest things."

Charlie gets down, too, and pats the wriggling bodies.

"How long have you known Marge?" I ask. It still feels weird to be able to ask her a question.

Mom looks up. "Since … well, since you were born. We met in a park, actually. She was walking Lancelot, her old dog, and you were screaming in the stroller …" She pauses and the dogs snuffle her hands. Her shoulders straighten, like the memory is uncurling her body. "We were both going through really hard things, and I guess we've always been indebted to each other."

"What hard things?" I ask.

She shifts around to sit cross-legged, wincing a little, and the dogs settle into her lap. They let Charlie play with their ears. "Her husband had just been diagnosed with ALS, and it progressed really fast. He only lived another year."

I kneel down. "And you?"

She's watching Charlie, maybe assessing how much to say. The muscles in her throat move as she swallows. "I was having a hard time adjusting. To new things."

Charlie makes Mozart's ears into bat wings. "Adjusting? Was that the depression Dad told us about?"

"He did?"

"When we were here last time," I say. "When they started searching the house we had to stay here."

The dogs jump out of Mom's lap, and she pulls her knees up to her chest. She hasn't just sat still with us in so long that it's both wonderful and disconcerting. And she's so thin that I keep expecting her to break. "Marge told me," she says. "I'm glad she could help. She's always great for that."

"You talked to her already?"

"On the phone from the medical center."

I hate that I'm still surprised by their friendship. That it makes me feel left out.

"I'm hungry," Charlie announces. "But not for cheese and crackers."

Mom ruffles his hair. "Of course you are. Should we see if there's anything else?"

They get up, and the dogs yap around us, their food radars on high alert.

Mom puts out her hand to help me up and her fingers are

cool, like they were when she touched me in the health unit. When I pull on her hand to stand up, I can feel how her muscles tense and she leans back for leverage. She's watching my face with that look Iris described ages ago — the one where she's looking into you, really seeing you. But I don't know what she's seeing, which part of me is there.

∗

Dad appears and confers with Charlie about dinner as Mom goes up to the bedroom with her phone.

"Why is the person with the most limited palate always in charge of food decisions?" I ask.

They both look up from the takeout flyers Dad's pulled from a drawer.

"Never mind," I mutter, and go in search of a place to text in peace. We've been warned that even though the story is out not to say much. Since we got here — just hours since we left Port Melandron — the story has been spreading on all media. I'm not supposed to contact my friends until someone says it's okay. Well, my best friend still hasn't replied to me, and the only other person I'd tell is Mylo, and I know he can keep a secret better than anyone.

I plop onto the blow-up mattress in Marge's office, where I've volunteered to sleep because I don't want to share a room with Charlie again, and take out my phone.

We're back.

It takes a while for the in-progress dots to start. God, I've missed texting people.

Good. Everything okay?

Yeah. Except the media are looking for us. We're hiding. Shhh.

How's your mom?

Thin. Quiet. Okay.

It's amazing.

Yeah.

A thought gnaws at me. I'm expecting more from this conversation. An energy, enthusiasm. Something.

How are you? I ask.

Good. Been working a lot. My mom's taking me to Montreal on Thursday. Her sister lives there.

Is that a surprise?

No. She planned it a few months ago.

You just never mentioned it. Something weird is happening and I don't know how to fix it. It's like we can't find our groove, when it was second nature just a few days ago. *I miss you.*

He doesn't hesitate. *Miss you, too.*

But it still feels different. I want to ask him — to be as honest as we were at Constance Pond. We know what's under each other's skin.

Will you be home before Thursday? he asks.

Maybe. Maybe not. I don't know.

Okay. I might not see you before I go. I'll let you know when I'm back.

Okay. Have fun. That's such a lame statement. A command to have a good time. Like he needs me to tell him that.

For sure. And you take care. Text me, okay?

I lie back on the air mattress and it squeaks in protest. *Yup.*

*

I wake up from an unexpected nap and wonder where I am.

I'm at Marge's. Again. Mom's home. Holy crap.

My next thought is Iris and how I want to see her so badly. To sit against the wall in her room and cross my legs over hers and tell her everything. I listen to the voices through the floor.

When I get out my phone, there's a message on the screen.

My eyes water. It's Iris. *I just heard the news. WOW! I miss you. I'm sorry. Where are you?*

Relief floods in as I type. *I'm sorry, too. So sorry for everything. We're at Marge's, and Mom's safe.*

I roll off the mattress as I wait for her reply. Maybe everything will be okay.

"Grace! Dinner!" Charlie's shout comes up through the floor.

I can hear Dad telling him to be quiet.

When will you be home?

A door hinge creaks down the hall and a voice rises and falls. I instinctively freeze to listen.

It's Mom.

Maybe tomorrow or the next day, I text Iris. *I'll let you know. Promise.*

I shuffle in my socks down the hall to Mom's door, which is not quite closed, holding in my breath.

"No, I don't want any more meds. I want to be able to think."

"But Dr. Bansal said —"

"He said I should trust my instincts."

Grandma's in there with her. "All right, but your instincts might be a little ... tired after everything you've been through."

"Stop being dramatic, Mom."

"Wasn't what happened up there dramatic? Not to mention you ripped out your IV!"

"Not so loud. Look, Dr. Bansal also said there would be ups and down. But since I saw Felipe, I feel better. More grounded. I mean it."

"I just can't understand that."

There is silence for a moment and I feel light-headed from breathing so little.

"I don't expect you to," Mom says. "But I needed to do it. He was ..." Her voice breaks and there's silence.

"Graaaace! Pizza!"

I jump and my elbow thuds against the wall. I sneak back toward my room and am about to throw myself through the door when Dad pokes his head up the stairwell. "What Charlie means is, would you like to join us for dinner?"

62

Mozart and Vivaldi's yapping signals that Marge must have pulled into the driveway. The pizza boxes are still open on the kitchen table, Dad and Charlie sprawled on the couch watching something on TV. Mom's drinking a glass of water, staring into the backyard. I'm picking the olives off the last slice of pizza and eating them. Grandma's upstairs somewhere, hiding from all the cheese.

The door opens and the dogs yip and scramble on the wooden floor.

"Oh, you sillies," Marge says in a motherly tone. "Yes, I'm home."

I'm struck by what it must be like for her to come home to this empty house every day, just those dogs greeting her like crazed fans. Sipping her after-work glass of wine.

"Hi," I say, walking around the corner. "How was work?"

"Grace, hello. Good to see you again. It was fine. Only half-boring." She straightens up from petting the dogs. "How is everyone? Your mother?"

"She's in the kitchen," I say, which isn't actually an answer to her question.

She puts her bag down beside me and pats my shoulder. She smells like floral soap. "You remember the last time you were here?"

"Yes."

"It was very different circumstances."

"I know. It feels like a different life."

She smiles. "It was. And you survived it."

"Marge." Mom's in the kitchen doorway.

They hug and I hear shoulder joints pop. They stay embraced for a while.

I step into the living room enough that they can't see me. The scene on the TV reflects off the window. It looks like Dad's asleep on the couch, Charlie snuggled under his arm.

"You wait until you're ready," I hear Marge say. "And it's okay to keep some things to yourself, you know. No one is entitled to know every one of our secrets."

"I keep swaying between open and closed," Mom says. "It's exhausting."

"Of course it is. After Len's diagnosis, I couldn't decide what I wanted to say, and to whom. It's your choice."

They walk into the kitchen and I lose the thread of conversation. I want to follow but can't think how it won't be obvious that I'm eavesdropping.

Grandma comes down the stairs. "Was that Marge getting home?"

"Yes."

"Are they talking now?"

I nod.

She looks into the kitchen.

Judging by the silence, only punctuated by shouts from the TV, they must have gone into the backyard.

"They'll have things to catch up on," she says.

"Duh."

She eyes me sharply.

"Sorry," I say. "I just meant … sorry."

She pats my arm. "We're all discombobulated."

"Did you eat anything?" I ask her. "There's probably salad around somewhere."

My phone rings as we're all sitting in Marge's living room, trying to seem interested in a wolf documentary Charlie needs us to see. The pack is tearing apart an elk in a way that is not G-rated.

I jump up when I see Iris's name and go out into the kitchen.

"I couldn't wait," she says. "Mom told me not to bother you because you're all trying to bond and everything, but she doesn't get it — I need to talk to you!"

"I know," I say. "It's fine." I'm not sure what I mean — I'm just so relieved to hear her voice. "And I feel so bad about what happened. I just — It was … awful."

"I'm sorry, too," she says. "I was stupid to shut you out. But, your mother — are you allowed to tell me?"

"Not really, but I'm going to anyway."

"Oh, thank God."

I take the stairs up to my air mattress, grateful for the privacy and for my best friend, for the jellybeans in my pocket, found by Charlie at the back of Marge's cupboard. And for Mom finally being in the same house as us.

*

Dad announces that we'll get to go home after the police hold their press conference and read the statement Mom and Dad have prepared. I don't watch, but I imagine Isabel standing in front of the cameras and microphones, telling the version of the story they've agreed on for the public. The reporters clamoring to ask questions. The buzz in the room. When I finally go online, the story is everywhere and it's all people are talking about. I don't even check Jungle because it's too much. Mylo texts a goodbye as if he's going to Antarctica, not just across the country. I command him to have a good time because there's nothing else I can think of to say. My chest feels heavy as I wait for him to say something back, but he doesn't. So I feel heavier.

The police have asked that people respect our privacy, but as we come around the curve in the road, it's clear our neighbors are prioritizing celebration over discretion.

Charlie's eyes are huge. "There are, like, a thousand balloons on our porch."

Isabel and Constable Baker are there, plus people from around our street. It feels like a homecoming for all of us. Charlie scampers up the lawn to the porch, and Mom and Dad head for the officers.

I stand in one spot and try to decide why my heart is pounding. There are voices everywhere. It's surprisingly overwhelming.

"Grace!"

That one voice cuts through the crowd and I instantly feel my eyes sting.

Iris hugs me from behind and pushes me down so we're enfolded in a tangle of limbs on the grass.

"You're here," I say. "You didn't tell me."

"I sneaked my mom's car. She'll be pretty pissed. But I couldn't *not* come!"

We're spooning on the ground, so I can't see her face. Her breath is in my ear.

"I never want that to happen again," I say. "It was awful."

She rests her chin on my shoulder. "I know. It sucked. Let's make a peace accord."

"I will sign that."

"So ... where's Mylo?"

We haven't talked about him yet — about the secrets or the fight. Or that he's been acting weird.

"In Montreal," I say.

"Random."

"Kind of. But not."

"Should we get up?"

I squeeze her arm and she squeezes me back. People are looking around like they might inquire about helping us. "No," I say. "This is nice."

She presses her cheek against the back of my neck. "Yeah, it is."

63

Grandma and Dad are packing the last of the second-generation lasagnas into the freezer when Isabel and Constable Baker walk into the kitchen, radios squawking. It hits me that we might not see them again. They did their job. There are other crises to attend to. It's strangely sad.

"Grace." Isabel comes to the table where Iris, Charlie and I are working through a bag of chips. "Everything good?"

"Yeah," I say. "So far. Chip?" I hold one up.

"Why not." She takes it.

"Are you here to interview us again?" Charlie asks with his mouth full.

"No." She smiles. "Just to tie things up and say goodbye. You'll be glad to get back to being a complete family."

Charlie grabs another handful of chips in reply.

"Was it harder than the others?" I ask.

"Was what harder?"

"This case."

She nibbles the chip. "Every investigation is challenging, but this one was ..." She searches for words.

I sit up. "What?"

She hesitates and then leans down to me. Charlie's rustling around in the chip bag, so only Iris and I can hear. "My mother died when I was young. I felt throughout this investigation that you needed your mother back, not just that she needed to be found. Does that make sense?"

"Yes," I say. "Thank you."

Iris grabs the chip bag and holds it out to her. "Here. You deserve this."

64

The hours pass and we wander around the house, trying to be normal when there's an invisible layer of abnormal covering everything. A security person is stationed in the driveway to ward off any sneaky media people. The house feels smaller somehow, with less empty space than before. It's still a shock to think about: Mom is home.

For part of the time, she has a really long bath. Grandma stays on the phone with her manager for what seems like all afternoon. Charlie hums to himself and hangs around the bathroom door, waiting for Mom to come out so he can show her his *Minecraft* masterpiece. Dinner involves Grandma sermonizing about what we should do to improve our diets — chickpeas, sunflower sprouts and lots of turmeric — and how she can't wait to get back to California — the weather, the food, the blah, blah, blah. I watch Mom because I can't not. She finishes her plate slowly, concentrating on each bite, the movement of her fork. I want to ask her about what she ate on the boat. Why she's lost so much weight. Whether she went with him or was forced.

After dinner, Charlie finally gets to take Mom up to his room to show her the *Minecraft* megalopolis.

I stack the dirty dishes on the table.

"You coming down with something, Grace?" Dad asks in front of the sink, where the water is running.

"Just tired," I say.

"Yeah, wouldn't a nap be really nice right now?"

"The best," I say.

Grandma leans around the doorframe. "I've got to take a call, otherwise I'd do those dishes."

"Sure, Patricia. We'll add it to your dishwashing tab," Dad mutters, but she's already gone.

"Is it me or is she generally more human now?" I say as I bring the dishes to the sink.

"As opposed to being orc?"

"Maybe not orc. Maybe … witch?"

He cringes. "I'm not going to acknowledge that comment. As a parent and son-in-law, I can't."

"Well, you're the one who said orc." I stack the dishes in the dishwasher, and Dad dumps the cooking pots in the sink with a squirt of dish soap. I like standing beside him, doing this. It feels good. Team-like.

Grandma's laugh floats in from the living room. The throaty laugh she uses with other show-business people.

"Dad," I say quietly, "has Mom told you anything?"

"About what?"

He knows what I mean. "Anything. Why she needed to see the body. What happened on the boat. What it was like. We all have a million questions."

He rinses a glass and puts it on the drying rack. "But it's up to her to tell."

"So she hasn't."

He puts his hands back in the soapy water. "Dr. Bansal says she needs time. We can't push her."

"No, I get it," I say, suddenly with no more plates to stack. I lean against the counter. "But did Dr. Bansal tell you anything?"

He rinses a wooden spoon. "No, but the police did."

I gasp. "What did they say?"

He looks at me. "They only told me what they found on the boat. Your mother's experience is hers to tell. And promise me this stays between us. I mean it."

"Promise."

He wrings out the dishcloth. "The boat had several mouse nests and was barely seaworthy. They were extremely lucky they didn't hit a bad storm out there. And the only thing that worked in the galley was the fridge."

I stare back at him, knowing he's waiting for me to connect some dots.

"They couldn't cook food," he says, "at least not at the end. Which means they were basically eating sashimi, because apparently Krause caught a lot of fish."

"Is that why she's so skinny? There was no other food?"

"Maybe. The police think Krause stayed away from the few coastal communities to avoid being found, so they didn't pick up supplies often. Only GG can tell us more about that." He drains the water from the sink. "But Gracie, we need to be careful. Dr. Bansal said she could be triggered by something that brings back the trauma. She could get upset like she did in Port Melandron."

"You mean when she ripped out her IV?"

His head snaps around. "How do you know about that?"

I close my mouth, then open it. "I overheard."

"Well, yes. And it'll be really traumatic for Charlie and Patricia — not to mention your mother — if something like that happens here."

There's footfall upstairs. Mom and Charlie must be coming back down.

How long are we going to be avoiding trauma for? I remember what I heard Marge say to Mom: No one is entitled to know all our secrets. But aren't there secrets we do need to know? "Dad," I say into his ear. "What if ..."

He waits, but I can't say it out loud. What if she wanted to go with him? What if she needed to see his body because she still cares about him? The thought makes me feel sick, especially after what Dad just described.

Footsteps on the stairs.

"What is it, Grace?" he asks.

He smells faintly of sweat. I shake my head. "Nothing."

"Dad! I didn't show you the last part of my fortress." Charlie bounds into the kitchen, all high-energy comet once more.

"It's incredible," Mom says behind him. "He must have spent weeks on it."

"Yup," I say. "Weeks and weeks."

65

There's a quiet knock on my door as I'm getting into bed early. Sleep seems like the easiest thing to do right now, if my body will cooperate.

"Grace, are you awake?"

It's still surreal to hear her voice. She's standing there, lit by the hallway. I think about the morning of the soccer game, how she stood in the sun and looked so miserable and how mean I was to her.

"Yes, I'm awake," I say. "You can come in." I've always wanted her to come in. But now it feels charged up with something — possibility and mystery. A kind of exposure that feels scary. An image flashes through my mind — a barely seaworthy boat, mouse droppings, the Pacific Ocean all around. Three months of that. I have no idea who she became on that boat.

She's wearing a T-shirt, long cardigan and leggings, her hair pulled back. She moves my swivel chair across the carpet and sits down beside the bed. "Hi," she says.

I sit cross-legged on top of my blankets. Try to take a normal breath. "Hi."

"I know you have questions."

I stare at my hands. "We all do."

"The thing is," she says, shifting in the chair.

I study her face, the faint lines around her mouth that are usually covered with makeup. She's going to look like Grandma when she's old.

"The thing is," she says again, blinking at the ceiling, "I'm still out there sometimes."

"What do you mean?"

She pulls her cardigan closed. "I'm not always sure where I am." She touches her forehead with one hand. "Some moments I wake up to the reality that I'm home all over again. And other moments I can hear the waves. His voice." Her chin quivers and she presses her lips together.

My throat starts to ache.

She covers her face with her hands. "Just a minute." She bends like a tree under the weight of snow.

I can feel the confusion radiating from her. I reach out and touch her knee, still an amazing thing to be able to do. "Do you need to breathe?"

"Yes, that's a good first step," she says from behind her fingers.

"A four count is good. From the chest. In and out." I demonstrate.

She straightens her back and tries it. I watch her collarbones rise and fall.

"Thank you," she says.

"You're welcome."

"Actually," she says, "I mean thank you for what you did to find us."

Us. I don't know what she's talking about.

"Corporal Sanchez explained it to me. The wood sculpture. You made that connection." She pulls on her fingers. I haven't seen her do that in ages. It's strangely comforting. "She told me you went to Ammonite because you had a hunch and that's what helped them connect things to Fortune Bay and the boat. It was you, Grace." She takes a breath and lets it out. "I'm so grateful for that. I can't even say how much." She leans forward and touches my socked toe, the only thing she can reach without getting up.

I think carefully about which question I'll ask. Which ones I'll keep for later. "Did you know about the wood sculpture before you disappeared?"

She tucks her hair behind her ears. "No."

There's a strain of muffled sound from downstairs — a voice, probably Grandma's.

"He told me about it a few days after we got on the boat," Mom says quietly.

My heart is beating in my ears. I want to know more, but I don't want to trigger something.

She braces her arms on her knees and touches my toes again, like it's easier to talk to a small part of me. "I'd given up hope of persuading him to take me to shore. He seemed to think it would make me feel better, telling me there was this monument to him and me in Ammonite." She looks out the window. "But I knew it was a clue and if someone could find the initials he carved, they might connect them to him."

She's so small and used up. Even more than before. It occurs to me that being used up might be why she's been so skinny.

There hasn't been enough of her, literally or figuratively.

Slowly, she stands. "I need another bath. You have no idea how amazing hot water is."

"Right now?" I ask, already missing her hand on my foot.

She hugs her arms against her. "I need time, Grace. It's like the waves keep going in and out. One minute I'm okay and the next ..."

I uncross my legs. "It's okay, Mom." Even though it isn't.

She pauses halfway to the door. "I still wake up feeling the rock of the boat and the rough blanket on my skin. It's so strange. Even the worst things can seem like a comfort if they're what you know."

66

I dream that I hear Mom and Dad talking through my wall, and
when I wake up I'm not so sure it wasn't real. There was a feeling
of dread, an aching in my stomach, as their voices rose and fell.

Mom doesn't come out of the bedroom until almost noon.
Charlie lets me decorate one of his houses on *Minecraft*, but he
keeps running out to check if her door is open yet.

I wonder what people from school are doing. People with
normal lives, normal summer plans, having normal, trivial
conversations with friends.

"Do you think she's actually sleeping?" Charlie asks for the
second time.

"Dad said if the door's closed, no go."

"But that wasn't the rule before."

"This isn't before."

"What do you think she'll want to do when she gets up?"

I make some curtains for a window and color them yellow.
"Dad said she's going to see Dr. Bansal."

"Ugh, make them blue. All afternoon?"

I shrug.

"Geez."

"She's kind of messed up, Charlie," I whisper. "You would be, too, if someone kept you on a boat for three months."

He blinks at the screen.

*

When Mom does come out, after hugging us and murmuring good morning, she goes downstairs in her sweatsuit and starts talking to Dad in a low voice. When we get to the kitchen, Dad's grabbing his keys. "I'll be right back," he says.

"Dr. Bansal?" I ask.

He gives me a tired look as he goes out the door.

The next day is mostly the same. Mom comes down late, eats a little lunch and goes out. When she gets back, she runs a bath. Charlie and I build a new castle and a moat around it. I go on Planet Hunters but don't find any transits. Text Mylo, *How's Montreal?* He replies with a photo of a park, his mother in one corner, at the edge of a lake.

How's your mother? I text.

Good, he replies. *How's yours?* I switch between feeling sad and feeling annoyed and feeling hopeless.

But the day after that she gets up when we're cleaning up breakfast and sits on the couch with Charlie and me before she goes to her appointment, and the next day she's having her bath early when I get out of bed. Through the chaos, a pattern emerges — or at least a lack of pattern that kind of points toward progress. Less time in her bedroom or in the bath, more time with us, even if it's doing nothing. A few more smiles than dazed looks. But it's like being on a boat at sea — you don't always know what the next wave will feel like, or how exactly to plant your feet.

67

I rewatch a video of Elizabeth Tasker talking about finding life on exoplanets. She stands in front of an audience and answers a question about how much more there is to know about the universe.

And this is the part where I get goose bumps.

"It's more of a question of how much we *don't* know," she says. "There's a fable about six blind men examining an elephant. Each reaches out to touch a different part of the unknown animal. One man finds the smooth membrane of the animal's ear. Another holds the curved tusk, while a third grasps the thin tail. The fourth man touches the elephant's trunk and the fifth wraps his hands around one leg. The final man presses his palms against the elephant's broad flank. An argument then erupts over what the elephant truly looks like, since each man has only found a part of the truth.

"This is how we're learning about the universe: a bit at a time and with only partial knowledge, which makes it both daunting and essential that we keep learning. We will never know everything, because 'everything' is probably an infinite term. But we can expand our understanding of the elephant, bit by bit. We already know a huge amount more than the first astronomers did, and we'll know exponentially more in fifty years than we do now. It's truly exciting to think of how much we're discovering."

68

After two other weird text exchanges with Mylo I decide to just call him. It's what we've always done best anyway. I want the old us back. If we have, in fact, moved from an "old" to a "new" us. "Hey," I say as soon as he picks up. "Are you back yet?"

"Uh, no. Tomorrow. Hi."

"Hi. So what's going on?"

"What do you mean?"

I sit down on my bed, feeling suddenly flushed. It's okay. I'm allowed to ask these questions. "This," I say. "How come there's this ... weirdness now?"

"Uh, I'm not sure."

"I never remember it being like this when we talked. I mean — Constance Pond. I know you. What's going on?"

"Just hold on, I need to move." There's silence and then a door shuts. "I'm going outside. My mom's kind of pissed at me right now."

"Why?"

"We had another fight."

"About what?"

"Uh, my dad."

"Is there news? Did they —"

"No. They didn't. There's nothing." His voice is flat in a way that makes me shudder.

"Oh."

"I told her I want the investigators to try to find him again," he says, his breath blowing into the phone. He must still be walking. "Why should we give up hope, right?"

"Right," I say. "Of course."

"But she won't do it. She says if he wanted to be found, he would have been. It's like she thinks it's his fault."

He breathes into the phone some more.

"Is there a fault?" I ask quietly.

"I don't know! Maybe. Maybe it's her fault. Maybe she drove him away. *I* feel like leaving sometimes."

"But she loves you," I blurt awkwardly. "At the fundraiser I could see the way she — and she told me —"

"You don't know her. You don't know what's going on. It's so fricking complicated. And I'm so tired of it." His voice gets gravelly. "I just want him back."

"I know," I say, my heart beating hard. "I totally understand."

He doesn't reply.

"Maybe she has a reason for not starting the search again," I say. "What do the police say?"

Silence.

"Mylo? I just mean your mom seems like a good person. I wasn't expecting it, and I was wrong. She really loves you. I'm not saying she's right, but if you can talk to her about it, maybe there's more to the situation than you know."

Silence again. He's not breathing into the phone anymore.

"Are you there?" I ask, feeling like I'm in a pitch-black room, trying to find him.

"I have to go," he says quietly.

"What? Wait. You have to answer me. Don't go."

"I have to get back."

"But, Mylo, what about —"

"You don't understand."

I feel like the air has been sucked from the pitch-black room. "What? Yes, I do. I know exactly what this feels like."

"Oh, yeah, right — you do. And now you're on the other side of it."

My skin goes cold. "What does that mean?"

"It means congratulations. You have your mother back."

69

Galaxies collide all the time, like cosmic car crashes. Even in the impossible vastness of space, the gravity of a bigger galaxy will pull a smaller one, suck in its dust and gas and its solar systems, absorbing them, morphing them. Over billions of years, at over one hundred kilometers per second: smash.

I'm looking at images of these crashes on my computer when it occurs to me that we slam into people around us, invisibly, all the time. Through the things we say and don't say. What we do and don't do. That we are slowly changed by the constant bombardment. That we consume and are consumed, until we become products of our interactions, made of old and new parts, simultaneously broken and healing.

70

Bruce and Moira ask me what they can make for dinner when I arrive; Iris is not even included in the decision. They corner me in the kitchen in the nicest way and offer cookbooks.

"I'm okay with whatever," I say. "Honestly."

"But do you eat tofu? I can't remember. Salmon?" Moira asks, getting out a frying pan.

"Yes, just not usually together."

"God, Mom," Iris says. "You can just surprise us, too. We have important business to attend to."

"I really don't mind," I say.

"I was wondering about this." Moira shows me a recipe on her tablet. Grilled tofu with a ginger-garlic sauce.

"Perfect," I say.

"We were going to bring out the bubbly," Bruce says from the fridge. "In celebration. Sparkling apple or cranberry?"

I tap the nearest bottle. "Cranberry."

"Okay, okay, thank you, you guys are amazing." Iris pulls me away and we go upstairs.

"You have the best family ever," I say once we're installed in her room with the door closed.

"Ugh, you see them, like, ten percent of the time. It's their best ten percent."

I lie on her bed and smell the smells of her stuff. It's deeply comforting.

She gets out the Take the Castle game and sets it up. I pass her my phone so she can check the photo for our last moves. It feels like it's been a year since we did this.

And the last time was when we argued about Zane, and she didn't even know about me and Mylo. Now she knows, but not about our phone call last night.

"So did you know Elizabeth Tasker's going to be in Seattle next month?"

"No."

"She's giving a lecture at a university. Just thought you might want to know."

"Thanks."

She looks at me sideways. "What?"

"Nothing. There's just a lot going on. I'm not one hundred percent focused on my future as an astronomer right now."

She puts the last game pieces on the board. "Why the hell not?"

I can't tell if she's joking.

"Okay," she says, "how about whoever's turn it is to play also has to divulge something. We have lots to catch up on, right?"

"Okay."

"You look tired."

I get down on the floor in front of the board. "Yeah. I didn't sleep much last night."

"Why's that?"

"You'll have to wait until it's my turn." I pick up the die to roll for who'll go first. I get a five. Even goes first. I sit back against the bed.

She studies her army. Most of them are still waiting to get into the moat. I recall thinking that was a bad strategy. "So you may be relieved to know that Zane is no longer in our fund-raising group."

"Really?"

She moves a unit of soldiers and frowns at them. "Yeah, he was probably not going to stay after I lit into him via text and and then left a similarly angry voicemail." She plays with the end of her braid.

"And how are you?"

She shrugs. "Meh. It sucked for a while, but it's better now."

"I was so sorry about it," I say. "When I heard him talking on the phone, I wanted to kick him."

"I did kick him," she says. "In my mind, a hundred times. And the thing is, you warned me about him."

"Well, not really. I don't remember what I said."

"You said I was blinded by love."

"Ugh, I'm so cliché." I point to the game rules and she passes them over.

"Yeah. But it turned out to be true, so." She's watching me. The rest is waiting to be talked about and it's my turn.

"Hey, did you make your target?" I ask, both wanting a diversion and actually curious.

"Target?"

"At the fundraiser. For the Iraqi family."

"Oh, right," she says, then stops. "Hey, is this an illegal question when it's actually your turn?"

I groan. "How many games with elaborate rules are we playing here? Can't you just tell me?"

She grins. "We made more than our target. The family's coming in three months. Your move, Carter."

I don't really care about the game, so I try something reckless and move my entire army to the castle gates. "So before we talk about what happened between Mylo and me, I want you to know we're kind of not talking anymore."

She crosses her legs. "Why?"

I take a moment because the shock of hanging up after that phone call is still fresh, still makes me feel like crying. "I think my situation's not helping him right now."

She narrows her eyes. "That's too vague. Explain."

I tell her about last night. Then I tell her about before, too — the times we kissed, all the phone calls. How I had liked him since the ice cream parlor. And then I keep going and tell her about his dad. About Constance Pond. It isn't my secret to tell, but what's the point in being honest with my best friend if I don't tell her this? It's a big part of the story. My story, too.

"Wow," she says. "This is a lot."

"I know. I'm sorry I kept it from you."

Her freckled forehead is smooth. She looks thoughtful, then gets up and opens a drawer in her desk, rummaging around. "Keep talking. I'm listening."

"That's it," I say. "I'm done. Now you know everything."

She comes back with something in her hand. A wrapped candy. "This is from my emergency stash. My dad refreshes the earthquake kit once a year, and I plunder the out-of-date snacks. And chocolate." She holds it out to me. "These are still totally fine, though. You'd never know."

I take the purple-wrapped chocolate. "Is this an emergency?"

"It seems like a moment when chocolate is needed."

I unwrap it.

She taps a game piece on the board pensively. "I don't think anyone's going to take this castle."

"I've been thinking that for months."

"This game is kind of ridiculous."

"Yup."

"Should we stop?"

"Sure."

"Does that make us quitters?"

I stretch my limbs out. "I think it makes us peace-loving and non-castle-coveting."

She gets herself a purple chocolate and sits on her exercise ball. "So I have some news."

I pull my legs up to my chest.

She throws her crumpled purple wrapper in the garbage can by her desk. "I've been accepted to an youth exchange program for next year."

"What?" This is not what I expected her to say, but suddenly it seems like it's the most inevitable thing in the world. Iris has always been destined for great and far-flung adventures. It's one of the things I love most about her. "Where? When? Is this instead of going to university?"

She grins. "It's in Tanzania, January, and I'll be back before university starts. Homeschooling benefit number thirty-five."

"This January, like in five months?"

"Yeah."

I wave my hands around stupidly. "When did this happen?"

"I applied in May, but I only found out last week."

"Why did I not know you applied?"

She reaches into the closet behind her and pulls on a cardigan. "I told you, but it was just after GG was abducted and, you know."

I try to figure out why I feel so unmoored. It's like she's been planning and dreaming for months without me. "God. I feel terrible."

"It's fine. You were obviously preoccupied."

"No, about you going." I lift myself up and onto her bed. "I just finished hoping we'd be friends again and now you're leaving?" I look at her. "For how long?"

"Six months."

I flop back on the bed. "Ugh, that's so long."

She comes over and lies next to me. "But it's not for a while. I'm not even thinking about preparing for it."

I stare at her gray ceiling. "But January will be here in no time and then you'll be in Tanzania and I'll be depressed."

"No, you won't. You'll be discovering your next exoplanet and writing a paper on it with Elizabeth Tasker and going on dates with Mylo McLean."

I'm filled with a weird dread. "Don't say that. It's not funny."

"Of course it's not funny. It's future fact."

I close my eyes. "He sounded so broken. Like there was this thing between us that would now always be there. And I guess it will." I don't say the *unless* part — the unless they miraculously find his dad and he's suddenly a functioning family member again part — because deep down I don't believe it's going to happen, and the fact that I don't believe it makes me ashamed.

She moves so her shoulders are in line with mine. "Forgive me for being optimistic, but I think Mylo will come around."

I exhale through my mouth. "You're so annoying."

"Are you mad at him?"

I think about it.

Below us, Bruce and Moira have turned on some music.

"Yeah," I say, "but also not."

"I mean, he was dumb to say those things."

"Yeah, yeah — I have to think about what he's going through, and his mom and everything."

She pats my leg. "Well, I was going to say that he's a good person. Good people do dumb things sometimes, right, exhibit A?"

I narrow my eyes at her.

She rolls onto her side and butts my shoulder with her forehead.

71

Nine days after we get home with Mom, Charlie and I find her in the kitchen mixing pancake batter. I can't remember the last time she made pancakes.

"Do we have blueberries in the freezer?" she asks. Just like it's a regular morning and we're used to coming down sleepy and hungry, ready for our mother's cooked breakfast like it's the 1950s.

Charlie gapes a little, then recovers joyfully. "I'll go check!"

"How did you sleep, Grace?" she asks me.

"Okay," I say. "What's with the pancakes?"

She takes a carton of orange juice out of the fridge. "I haven't had them in ages and I woke up thinking I should. That we all should. Right?"

It's nice. I know it's nice that she's this chipper and committed to weekend breakfast food. But it's also uncharacteristic and bewildering, all the cups and flour dust everywhere. There are smears on her shirt.

"I found raspberries but no blueberries," Charlie says, coming in with a freezer bag.

"Can we put raspberries into pancakes?" Mom asks, looking

at the cookbook on the counter as if it will tell her.

"I think so," I say. "Want me to ask the internet?"

Then Charlie rushes at her and almost topples her over in his enthusiastic hug, and she pats his shoulder. "Hey, you."

"This is great," he says, his arms around her, his chin against her ribs.

She pulls me against her, more strength in her arm than I expect.

"Is this Grandma?" I ask.

"What do you mean?"

"I mean, did Grandma tell you how healing it is to work with food or something? It's like you're channeling her."

Of course, Grandma walks into the kitchen then and says, "My goodness, what a mess."

"Remember that time with the chili?" Mom says to Grandma and they both groan.

Charlie and I look at each other.

Grandma comes around the counter and peers at the bowl of batter. "Your mother tried to make chili for a barbecue when she was your age, and it ended up all over the kitchen."

"It literally exploded," Mom says.

"How come we haven't heard this story?" Charlie asks.

"Or the one about the snake," I say.

Grandma looks horrified. "What snake?"

Mom smiles and eats a frozen raspberry. "Your dad told you about that?"

"He didn't tell *me*!" Charlie pulls on her arm.

"And about the perm, too," I say, nabbing a few raspberries for myself.

She's laughing, and this time Grandma knows what I'm talking about.

"Oh God, that awful perm she had in the early nineties?"

"You had one, too!" Mom says to her.

Grandma crosses her arms over her chest. "I did not. You're delusional."

"I remember it. I swear. I'll dig up a photo somehow. There must be some online."

"But what about the *snake*?" Charlie yells.

As we're all finishing our plates, a stack of uneaten, half-cooked pancakes in the middle of the table, Mom's phone rings. It's an unexpected noise because it's been months since we've heard its ring. It instantly takes me back to mornings before school, Mom rushing around looking for shoes or a lost note or her keys. Her phone jangling on the counter, making her stop whatever she was doing to answer it. Going into the garage or basement or upstairs to talk.

Now she slowly gets up and checks the display.

Grandma *tsks* and watches her. Like *she* doesn't jump up the moment hers rings.

It can't be him, I remind myself. This is a different time. Different everything.

"It's the station," Mom says to Dad. "I'll be right back."

"Can't it wait?" Grandma says. "Honestly, GG, you're still recovering."

"It's fine," Mom says. "Just a quick call. Be right back."

"She's talking to work people already?" Charlie mutters.

"They were closely involved in the investigation," Dad says as he stacks our plates. "Roger was the third person she talked to when she was at the medical center."

"I hope you were the first," I say.

"It doesn't mean she's going back to work, Charlie. They're her colleagues. They've been worried for her."

But as we're finishing the dishes and Grandma's watching a show about vacation homes in St. Maarten and Charlie's telling Mom about the drawbridge he wants to build, there's a knock at the front door.

Mom dries her hands on a tea towel. "It's just Yasmin Brouwer," she says and walks out.

"Yasmin from the station?" I ask Dad.

He looks mildly surprised.

A moment later, Yasmin Brouwer, tall and model-y in a bright flowered dress, walks into the kitchen behind Mom, who holds a huge bunch of flowers in one hand.

Dad pulls the plug out of the sink, where the water gurgles as it escapes.

"Grace, do you remember Yasmin, the assistant news director at ITV?" Mom says, touching Yasmin's smooth arm. "I don't know if you remember the documentary we did on cricket farms?"

"God, you *are* going back to work," Charlie says.

"Honey, the station wanted to send someone over to talk about the media. It's important that we understand what's going on and how to respond to questions."

"Questions?"

"There'll be interviews and press conferences. Media people

might try to stop you on the street," Mom says in a tone meant for Charlie, overly emphatic, which I immediately resent.

"But this is the first day you've actually been around." Charlie looks at Dad, as if for support.

"If I may?" Yasmin holds up a slender finger. "Everyone wants to talk to your mother right now. We have requests from the U.S., from the European press. It's a crazy time. We just want to brief you all on what's going on."

"All of us?"

Mom is still holding the flowers Yasmin gave her. An elaborate bouquet with ferns and twigs and lilies, that waxy kind with the white stamen. "You and Charlie might get approached and you need to be prepared to answer appropriately. Or to know what you shouldn't say."

"They're going to be hiding in the bushes?" Charlie's eyes are wide with excitement.

"Hopefully not," Yasmin says. "There are rules in place about how close to schools reporters can go, but we need to talk about the different scenarios. Shall we sit?" She indicates the living room.

She goes through the standard answers we should give if barraged with questions on the street or online, what we should say if someone at school asks.

I watch Mom watching her, the way she sits with her back straight and her chin up as Yasmin talks. Mom's eyes have tiny lines at the sides, while Yasmin is fresh, less weary. I never thought about how much older Mom is than her, maybe because I never noticed it before. Or maybe the biggest changes have happened since she's been gone.

"And how are you two feeling having your mom back?" Yasmin asks.

It's a stupid question, so I let Charlie take it. He gives Mom a hug and enthuses about her pancakes and showing her his fortress.

"It must be so good to be a family again," Yasmin says, trying to pull me into the conversation. "You must be loving all the catch-up time with your mother at home."

"As opposed to what?" I ask.

Yasmin looks startled.

"As opposed to her being back at work?"

"Grace," Mom says. "That's not what Yasmin meant."

"You said you weren't going back," Charlie says.

"I already told you," Mom says. "Nothing has been decided."

"So things are open," I say. "You might go back."

Mom covers her face with her hands, and I see the calm energy of the morning evaporating. She'll probably need to see Dr. Bansal after this.

"I have to get back," Yasmin says, getting up from the couch. "Thank you for listening so well, you guys. You'll be pros with the media, I'm sure."

She and Mom murmur at the front door, clearly not finished, but Charlie barks something in my ear, so I can't hear what they're saying. I push him away and he rams into my hip. The only thing I catch is something about "time-sensitive."

I hiss at Charlie to stop and he makes a face at me.

"Of course. It's up to you," Yasmin is saying to Mom. She pulls the door open and tries to catch my eye. "Have a good day, you two."

"*You two*," Charlie scoffs once the door is closed. "We have names."

"What on earth are you talking about?" Mom asks, grabbing him into a hug. "Yasmin knows your names."

Charlie squirms like a puppy in her arms. "Okay, now can I show you how I'm going to build my drawbridge?"

72

The next morning Mom doesn't join us for breakfast. Dad says she has to move up her appointment with Dr. Bansal, and she comes down in sweats again, kissing us both on the cheek before going out to the car.

"Why is she going backward?" Charlie asks.

"Maybe it's not backward," I say. "Maybe it's sideways."

He looks at me like I'm crazy.

That night I hear them talking through the wall of my room. I can't tell if Mom is crying or not.

I develop a habit of checking Mylo's social media to see if he's posting anything new. Where he is. Who he's interacting with. I'm kind of stalking him. But each time I look and see no new photos or comments or posts, I feel worse about not contacting him. Iris's probably right, but I still can't do it. I imagine us talking on the phone like we used to and Mom coming up in conversation, and therefore the absence of his dad coming up, too, and I don't know what happens from

there. What do I say? What does he say? I can't see a way
where it won't hurt.

73

And then, because there needs to be something else to make life more complicated, August ends and we're at the start of school. I try asking my parents to let me homeschool, or at least do correspondence again, but they refuse. I reluctantly collect the school supplies I need and let Mom buy me the token back-to-school clothes, which Grandma goes with me to find because Mom's doing some intense sessions with meditation or something and is occupied half the day. I force myself to answer comments and messages on Jungle because these are the people I'll soon be surrounded by five days a week. It feels like more of a survival strategy than anything else.

The night before the first day of school, an email comes into my inbox from Elizabeth Tasker. I see the name and do a double take, wondering if it's a form email from her website or something. The subject is A Lecture Near You.

Hi Grace, she writes. *It was so nice to connect with you over Skype in July. I've had a last-minute invitation to give a talk in* the astronomy department at Heaton. *Claudia tells me it won't work for your club to come, but I wanted to extend a personal invitation. It would be nice to actually meet you and chat about your next steps.*

I read the letter twice. Elizabeth Tasker is writing to me. Wanting to be my astronomy-life coach. I forward the email to Iris, who sends back a one-word reply that takes up a whole line.

Go!!!

74

During English, my first class, I wonder if there was a meeting about me or something, because no one mobs me for information and Ms. Tchenko calmly leads us through the long list of writers we'll be studying until Christmas without having to stare anyone down for misbehavior. When I look around the room, a few pairs of eyes follow me, but no one gawks. I still can't get completely comfortable.

The halls have their usual buzz and shuffle, people moving around like wildebeests preparing for the migration, and it calms me somewhat, being lost in the herd. A girl from last year's gym class waves in a vaguely embarrassed way. A guy who once helped me get my locker unstuck catches my eye briefly. I leave the herd to exchange stuff at my locker and take a few slow breaths with my head stuck inside.

When I turn around to go, the hallway has cleared somewhat, and there he is by the water fountain, talking with Trent, who's grown his hair out over the summer and looks like a surfer. Mylo glances over, pausing in midsentence. His eyebrows rise in instinctual surprise, but three girls walk in front of him and then he's gone.

I'm not sure what I would have said anyway. Seeing him at school is disorienting enough as it is.

There are murmurs behind me, and then someone taps my shoulder.

"Uh, hey, Grace." It's Melissa Urquhart, the tattletale Mom brought up during our fight at Star Club. She of the drug-use rumor. She smiles and her teeth are really white. "So how was your summer?"

I resist the urge to roll my eyes. "Pretty relaxing and fun, thanks."

She pushes her brown hair out of her eyes and it falls right back. "God, that's so great. You sound so well adjusted. I can't imagine. Hey, do you want to eat lunch with Camryn and me?"

"Uh, no, thanks," I say. "I'm not hungry."

"But you could just sit with us —"

"I have to go now." I wave to make myself clear. "See you, Melissa." I walk out into the courtyard for some air, the greasy smell of the cafeteria revolting. Unfortunately, Sasha's there, and she sees me right away, as if my orange tank top is the beacon she's been searching for. Should have gone for a more subdued color.

"Oh my God, there she is!" She tosses her dark hair behind her shoulders and strides over. She has one of those bodies that any clothes look good on. She moves like a dancer, like someone who's confident in the space she takes up. "Hey, you," she says. "Come and sit with us. They've been asking if you were coming and I said, yes, you totally were, but someone thought maybe you were doing homeschooling again or something."

"It was correspondence."

"Whatever!" She turns to the group arranged on the concrete picnic table. I only know two of them by first name — Connor Something-son and Annie O'Something — but I've never spoken two words to any of them. These are Mylo's people. He and Trent go to their parties and they drive one another to school. He used to talk about them when we spoke on the phone. This is the top echelon of the school, and they're looking at me like I'm fascinating.

"How are you feeling?" Annie asks. "Is it weird to be back?"

"Yeah, pretty weird," I say, because I don't care enough to lie to them.

Another girl whose name escapes me comes up and leans against the edge of the table. "Your mom is my hero. I thought she was great before, but now it's like she made it back from hell, you know?"

"Yeah," I say. "Sure."

"Is she okay now?"

"She's doing well," I say, knowing she wants more, but I'm not going to give these people anything.

Sasha's eyes are on me. Her nails are a perfectly painted dark purple. "If you need something, just call, okay? Seriously." She manages to look both empathetic and regal at the same time. "It must be super strange to be you right now."

I'm taken aback enough to take the scrap of paper she hands me with her number on it.

"Is Mylo in class?" Connor asks the group in general. "Dude has my chem textbook."

"He said he was coming," Annie says, pulling out a bottle of fruit smoothie and twisting off the cap.

Sasha's still watching me. She smiles.

"I'm going to go for a walk," I say, but none of them are paying attention anymore except Sasha, who waves and makes me wonder if I've been wrong about her, or if she's just good at getting what she wants.

I go outside and down the steps and into the park that borders the school. I find a log to sit on and eat the crackers and hummus Grandma packaged up for me with the enthusiasm of someone who finds school lunches adorable. Birds hop and chirp. They tweet like they're discussing the latest gossip.

75

Mom's home when I get there. She's staring at her tablet screen with a furrowed brow, only disengaging to answer my question. "No, I'm not seeing Dr. Bansal today."

"Why not?"

She sits up straight on the kitchen stool. "I'm making progress, he says, so we're trying less frequent sessions. I'm doing mindfulness exercises and yoga and I've got some books."

I lower my backpack to the floor. "And are you feeling present?"

"Sometimes."

"Oh — Grace. How was school?" Grandma's perfume wafts in with her, and I don't have to turn to know her outfit outdoes both of ours. "I can only imagine you're relieved to be back after all this time."

"Are you going out?" Mom asks her.

Grandma taps her painted nails on the countertop. "Just to get a few things. Nothing special."

"This is how you dress for nothing special?" I ask.

She looks down her nose at me, which is a feat considering I'm taller than her. "Didn't we have the conversation about personal presentation?"

"Oh, yeah. Right."

"What conversation?" Mom asks.

"I gave Grace my little diamond pendant."

Mom's forehead creases. "The Grace Kelly one?"

"I thought it was a good moment," Grandma says. "You once suggested I give it to someone else."

Mom's face clouds over.

"What?" I ask. "Why is it called the Grace Kelly one?"

Grandma's watching Mom. There's suddenly an energy, the buzzing charge of a magnetic field. I'd almost forgotten it was like this between them. "Well," Grandma says, closing her eyes in sermon-preparation, "the story is that the actress Grace Kelly wore a very similar necklace once and mine was a copy, although I don't know how true that is. What I do know is I wanted to pass it down to your mother, but she wasn't interested." She shifts her weight to her other hip and sighs. "We had a big argument and I was a terrible mother for expecting her to like it and be grateful for all the things I'd done for her. The fact that I wanted to give her a piece of my favorite jewelry — well, I was practically trying to brainwash her."

"Mom," Mom says quietly.

"At any rate," Grandma goes on, "you weren't here, GG, and I thought I should pass it on to the third Grace if the second one didn't want it."

"Second one," I say. "But you said Grace Kelly didn't own that necklace."

"She means herself," Mom says.

Right. Grandma's first name is Grace, too — it's just that everyone knows her by her middle name.

"We're a dynasty," Grandma says with a sweep of her hand.

"I was twenty," Mom says, finally looking at me. Her skin is slightly pale, and I wonder if we're headed for something triggering. "I was trying to figure out what I wanted. To be independent and my own person. That's not easy when your mother's Patricia Forsythe."

Grandma sniffs. "As I recall, you threw the necklace at me."

"There was so much more to it than that," Mom says. She seems to be holding back a ton of baggage. Her jaw is tight.

"Maybe you guys need to talk this through," I say, stepping away. "I don't want to get in the middle."

"There's nothing to get in the middle of," Grandma says, swinging her purse over one shoulder. "It's ancient history, and here we are today with completely different problems." She stares at Mom.

"Such as?" Mom glares back at her.

The hair on my arms rises and the magnetic force that repels them from each other becomes almost tangible.

Grandma still hasn't spoken.

"Never mind," Mom says, the words rushing out of her. "I don't want to get into it. I'm trying to stay centered."

Grandma clears her throat. "Good idea. I'll find my center by going shopping. What about you, Grace?"

They're both looking at me, and I realize that for a second I wasn't sure which one of us she meant.

*

The women in my family are scary, I text Iris in the aftermath.

??

Grandma and Mom went at it about an old fight they had. I don't know how long they'll last in the same house. They'll hurt each other or something.

They're both kind of too big for the space around them.

Yeah, I guess.

You think Patricia will leave soon?

I can't see her staying much longer. And it's weird.

What is?

I kind of think I'll miss her.

76

Dad has to rush off to a meeting, so I tell him to drop me a few blocks from school and I'll walk. I'm replying to a text from Iris and kind of watching where I'm going when a guy in a polo shirt and dark-rimmed glasses sidles up to me with a smile so eager my radar beeps "reporter" before he opens his mouth.

"No," I say, Yasmin's training actually coming in handy. "I won't talk to you."

"I'm just wondering how you've been doing the past few weeks. How you're adjusting. You were so —"

"Stop. I'm late for school." I walk faster.

He looks ahead, where people are milling around and climbing the front steps. "There's ten minutes until the bell."

"Oh my God, how do you know that?" I adjust my bag and start speed-walking.

He shrugs and keeps pace with me. "I graduated from here four years ago."

I glare at him. "Screw off or I'll call the police."

He stops suddenly and for some stupid reason I pause, too, and in the second before I get my stride again, he says, "Isn't it strange that your mother hasn't demonized Philip Krause?"

I keep walking but my face is instantly hot. "Go away!"

"That she hasn't spoken out about him in the press? No one knows their real relationship, but I —"

"Shut up! Just go away!" I turn, expecting him right behind me, but he is ten feet back, arms at his sides.

"Shouldn't we all know the truth?" he asks, cocking his head with a smile I want to kick off his face.

"You okay, Grace?" a voice says beside me.

"Who is this guy?"

Feet shuffle on the asphalt around me.

Sasha's there; she puts a hand on my arm and Connor What's-his-name, plus some other guy, walk toward the reporter, who backs up, tipping an invisible hat in my direction.

"What an asshole," Sasha breathes into my ear. "That was intense. You really freaked on him." She pulls on my arm, and I let her lead me down the sidewalk. "He's not supposed to be within a block of the school," she says. "Plus, reporters aren't supposed to question any students."

"How do you know that?" I ask.

"Mr. Shand sent out an email," Connor says.

"What did he ask you?" Sasha whispers.

"Nothing," I say. "Nothing."

77

Mom is shrugging on her coat when I walk into the kitchen to get a glass of water. I managed to pick the movie this time, but Charlie insisted on making a dent in our ridiculous stash of fake-butter-covered microwave popcorn, and now I'm severely dehydrated.

"I have to pick up some medication," Mom says, tying the belt of her coat. "I'll be twenty minutes."

I try to assess her level of normality.

Charlie wanders in. "But Dad said you're supposed to stay here until the buzz dies down."

She walks over and kisses his head. "Time for bed, buddy. It's late."

"The pharmacy won't be open," I say. "It's almost ten."

She picks up her bag. "I'll go to the one at Tanglemere."

"That's twenty minutes one way."

She looks the tiniest bit impatient. "I know."

"So you'll be forty minutes, plus waiting time."

"Is that Dad snoring?" Charlie asks, sticking his head up the stairwell.

"He's got a cold," Mom says. "Don't wake him up, okay?"

Charlie turns back, eyes bright. "Okay. Have fun."

"Charlie." She's watching him.

"What?"

"No *Minecraft*, okay? Straight to bed."

"Okay."

"I mean it."

"I know."

We both wave as she opens the door.

"Who was that? Did someone come over?" Grandma sticks her plastic-bag-covered head out of her room.

"Mom just went to get something at the pharmacy," I say as Charlie bounds up the stairs to *Minecraft*.

Grandma's face goes tight. "She's going on her own? Go with her, Grace."

"Why? She seemed fine."

She steps out of the room in her green dressing gown, waving her hand at me. "Go, Grace, before she drives away. She shouldn't drive alone, not this late at night."

"But —"

"Go!"

I grab my coat and run out the door as Mom turns the ignition in the Acura.

∗

She drives with her window cracked open so that her hair flutters around her face. The lights from passing cars slide over her.

"It's a sleep aid," she says. "Something with melatonin."

I turn the heat on low.

"Dr. Bansal suggested it," she says.

"It helps?"

"Yes." She shoulder-checks and changes lanes. "But it's also nice to get out of the house. I've had enough of prisons for a lifetime."

"What if there's a reporter?"

"Oh, there won't be. It's ten o'clock at night and the place is in a strip mall."

"You're not wearing a hat or anything."

"I have one in the trunk. I always keep one in the car."

I should have known that. "A reporter found me at school," I say.

Her head whips around. "What? Were they on school grounds?"

"No, I was a block away."

"Damn — did they give you their name? A card?"

"No."

"I'll call Roger in the morning. And Corporal Sanchez. It's not okay for them to harass you like that." She looks at me as we stop at an intersection. "Did you tell them anything?"

"No."

"Good." She stares ahead, lost in the conversations she's going to have with the people in charge.

An ambulance flies past us, lights flashing but without its siren.

I wonder what to say next. There are so many things to choose from.

"Listen, Grace," she says in a low voice, as if someone might be listening in. "I want to apologize for the argument we had at your photography show in April."

I'm surprised enough not to comment.

"I shouldn't have flown off the handle the way I did. You were right. You deserved more respect, more of a chance to explain yourself."

She moves the car through the intersection but doesn't say anything else, maybe waiting for me to respond.

I still say nothing. Does it even matter, that stupid part of the argument? Is that all she thinks it was about? "Why would you even take a call at your kid's event?" I ask.

Her hands grip the wheel. "I recognized the name on the display from your class list. I thought it might be important."

"But the first call," I say. "The police said there was one before. When I was up presenting."

She doesn't answer.

"Was it him?"

The words sit heavy between us.

Her mouth opens for a moment, but no sound comes out. "I was so angry that he interrupted the show."

I feel punched in the gut. He is suddenly in the car with us.

"I told him he crossed the line and I hung up on him. I was so angry."

She pulls to the side of the road and the Acura jerks to a stop.

I get ready for shouting, ready to unclip my seat belt — panic starts to freeze my muscles. Has she been triggered?

But she stares at the steering wheel as if not seeing it, and the air turbulence from passing vehicles shakes the car.

"Mom?"

"I was so angry at him," she says. "I still am. Sometimes I hated him so intensely. The times he wouldn't speak to me for days for saying something he didn't agree with. Or not let me eat." She rubs her face with both hands. "But he was also right about some things. He was the only one who …" She looks at me and her face is wet. "He knew a me that no one else did. It might be impossible to understand, but it's true."

My ears ring. Nothing feels quite real. The car shakes again. "But, Mom," I say. "Did he hurt you?"

Her breathing quiets and I realize she's been taking quick, shallow breaths. She pulls on her fingers. "Sometimes."

There's nothing but the sound of the Acura's engine ticking as it cools, a car swiping past us. Mom's admission hanging in the air.

I feel like I'm unlearning who she is, what happened while she was gone — taking down the bricks of who I've always known her to be, one by one. But I don't know if I can handle the things I'll have to know in order to rebuild.

She seems somewhere else, her eyes searching the dark on the other side of the windshield. "He pushed me once and I hit my head and passed out. I woke up on the deck, in the rain." She closes her eyes. "The drops felt like cold needles. It's the most alone I've ever felt."

I want to cry but I force it down. This is more important. I'll cry later. "Mom," I whisper, thinking she might be disoriented, "you're safe now."

The car is still and for a moment the road beside us is deserted. Far off, lights from a dealership flash red and blue.

Then her sobbing is like a desperate animal, and her

shoulders hunch around the sound. She shrinks in the seat. Seeing her, hearing her, makes me desperate in my skin, itching to get out, to get away. I should be comforting her, hugging her, but I can't. If I touch her, I might dissolve, too.

"I'm sorry," I say, my body shaking. "It's okay. You're safe now. I'm sorry."

She wipes her eyes and inhales deeply. Exhales, and I hear her lungs shudder. "I shouldn't have told you that."

"It's okay."

"It's not. There are things that are more damaging to know than not know. For you and Charlie."

I can't say I want to know it all, because suddenly I don't know that I do. It's worse than I thought, and not just the details. It's worse because of the deconstructed mother I currently have. The certainty I used to carry around is gone, a bunch of painful questions in its place. "Let's go home," I say. I wonder what Dr. Bansal would say if he were here.

"No." She finds a tissue and blows her nose. "I need the sleep aid."

"It'll be there tomorrow."

"I need to sleep tonight."

Silence fills the car. She presses her fingers to her eyes.

"Do you have nightmares?"

She nods. "But they've been getting a little better since I started the new therapy." She puts the tissue back in her pocket. "I'm sorry to scare you like that." She puts the car in Drive and grips the wheel. "I'm all right." We drive quietly for a few moments and then she says, "I'd like to put some music on, if that's okay."

"Sure."

She finds a station with a weird jazz song, lots of offbeat drumming. Complicated enough that I can't follow the rhythm.

78

The hallway simmers with Friday afternoon conversations — everyone ready to escape, the idea of the weekend already influencing noise level. I keep my head down as Trent appears on my right, laughing and oblivious to me. His voice is both joyous and hyena-like. Two more doorways and I'll be at my locker. After my locker I can get out of here.

Then Trent calls out, "Hey, My! Are you coming to Sasha's tomorrow night?"

I stop and become a rock in the stream, people flowing around me.

Mylo's three feet away, watching me. He looks as surprised as I probably do, but he pulls his face together more quickly. His eyebrows unbunch and one corner of his mouth curves up. Is he smiling at me?

Trent reaches him and claps his shoulder. "Hey, you coming?"

Mylo turns away and says something in reply that I can't hear.

Then the stream sweeps us in opposite directions.

✳

Sasha's sent me a message on Jungle: *I'm having a party at my house Saturday night. Want to come? It would be fun to hang out!*

I wonder if Mylo's told her anything about me, or if my life is just elevating me to a new status. Or maybe Sasha's just being nice — I guess that's possible, too. But the idea of being in a house filled with people from school who all have distorted theories about my drama and want to know which one of them is right seems like the worst way to spend an evening.

I can't, I reply. *Thanks, though. See you Monday.*

79

I don't eavesdrop so much as pass by Grandma's room as they're talking, a conversation whose perimeter I walk through unknowingly until I'm already inside its gravitational pull.

"But things don't have to be like that," Mom is saying.

"Don't they? I have a job to get to — they've been waiting for me — and you have the job of getting your life on track."

I stand back from the doorway, out of view.

"But can't you push it back a few weeks? They've been flexible before."

There's a pause. "They've been waiting this whole time." Grandma sighs. "I know those months were out of everyone's control, honey. But I have to do it now."

"Is this about money? Don't lie to me."

I hold my breath. I've never imagined Grandma having a problem with money.

"I lost quite a bit last year when the Argentina thing fell through." Grandma has lowered her voice. "At this point I either go or I break the contract, and I can't afford to break it."

Another pause.

"I'll cover the cost."

"No. I can manage it. It's not the worst timing, anyway. You need to be focusing on your family and getting back into the game."

"It's not a game."

"Come now, you know what I mean. Roger's itching to get you back at work. It's a wonderful opportunity, a chance to really move on."

One of them walks across the room and I press myself against the wall.

"At any rate, I've booked a flight for next week. They've given me until Thursday, which is very generous."

"Mom, let me help you. Just let me think about everything, okay? I'm sure there's a way."

"Honey." Grandma's voice is soft. "Is it really so important that I stay?"

"Yes," Mom says. "I'm making progress, and Grace — I see how you two have bonded. It means a lot. Doesn't it?"

"Of course it does."

It sounds like they're hugging. I can't remember the last time they've talked like this.

One of them walks to the door and I slip down the hall and around the corner.

80

It's a jailbreak of sorts, except we don't call it that.

Iris picks me up and we drive to Camas Hill. There's a grocery bag full of snacks on the backseat. I wonder if some of them are expired earthquake supplies.

"So have you talked to Mylo yet?" Iris's hair is bunned on top of her head and her freckles stand out in the gray, overcast light.

"No."

"Why not?"

"We made eye contact in the hall the other day."

"And?"

"That's it."

"He hasn't been to HackAttack in weeks. I texted him and apologized for freaking out at the fundraiser and I thought we were cool. He seemed fine with it. But now, nothing. I'm kind of worried about him."

That makes me feel horrible. I shrug.

She pulls into a parking spot at the top of the hill. "Do you think he has anyone else to talk to? Like, besides his entourage at school, who you told me aren't sensitive types?"

Now I feel bad about describing Sasha & Co. that way. I'm not sure how I feel about them anymore. I shrug again.

"Shrugging is not an answer."

"It's what I do when I don't want to reply."

"What are you, six?"

I reach back for the snacks and pull them onto my lap. In the middle of the parking lot, a couple of crows are harassing an empty chip bag. "So you think I should just call him like everything's normal and nothing happened?"

"No, I don't think that."

"Then what?" I've had this feeling before. The uncomfortable reminder that Iris is smarter than me when it comes to a lot of things.

She puts her keys in her jacket pocket and opens her door. "Well, just think about it, I guess."

We hike up to our spot — a flat area with views of the Salish Sea and the smaller islands between us and the mainland. This is where we sometimes imagine our homestead would be. There's a Garry oak meadow below and an outcrop of rock above that blocks some of the wind. We sit on the gravelly ground and go through the snack bag. The clouds are a soft white ceiling above us. It's not summer anymore.

"I think she's going to go back to work," I say, tearing into a bag of pretzels.

"Already?"

"I don't know when, but I heard her and Grandma talking. They want her back badly."

"And you think she'll go?"

I start to shrug and stop myself. "It's weird — before she was abducted, I would have said of course she'd go back to work — it's her life, it's what makes her *her*."

Iris chews on a chocolate bar. "And now?"

"I don't know," I say. "It feels like there's more going on. She seems really conflicted but not just because of recovering." I haven't told her about the trip to the pharmacy because it still feels too fresh, too personal. Plus, I don't really want to say out loud what Mom told me. It still gives me waking nightmares when the images flash through my mind.

I shut my eyes as the wind blows cold in our faces. "Now I kind of can't imagine her back at work, which is so weird. Right?"

She doesn't reply to that but taps me with her half-eaten chocolate. "Trade."

I pass her the pretzels.

"So I've been wondering something," she says after a while.

I take one bite of chocolate and my mouth feels uncomfortably sweet. "What?"

"You've never really explained why you don't like what she does for a living."

I look at her. "Who says I don't like it?"

It's her turn to shrug. "It's just a vibe I got."

"Well, it's wrong." Now I'm annoyed with her again.

"Okay," she says and crunches a pretzel.

I don't feel like eating the chocolate anymore, so I wrap it up and put it back in the bag.

A motorbike starts up in the parking lot, grumbling and then roaring down the hill.

"But seriously," she says. "You have not one but two celebrity family members. Isn't it a little odd that you dislike what they do so much?"

"I don't dislike it!" I don't mean to raise my voice, but I have. "I just don't find that kind of thing particularly thrilling. Kind of like how my mother and grandmother can't understand my attraction to astronomy. We're different people."

Iris is watching me, a pretzel in her hand. The wind blows the baby hairs around her face.

"Can we not talk about this right now?" I say. "I need a break from family analysis."

"Sure," she says.

"Are you packed yet?" I ask, throwing a rock into the scrubby grass.

"Come on. Don't be like that."

Somewhere behind us, the crows are cawing to each other. "Sorry. I want a take back."

"Granted." She rustles in the bag. Her face is focused as she searches.

I look away down the hill. "I'm already missing you."

"I know. But I'm not even a little bit gone. Besides, you might get into a university on the other side of the country. What will I do if I get back and you're in Toronto?"

"Be depressed."

"Terribly. And it'll be all your fault."

"I'm hopeless."

"The worst."

"But it's actually true," I say and the weight of it sits on me.

"What?"

I rest my forehead on my bent knees. "I have this horrible

feeling that I've been blind to so many things for months. I can't rely on my perceptions anymore — it's like all my understanding of people has been wrong. I've used the wrong lenses or data or something." She's watching me, confused. "Never mind," I say.

She brushes dirt off her pants. "What do you really want right now?"

"I don't know."

"Try."

I massage my temples. "Kombucha."

"Really?"

"And to have a superpower where I could understand what everyone is thinking."

She crosses her legs into Lotus pose. "I don't think that would always be so great."

"Probably not."

The wind rustles the bag between us and Iris pats my knee. "But if you really want kombucha, we can make that happen."

81

Mom's in the kitchen when I get home, a sight I'm kind of getting used to now. There's something boiling on the stove, and she looks up from a heap of vegetables on the counter to smile at me. "How's Iris?"

I reach for a carrot. "Good. Fun. Perceptive."

She pauses in her chopping to ponder that. "She is. I've missed seeing her." She puts the knife down. The same one Grandma wielded with such terrifying ineptitude. "And you? How are you, honey?"

I shrug because apparently that's what I do now when there's too much to say.

"I didn't consider how long this would take," she says, pointing to the open cookbook on the counter. "Vegetable lasagna seemed like a good idea an hour ago, but now I'm not so sure."

Being overambitious in the kitchen must be genetic. "Uh, Mom," I say, "you know we have, like, eighteen lasagnas in the freezer? It was the go-to condolence-slash-celebration dinner from all the neighbors."

"Oh God, really?"

"Plus, Charlie won't even go near it."

"I was going to make mac and cheese for him."

"Good plan. But we kind of developed an aversion to lasagna while you were gone. It was ..." I lean on the counter and crunch my carrot. "You kind of had to be there."

She looks at me in bewilderment, but then a smile sneaks the corners of her mouth up. Then she starts laughing.

I start laughing, too, and almost choke on a mouthful of carrot.

*

We work on the lasagna together — two sauces, three kinds of cheese, sautéed vegetables and boiled pasta laid out on the pan to receive it all. It smells good and I suspect I'll want to eat it when it comes out of the oven, regardless of my last experience with this dish.

"You know, we used to cook together when you were little," Mom says as we're cleaning up the mess. "At first you loved inventing your own recipes and cooking them in the microwave."

I can't remember this at all. "How old was I?"

She tosses carrot peelings in the compost. "Four or five, maybe."

"What did I make?"

"Oh, sludges made from flour and milk and sugar. You'd bring them to me with a spoon and I'd have to eat this congealed mass of starch like it was delicious. You were so proud, how could I not?" She wipes the counter with a cloth. "I can still see your little face grinning at me."

I don't know how to feel about this me I can't remember. And the her I hadn't expected.

"After that I got you a baking kit and we made things together."

"Like what?"

"Cookies and cakes and smoothies. We made fruit salad a few times, and I taught you how to use a knife safely."

I've never thought about where and when I learned that. And to think I gave Grandma a knife lesson just a few weeks ago.

She peers through the oven window at the lasagna. "I thought it was important that you do it right, especially since you were hell-bent on cooking all the time. You'd get the stool and find your baking kit and start cutting things all by yourself. I was terrified you'd cut off a finger."

I stare at my hands. "How come I don't remember any of this? I had no idea I was so into cooking."

"No one remembers everything from childhood. Apparently I loved running naked through the house when I was four, which I have no memory of, but your grandmother won't let me forget it."

I open the fridge for orange juice. "Ugh, Grandma." I pull out the jug and get a glass, gesturing to Mom to see if she wants one. She nods. "It feels like that was a totally different person," I say. "That kid who baked and cut up things and microwaved paste." I don't have the courage to add, *and a different kind of you for helping me do it.*

She's quiet for a moment, and I start worrying that the easy conversation we've just had — the first one in a long time — has led to another emotional wall. But then she says, "We're all made up of different versions of ourselves, Grace. Different parts that we outgrow or hang on to or hide." She tucks her hair behind her ears. "Dr. Bansal and I have been talking about that a lot."

There it is: the open door and the answers beyond it. What has she been talking about in therapy? What do the different versions of her have to do with her abduction?

I'm about to open my mouth when she says, "The first time you came to the station you were about the same age — maybe six. Do you remember that?"

I shake my head.

"You were so excited to see it. I'd just gotten a promotion and a new office and you ran around peeking into all the rooms, trying to guess which one was mine."

I lean over the counter as the smell of baking lasagna fills the kitchen.

"And at one point we lost sight of you, which was odd because you were kind of a timid kid — you didn't like exploring where I couldn't see you. We searched everywhere, and finally someone told us you were in the production studio." Mom takes a sip of juice, looking at me. "You were sitting behind the desk, pretending to read the news."

"You're joking," I say in shock.

"I'm serious. Yasmin could tell you. She was there."

I push off from the counter. "But why would I do that? I never liked anything to do with your job."

Mom's watching me.

I drop my head. "I'm sorry. I didn't mean it like that. I'm just surprised."

She comes around the counter. "So was everyone there. You were usually shy and there you were, pretending to read from this piece of paper in this huge studio with the lights shining down."

It's kind of unnerving to know this. I think back to the other versions of me there were — the spelunker me, the fossil hunter me. It's like they were outfits I tried on and then discarded.

Now she's standing there studying me in that way Iris described all that time ago in her car. She's looking into me, so far that I feel exposed.

"I can't believe you're in your last year of high school," she says in that way adults do when they're actually thinking about how old they've become in comparison. "It's not fair."

"I know," I say, because I can understand what she means. "But fairness is a social construct. Like time."

82

It's a butterfly wing, iridescent green with brown underneath, divided into delicate segments that curve down and escape the photo's edge. I'm sitting at my desk, trying to get into some biology homework, but all I can do is stare at his picture on my phone.

Then the in-progress dots start blinking and my pulse beats against my skull. Just like there's been no distance, no argument. *I didn't take this one. I found it online. It's a green-banded swallowtail.*

I know what this is. I've felt it, too: the need to show someone this amazing thing you've found, to share the astounding existence of it, or else you might explode. I've been like that with space stuff for years. *It's beautiful*, I text back.

He replies right away. *I'm going to Constance Pond in an hour. Will you meet me?*

*

It's September, so the sun is still bright but the warm air has that undercurrent of coolness. The sun sparkles on the water, but I'm sure it's too cold for swimming, and anyway, that's not why I'm here. It feels like that time we swam was in an alternate universe. So many things were different. The light and the dark have been reversed — my mother was missing, but we found each other, and now she's back, but we're the ones who are broken.

He sits on the grass beside the water, his legs crossed and his phone in his hand. The wind ruffles his hair. It's grown longer than I've ever seen it, down almost over his ears, touching the base of his neck. I hope he's not following Trent's hair advice.

"Hey," I say.

He turns and his eyebrows rise up and I am filled with the urge to go over and touch them with my thumbs. "You came," he says.

I walk over and sit beside him, leaving a a bit of space between us. He smells like herby soap.

"So," I say, looking at the rippling water. I'm glad I wore my cardigan.

"Yeah," he says.

I want to ask if there's anything new on his dad, if his mom changed her mind about the search, but judging by Mylo's energy, there's no happy reunion around the corner.

I get why he said what he did on the phone. It was awful, but I get it. I left the Perpetual Waiting Room. We were there together, and then I got to leave. My person came back. I can feel the loneliness he must have felt, suddenly being in there alone again. I reach out and touch his knee with the tips of my fingers.

He closes his eyes. "I'm sorry," he says. "I was such an asshole."

His phone is cradled in his hands, the image of a red butterfly on the screen.

"It's okay."

"It's not okay."

I take his hand and lace my fingers between his. "The level of okayness has fluctuated over the past few months, but at the moment it's good."

The wind picks up and the long grass around the pond waves and hisses. Clouds wander through the atmosphere.

"What are you thinking?" he asks.

I look at the sky. "That we're so lucky we have an envelope of gases protecting us from radiation and the harshness of space. You?"

He holds up the image on his phone. "How insane it would be to have six thousand lenses per eye."

"Yeah, amazing."

Somewhere far off, a dog barks.

"I've been coming here a lot since I got back from Montreal," he says. "It's kind of become the place where I sit with my dad and just be. I feel him here, you know?"

"Yeah. I know."

He puts his phone down on the grass. "He never saw my photos."

I lean slowly until our shoulders press together.

"Sometimes," he whispers, "it feels like it's too big to handle."

I squeeze his hand, put my head against his and listen to the wind in the cottonwood trees.

83

Mom's not there when I come home from school the next day. Charlie's watching a show in the TV room and Dad's printing something in his office. Grandma's out at some spa and won't be home until later. The house smells thickly of chili.

"Where is she?" I ask loudly enough that Dad can hear me. She's been going to her appointments by herself for a while, but they're usually earlier in the day and she comes straight home. It's strange to think of her wandering around town like a normal person.

"She had a meeting at ITV today," Dad says. "She's probably still there."

I stand in his office doorway with my bag dragging on the floor. "So she really is working again. She lied."

"She's not working," he says, swinging around. "It's a meeting."

"That's a euphemism for working."

At five forty-five she comes in the door, her coat over one arm, her hair pinned back smoothly. She may not have "worked" today, but she's GG Carter, Broadcaster. She's wearing heels.

I try to find something in her face that will give me information. It just looks smooth and made up.

"The meeting went much longer than expected," she says. "I'm sorry."

"Oh, no — are you going back to work now?" Charlie pads into the hallway.

She exhales and takes out a hanger for her coat. "No, it's not what you think."

"So what was the meeting about?"

She closes the closet and walks past us, touching Charlie's shoulder. "Have you eaten?"

Dad's gone to the sink and is washing lettuce. "Dinner's almost ready."

"I'm having PB&J," Charlie says.

I lean against the wall and watch her. She surveys the kitchen as if she's looking for something. Her eyes don't rest on any one thing. Then she starts pulling on her fingers one by one. She sees me watching.

"What happened?" I ask.

She looks confused, worried. Unfocused. "What do you mean?"

"You're stressed about something. Is it the meeting?"

Dad's watching her, too.

She clasps her hands together. "We discussed something at ITV that I want to explain to you."

Dad puts down the salad bowl.

Charlie hangs on the edge of the counter.

We all stay in our spots around the kitchen, anchored like stars in a constellation, waiting.

Mom touches her hair. I'm reminded of Grandma, the way they both reach with their long fingers. There are silver hairs among the blond, at the front, near her face. I wonder why she hasn't colored them away.

"What is it, GG?" Dad asks.

"We discussed doing a one-hour documentary special about my experience. Our experience. Done live-to-tape in studio with some footage filmed here in the house beforehand. It would be mostly me, of course, but everyone would be there. It sounds scary, I know, but I think you'll see it's not that big a deal …" She looks at Dad as she trails off.

She can't be serious.

"It would have to air in about a week," she continues. "It's soon, but that's the nature of the news."

"Really, GG?" Dad says slowly. "On prime time? Are there other networks involved?"

"A documentary. You're going to interview someone?" Charlie says.

"No, stupid, she's going to *be* interviewed," I say, not caring how vicious my voice sounds. "They want to publicize everything about her abduction so the world can know every detail." Even though we don't.

Mom puts her hand up more calmly than I expect. "Grace, just wait a minute."

But I can't wait. "How can you do something like this when not long ago you were unable to sleep at night?"

"You're going to tell everyone what happened on live TV?" Charlie asks.

"Everything will be prepared," Mom says. "There'll be a contract and exclusivity agreement. The interview will be carefully thought out."

The words she's using are all too familiar. She's gone back and has lied about it. "This is insane!" I shout. "I can't believe I thought you'd changed."

I see my words' moment of impact. Mom takes a step back. She swallows whatever she was going to say.

"Should we all sit down to talk about this?" Dad asks quietly.

The chili splutters on the stove as we stand there looking at one another.

*

A one-hour special. Extra staff on the project, a top national broadcaster flown in for the interview. It's time-sensitive, so the taping will be in six days. We'll all have to be made presentable — wardrobe and makeup. We'll be at the station for several hours before the taping to get acquainted with everything. It's all incredibly elaborate bullshit.

We're sitting at the table, our dinner still unserved on the counter, and she's spelling it out, deepening my dread. "I know it's overwhelming and sudden, but I promise it will be okay. This will be good for us, I just know it."

The "woulds" have changed to "wills," meaning this is already a done deal; she's not asking us for our buy-in. "So we're hostage to whatever you want to do?" I say. "We have to be a united family on TV, *'coming together to heal.'*" I do exaggerated air quotes. "That's the story you want to project?"

"Grace." It's Dad, looking at me from across the table, but I can tell he's conflicted, too. His hair is up on end where he's been raking his hand through it. "Is this a financial move, GG? Are they pressuring you with money?"

"No, honey. It's not about that."

"Is it a promotion thing for Roger? This will be incredible for his ratings."

"It's a story that needs telling. He knows that." She pauses. "I know that."

"Good God!" I say. "So now it's just a story for people to consume. Not *our* lives, *our* nightmares. We'll be displayed for everyone to see and talk about. Why not write a fricking book while you're at it?"

She folds her hands on the table. Her nails weren't painted yesterday.

"Holy crap," I say. "Are you going to write a book *as well*? This is unbelievable."

Dad puts his hand up as if he's a cop who can stop my words in midair.

"There's no book," Mom says. "But you're right about the story part. I know this might seem strange, but it's actually the most efficient way to get the truth across. This is my chance to tell what happened. Yes, we'll have to be on TV and the world will see us, but after that it's done. We will have set the record straight."

I think about the comments online, gossip in the hallways at school, Sasha and Melissa always asking, watching. I think about all the things I still don't know myself. She won't be able to hide from questions in the recording studio. Maybe we'll finally get the truth. All of us. I just wish it didn't have to be like this.

She sits back in her chair, eyes on me. "It's a way to be in control of the story because people will hear it from the source."

"A kid at my school said his dad said you were a spy," Charlie pipes up.

"That's exactly what I mean," Mom says.

"You *are* a spy?"

"No, honey. But there are all kinds of stories out there, and no one can set the record straight but me. Us."

Dad says nothing, just stares at the crack in the table where the middle leaf fits in.

Then the front door opens and shuts. A voice calls, "Grace? Andrew? Hello?"

We all look at each other.

"What's going on?" Grandma stands in the doorway smelling of coconut and mango and holding a bag full of spa products.

84

Mom goes to bed early with a headache, and I escape to my room to tell Mylo about the interview. He's just gotten home from HackAttack, which he's finally returned to after Iris prodded him for the twentieth time. I suspect it also has to do with Constance Pond and the afternoon we spent there talking. Whatever it is, I'm glad he's back, that we're moving further away from the weirdness. I've missed talking to him on the phone.

"This is nuts," he says when I finish describing what will happen six days from now. "And you're obviously not happy about it."

"You got that from my enthusiastic tone?"

"And the swearing."

"It's a nightmare and I have to be in it. I just want to wake up and find it was something my brain invented."

"But ..." he says.

"But *what*?"

"Uh, don't do that."

"Do what?"

"You're getting ready to bite and I haven't even spoken."

"I'm not going to bite. I'm just furious."

"I know. But … what if your mom's right?"

I growl into the phone.

"Nice kitty. I'm just saying, she has a point. My mom's dealt with setting records straight, too."

"But my mother could do that on her own, couldn't she?"

"Yeah, but aren't you part of the story? Your whole family?"

"But it wasn't our choice to be in it!"

"Was it hers?"

His question stops me. My heart beating in my chest feels like the only moving thing in the house. Was it her choice? This is the question. *The* question. I can't answer it. Only she can.

"Grace?"

And maybe she'll have to answer it in front of millions of people. And I'll have to be there watching her when she answers and that means *everyone will know.* Oh my God.

"Hello?"

"I'm here," I say.

"Are you still an angry tiger or whatever?"

"No," I say. "I'm just angry me."

85

Sasha's at my locker when I get there on Monday morning. The weather has finally cooled off, and she's wearing an immaculate blue sweater and smoky eyes. It's too much perfection this early in the day.

"I heard something," she half whispers, "about an interview your mom might do? My cousin's girlfriend works at ITV." Her fake eyelashes flutter. "She's just a receptionist, but it was a rumor she heard."

I close my locker so hard that it bounces open again. "And you want to know if it's true."

She takes a jumpy step back. "Well, I didn't believe her, obviously. I wanted to hear it from you."

"Hear what?" Mylo appears beside us and smiles, catching my eye. "Some hot gossip, Sasha?"

I can't think of a quick comeback. This is the first time he's come up to me at school, and I'm not prepared for his magnetism. The stomach butterflies are back.

"Oh, hey," Sasha says, batting him away. "We were just talking about some girl stuff. Never mind." She winks at me. "I'll see you in chemistry, Mylo?"

"Yeah, I guess." He leans past her and kisses me slowly on the mouth. "But maybe Grace doesn't need girl stuff right now, okay, Sash? Just cool it." He winks at me and walks away down the hall.

I allow Sasha two seconds of shocked silence before I walk in the other direction, to history.

86

That night I hear their voices sparring on the other side of my wall. There's a pause and then more heated words too muffled to hear. The dull thud of the en-suite door closing.

It's late and no one else is up. I pad out into the hall and stand a few feet from their door, which is pulled against the frame but not all the way closed.

"Andrew," Mom says in a murmur that's supposed to carry across the room. Dad must be in the en suite. "Dr. Bansal agreed. I wouldn't say yes to this if he hadn't said it was all right."

"But that doesn't make it a good idea. Psychiatrists have been wrong before."

"An hour ago you told Roger you were supportive of the special!"

"He's your boss, GG. I'm not going to tell him I don't want you to do something. Don't put me in that position."

"But —"

"I just don't think it's the right time for this. Maybe in a few months, when the kids have settled more and you're more secure emotionally."

"I'm doing fine —"

"But what about the rest of us?"

She doesn't answer.

I measure the silence in breaths. One, two.

"Maybe this has been just as hard on me and the kids as it has been on you. The times I almost couldn't ..." His voice cracks and trails off and I find my throat aching for him, this guy who tried so hard to hold it together for us.

She's murmuring something. It sounds like they're touching.

"It just seems like such bad timing, GG."

"The worst and the best. It has to be now, Andrew, while the story is still in the headlines."

"Always about headlines."

"Honey, that's the way the industry works. Plus, with the things that are going around on social media right now, the story needs to be set straight."

He clears his throat. "And our kids? What the hell are they going to be asked?"

"I've made sure there'll be no inappropriate questions. I was very clear about that. It's airing at 7:00 p.m."

A small silence. "You've been so quiet about everything that happened, GG."

"I know."

"What makes you think you can just blurt everything out on live TV? This isn't the same as broadcasting. I just don't get it. Are they pressuring you or something? Is it about the money? You can tell me."

She doesn't answer and I lean in closer. Her voice, when she speaks, is almost too quiet to hear. "I negotiated the deal with them today. They agreed to my terms. It's done."

"The deal?"

"My new plan."

"But," Dad says, "I thought that was just thinking out loud. You said it was a wild idea. You were scared."

"You said you supported it."

"Of course I do. One hundred percent, if it's what you want. But …"

I put my ear as close as possible to the crack without touching it.

"I need to do this," she says. "I've been waiting all my life to."

87

The unimaginable thing is, we could be living inside a black hole. We know so little about what's inside one that almost anything is a good guess. But one guess is that black holes contain countless universes, like bubbles in a jar, and we are just one solar system in one galaxy in a supercluster among thousands inside a universe that could be one of such a huge number of universes we can't even imagine it. The multiverse. And all that inside a black hole.

I find this strangely calming. Or maybe it's the mind-bendingness that makes my brain give up on trying to rationalize anything. There's something meditative about it. Just millions of bubbles in a jar: universes upon universes. Containing mysteries.

*

I don't know what it is, I text to Iris, *but she's got some plan. I think she might be trying to get a bigger job or something. Using this stupid interview as a way to market herself.*

Do you know that?

No. I'm theorizing.

But theories require more than blind guesses.

What else do I have at this point? But I know the answer to that and I'm glad Iris doesn't answer. I have Mom, in the flesh. If I really want to know, I could ask.

But when you upset the jar of mysteries, all the bubbles spill out on the floor.

88

I'm a mess in first period — five hours' sleep, a bad-hair day and a knot in my back from lying funny in bed. I forgot to do my physics homework, and my good-student reflex is to feel bad, but really, who cares? I already know this stuff anyway.

The more immediately consequential thing is that everyone seems to know about me and Mylo now. I'm getting more looks and murmurs than the first day I was back at school. Mylo was going to meet me before class, but he texted to say he was running late and could we meet after. But Sasha's in my physics class and she's on me like a proton to an electron.

"So, hey, why didn't you tell me?" She's in my face and I can smell her toothpaste.

I'm filled with prickly annoyance. "Tell you what?"

"Uh, hello? How long have you two been hiding that?"

The annoyance starts to boil my insides. "I didn't know I owed you an explanation. For anything."

"Yeah, sure, you don't. But he's my friend and you're —"

"Not."

She stops and I can see her searching for another way in.

"Look, you've been nice to me," I say in a low voice, because even though there's the usual pre-class chatter in the room, people are watching us. "I think we have a decent rapport as far as acquaintances go. But I'm under no obligation to tell you anything and I probably won't. My business is mine. Yours is yours. Sound good?"

She doesn't walk away. "Yeah, okay." I have to give her points for being so chill. She surveys me from under her feathery eyelashes. "Holy crap, I get it."

I don't know that I want to hear this, but I raise my eyebrows in question.

She leans in again. "You're perfect for Mylo. I can totally see it. He needs someone who knows who they are, you know?"

Mr. Pierce calls out for everyone to settle down.

She takes a step toward her table. Despite her ridiculous lashes, she's hard to dislike up close. "Thank you," I tell her and she smiles back.

After biology I have a spare, and Mylo texts that he's in the parking lot waiting for me.

Why are you waiting outside? I reply.

Do you really want to spend the next eighty minutes in there?

Nope.

Me neither.

*

His car smells like spearmint gum. He's superhot in a gray jacket with a green T-shirt underneath. I just want to touch him, to put my face against his. It feels like it used to — like sanctuary and adventure and surprise, but also deeper. There are layers I didn't anticipate.

"Hey," he says, leaning over to kiss me. "I need donuts."

*

We drive for a while listening to pop songs in a Scandinavian language, and then we come around the corner of the strip mall and the sign — Mabel Bakes — comes into view behind a flapping banner for a dry cleaner.

"It looks kind of sketchy, but I promise it's not." He opens his door. "Coming?"

The bakery is small, old and empty of people except for a gray-haired woman who wears one of those old-fashioned aprons that has frills on the shoulders.

"Hey, Mabel," Mylo says. "A raspberry jam and" — he turns to me — "what will you have?"

I survey the racks, overwhelmed by choice and the smell of baked goods. "I'll have raspberry, too."

Mabel smiles at us and bags our donuts. "On a break from school?"

"You know this is where I come for sanity," Mylo says, handing her coins.

"Gosh, you're so like him." Mabel gives him a sad smile. She closes the old cash register and it pings. "And you're Grace, I assume? Mylo's told me a lot about you."

"He has?" I look at him. He's blushing the tiniest bit. I wonder exactly how much time he spends here.

"You've both been through a lot," Mabel says, her wrinkled hands on the glass counter between us. "You take care of each other, all right?"

*

Back in the car, the smell of dough filling the space, he takes a bite without explaining anything.

"What was that about?" I ask, my donut warming my lap.

"The best-kept secret in town," he answers with his mouth full. "They've been here for years but the sketchy location keeps them from becoming famous."

"And your dad …?"

He stops chewing to swallow. "He brought me here all the time. Mabel was his babysitter when he was a kid."

"Seriously?"

"So I go pretty often."

"And apparently you tell her about me."

He looks over. "Are you mad?"

"No, not at all. I just …" I don't know what I feel.

He crumples his now-empty bag and tosses it into the back-seat. "Can we jailbreak it up right now?"

"We kind of already are." I lick sugar off my fingers. The donut is really, really good. "Where were you thinking?"

He starts the car. "I have a place in mind."

*

We pull into the gravel lot at Hawksley Heights, a housing development that's been cleared of all plant life but apparently delayed in construction. White pickets poke out of the ground every few feet, and orange taping flutters in the wind. Clouds press in and most of the city is obscured. It looks cold and moonlike outside the car.

He cuts the engine and the car goes still.

"It's kind of lonely up here," I say.

He stares out the windshield, disappointed. "Yeah, sorry. I thought it would be clear." He watches the orange flagging tape flutter. "I like coming here for the view. You can see the Olympic Mountains and this big stretch of ocean, and it just reminds me to breathe, you know?"

"Yeah," I say, thinking of Camas Hill.

"My mom's decided to move on with her life," he says. "She told me she's never going to ask them to reopen the investigation, and that I should stop bothering her about it."

I touch the sleeve of his jacket.

"She says we need to go forward and she's doing it for me, but that just feels like such crap. She's doing it for herself, and she's delusional."

"Maybe she thinks it's what's best for you."

His eyes are bleak. "But does that mean she *knows* what's best? You can't just forget a parent — or a husband. Remember when you were a little kid and you thought your parents knew everything?"

"Yeah."

"It turns out they're just as messed up as we are." He stares out the windshield at the grayness. "So what's the fucking point?"

The black shape of a bird floats by in the distance, then disappears into the clouds.

"Mylo," I say. "Come here."

He leans his head over and I kiss the soft skin at his temple, his hair smelling of salon shampoo made too sweet in a lab. I whisper into his ear, "I get you." But I mean it in multiple ways. I mean *I understand*, but also *I'm lucky I have you*. Eloquence has deserted me, so I say, "I'm here," against his earlobe.

And he turns his face to me and says, "I love you."

Then our mouths are pressing together with the same left-over sugary bite. He breathes into me and I breathe back. The breaths we've been coaching each other on taking all these months. We are here. It's this. I consider that maybe there *is* nothing else.

We fumble our way into the backseat and fold ourselves into a tangle of limbs, our mouths searching and finding the other. His hands are warm on my back, my stomach. I reach under his shirt and feel the ladder of his ribs. It's not enough though, so we pull at each other's clothes, needing to be closer. Finally we're both shirtless and I can feel his heart beating against mine, these muscles that keep us alive, that never stop until we're dead. I read a stat once on how many beats the average heart makes in a lifetime. Something over three million. How many beats are we using up just staring at each other, trying to catch our breath?

His fingers run down my face, barely touching my skin. It's so gentle it makes me want to cry.

"I love you," I whisper. I kiss him, wanting to find enough, to be satisfied, but I'm not. I need more, and I know he does, too.

And it's fine — it's the rightest thing in the world — to be with him like this, to feel him speak against my ear and to answer and to do this together. It's what this now is for.

*

There's no way we'll make it back for our next classes, so we lie together in the backseat with our clothes back on and he presses his palm flat against mine. "Do you ever want to take off?" he asks.

"Run away?"

"I guess I mean it more theoretically. Some kind of escape that we don't currently have. Maybe time travel."

I push against his hand and he pushes back. At Star Club we talk about astronomy as time travel. Looking at light from space is by definition looking at the past. But he's talking about the kind of time travel that can never actually happen. The universe just isn't set up that way. "What would you do if you could travel back in time?" I ask, but I already know what he'll say.

"Go back to when my dad was still here and tell him not to go. Or go further back and stop him from drinking so much." He traces the lines on my palm. "What about you?"

I hesitate. "I don't know."

"Would you stop your mother from being abducted?"

I sit up a little higher. "Yeah, of course." But it feels like I'm saying that for the wrong reason. Because it's what I know he wants to hear.

The clouds have risen over the edge of the moon-scaped

hill and surrounded the car, pressing like they're actually solid.

I don't know how I feel about my answer. It's not so clear anymore.

89

I wake up to someone compressing the edge of my bed so that I roll toward them. I open my eyes to the autumn sun streaming through my window and see Mom in it, wearing a gray turtleneck.

"Morning," she says.

I mumble something back.

"Can we talk?"

"About what?" I croak.

She adjusts her position on the mattress. "Yasmin just called me to say there's some misleading information online right now about Felipe, and I wondered if you'd seen it."

"I haven't."

She doesn't look that relieved. "Well, you might hear about it at school."

I roll onto my side. "Why don't you just wait until the interview and then you can clear his name for the whole world. You're kind of the only Felipe expert there is."

"Grace." She puts a hand on my blanket-covered hip. "I want to talk to you."

This is exactly what I wanted. What I know I need. But I'm

afraid — afraid of what people are saying online and what she's going to tell me. What if it changes everything? It's amazing how comfortable the status quo is, even when I know better.

"He was a complicated person, more complicated than the media or online theorists could imagine."

I rub away the sleep from my eyes and sit up. If we're going to do this now, I need to be ready, not lying around in a post-sleep haze. When I'm settled, she holds out the glass of water from beside my bed. I down it and then say, "Okay, but if you're going to tell me all about his abusive childhood or something, I don't want to hear it. I'm not interested in feeling sorry for him."

"Well —"

"He hurt you, Mom. He imprisoned you for months and deprived you of food. I'm glad he's dead. I don't care how much Stockholm Syndrome you have. You won't change my mind."

She studies the rumpled fabric of my blanket. "I don't have Stockholm Syndrome."

"I didn't mean … I just know what you're trying to do."

She looks at me. "Do you? You know what I'm trying to do?"

I let out a breath. "No."

Somewhere downstairs, Charlie laughs at the top of his lungs.

"What time is it?" I ask.

"After nine." She gets up from the bed and brings my swivel chair over to sit on.

I kick the blanket off my legs. "Fine. What are people saying about him?"

"Yasmin says there's a lot of talk of him being a murderer. There are a number of cold cases that people want to link him to. It's really disturbing, the things they're saying he did."

I can't contain my frustration. "Mom, the things he did to *you* are disturbing. What difference does it make if people try to link him to a murder? He's dead, and the murdered people are dead. If it's not true, it's not true, but it's nothing to do with us."

She's horrified. "What do you think those families will go through, trying to find out? Don't you understand what happens with stories like these? They develop a life of their own online, but real people are affected. I know — I've reported on them."

"But you don't think there's any chance he's connected to those cases?"

"He wasn't. I'm sure of it."

She seems to be waiting for me, or for some unknown thing, so I say, "Okay, so what do you want me to know?"

She leans forward so her elbows are on her knees. "I met him in 1992. He'd gotten his bachelor's degree in two and a half years and was doing his master's when I knew him, and we were both twenty-three."

"Intelligence doesn't make someone a good person," I point out.

"But Felipe was like no one I'd ever met. He had this energy. He was always moving, always thinking. And he made things — furniture, sculptures out of any material; once he made a tiny splint for a bird with a broken leg." She pauses and rubs her arms like she's cold. "He volunteered at a hospice and collected sea glass. He was an amazing human, Grace." She looks unspeakably sad. "I don't expect you to believe me because that Felipe was long gone when he drove me away in his car. But it was him, once."

"How is anyone going to believe you?" I ask. *And what does it matter?*

She clasps her hands together. "I've gotten in touch with some of the people we knew in university. They contacted me, actually. The police found a lot of people during the investigation. We remember the same fun, bright person. It's just that they all thought he was dead."

"How can he have changed so much?" I ask. "It seems impossible."

"He was intense even back then in a way that made me wonder sometimes. He'd obsess about things and get in these moods for days at a time. He had a temper. In hindsight, something was a little off."

"Did he hurt you then?"

"No." She's looking at my wall, the glossy posters of planets and the Crab Nebula that have been there for years now. I really need to update them. "He so badly wanted me to be happy. It was like his personal mission. I was flattered by it."

"So did he go crazy or something?" I ask. "Is that how you can explain the difference between the past and later him?"

"Dr. Bansal thinks he had several disorders. These things can take years to come out. But we'll never know for sure." She pulls on her fingers.

I want to ask her about the body. About why she had to see it. The questions push at my insides.

"My God," she says, "the day I got that email that he'd died in the boating accident ..." She pulls on a finger. "My whole body felt it. I hadn't expected to be so devastated."

"Why were you?"

She takes out a tissue and blows her nose. "He was a remnant of the time in my life when anything was possible. He'd wanted that for me. I didn't make the choice he expected and that's when we fought and drifted apart, but I never forgot him. I think I imagined sometime in the future I'd find him and we'd be friends or something." She crosses her legs. "But I got the email from his friend in Portugal and it leveled me."

"When was that?"

She chews her lip and the silence stretches out. I wonder if she's hitting her emotional wall. But then she looks me in the eye and says, "I got the email about his death three days after you were born, Grace."

I stare at her hands, so like Grandma's. Realization dawning like an electric charge on my skin.

"I had no idea it would hit me so hard. I grieved for weeks. And I was so shocked at my own reaction, I didn't want your father to think I still loved Felipe or something. Because I didn't."

"Oh my God," I say, sitting up straight. "It wasn't postpartum depression. You were sad about *him*."

She reaches out but I move away. "It was all mixed together. Nothing's ever clear during that time after birth. I was sleep deprived and hormonal and knowing he was gone, that the person who really knew the pre-journalism me was gone — it was like that part of me died, too."

"And what, you've been someone else ever since?" I get up from the bed and pace around, unable to be still. "Is that why you had to see his body? You cared that much, after what he did to you? Holy shit, Mom."

"You don't understand," she says. "I needed closure. He'd already died once for me. After everything that happened, even after all the horrible things he did, he was still my connection to the past, like it or not."

I don't want to sit or stand. I can't figure out where to put myself. "This is crazy. It's not normal."

"Honey, things are not always rational —"

I hold up my hand. "You say he was the only one who really knew you. What the hell does that mean? Have you told Dad this?"

"Your father and I have had long conversations about everything. He understands. He knows —"

"How can he understand? The way you're talking, it sounds like you never got over Felipe."

"That's not true." She swivels around to face me. "It's so much more complicated than that."

"I don't want complicated!" I shout. "I want simple and clear. And I don't want to know that for all this time we thought you had PPD, but you were actually grieving your long-lost boyfriend, who you cared about so much that you went nuts just to see his dead body. I don't want to know any more!" I walk out of my room and take the stairs two at a time. I don't stop, and then I'm out the door, walking up the sidewalk with no destination in mind. Just away.

Oh my God, she's going to say all this in front of the world. She's going to lay bare our whole family history. And we have to sit there and look supportive.

I reach into my pocket for my phone. This necessitates an emergency call to Iris. But after checking all possible pockets I let out a string of expletives and keep walking. I left my phone in my room.

90

I manage to stay out of conversation range with Mom for the rest of the day, and the next morning she and Dad take Charlie out to run errands. The house is quiet and bright with sunlight and it's easier to breathe with it to myself. I start to unload and then reload the dishwasher, the chore I agreed to do in order to stay home.

"Need some help?" Grandma stands in the hallway.

"I didn't know you were here," I say, then feel bad that I assumed she wasn't. "I mean, yeah. Help would be good."

"I had some emails to send." She comes closer and indicates the dishwasher. "Are we loading that thing?"

I hand her a stack of plates to put in. Something seems unusual, odd, until I realize she has a totally different perfume on. It's floral and fresh. Pleasant. "You smell ... unlike you," I say.

She raises a penciled eyebrow.

"Did you run out of your usual perfume?" I ask.

"What is it you like to call it? Eau de Toxic Fumes?" she asks, slapping my arm with the back of her hand. "I found a new one downtown. You like it?"

"It's acceptable," I say.

"Well, thank God."

We put the dishes away, something Grandma's managed to avoid almost the whole time she's been with us. I'm kind of impressed by her avoidance tactics.

She announced at breakfast that she's leaving this afternoon for L.A. Given what I overheard last week, I wasn't surprised, but I pretended to be because she looked like she wanted that. Even Charlie did a decent job of being sad.

Grandma puts a stack of side plates in the cupboard and closes the door. "I sense you and your mother are having trouble right now."

"No more than usual," I say, focusing on wiping a spot on a plate.

"She told me you walked out on a conversation."

She described it as a *conversation*? I put the plate away indelicately. "You weren't there."

She comes over and takes the cloth from me. "Grace, this is important."

I can't meet her eyes and I hate that. I'm not willing to cry right now.

"Honey, you need to listen to each other."

"Stop."

She holds my shoulders firmly. "Grace, it's all going to come out and it's going to be okay."

"At the stupid taping, yeah, in front of everyone." I wipe my eyes with the back of my hand. "How can she feel those things for him? Did she tell you? I don't know what story to believe anymore. I don't know who she is."

Grandma pulls me closer. "Honey, ask her. Listen to her. Now is the time."

I push away. "You keep saying that. What's happened to you? You were never this ... enlightened."

She laughs. "Grace, honey. Here's the thing I learned years ago, when your mother was young." She holds her hands out, as if demonstrating something. "Mothers and daughters exist in a relationship that's always moving. There's pushing and pulling, a back and forth, a circling around of arguments that never ends, and you know why? Because we're made of the same stuff. We know each other, we see ourselves in the other. It's how we're built."

I press my fingers against my eyes and count breaths.

She's still there in front of me when I'm done. "I'm old and annoying and leaving, but I can still be right about some things."

"Okay, Grandma," I say, letting her hug me.

"Okay what?"

"I'll think about your unsolicited advice."

She pats my cheek. "You're several steps ahead of her, you know. You'll see."

91

But there's no time to smooth things over with my mother before the camera crew shows up first thing the next morning to film the happy-family footage. Mom is frantically trying to put away magazines and shove the laundry room door closed. Dad is wiping the kitchen counter as if a few stray crumbs will show up on camera. Maybe they will. Who the hell cares.

The stylist has been here since before breakfast, her short, rotund frame somehow in all my sightlines no matter where I look. She complimented me on my long, thick hair and waited for me to be flattered. I pretended not to hear her.

Charlie has been instructed what to wear and his hair is brushed awkwardly to the side. He sits on the couch with the tablet, his socks too argyle to look at.

"Can you get dressed, Grace?" Mom asks breathlessly, flying past me as the crew comes in the door, darkly clothed and carrying cameras and fuzzy microphones, shouldering bags.

"I'm wearing what you asked."

She appraises me again. "I asked you to wear something seasonal and tasteful. A cardigan, maybe."

I'm wearing a gray dress and leggings. I am neutral and unassuming. I should be in a church right now.

"It's too sad," she says. "Can't you put on some color?"

"What do you want, me to match the fall leaves?" But she's already gone into the kitchen, where the crew are setting down their equipment and telling Dad that yes, they'd love some coffee.

Twenty minutes later, we are all assembled on the couch in the living room, shoulders back, heads turned the right angle. Yuri, the cameraman, jokes with Mom about lighting and some hilarious incident that happened on a shoot once. Mom laughs so warmly that it's impossible to tell she was stressed and nervous thirty minutes ago. She holds her hands in her lap so she can't pull her fingers.

"Now, this is just for an opening shot," Yuri says. "We'll do a bit where you laugh at something — Corbyn here is great at cracking people up — and then we can move on to shots around the house."

"Can you move over, Mom?" Charlie asks. "My leg's getting squished."

"We need you all on the same couch for this," Yuri says. "It'll be quick, I promise. Now, Corbyn, give them something to laugh about."

They film us in the kitchen, pretending that we always work together to make a fruit salad. Mom does the chopping. Charlie separates each grape from its stem. Then out in the front yard with our coats on, raking leaves they've had to pull off the trees because they haven't actually started falling yet. Charlie steps out of line at one point and jumps in the leaves and the crew think it's great and zoom in on him.

After an hour of demented faking it, the crew take a break to look over their footage and Mom and Dad murmur quietly in the TV room.

"Are we going to be done soon?" Charlie asks behind me, and I hit my arm on the door frame.

Mom emerges calmly. "Soon. There's just one more thing they want to get."

"What's that?" Charlie asks.

"They'd like to film you and Grace."

"Doing what?"

"Go have a look in the backyard."

I don't go, but a moment later Charlie's shout implies something unexpected.

Someone has set up a trampoline, walled like the safest possible castle, in the middle of the lawn. Charlie's already inside, scrambling to his feet and hollering his delight.

"Where the hell did that come from?" I ask. We stand at the sliding door and watch him.

"The crew brought it."

"So there's been a dedicated trampoline setup person here all this time?"

Dad whistles. "And those things are a pain in the butt, too."

"What are we supposed to do?" I ask. But I know the answer.

"Okay, GG," Yuri says behind us. "We're ready."

*

"I can't believe it." Charlie grins as I crawl onto the surface of the trampoline. "How cool is this?"

"Do *not* double bounce me."

"So just have fun for a minute," Yuri calls. "Then we'll get you to lie on your backs or something and be still."

"Do we get to keep it?" Charlie asks me as he bounces.

"Of course not. It's probably a rental." I keep my back to the camera. I don't give a crap what they say.

The camera guy moves around and catches me from the side.

I hate myself more with each bounce. I am a trained monkey in the circus. A soon-to-be televised circus.

"Okay, great. Now can you lie down together? You don't have to touch if you don't want to."

Mom and Dad are standing at the edge of the lawn, watching. I hate them for letting this happen. We're actors playing ourselves in a TV special. It's insane.

"This is kind of weird, right?" Charlie whispers. "The cameras."

"Understatement."

"You're mad at them."

"You should be, too."

He sighs. "Can't we just enjoy this beautiful trampoline?"

92

"It was so bad," I tell Mylo on the phone later. "So, so bad. I need you to save me."

"I wish I could."

"Just drive over here and take me away."

He laughs. "I can't."

"God, you're so decent. I hate that."

"But I love you."

I let the shiver reaction dissipate, then get it together and say, "I know, but that's not enough."

"It's not?"

"I mean, it's totally enough, but it's not going to help me with this problem."

"Maybe it will."

"Ugh."

"Are you nervous?"

"Yeah," I say. "It's terrifying."

"I know."

"I love you. Come over right now."

"I can't."

"Goddammit."

*

So, Grace, Iris's message ends abruptly, as if she's forgotten what she wants to say.

It's maybe thirty minutes since I hung up with Mylo. I'm eating leftover fruit salad out of a mixing bowl in my room because interaction with my family members right now will cause a fission reaction that could explode the house.

So, Iris, I text back. *I hate my life.*

She replies right away. *Mylo and I have been in discussion and we feel a jailbreak is needed.*

How about a lifebreak? Want to escape to Fiji?

We were thinking something with less plane involved. Your job is to make yourself free tomorrow at noon.

Tomorrow's the taping, Iris. There are like five super annoying and important things that have to happen.

But it's not until the evening, right? We thought you could use a break. A jailbreak.

I eat the last bite of fruit from the bowl. *I'll ask.*

Make it happen, Carter. We're counting on you.

Yes, sir.

93

After a dinner of takeout Chinese food, which no one really eats, Mom finds me in the hallway as we're heading for our respective rooms. She's changed into more comfortable clothes and pulled her hair back, and I think about what Grandma said. I try to see what part of me is in her. It must be well below the surface right now.

"Are you okay?" she asks, putting a hand on my arm. "I know that was a lot today."

"It was too much," I say, "but at least it's done."

"And after tomorrow it'll be finished. All behind us."

Except it won't be. The Mom who's returned from the abduction will always be here, so the abduction will be, too. The hope that this could fix everything is a crazy delusion, and the reality of that hits me like cold water.

"Grace?" She's watching me, searching my face.

"I need a break tomorrow," I say. "Iris wants to hang out, just for a little while, and I think it would help me de-stress."

Mom frowns. "It's going to be a busy day. Could it wait until Sunday?"

"Not really. It's kind of the point — she wants to be a source of calm in the crazy. It's just for, like, an hour. Please."

Mom takes out her phone and appears to be checking some kind of schedule. "The read-through of the interview questions is at two o'clock. Can it be before that?"

"Yes, totally. Thank you." I hug her and for a millisecond her body is frozen, then her arms come around me and I can't remember the last time we hugged like this. We've touched in so many other ways but not hugged. She rubs my back and I smell her hair and it all gets too intense, so I pull away.

"Just please make sure you're back before two," she says, clearing her throat.

"Yes," I say, already going down the hall to my room, ready to text Iris back. "Of course. I will be."

And half an hour later, when I hear her in the hall again, explaining to Charlie that Roger needs her for something at the station and she'll just be a few hours, I wonder how she's feeling about tomorrow. She must be more nervous than any of us. Or maybe she's not. Maybe this is the culmination of everything, the only way she knows how to process stories, things that happen to her.

I look out my window at the clear night sky, the brightest stars visible and the dimmest ones there but obscured by light pollution and smog and the atmosphere.

I grab my hoodie and the backpack containing my scope. It's been too long and I need to be out there.

This is how I process things that happen to me.

*

The air is cool and clear and I can breathe better outside than anywhere, so I sit on a rock in my fake-fur-lined winter boots, which is overkill because it's not that cold, and stare across the land to the shadows of hills in the distance. The crickets of summer have died and the only sound is a car now and then on a hidden road.

I set up the scope slowly, enjoying the familiar movements and clicks as parts slide into place. I love this machine. I love what it lets me see. I'm filled with affection for this inanimate object made of metal and mirrors that only works if a human eye looks through it.

I adjust things until I find the moon and fiddle with the focus. It's a waning gibbous moon, so a small portion on the right side is dark as the sun's light moves across to the left.

I remember the first time I really saw the moon through a telescope. It was at the planetarium, before I joined Star Club. The detail — all the valleys and craters, ridges and mountains — shocked me. I'd seen flat, two-dimensional pictures of it a thousand times but never really *seen* it. It's the closest thing to us, the object that creates our tides, our months, but we still know so little about it.

Something stirs the leaves below me. A deer maybe. They're around all the time, either sleeping tucked away somewhere or slipping silently through the trees to peer at you with their big eyes. I like knowing they're around.

I lean down to look through the eyepiece again. Wonder what my life will be like in twenty-four hours — the next time this part of our planet is in darkness, the moon a little less bright, one day closer to new.

94

My phone buzzes me awake the next morning.

It's Iris. *OMG*

I roll over and text back, *Why are you waking me up so early? Why are YOU up this early? You're not jailbreaking me now, are you?*

I just remembered today's Elizabeth Tasker's lecture. Did you ever reply to her email?

Crap. *No. I forgot.*

My parents are making me go to this stupid family thing, but you need to go. GO.

Iris, it's the taping. I got a pass for the jailbreak but I can't ask for more.

But ... maybe you could pop into the lecture for half an hour?

I wish. I doubt it.

But this is a one-time thing! It's HER! Are you scared to meet ET or something? Eeek, look what her initials spell!!

Crap. She knows me too well. I don't reply, which is itself a reply.

GET OVER YOURSELF AND GO!

*

Yasmin's in the kitchen when I come downstairs after debating with myself forever about how to ask if I can go to the lecture. The process is not going to be more fun with Yasmin here.

Dad's cooking scrambled eggs, one of his signature dishes, and Mom's reading something at the table while Yasmin looks over her shoulder.

"Morning," Dad says. "Got any plans on this regular old Saturday?"

I roll my eyes and take the plate of toast he holds out.

He leans in and murmurs, "It'll be okay, Gracie. I promise."

"You been talking to Grandma?" I mutter.

"What?"

"Nothing. She just said the same ridiculous thing to me before she left."

"It's going to be better after you've had breakfast, anyway."

"Why is *she* here?" I whisper.

"Yasmin? She's brought some notes from the meeting they had last night. Your mother's reading through some contract stuff."

I see Yasmin squeeze Mom's arm. They talk so quietly that it must be something important. "Dad," I say, pressing my forehead against his shoulder, "can we go see your glacier sometime?"

He shifts position and his arm goes around me. "My glacier?"

"The one you told me about that's receding. Maybe that doesn't narrow it down. The one on the mainland. I guess that doesn't help either."

He thinks for a moment. "The Stave Glacier? Yeah, sure. It's beautiful up there. But why?"

I push closer into him. "I'd just like to see it. Thanks for the eggs."

He kisses my hair.

Mom sees us and comes over. "You okay, honey?"

"Yeah, I'm fine." I walk to the kitchen table and set my plate down. "Actually ..."

Everyone's looking at me, which is not something I enjoy. "I need to go to a lecture," I say.

"A what?"

"There's a lecture today at Heaton by this amazing astrophysicist who I've been in touch with and I forgot to tell you it was today. She invited me personally and I really want to go. Just for a bit — not even the whole thing. I promise I'll be back in time."

Mom's trying to process; her forehead is furrowed. "Oh, honey, that's just not possible. You're already going out with Iris. We need to go over the interview and get everything ready. It's going to be too rushed."

"It won't be — I'll make sure I'm back. This is really important. She's so amazing and she's here all the way from Japan to talk."

"She's Japanese?" Dad asks.

"No, she works for JAXA," I say. "She's British."

Yasmin shuffles the papers on the table. "What's JAXA?"

"It's like the Japanese NASA."

She looks confused. "Oh."

"Grace, the answer is no." Mom crosses her arms over her chest. "It's too much today. I'm sorry. Can we get this person on the phone or Skype to talk with you?"

"Already done that."

"Well, I'm sorry, it can't happen today."

"GG." Dad takes Mom's hands. "Would it really complicate things so much?"

But Mom's face is set. "She needs to be at the read-through. It's important."

Yasmin's trying not to get involved; I see the way she's sorting the already-sorted papers. Like a news anchor does on TV.

"Yasmin," I say. "If I miss forty minutes of the read-through, will that ruin everything?"

She's half-startled, half-worried. "Oh, I don't know. It's not my place to say ..."

"But aren't you in charge of the schedule and everything?"

Mom steps in front of me, blocking my view. "Grace, I already gave you the answer. You'll have to find another time to talk with your scientist."

No one moves as we stare at each other. I can't tell what she's thinking, but I'm ready to stomp on her foot.

"Astrophysicist," I spit instead, slipping past her and past Yasmin, whose head is down in the papers again. "You can at least get that part right."

95

"So are you going to tell me where we're going or do I have to wait in suspense until we get there?"

Iris has all six bangles on. Actually, I count seven — the scale has officially been broken. Her hair is big and wild around her shoulders, and she's nodding along to the super upbeat music she's cranked on the stereo.

"Hello?" I ask. "Did you hear me?"

"I think suspense is a good strategy. It keeps it more interesting. But first we have to pick up your boyfriend."

That word momentarily disrupts my thoughts.

"It was his idea, you know." She finally turns the music down so we don't have to yell at each other. "He is sooo in love with you."

I look out the window as my face heats up.

"And I'm so in support of it," she says. "Just saying. Didn't I predict you'd be with him, way back when?"

"Yeah, you did."

"And am I not amazing at predictions in general?"

"Yes, you are."

"So by my careful calculations, you will be in a kick-ass

astronomy program by the time I get back from Tanzania and you and Elizabeth Tasker will be, like, doing some research together, or at least be friends. How's that?"

"Got any lottery number predictions?"

"Not at this time."

I sigh. "Iris, I just had a fight with my mom and I'm not even going to the lecture. I'm not" — I wave my hands around — "even a two on the bangle scale."

"The what?"

I point at her arm. "You're a seven today, which is rare."

She looks down at her arm, then back at me. "You measure my mood by the number of bangles I wear?"

"Listen, I want all those things to come true, but right now what I really want is for this day to be over. Tomorrow will be so much less complicated and awful."

She watches the road.

"I'm sorry," I say. "I don't want to ruin the fun. I love this. I love you."

"I know what you mean," she says. She turns onto Mylo's street. "How about we take it in small chunks. Hours. My mom does it this way with deadlines." She raises a hand from the wheel to count on her fingers. "This hour is for the jailbreak. The next hour is for you going home and getting ready for the read-through. The next is for eating a lot of sugary snacks, because, anxiety binge. The hour after that is for doing what-ever you have to do to be ready for the taping. The hour after that will be makeup and hair and whatever ..." She looks over at me. "Does this make sense?"

"Yeah."

"Can we try it?"

"Sure."

"Hey, there's your boyfriend. Go kiss him."

Mylo's waiting by the side of the road, a bunch of purple flowers in his hand. He looks so good that it makes me ache.

"For you," he says, holding out the bouquet when I get out of the car. "For, you know, luck."

I kiss him and wish we were alone. His arms wrap around me. My body's trying to tell me it will all be okay. Somehow.

As we drive to wherever we're going, the music loud again, my best friend and my boyfriend in the front, grooving to the beat, I look out the window and try to remember that everything's still happening in the galaxy right now. All the exoplanets going about their orbits and stars burning through their fuel supplies and asteroids shooting through space. It's all happening, all in motion right now. We're just three small life forms inside a metal frame going an infinitesimal distance at a spectacularly slow speed. I close my eyes and name the moons of Saturn.

"Grace?" Mylo has twisted around in the front seat. "We're here."

We're at the ice cream parlor. The place where we first sat together and I noticed how enchanting Mylo's eyebrows were. The place where he became a neutron star, which he has remained. He opens my door for me.

We all order sundaes with different things on top. Mylo and I share one side of the bench, my leg slung over his under the table. Iris keeps stealing my raspberries, so I take one of her brownie pieces. We talk about school and Iris's trip and

Mylo's photos, which he's just made a website for, and the people sitting next to us shoot us glares because we're too loud.

It's perfect, and I feel teary because no way was I going to get through today without being emotional at least five times.

"You okay?" Mylo says into my ear.

"Yeah."

"Do you need to go soon?"

"Yeah," I say. "Pretty soon."

"We'll be watching and cheering you on," Iris says, scraping the last bit of ice cream from her bowl.

"You could imagine us in the room, if that helps," Mylo says.

"It doesn't help." I push my half-finished sundae away. "I'd rather no one was there. But thank you, guys. You're the best of the best."

*

When they drop me off at home, they both hug me and say supportive things, but it feels like I'm going into battle alone. A battle I don't want to fight. As the car drives away, I feel a sickening dread. Another hour gone.

I walk into the house and there are voices and it takes me a moment to differentiate them. The TV's on. Charlie says something that sounds like he's arguing with it. Dad's on the phone in his office. I walk down the hallway and find Mom and Yasmin talking at the table. I guess she's staying all day. They both look up from pages of notes and stop midsentence.

"Hi," I say. "I'm back, so."

"Grace." Mom gets up, leaving everything where it is, and

taking my arm leads me out of the kitchen. "I wasn't sure if you'd come back," she says in a low voice.

"You said before two." I see she hasn't covered up the dark circles under her eyes yet. I guess the heavy TV makeup will be in a few hours.

"I know, but I wondered if you'd just …" She looks me in the eye. "I'm sorry about before."

I study the floor. I don't have any more energy to argue. I just want to get through this day.

"Your grandmother called me," Mom says. "To wish me luck and everything." She pulls on her fingers.

"Yeah, so?"

She tucks her hair behind her ear. "You should go to the lecture at Heaton. We can fit it in as long as you're back by five at the latest."

I stare at her. "Serious?"

"Yes," she says. "But on one condition."

"What?"

She clears her throat. "I come with you."

96

The sign outside the Douglas Building says, "Elizabeth Tasker, Astrophysicist, Finding Tatooine: Worlds with Many Suns, September 29 from 3 to 4 p.m."

The room is pretty full and there are still a few minutes before it starts. We inch along a row of four bearded men, probably university professors, and take the last two seats. On the other side of us are a woman and a girl maybe a few years younger than me.

Before we left the house I told Mom this was a stupid idea. Did she really think it was advisable to go out in public on the day of the taping when the documentary had been hyped all week? Her face was on promo things all over town. But she refused to change her mind.

As we sit down, I scan to see who might be watching us. I know it's a matter of time until she's recognized, and I can't tell if she sees this as a weird challenge or some kind of statement of what she's willing to do to be here. I'm torn either way.

The woman on my left says something to the girl, and my attention is pulled to them. She's talking about exoplanets. The girl rolls her eyes.

"Did you watch the video I sent you?" the woman asks.

"Just the first thirty seconds," the girl says.

Mom's rummaging in her purse on my other side, so I keep listening to them.

"Maybe you're out of your science phase," the woman's saying. "Your mother said you still liked space."

The girl crosses her arms over her chest. "I still like it, but planets are kind of boring."

"Exoplanets are amazing," I butt in. They both look at me. "I find real ones through a website that offers datasets to the public to analyze. Did you know some exoplanets have oceans made of tar?"

The girl blinks at me. The woman beams. "Well, that's fascinating," she says. "How long have you been studying space?"

"Since I was thirteen."

The woman nudges the girl, who scowls. "This is my niece, Emily," the woman says.

"I'm Grace," I say.

Mom fiddles with the zipper on her purse. She's trying to keep her head down, and I realize I might have just endangered that process. Crap.

Emily's aunt peers past me and says, "Are you Grace's mother? You seem familiar."

Shit.

Mom slowly looks at her, a finger to her lips.

"Oh my," the woman whispers. "G — is it you?"

Mom leans over me to say, "My daughter knows the astrophysicist presenting, so we had to come."

"But what about the show — aren't you ... on TV tonight?"

Mom puts a hand on my leg as she leans farther, trying to keep it quiet. "We've got to go to ITV after this. Luckily there was time in the schedule."

I clear my throat.

"That's so lovely that you made time for your daughter today. Isn't it, Em?" The woman turns to her niece, who looks a little blank, or bored, or both.

"Time in the schedule," I whisper to Mom. "Really?"

"Technically, yes," she whispers back.

Emily's aunt turns back and leans over me. "Would you mind signing something for us? I hate to ask, but it would mean so much to me and my sister." She holds out two business cards for a real estate office.

Mom signs them on my lap and leans in again. I feel like a table. "Is this you?"

The aunt nods vigorously. "Yes. I serve the whole Southern Island area. And I love your show!"

A man wearing a cardigan raises his hands at the front and steps to the mic.

Mom sits back and folds her hands over her purse. She actually looks interested in being here, or at least relieved that the fan encounter went well.

"Your mother is amazing, isn't she?" the aunt says in my ear, startling me.

Cardigan Man is introducing Elizabeth Tasker, and I'm kind of annoyed that this woman is still talking.

"After everything she went through, here she is. That's resilience." She sighs. "This makes tonight's show that much more amazing — she's sitting *right here*."

Emily shushes her aunt, giving me an apologetic look.

I smile at her.

Elizabeth Tasker walks to the lectern to a roomful of applause, and it's my turn to feel like a giddy fan. She's shorter in person than I expected, and her hair is blonder. She adjusts the mic and says something quietly to Cardigan Man.

Mom pats my leg.

"I'm going to talk about a kind of star system that many people aren't aware of," Elizabeth begins, "which is two or more stars orbiting each other, and with an array of exoplanets and moons in turn orbiting them. A binary system, which obviously has two stars, is common in our galaxy. In fact, it's estimated that up to half of all star systems in the Milky Way have multiple stars. Which is quite a lot, if you think about it. That's millions of binary star systems in our galactic neighborhood."

It's happening — I'm here and she's up there and all these people are listening to her talk about stars. I'm a seven on the bangle scale.

"Now," Elizabeth continues, "my interest is in exoplanets, which, it turns out, are found doing all kinds of crazy things around binaries. You'll recall the name of my talk said something about Tatooine, and you'll probably remember Tatooine as the home planet of Luke Skywalker. Does anyone know what was unique about Skywalker's planet?" An image of desert-covered Tatooine comes up on the projector behind her. "Right — there are two suns in the sky. Tatooine was a planet in a binary star system. The thing is, when *Star Wars* was created, we didn't know if something like this was possible. But sometimes science fiction leads science, and now we know that worlds like this are probably out there."

She goes on to talk about different kinds of binaries, and triplet and quadruplet star systems, and not once do I see Mom check her phone or look disinterested. I can't believe she's actually sitting still for this. It's super-geeky stuff and she doesn't seem to care. It's all totally surreal.

The talk ends and we get up, Mom probably eager to find a place to blend into the wall while I find the courage to talk to Elizabeth Tasker.

"You go chat," she says, pulling her hat down. "I'll be outside for a few minutes. Roger left me a message and I need to return his call."

"You're okay?" I ask, thinking this will be the worst time for her to be out in public, dispersing crowd and all.

"I'm fine, honey. I noticed a patch of trees out there I can stand in." She leans over and kisses my cheek before I even know it's happening. "Go talk to your astrophysicist."

"Okay," I say, flustered. "You're sure?"

She pats my arm. "You'll be fine. I know you will." She walks away, her phone already at her ear.

I have a fleeting memory of the last time she went away to take a call in a place filled with people. But this is different. So many things have changed.

I walk up to the front and stand behind the woman who's talking to Elizabeth Tasker, my pulse beating in my ears. She's not a rock star, I tell myself. There's no need to feel this shaky. But then I think, what makes a rock star worthy of shakiness and a scientist not?

The woman has walked away and I'm up. I'm not entirely sure I'll be able to talk.

Elizabeth Tasker is smiling at me. "Are you Grace Carter?"

"Yes," I say. "I loved your lecture."

"Thank you. It's one of my favorite talks to give." She leans on the stool that's behind the lectern. "I'm glad you came."

I pick at a hangnail. "So what's new in exoplanet research?" Stupid, stupid. I want a take back.

She smiles. "Well, a system with two planets made mostly of carbon were discovered last month. Which means that just below their surfaces they could have thick layers of diamonds. So that's fun to imagine."

We talk about her exoplanet modeling and how she got her job at JAXA. She asks about what kind of telescope I have, and what the sky viewing is like here. She's nice and funny and easy to talk to. I don't want to leave, but there's someone behind me. I'll have to go soon.

"It's so nice to meet you in person, Grace," she says. "I was hoping you'd come."

"I want to do something like you," I blurt out. She blinks at me and I stumble on: "I've wanted to be an astronomer for a long time and meeting someone who actually *is* — who's doing such amazing research — I just ..." I suddenly run out of words and stand there with nothing.

Her eyes crinkle at the corners as she smiles. "I know how you feel."

I finally breathe and the oxygen calms my brain.

"It's a great ambition," she says. "It's also a long road, so be prepared for struggle and years of uncertainty." She looks around the room at the now-empty seats. "It might seem like the only thing you want now, but the world is a huge place, even if it doesn't seem like it when you're studying space. It's completely okay to love astronomy and have a career doing something else."

I stare at the half-erased words on the chalkboard behind her, not sure what to say. What to think. How did we get to *not* doing astronomy?

"My intention isn't to dash your hopes," she says, holding up a hand. "I'm trying to arm you with perspective. Which is what astronomy gives us, right?"

"Yeah," I say, still totally confused. "Right."

"The thing is, I wasn't at all certain I was going to make it in the field, Grace. No astrophysics student is, and many don't find jobs. But I always knew I could go back home and find something else if I needed to. And maybe that helped me, in a way. Do you know what I mean?"

The sounds of the room come to me in snatches — a conversation going on behind me, a guy laughing by the door. Someone shifting chairs around.

Elizabeth Tasker leans toward me. "I guess I'm saying this because I see something in you, Grace. It might not seem like it, based on what I just said, but I really hope you succeed."

"Thanks," I say, because I can't think of another response.

"Let's keep in touch, okay?" She pushes a strand of hair out of her face. "Email me any questions you have, and I'll let you know when I'm next in the area. Or if you ever come to Japan." She smiles. "I know a good sushi place or two."

"Thanks," I say again, wishing I had a bigger vocabulary at

this moment. It seems really important, but I can't get it right.

She holds out her hand. "Keep up the planet hunting, Grace. I'll look forward to our next conversation."

97

I'm a little numb with what just happened, unable to process how it was good or bad or a mix of both. She wants to stay in touch. She wants me to think about other options. My hands are still a little shaky and my head feels full of fog. When I get outside and walk to the clump of trees, Mom's not there and a tingle of panic starts to creep over me. I send her a text: *I'm done. Where are you?*

I walk back into the building. The hallway is mostly empty now, only a few people still hanging around to talk outside the room.

Be right there, she replies.

Relieved, I walk to the end of the hall and then turn around. Being in a university always feels intimidating as well as comforting. It's like seeing a future you want when you're not quite ready for it.

My phone buzzes again. It's Iris. *How WAS it?? Amazing?*

How was it? I'm not sure.

Outside, a clump of university students laugh together so loudly that I can hear them through the glass. They hold one another's arms as if the thing they're laughing about might make them fall down.

Yes, amazing, I type. *Elizabeth's great. She told us all this cool stuff about binary stars. And she wants to keep in touch.*

You guys are buds now!

I think buds is too strong. I consider telling her about Elizabeth's advice. Decide not to. *But she's awesome,* I reply.

I'm really happy for you.

Oh, and my mom came.

What??

"There you are, Grace." Mom's walking toward me. There's something heavy in her face.

"What's wrong?" I ask.

She touches her hat and looks around. "I'll tell you in a moment. Let's go this way."

We walk back toward the lecture room and Elizabeth and Cardigan Man emerge from it, grinning.

"Excuse me," Mom says, "is this room free for a short time?"

Cardigan Man checks his phone. "It's empty until six, I think."

"Grace, is this your mother?" Elizabeth asks me. She doesn't seem to recognize her, which is both refreshing and a relief.

"Yes," I say, and introduce them without giving Mom's name.

There's a moment of awkward silence and then Mom says, "Well, thank you for a wonderful lecture. It reminded me of my university days, and that's what I need right now."

Once we've said goodbye and Mom's closed the door to the room, I turn to her and say, "What's going on?"

She walks to the back and sits on the second chair in the row, gesturing for me to sit beside her. "I just had a conversation with Roger and it made a few things extra clear."

I sit. "What things?"

"His motives and level of understanding. But it doesn't really surprise me, knowing him. I was just hoping for better." She scratches under the hat and then takes it off, shaking out her hat hair. I guess sitting with her back to the door in an empty classroom feels secure enough. Or maybe she doesn't care anymore. Whichever it is, something's changed. "He's pushing me to talk about how the trauma of the abduction drove my decision to take time away from TV to recover. He's not interested in much of the truth."

I watch her play with the rim of her hat. "And what is the truth?" I ask.

"That none of that is what it seems." Her gaze wanders around the room. Then she looks me in the eye. "I'm going to have to lie in the interview, and I hate having to do that in front of my family. So I want to tell you the truth now."

"But why is he doing this?"

She shrugs. "Your dad was right. Ratings, pressure from his boss. I thought I knew how it would go, but in the end he's got his priorities. And they're not mine. Not anymore."

We sit a moment without talking, and my fingers find a rough spot on the hem of my jacket. I pick at the bunched thread.

"Grace, there's so much I haven't told you. Or anyone, except my therapist and your father." She exhales. There's no other sound in the room. This place where sixty people sat just half an hour ago, listening to a lecture about gravitationally locked stars.

A question — *the* question — pokes at my insides, prodding me until I open my mouth. I don't keep it in this time. I can't. "Was it your choice?" I ask. "Did you choose to go?" Just in saying it, a kind of relief sweeps over me, followed by the heaviest dread I've ever felt.

She closes her eyes. "It's not as simple as yes or no."

"Give me the simplest version. Please."

Somewhere outside, a car engine starts, reminding me that we're still in the real world. Whatever happens here, it's real.

Mom tucks her hair behind her ear. "He'd lift me up by talking about what was possible, what my life could be ... I'd felt so drained and worn out, Grace, and he made it sound so good." She closes her eyes.

I wait with my throat closed up.

"But then your dad and I had a terrible argument. Marriage even to your best friend is one of the toughest things you ever do. And when Felipe showed up at the soccer game, I was still angry. And lost. He offered to drive me around the block, help clear my head. I was stuck inside my problems and I couldn't see clearly. I couldn't see all the ways he'd subtly taken control of the situation. I know that now. It was a big mistake."

"But did he force you ..."

She looks steadily at me and I know what she's going to say before she says it. "It was my choice to get in the car. And that's a huge regret."

My hearing suddenly gets so acute that I can hear the air rushing into my lungs. There's a soft tapping on the window beside us and I see it's started to rain.

"For the first day or so, I still had hope he'd bring me back. He acted like he was giving me a break from everything, a vacation, like I'd told him I needed so badly. He'd taken my phone when we left Fletcher Field, but on the second night, he made me unlock it and then he sent a message to your father pretending to be me. I saw what he wrote. And I knew he wasn't going to drive me home." She rubs her arms. "I still feel cold thinking about it."

"I saw it, too," I say. "The text Dad got."

She closes her eyes.

I think about that moment — Dad's stricken face, the charged air in the bedroom — and then imagine Mom, somewhere far away, knowing we were receiving it thinking it was her. "But it's what made him call the police," I say. "He knew it wasn't you. He was so sure."

Her chin suddenly wobbles. "I know. Being with your father was the best decision I ever made. Everything good has come from that." She searches my face, maybe to see if I understand what she means. "But there's more I want to tell you. Do you remember what I said about Felipe when he and I were young?"

I nod.

"He was a different person. In a way it feels like a dream now. He knew what I really needed when we first met, even more than I did at the time. He persuaded me to apply for the program I wanted."

"Journalism?"

"No," she says. "Anthropology."

"What?" I stare at her.

"I got accepted into a program with an exchange to South Africa, and he knew it was what I wanted more than anything. He knew it was perfect for me. For years I'd tried different things, jumped around, annoying the hell out of my mother. Finally, I found a fit. It felt … like coming alive." Her angles have softened. Yes, she's been gaining weight, but this is about more than that. I can see how alive she felt back then. I know that feeling. "When your grandmother found out about the program, she went ballistic. Too far, too dangerous, too out of left field for her."

"So you didn't go."

"It's what started the fight that broke Felipe and me up. He wanted me to go anyway, to ignore my mother. And I chose not to."

"Why?"

She pulls on the fingers of her right hand. "For one thing, she threatened to tell admissions that I hadn't passed all my Grade 12 courses."

God, Grandma. I wonder if I should tell her I know. Decide not to.

"She was scared," Mom says. "She didn't understand what I wanted. She wanted something different for me."

"To go into TV."

"I went to Ryerson for journalism and it felt good. It *was* good. I thought maybe I could make it work. After I graduated, she got me a job interning for a major TV news producer, and from there I just seemed to go up and up. Things came easily, and within a short time I was doing segments on camera. I actually convinced myself that I could still get to South Africa. If I worked at the right places, with the right people, I could become a reporter covering that area or do a documentary somewhere. But of course that never happened."

We both look at things that are not each other.

"When did you first see him again?" I ask.

"He showed up at the station one day. I almost had a heart attack. He was just like him, but older." She takes a packet of throat lozenges out of her purse and offers it to me. I've seen her use them before she has to speak a lot. We both take one. "I don't think he was ever honest about why he faked his death. He said it began as a prank and then he liked the idea of starting over. It seems unthinkable, but then those months on the boat were unthinkable, too." She sucks on the lozenge. "At first he said he just wanted to be near me. He showed me things he was carving, brought me presents. Sent me pictures of the shop he was using." She studies the walls. "He started talking to me about the goals I'd had when we were young. Going to a place to study culture and people. He had these elaborate plans I didn't really take seriously, but it was nice to fantasize about them. They made me happy. Except he drove me away and said he was doing it for my own good." She straightens her back and looks at me. "And things got really bad — life-or-death bad, Grace — but they also … shifted. Transformed. I have control over my life now. I decide where I want to go from here."

"So what does Roger want you to say?"

She flips her hat over on the table. "Roger thinks the trauma of the abduction and recovery has made me rethink my career in television, made me want privacy and a life that's not on camera. He wants me to say that the corporation is allowing me to go. And that's what I'm going to tell the country tonight, because the truth is too complicated and personal, and I think you know what the media does with complicated and personal."

"So what's the truth?" I ask.

The rain hits the window harder.

481

"The truth is that Felipe, and being stuck on that boat, and being away from you, and having days and days to think has made me reconsider what I want, and I've negotiated a deal with ITV to let me out of my contract early. I'm giving them this interview and they've agreed to my terms. And I have terms for myself, too — this feels like a second chance I have to take."

I've been picking at the hem of my jacket and now a long thread is loose. I twist it between my thumb and finger. "So that's why you needed us to agree to it."

"I'm sorry, Grace. I haven't been truthful about that and I know you don't want to have anything to do with it. There's a confidentiality agreement on all of it and I only told your dad. Your grandmother doesn't even know."

"But why have you rethought your career?" I ask.

She sucks on the lozenge for a moment. "I've been unhappy at work for years. I managed to convince myself I liked it and I was doing some good, but it was never my passion. It was something I was good at, which isn't always the same as something you love. And the abduction made me think hard about what I wanted. What I would do differently if I got the chance. After I got back, I told myself I wouldn't be afraid anymore."

"Afraid of what?"

"Being found to be a fraud, wasting time on a job I didn't love. Letting myself be who I want to be."

A thought occurs to me. Maybe this is why I haven't been able to understand her, to know who she is. Because she hasn't known either. "And who do you want to be?" I ask.

"Like the me who was with Felipe in university," she says, and then emotion floods her face. "Ready to take chances and feel free. To be open about my past and have no more secrets from you and Charlie and your dad. When I was on that boat, there was no GG Carter. There was just me and an unstable man who thought he was doing something heroic when he was doing something traumatizing and abusive. I remembered things I'd forgotten, I drew on experiences I'd had two decades ago. To survive those months, I had to be who I used to be. GG Carter couldn't have done that." She takes out a tissue and blows her nose. "She didn't really make it off the boat at all."

I lean forward and rest my elbows on my knees. The rain pelts the window and I realize neither of us brought an umbrella.

"Do you know what I thought about most on the boat?" she asks.

I don't think I can produce words, so I just wait.

"I thought about you. How negligent I've been at knowing you. How scared I've been. To have a daughter who's so intelligent — from the very beginning, just brimming with imagination and spark. A daughter who has passions and dreams and wants to do so much. You reminded me of the me I could have been."

My eyes sting and I look away, but she keeps talking. "I've always been pushed to move further from what I want," she says. "By my mother, my employers, myself. I didn't know how to connect with you, Grace. You were being the me I always wanted to be. I didn't know how to touch you without shattering the box I'd been living in for years." She strokes the back of my hand with the tips of her fingers. "But look at you. Going to university lectures about binary star systems. Coauthoring research papers. I read the copy your dad keeps in his office. You are a wonder, Grace."

I can't see anything but a blur of color, but I feel her touch my face.

"Can you forgive me for not understanding, for not being there, if I'm here now?"

I lean forward until my head is resting against her collarbone, which isn't as sharp as it once was. Her hands are warm on my back. She smells like Sunday mornings when I was little. She smells like her.

It's not enough to say I'm relieved that my questions are finally answered. It's inaccurate to say I'm happy, because it's not that. I'm dissolved with the realization that she's telling me more truth than I imagined there was. That she's telling me who she is.

I'm fragmented by it. I'm deconstructed to nothing but stardust, pure elements, the same elements she's made of — because we are made of the same stuff.

98

We get to Mom's car soaking wet, but it feels somehow appropriate and kind of funny. The rain drums on the roof and windshield and water condenses on the inside as we breathe and laugh and try to do our seat belts up.

"We'll be a few minutes late," she gasps, "but they can just deal with it."

"What about the read-through questions?" I ask. "Weren't you supposed to go over them with me?"

She starts the engine. "Yeah, but you already know what's going to happen. There's nothing in the questions that will surprise you now. And now you know why they're set up the way they are."

We pull out of the wet parking lot.

"But what if you get emotional — what if you get triggered by something? You said Roger wants you to talk about traumatic stuff."

"Only what I choose to talk about. You and Charlie will be there — it's airing during prime time — the contract is specific about those things. Plus, Dr. Bansal's going to be there, and my lawyer."

"You have a lawyer?"

"You bet. He's very good." She turns left onto the main road.

The rain lets up a little as we drive past strip malls and office buildings on the way to the station. The windshield wipers provide a steady rhythm and the blowing heat makes me sleepy.

"Can I ask you to do something?" she says after a while, startling me.

"What?"

She glances over. "Tell me your favorite fact about space."

I stare out my window for a moment. "Uh, that's kind of hard to answer."

"Just pick one thing. What's something that blows your mind?"

I rest my forehead against the cool glass of the window. Silica grains forged together into a smooth sheet. "Well," I say, "the universe is expanding, right?"

"Is it?"

"Yeah, from the Big Bang. But what's actually expanding is space itself, which was also made at the time of the Big Bang."

"Okay," she says slowly.

"So what that means is there is no center of the universe. Everywhere is the center — which means nowhere is. It just doesn't fit our expectations of how things work. We naturally want there to be a starting point, but anywhere I stand in the universe is the middle, even as it's growing. Like, right now, here is the center. And so is a hundred thousand light-years away. Which is so crazy to think about." I turn and look at her profile as the streetlights illuminate it. It's gotten dark out when I wasn't paying attention.

The corner of her mouth curves up. "So this is more about how hard it is for a human brain to comprehend reality than solving a physical problem."

"For me, yeah. Reality is badass."

She watches at the road ahead, smiling. "Wow."

We drive for a few blocks without speaking, but it's good. It's new.

My phone buzzes and I take it out of my pocket.

It's Mylo. *You'll be great. Tomorrow we're going for pancakes, okay?*

"Who is it?" Mom asks, and the curiosity in her voice makes me think she's seen my face redden.

I laugh. "Remember the guy who wanted to interview you at the soccer game?"

"Yes?"

My grin spreads across my face like an unstoppable force. "His name's Mylo."

99

The station is all lit up, and half the parking lot is full. A cameraman stands at the main entrance, but we drive around the back and Roger plus another guy come out a door and escort us inside.

The hallway is dazzlingly bright and I have to squint.

"Grace!" Charlie gallops down the corridor, all decked out in a striped shirt and dress pants, his hair gelled into place. He smells like cinnamon and he's chewing a huge wad of gum. "You only have, like, ten minutes."

"No, more than that," Yasmin says, coming up behind him.

She and Mom exchange broadcasting jargon and Mom turns to go into a room on the left. "Is your dad in the green room?" she asks Charlie.

"Yeah, but we're calling it the taupe room."

"Much more accurate."

"Where are you going?" Charlie asks, shuffling over in his shiny black shoes to grab her sleeve.

"I have to get ready. Grace and I got a little caught in the rain. I'll meet you in the studio, okay? Yasmin will show you." She turns to me. "Are you okay to go?"

We look at each other under the fluorescent lights and I know she means, "Are you ready to do this?"

"I'm okay," I say. "I'm ready."

100

We're all seated on the couch, Dad, Charlie and I, with Mom beside me in an armchair by a potted plant that looks equally real and fake. Her back is straight, her shoulders pulled back, and we haven't even started. She chats quietly to Roger, who's got his headset on and pit stains under his arms. She's the Fabulous GG Carter. I think of all the years she's been this person in this place, all the people who think this is who she is. The advertisements and commercials and articles that shout, "This is GG Carter!" And I know it's all a lie. A box.

Charlie kicks me with his heavy shoe.

"Ow."

"Sorry. These things make my feet clumsy or something."

I nudge him with my elbow. "Mine pinch my toes."

He stares down at the purple ballet flats I picked out in Wardrobe. "They're nice, though."

"Nice for now. Then I'm done."

"What if I have to pee?" he asks.

"Do you?" Dad asks.

"No. But I drank a Coke in the taupe room."

"I asked you not to do that," Dad whispers.

"Won't there be commercial breaks?" I ask.

"Yes," Mom says on my other side, her GG Carter smile slipping into a grin. "The nearest washroom is just out the door. Yasmin or Dad can whisk you out and back in time."

Then they're telling us we're two minutes out. Then one.

Dad clears his throat for the eighth time and Charlie fidgets between us. Dad presses his hand on Charlie's fluttering ones.

Mom adjusts the mic on her blouse, presses her lips together and looks over at me. Behind her makeup and hair, I think I see a nervousness, maybe even a sadness. This is what she knows how to do, and it's the last time.

"It's okay, Mom," I whisper, the sounds around us drowning out the words.

The lights shift. The interviewer, a woman from Toronto I know nothing about except that her hair is improbably red, crosses her legs at the ankle and taps her pages of notes on her knee.

Roger calls down the seconds and then we're on, the music rising, my pulse beating in my head, the lights flooding everything with photons.

Then the interviewer opens her mouth and welcomes us. She says our names and something about being fortunate to be here. I can't decide if she means we're fortunate or she is. Everything starts happening in slow motion, on mute. Mom's hand comes up on my right and squeezes my arm. Her mouth moves.

I'm not supposed to look around the room — the cameras are watching — but I glance at Mom, at the interviewer, at the chairs they're sitting in. Soft brown leather. Their hands gesturing, then returning to rest on the chairs. Thousands of people are watching this. Thousands of questions swirling in their heads.

Words start coming back to my ears. "Unbelievable … Rescue … Traumatic … Family … Mentally ill."

Charlie squirms beside me.

Dad's voice booms in my head and I snap back into full speed, regular volume.

"It was the most difficult time of our lives," Dad's saying, "but we got through it together. I'd say it's brought us closer."

The interviewer's eyes lock on to mine. "And how do you feel about having your mother home, Grace?"

My throat constricts. Loosens. I swallow and take the slow breath Mylo would be telling me to take. "It was hard at first," I say, and my voice is louder than I expect. "I think we expected things to go back to normal right away. But I know now that was never going to happen because we've all changed. And it's better. Better than before." I can feel them all watching me — my family sitting around me, the people in the studio, in the darkness behind the lights. Mylo and Iris, sitting at home with the rest of the country. Who would have thought I'd be doing this? Not the six-year-old me playing make-believe sitting at a desk in this studio.

The interviewer's nodding her head, ready to move on to the next question. Her pink lipsticked mouth opens.

But I beat her to it. "And I want to say that I'm proud of her." I can't look at Mom or I won't be able to finish. I stare straight into the nearest camera. "She's the bravest person I know."

I understand what Grandma was saying. What Elizabeth Tasker explained, even though she didn't know it.

My mother and I are stars in a binary, circling each other, pulled by our mutual gravity. We will always be this way. It's how the universe works.

ALCOR

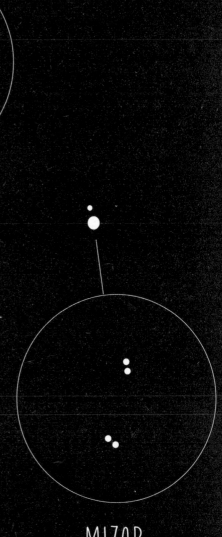

MIZAR

AN INTERVIEW WITH DR. ELIZABETH TASKER

One day when I was working on a later draft of this book, I walked into my local bookstore and saw *The Planet Factory*, Dr. Elizabeth Tasker's book about exoplanets, on the Read This! table. I knew I had found the astrophysicist for *The Center of the Universe*. Luckily for me, Elizabeth was happy not only to be turned into a fictional version of herself, but also to be interviewed about her career and thoughts on space science. I'm thrilled to share her responses here.

1. How did you come to pursue a career in astrophysics? Did you always want to be a space scientist?

When I was a kid, I was absolutely certain I wanted to be a country veterinarian, but in truth, there was little about a rural vet's life that actually matched my skill set or temperament. I enjoyed the theoretical models and ideas of all the sciences, but I was a hazard in the lab (which would likely have extended to the stall where a poor cow was trying to give birth).

But since the age of nine, I'd also been captivated by space. My dad had taken me to the London Planetarium as a birthday treat and bought the picture of Saturn that is mentioned in The Center of the Universe *(it's all true!). I'd done school projects on the solar system and bored everyone to death with strange facts about black holes.*

When I was thirteen, my school gave everyone a careers assessment test where this stood out clearly in both my aptitudes (physics all the way) and interests (astronomy and writing). After that, I started to re-think the cow idea.

2. What is your favorite piece of space trivia?

That the surface of Venus can melt lead and the longest a space-craft has survived on the Venusian surface (to date) is about two hours. I like this one because Venus is a planet almost exactly the same size as the Earth. If we were to see Venus as an exoplanet and make an estimate of its surface temperature based on its distance from the sun, we might guess about 27°C (80°F) — a nice temperature for a beach trip! The fact that Venus is so much hotter shows how much there is to learn about Earth-sized planets in our galaxy. Why do we have two planets, nearly the same size, around the same star (our sun) that are so completely different? What does this tell us about the chances of finding another habit-able planet? I find this all very exciting.

I also like the trivia that there are more stars in the universe than grains of sand on the beach. I was once asked how many stars there were when I told a border control guard for the United States that I was an astrophysicist. I replied with this trivia and he asked me which beach I meant. I said, "All the beaches! There are more stars than the sand on all the beaches in the world." He refused to believe me and I worried for one nasty moment that he wouldn't let me into the country! (He did.)

3. What excites you about your field right now?

In the last twenty-five years, we have gone from knowing just the planets in our solar system to thousands around neighboring stars. This told us our little system of planets is not alone, but what we don't know yet is what these new worlds are really like. I think the next twenty-five years will change this, as new telescopes will be built that can detect the atmosphere around exoplanets. The gases in the atmosphere are a real indication of how a planet forms and what might be going on at the surface. We've found many Earth-sized worlds, but will any of them really be like our Earth, or did they form in wildly different ways?

4. What is the coolest thing about your research?

I really like computer programming. When I began my PhD in the early 2000s, I was captivated by the idea that you could build whole sections of a universe in a computer. It is like making physics your giant toy box: you can turn on and off effects such as magnetic fields, star formation — even gravity — and watch what happens. Using powerful telescopes is of course amazing, but you don't get to play around with the universe. Learning how to code models for supercomputers (room-sized computers that have thousands of processors) was a huge draw to the field for me.

5. What has been your most surprising finding?

In truth, science research is rather sparse on the "Eureka!" moments, but the reality is actually even more satisfying. In research, you explore one aspect of a problem that might not tell you much on its own, but when combined with the work of other researchers can reveal something amazing. One of my favorite debates is from my studies in star formation, where I ran computer simulations showing that cold star-forming clouds of gas in our galaxy may frequently collide. Another research team had previously suggested that such collisions could be responsible for creating massive stars, much bigger than our own sun. A different group were observing evidence that this might actually occur. All together, our work suggested that these so-called cloud collisions might really be responsible for quite a bit of star formation. It was not a single person, but the results from researchers all around the globe.

6. What advice do you have for young adults interested in studying space sciences?

I actually love the advice my character gives Grace when she tells her she wants to be an astronomer. In the book I tell her she can still find astronomy fascinating but not pursue it as a career. Astronomy is indeed a wonderfully exciting field and I would encourage anyone with an interest to explore their curiosity to their heart's content. But life is full of opportunities and it's always worth keeping an open mind to what else might be out there. If I had not done this, I would have probably been a very bad and unhappy vet!

Even when I went to university, I intentionally studied physics for my undergraduate degree, rather than looking to specialize in astronomy or astrophysics early. This was because I knew there were many areas of physics we don't hear much about at school and these would be fascinating.

So I would say if you want to do space science — go for it. I have complete faith you'd make an amazing scientist. But don't hold yourself back by not exploring other areas that also catch your interest. As my character tells Grace, you can still love astronomy but not be an astronomer. I would add that it is also possible not to be a research astronomer, but still make a huge impact on the field.

7. Who do you admire in space sciences?

When writing my answer here, I kept changing my mind! This isn't because I'm very indecisive (okay, it's maybe a little bit because I'm indecisive) or because I've not felt the same thrill as Grace when I've attended a talk by a scientist I'd heard about (I certainly have). It is because it takes the enthusiasm, passion and commitment of so many different people in many different areas to advance science, from research to communication to politics.

For example, when I was Grace's age, I loved hearing the story of how Jocelyn Bell Burnell discovered pulsars (a type of dead star) during her PhD. Pulsars emit a flash that is so regular that Bell Burnell and her adviser first thought it was possible this was a signature from an extraterrestrial life form. My love of computers meant I was also in awe of Margaret Hamilton, who developed the software for the Apollo space program and is often pictured with a printout of her code that towers over her head.

And then, I keep up with much of my space and astronomy news from great science communicators such as Phil Plait and Emily Lakdawalla. I also avidly read the blog posts by Italian astronaut Samantha Cristoforetti when she described life on the International Space Station.

8. If you could give your teenage self a piece of advice about anything, what would you say?

I would tell her not to worry that she might not be good enough. In science we often talk about something called "imposter syndrome." It means that you think everyone around you is better than you. Of course, it's absolutely not true, but almost everyone tends to suspect this is the case and that sooner or later, they'll be "found out" to be not worthy of their position or degree or people's respect.

I definitely felt this way: I didn't find school easy and I wasn't top of my class; in fact, I was bottom at math when I was eleven years old (and let's never talk about French tests). I really wanted to study science but even as I became a stronger student, I

502

suspected my good grades were just due to luck that would one day run out. I am really glad that this common insecurity is now something that is being talked about a lot more in the field. Success depends on many things and it's very rarely about raw, born-with-it ability. It's passion and hard work all the way.

You can learn more about Dr. Elizabeth Tasker's work at www.elizabethtasker.com.

ACKNOWLEDGMENTS

This book started out as a what-if. A what-if about a mother and daughter, about a relationship and a family and a future changed by abduction. It's been five years since I started playing with those what-ifs and almost nothing is the same as when I began the story. I love that magic.

My stellar agent, Louise Lamont, read this story when it was only the first forty pages, then cheered and guided it into what it has become. Agents Allison Hellegers and Alexandra Devlin also steered it toward its home. My amazing first readers have all given me their sage advice and support: Claire Tacon, Kellee Ngan, Rachelle Delaney and Hannah Tunnicliffe. My teen readers, Hailey Johnson and Emma Mackay, gave valuable, detailed feedback.

My editor at KCP Loft, Kate Egan, has been so thoughtful and skilled and has helped me bring the story to a new level. She encouraged my geekiness and wild ideas and I am thoroughly grateful for the chance to work with her.

On things technical, I thank Peggy Aspinall and Janis Carmena for police and investigative details around abduction. Gilles Plante kindly supplied the answers to some of my early broadcasting and production questions. I also thank Heather

Mont for counseling and advice on the psychology of abduction. Any errors in these areas are mine alone.

Thank you to Dr. Elizabeth Tasker, who generously agreed to appear as herself in this book and also to be pelted with questions afterward. Also to Anna MacDiarmid at Bloomsbury UK for letting me use Elizabeth's words. To become barely conversant with space science, I watched many hours of *Crash Course Astronomy*, and I'm grateful to the amazing creators of that YouTube channel and the host, Phil Plait.

Everyone in the KCP Loft team who works so hard to make beautiful, intelligent and thought-provoking books — thank you. A grant from the Canada Council for the Arts was also instrumental to my having the time to write.

And this book would not have been possible if I didn't have the support of my family. It is a universal truth that a writer who is a parent is only as productive as their childcare provider. Thank you to my parents for providing babysitting during the early drafts of this book, and for their continued love and support. To my children, who inspire me to be a better parent and to keep showing them what working hard for your dreams looks like. And to my husband, for countless evenings of doing the kids-dishes-cleanup routine alone, and for always believing in me, I offer my love, gratitude and the guarantee that all of this will happen again as soon as I get started on the next book.

RIA VOROS is the author of middle grade and young adult novels that have been finalists for the White Pine Award and the Rocky Mountain Book Award, as well as a Best Books for Kids and Teens selection. She has an MFA in creative writing from the University of British Columbia. She is often a college instructor, sometimes an elementary school teacher and always a dessert-maker/consumer.

When she's not writing, teaching or eating sweet things, Ria can be found hiking to the tops of mountains or continuously getting the sand out of her children's shoes at the beach. She lives in Victoria, British Columbia, Canada, with her husband, daughter and son.

Find her at www.riavoros.com.

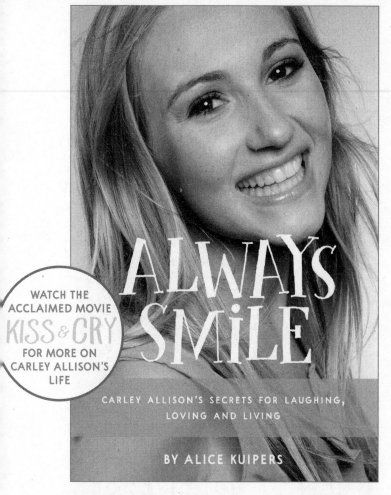

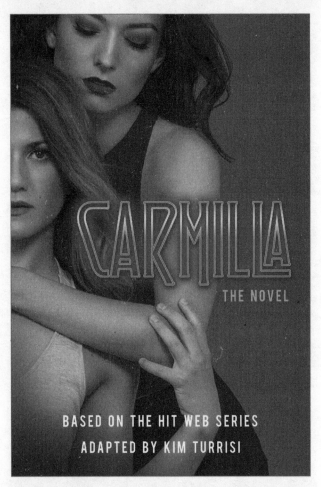

WHAT ARE YOU READING NEXT?

ANNA MAINWARING

REBEL WITH A CUPCAKE

To eat or not to eat —
is that even a question?

WHAT IF ONE TOUCH
COULD TELL YOU EVERYTHING?

ZENN DIAGRAM

WENDY BRANT

Kim Turrisi

Just a Normal Tuesday

Where you lose everything and still get

Keeping the Beat

FAME. LOVE. FRIENDS. PICK ANY TWO.

MARIE POWELL
& JEFF NORTON

THE LAST WISH OF SASHA CADE

How far would you go to save your best friend?

CHEYANNE YOUNG

Can you fall in ♥ with someone you've never met?

TEXTROVERT

Lindsey Summers

wattpad

KCP Loft

kcploft.com

 @KCPLoft

FALL IN LOVE

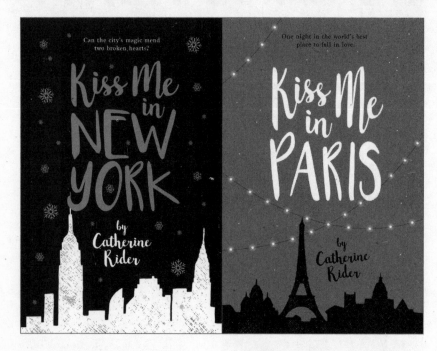